THE RISE OF THE WESTERN KINGDOM

A Prequel to
THE FALL OF DAORADH

The Rise of the Western Kingdom

Book Two of the Sword of the Watch

*To Mia —
Love Dad*

A NOVEL BY
John Montgomery

iUniverse, Inc.
Bloomington

The Rise of the Western Kingdom
Book Two of the Sword of the Watch

Copyright © 2012 by John Montgomery.
Auhtor Credits: The Sword of the Watch - The Fall of Daoradh

All rights reserved. No part of this book may be used or reproduced by any means, graphic, electronic, or mechanical, including photocopying, recording, taping or by any information storage retrieval system without the written permission of the publisher except in the case of brief quotations embodied in critical articles and reviews.

This is a work of fiction. All of the characters, names, incidents, organizations, and dialogue in this novel are either the products of the author's imagination or are used fictitiously.

iUniverse books may be ordered through booksellers or by contacting:

iUniverse
1663 Liberty Drive
Bloomington, IN 47403
www.iuniverse.com
1-800-Authors (1-800-288-4677)

Because of the dynamic nature of the Internet, any web addresses or links contained in this book may have changed since publication and may no longer be valid. The views expressed in this work are solely those of the author and do not necessarily reflect the views of the publisher, and the publisher hereby disclaims any responsibility for them.

Any people depicted in stock imagery provided by Thinkstock are models, and such images are being used for illustrative purposes only.
Certain stock imagery © Thinkstock.

ISBN: 978-1-4697-9290-3 (sc)
ISBN: 978-1-4697-9291-0 (hc)
ISBN: 978-1-4697-9292-7 (ebk)

Library of Congress Control Number: 2012907258

Printed in the United States of America

iUniverse rev. date: 05/11/2012

For Mom & Dad

Contents

Illustrations ix
Acknowledgments xi
The Song of Isha xv
Prologue xvii

PART ONE 1

  1. Harm's Way 3
  2. The End of the First Age 12
  3. Boundland 29
  4. Discovery 38
  5. Journey to the Western Coast 55
  6. The Northern Fields 71
  7. Power Revealed 79
  8. Shintower 91
  9. The Hunt Begins 105
10. Missing Scouts 118
11. Irreconcilable Differences 127
12. Witch of Southwood 141
13. The Faceless Mountains 149
14. Autonomy 157
15. Altar for the Sword 165
16. Imperfect Cage 182
17. Uneasy Peace 189

PART TWO 201

    18. New Paths.. 203
    19. Amphileph's Revenge 227
    20. War Begins 252
    21. Costly Protection 269
    22. Attack on Shintower 297

Epilogue 347

Illustrations

Map of Etharath	xii
Rionese Solar System and Calendar	xiii
Rionese Phonemes	xiv
Deceived	Chapter 1
Amphileph	Chapter 3
Cayden on the deck of the Nurium	Chapter 5
Galbard denied passage	Chapter 7
Mategaladh	Chapter 9
Mordher returns to Rion	Chapter 11
The Camonra Attack	Chapter 13
An Altar for the Sword	Chapter 15
Tobor	Chapter 17
Black Death	Chapter 19
Adheron surveys Highwood	Chapter 21
Rendaya and Bellows	Epilogue

ACKNOWLEDGMENTS

To my wife Bobbi, who doubles my joys and halves my sorrows.

To Ryan Ness, for helping to bring the vision of Erathe to life with your illustrations.

To all the fans that stopped at a tradeshow booth, a book signing, or an author coffee, or just wrote an email to say how much you loved the story of *The Fall of Daoradh*: know that your encouraging words provided the spark I needed to bring *The Rise of the Western Kingdom* to paper.

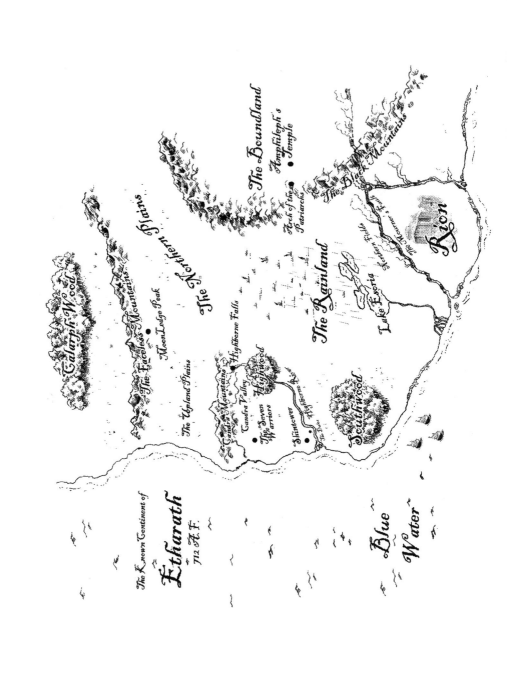

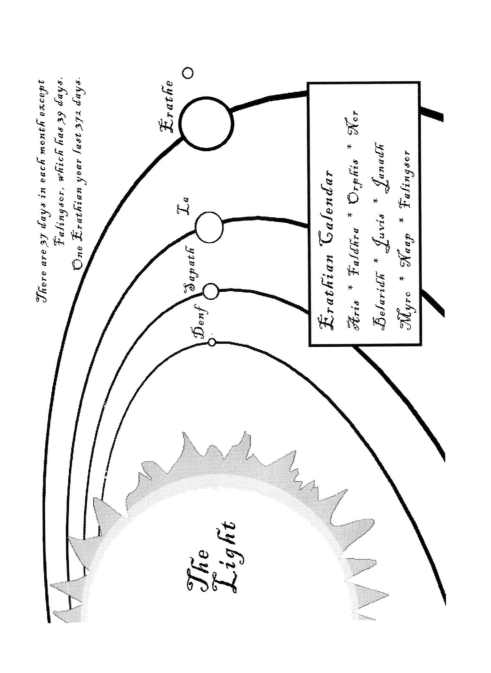

Rionese Phonemes

ā   ä   b   k   ŭr   ĕr   i

ī   ſ   ph/f   sh   j   th   n

d   e   s   t   r   w   kw

h   m   g   ō   ōō

The Song of Isha

Creator, let your Watchers know that patiently we wait,
We pray to have great strength of heart before it is too late.

"Rion! Our hearts, our homes, our loves! Where are your temples great?
All gone!" decried the bard in song, "but why this awful fate?"

"Failed grace" did take the tongue of most
Who spoke of such a thing,
Begged we the Guard to make riposte,
Lest heads find Camon's ring.

Now rages Watchers' war on them beyond the nearest gate,
While Rion's Guard, our holy guard, a chance for us create.

We fled Rion by craggy coast,
That fateful day of Spring,
We swear it now and drink the toast!
They'll feel The Sword's good sting.

Oh, Book, my Holy Book of Time, did not you once narrate
That Men one day would indeed proclaim that they with Him equate?

Creator, let your Watchers know that patiently we wait,
We pray to have great strength of heart before it is too late.

PROLOGUE

In the time after the Foundation of Rion, the people had flourished under the guidance of the immortals, the Watchers, led by the prophet Evliit, who controlled the destiny of men through one holy weapon, the Sword of the Watch, forged by the Bhre-Nora in the Third Domain, the realm of the Creator himself.

War and pestilence were unheard of, but by fate or by works, some did fare better than others, and soon envy turned to anger, and anger to murder and pillage, and man became set against man.

The Elders, the ancient followers of the Watchers, reined in the chaos by creating an army of paladins known as the Rion Guard, taking Rion's young and disciplining them in the arts of battle, music, and philosophy, while instilling in them a deep love for their Creator. For a time, peace came again to the land of Etharath, but as with all societies that live by the sword, even the poor did find a blade and the hatred to use it, and soon the world teetered on chaos again.

A division formed within the immortals, for some had seen these signs of humankind's corruption as an incurable condition and sought radical change through their mastery of alchemy and wizardry. Evliit called them Spellmakers and sought to temper their vengeance.

The Spellmakers would hear none of it, demanding that Evliit forever alter man's destiny through the powers of the Sword of the Watch. When he refused, Amphileph, the leader of the Spellmakers, created the Camonra, swearing his superior race would destroy mankind and repopulate the planet of Erathe.

The War of the Watchers ensued, and as Amphileph threatened the southern kingdom of Rion with extinction, refugees scattered across the continent, in hopes of finding some shred of hope and a rallying cry.

PART ONE

Chapter One

Harm's Way

Galbard walked toward the main temple of Amphileph, dwarfed by the jailer that walked in front of him. Slavery had both tattered his shirt and filled it with a muscular frame, and his wrist chains thumped against his leather loincloth in syncopation to the slap of his sandals on the stone path.

He walked a few paces behind his jailer, looking straight ahead at his back or down at the floor, the behavior demanded of a slave. The jailer was a Camon, a member of the race collectively known as the *Camonra*. They were the creation of Amphileph, master of the Spellmakers, and Amphileph had absolute dominion over them. Though they shared many of the characteristics of humans, most were over seven feet tall, and their slow gait, broad sloping shoulders, and thick limbs were deceiving, for when they wanted to be, they were as swift as they were strong. That three of the Camonra would roust a human slave in the middle of the night told Galbard that Amphileph himself must have taken some kind of interest in him, and that was frightening. It was better for a slave to remain unnoticed.

Two of the Camonra walked behind Galbard, and the jailer led the way through the Camonra encampments, toward the immense temple at their center. The group came to a stop before the temple entrance, and one of them exhaled his boredom on the back of Galbard's neck. The warm stench of it surrounded him, and Galbard curled his nose. He wanted to step away, but he did not dare move.

Galbard had rarely seen the Camonra without their helmets, so he caught himself glancing up when he was sure no one was looking. The Camon in the front of him had been roughly shorn, his short, jet black hair exposing one ear that had cartilage crumpled from a blow. The other ear had a more pointed tip that flopped a bit with each step the Camon took.

His wide-necked chainmail revealed his upper back, where whip marks crisscrossed the bared area at various widths and depths, some of them edged by the dots of scar tissue that a course needle might leave. When the Camon turned, Galbard could see deep frown lines that made his face look as though it might never have smiled. A large scar ran from the crumpled ear to the edge of his chin.

"Enter!" a voice called from within the temple.

The Camon in front of him snorted through his snub nose and motioned with his head for Galbard to enter, and Galbard momentarily looked at the Camon's face. He did not seem to notice Galbard's mistake, and Galbard quickly looked at the floor again, but the flash of an image stuck in his mind: the bloodshot eyes under the heavy brow, the flat square face, the pug nose and large carved chin, and the gold beads that adorned some of the dreadlocks in the creature's beard.

When the Camon turned to face the temple door, Galbard looked up at him again. The massive creature raised his thick, somewhat elongated arms and slowly pushed open the heavy door of the temple entrance. His tree-trunk legs lumbered ahead of Galbard through the temple doorway, and his chainmail *chinked* with each step. Galbard tried to walk in time with the Camon's steps, but he had to take two steps for each of his.

The two other Camonra took their posts on either side of the entrance, and Galbard followed the jailer inside. He heard the doors closing behind him, and then his escort pushed him forward through an arched opening, an entryway into the domed temple sanctum. They shuffled to a halt at its center.

The domed ceiling had a central opening, allowing a column of moonlight to illuminate the temple floor, and when Galbard stood still in its light blue beams, the walls of the room seemed to sink away into the darkness.

"Father, I have brought you the human," the Camon said.

Out of the darkness, a thin man in a long, flowing red robe appeared. Galbard caught his breath. It was Amphileph! Amphileph looked at his fingernails, cocking his head to one side, his long, jet black bangs hiding his eyes. He leaned his head back and pushed his bangs back with both hands. His skin was pale, and his dark green eyes were piercing.

"You are the one called Galbard?" Amphileph asked.

The Camon swatted Galbard to the ground. "Bow down before the Father, dog!" he said.

"Yes, master," Galbard managed.

"Now, now, let's not mistreat our guest," Amphileph said. "Help him to his feet."

The Camon's massive hand grabbed Galbard's shoulder and lifted him up, dropping him back upon his feet.

"I am told that you can speak the old language, Galbard. Is that true?" Amphileph asked.

"Yes, master," answered Galbard.

Amphileph circled him in the shadows. "A slave's life is unbecoming to such an educated man. Wouldn't you like to go free? All I have to do is speak it, and it will be so," Amphileph said.

The hair rose on Galbard's neck. "Yes, master, of course."

"Then you must do something for me. You will find a man in the foothills of the Black Mountains, asleep under the Arch of the Patriarchs. Do you know this place?"

"Yes, master," Galbard responded.

"Kill the man and bring me his belongings, and I will set you free."

Galbard's heart raced at the mere thought of freedom, but he sucked in a quick breath and fought to remain silent. Killing for freedom would bring him only a new prison of guilt, but it was sure death to refuse Amphileph. Silence was the better option.

Amphileph's hand emerged from the shadows, a single finger pointed in Galbard's direction. His nails were manicured and his red garment shimmered in the moonlight.

"*Ara Libre Cudhara,*" Amphileph said, and the shackles fell away from Galbard's hands and feet. Amphileph raised his hood, and his face disappeared in its shadow. His eyes seemed to glow from within the hood. "Run, and I will find you, no matter where you go."

Amphileph turned to exit the room and waved them away. "Dress him properly and see him to the western gate," he said, before completely disappearing in the darkness.

Galbard allowed himself to exhale, but before he could relax in the least, the Camon's large hand grabbed him up and dropped him facing the opposite direction. He flicked his fingers against Galbard's back, pushing him toward the exit.

The three Camonra escorted Galbard to the western gate as Amphileph had commanded, stopping just long enough to remove the large timber that barred it. The Camonra gave him clothing fit for traveling: leather boots and a long coat, a dagger, and a pack with a day's supplies. Galbard waited for them to say something, but instead, the largest jailer pushed him out of the gate rather unceremoniously, and the Camonra turned and walked away. Galbard picked himself up and watched them push the gate back closed. The timber fell back in its place with a great crashing sound.

Galbard was a little stunned. After more than a year of imprisonment, they had just left him at the western gate without even a second thought, like so much trash. He pulled his hood over his head and tightened his belt, turned and walked toward the Arch of the Patriarchs, a holy place of prayer west of Amphileph's temple and high in the Black Mountains.

He had always told himself that he would do anything to escape his enslavers. He had often thought of killing one of the Camonra and escaping, especially when they had been unusually cruel, but he acknowledged to himself that it was only a crutch, a way to keep some thread of hope alive in his hopeless life. Still, a Camon was one thing; never once had he imagined killing a human being, and it was unthinkable in a holy place where the Creator himself watched over them. It was not in him to murder, or at least that's what he had thought, but failure to do as Amphileph asked was toying with death, and likely a horrible death at that. He repeated Amphileph's words in his head, *Run, and I will find you, no matter where you go,* until in the distance, he could see the arch above the horizon about two-thirds the way up the Black Mountains.

Galbard climbed higher still, and when he pulled himself onto the arch's plateau, he could see a man, just as Amphileph had said, motionless, leaning over the large, flat, knee-high stone table centered under the arch. His hair and robes were dirty and disheveled. It appeared to Galbard that the man had been kneeling in prayer, maybe throughout the night, and he had fallen asleep out of exhaustion.

Galbard approached the prayer circle. The man's shoes sat beside a small bag and an old sword. Staring at their worn soles and the dusty bag, he wondered what guilt this man was carrying that qualified him for death, especially death at his hand.

He stood there for what seemed like an eternity, wrestling with the repercussions of not doing as Amphileph commanded. Galbard put his hands upon the sword and removed it from its scabbard. He tried to remove it slowly, silently, but the blade seemed to scrape the scabbard along its entire length, making Galbard sure the man would wake. His heart began to race, and he moved closer to the prone man's head, raising the sword above him. Its tip pointed precariously toward the man's temple.

Galbard couldn't move. Sweat began to bead upon his forehead.

What am I doing? he thought. "Creator, forgive me," he whispered, looking to the skies above. He lowered the sword and backed away, and then he returned the sword to its scabbard, his hands shaking so badly then that the length of it made a *tink, tink, tink* sound sliding into the scabbard. He tried to regain his calm, but the noise seemed as loud as a dinner bell. He stopped for a moment and closed his eyes, exhaling deeply.

He turned and looked down the mountain toward Amphileph's temple. "Under penalty of death, I'll not bring this shame upon my forefathers," he said. "When I stand in judgment in the Third Domain, my soul will blacken with things for which I am ashamed, but this will not be one of them."

He carefully placed the sword back where he had found it and returned to the man's side. To Galbard's relief, the man had not awakened throughout the entire ordeal. "I don't see a bottle, my friend, but whatever it was that you drank, you should probably not drink it again."

Galbard shook him, attempting to awaken him.

"Wake up!" Galbard said. "Wake up!"

The man's eyes flickered open.

"You must run! Run away, far from here!"

The man's eyes were dazed. He didn't seem fully aware of what was happening. Galbard stood back from him and yelled, pointing to the temple in the valley below. "Listen to me! Sober up! I don't know what you've done, but the master of that temple wants your head on a spear. I was sent to kill you, and now that I haven't, I've made my own doom! Flee before I come to my senses!"

The man's facial features suddenly began to shift and his clothes changed in a flash of blinding light as he slowly rose before the stunned Galbard. The pauper clothing had transformed to white, flowing robes that floated around the holy man.

Galbard stumbled back and fell to the ground. He knew immediately who it was: the great prophet Evliit, the leader of the Watchers, who could consult directly with the Creator and call down his favor or his wrath.

The former slave spat on the ground with his misfortune. "How can it be that I've angered both a Spellmaker and a Watcher in a single day?"

Evliit hovered above the ground, his face shining. He raised his hand, and the sword flew from its scabbard into it. The sword began to glow, giving off such an intense heat that Galbard had to cover his face. He prepared for his doom. The winds gasped like the gods drawing a breath, and the light suddenly dimmed.

Galbard dared to look again. Evliit and his robes slowly sank back to the earth. He was teetering as if he might fall.

"Help me," Evliit managed, reaching out to his would-be killer.

Galbard hesitated in bewilderment, but then instinctively moved to catch him as the prophet fell forward.

Evliit clutched Galbard's arm to regain his balance, searching his face with what Galbard thought was a mixture of sadness and terror in his eyes. "It has come to this," Evliit said. "The Spellmakers would take the Sword of the Watch from me by force?"

Awkwardly, Galbard helped him to sit upon the edge of the altar table, and then he looked away. A slave should not have even touched the same ground as a Watcher, especially in a prayer circle.

Amphileph had sent him to kill the prophet of the Creator! His soul was likely cursed just having agreed to make the trip to the Arch of the Patriarchs. His mind reeled with the thought that the actions of the past few minutes might actually have doomed him forever.

"Your things, master," Galbard said, and then he hurried to bring the prophet his scabbard, bag, and shoes. Galbard stopped and knelt at the edge of the prayer circle, and he placed the shoes so that Evliit might slip them on immediately upon his exit.

"I accept my fate," Galbard said, entering the prayer circle with his head down and Evliit's scabbard and bag outstretched before him. He waited for Evliit to take his things, and then Galbard quickly backed away from him outside the prayer circle.

Evliit placed the sword back in its scabbard. He removed a small vial from the bag, drank it, and put it away, and then he heaved a deep breath and slowly looked over the length of the sword.

"Come here," Evliit said. Galbard moved to kneel some ten feet away. "Closer, come closer."

Galbard glanced up at him, and then kneeled at Evliit's feet, expecting the worse.

"You are Galbard, a slave of Amphileph," said Evliit.

"Yes, lord."

"Stand up, and hold out your hands."

Galbard stood up and looked in Evliit's eyes then, extending his hands. To his astonishment, Evliit placed the sword in them, walked past him to the edge of the prayer circle, and slipped on his shoes.

Galbard could not move. A strange tingling sensation ran from his hands throughout his body. The tingling intensified. The golden color of the scabbard and tang began to blur together, becoming luminous. Memories raced through his mind, memories of Rion and the life he once had there, and then flashes of the rolling grasses in the fields north of the city. His head began to pitch slightly, and his eyes flickered closed. He was sure the Watcher could see his expression change from surprise to concern, and when Evliit spoke, the words seemed to pierce Galbard's soul.

"I can wait no longer," Evliit said. "My brethren and I have one last chance to confront the Spellmakers. We will bind them to the lands beyond the Black Mountains, and I will send the sword away from here with you. It has chosen you."

With those last words, the intense pain stopped. Galbard's arms relaxed, and he nearly dropped the sword. He immediately motioned to Evliit to take it back.

"Send the sword away with me? Oh no, my lord, please don't set this task upon me!" Galbard pleaded. "I have no business in the affairs of Watchers. I am nothing, and I must go to ask the Priests of Rion to cleanse me for the evil that I have already done. I swear to you that my eyes were covered by a strange spell, and I did not see you as you were." He lowered his head and held the sword out toward Evliit.

Evliit shook his head. "You didn't see a Watcher, and yet you spared my life. This is not the act of an evil man." Galbard felt Evliit place his hand on the sword and gently push it away. Galbard fixed his eyes upon it and accepted Evliit's charge. A surge of energy coursed through his body, as if every nerve was firing at once. It was exhilarating, and when Galbard looked up, he saw the Watcher's gentle face smiling back at him.

"You are worthy," he said, and the words seemed to melt away Galbard's anxiety.

Evliit turned away and looked westward. The winds began to stir up, and dark clouds formed above the Black Mountain valley. Evliit stared down at the valley for the better part of a minute, his eyes piercing, unflinching in the wind, his beard and hair blown back wildly. Galbard thought him sorely vexed, and he waited in silence for the Watcher's next command.

"Your former master has grown strong. A spell to bind him will come at great cost, consuming the life force of all but the strongest among us. We can take no chance of the sword falling into his hands, for with it, Amphileph would surely end the time of men. You must take it far away. My brothers and I will not be able to bind the Camonra who already move upon Rion, and Amphileph will give them no rest until they have captured the sword for their master."

"I understand," replied Galbard.

"Your heart is true, Galbard. The Creator has crossed our paths for a reason. Take the sword far away into the western lands, throw it into the depths of the ocean that lies beyond if you must, but keep it safe from the evil of Amphileph! I have said my prayer for you. I have asked the Creator to show you the path and give you sanctuary. Go now and pray for *us*. Pray that we can still bind Amphileph!"

Evliit began to chant then in the ancient tongue, and the hair rose on Galbard's neck. There was power in each utterance. The clouds above the valley began to turn slowly. Beams of light shot out from between their wispy turnings. There was a flash from within them, and a great clap of thunder.

Galbard felt a wave of energy pass over him, moving inward toward the valley. It almost pushed him over, and then there was a second flash and Galbard saw it—a sphere of energy was closing in slowly from miles above and around the valley, closing on Amphileph's temple.

Galbard took the Sword and ran, ran as fast as he could northwest to the crest of the Black Mountains on the northern side of the valley. Far below him, he saw the battle for Rion unfolding. Ten thousand Camonra poured across the northern fields toward the city. There were five, maybe six columns of the Rion Guard's cavalry rushing to meet them, flags flying in the wind, and then suddenly, the entire mountain began to shake violently.

Galbard lost his footing and fell against the mountainside, holding onto the stone with all his strength. The Black Mountain Valley split open. A fiery rift crossed southwest through the Black Mountains, where it forked west across the battlefield and south around the east side of Rion. The sky filled with plumes of lava and jets of superheated air, magma, and ash.

Galbard struggled to his feet to look toward Rion, but black clouds of ash and smoke obscured the horizon. The battle drum and the trumpet were silenced. Gone were the long battle lines of the Camonra. Gone were the ordered battlements of the Rion Guard who opposed the sacking of their beloved city. In mere moments, it seemed that everything Galbard knew of his world had changed.

Chapter Two

The End of the First Age

Cayden beat his hands together to knock the dust from them. He loosened the dirty rags that he had tied around them to protect them from the unfinished stone he'd been working into the base of the railing surrounding one of the lower temple's verandas. Masonry work in Rion had thinned since the evacuation of the outer city, and rough stone or not, Cayden's hunger made him happy to have the work.

It had been especially hard to stay focused when he had started setting the stone around the side of the veranda closest to the market. The sounds and smells and the constant flow of people there kept dragging his attention away. The middle of the morning always seemed to be the best time to take a short break and watch the spectacle unfold on the cobblestone streets of Etharath's largest city. Now was close enough to mid-morning for his taste. He removed his leather apron, wrapped his chisels and short-handled sledgehammer in it, and set the bundle just out of sight behind the railing. He pushed his sandy brown hair out of his eyes and lifted up his shirttail to remove the coin pouch tied to his leather belt. He dug around in it and found a small coin, put a smile on his face and walked toward the marketplace in hopes of buying a couple of apples or possibly some bread.

Cayden made his way toward a little stand where he'd found apples the day before, basking in the carnival atmosphere of Rion's central market. Traders making their way through the causeways between the temples shouted out their barter in almost barbaric cries.

Suddenly, above the din, there was a clap of sound so thunderous that the marketplace came to a standstill. Faces turned to the skies in amazement, and a deep red sunlight cast an eerie shadow over the traders and their customers.

"What is this?" one asked, pointing out the blood red and blackening sky. Before Cayden could answer, a second burst of energy came across the land. This one pushed them all from their feet in a wave.

The great Temple of Rion rocked on its foundations, breaking the relief of heroes stretched across its pediment from its mounting. The huge stone relief flipped over in mid-air, and crashed upon dozens of onlookers with a sickening thud. It sank in the cobblestone face up, carnage spraying from beneath its weight.

Cayden staggered to his feet. He felt something warm and sticky on his cheek and looked down at the spatter of blood on his boots. Everything inside him said to run, but he could not move. Those fleeing zigzagged around him in a blur, but he could only look across the horizon at the toppling structures that signaled the end of an age.

Someone collided with Cayden and nearly knocked him off his feet, but the force of the collision seemed to snap him back to reality. He spun around disoriented, and then a crowd moving toward the temple swept upon him.

"No! Get away from the temple!" he yelled, trying to dig in and hold his ground. But the wave of bodies, almost knocking him down, continued pushing him toward the temple steps until a loud popping sound made all of them freeze where they stood.

Sandy dust sprayed his face from above. The columns on either side of the temple entrance were cracking under the stress. Before he could make a sound, a large shard of marble broke away from the column, careened off the temple steps, and cut effortlessly through the crowd, narrowly missing him.

Bodies pinned him to the ground, almost smothering him. He had always been a little claustrophobic, and the weight of the bodies was crushing him. There was crying and moaning, and the knot of people writhed on top of him. He heard a voice yelling to get up; it might have been his. Using all his might and will, Cayden pushed a limp body out of the way. He pushed his head out into the air, clawed his way out of the pile, and crawled over stunned, wounded, and dying people to get to his feet. He began running toward the southern side of the city with abandon.

On either side of him, the great architecture of Rion was falling like wheat to the great scythe that was the fury of the Mourner's Fault. A billowing cloud of ash rushed in from the north and engulfed them, and

Cayden had to feel his way along in front of him, blindly stumbling along the path between the row houses. To his left, a mother screamed for her children. Somewhere south of him, a man was shouting curses.

There was suddenly a clearing in the haze and Cayden could see where he was.

"The end is upon us!" a man with his hands raised to the sky cried. "Our sins have convicted us!"

A second man appeared beside him and fell upon his knees. "We are doomed!" he yelled. "We have forgotten our heritage with the Creator, and now we reap our penance!"

Cayden darted past them in a dead run, screaming, "Run you fools!"

The two men tore their clothes, ignoring him. They pounded their hands against their foreheads in repentance, never seeing the massive column that silently lumbered forward on its pedestal, crushing them where they knelt.

Another rolling spasm of the land threw Cayden in the air. He skidded to a landing on his back and opened his eyes. The blood red skies were streaked with smoky trails of flaming magma shooting into the air north of Rion. *I must make it to the sea,* he thought, forcing himself to get up and run south again.

Molten stone began to drop around him. A small piece landed on his shoulder and burned through his leather vest, searing his skin. He kept running, scratching and clawing at the incredible pain coming from the burning hole in his vest. He scraped the small, greyish stone out with his fingernails, oblivious to the burning sensations in his fingers, and he flew toward the cliffs of Rion.

Exhaustion slowed his pace, and then the sound of the masses exiting Rion behind him became deafening. Cayden pushed himself even harder to avoid them trampling him.

Rifts suddenly split the ground. Some were tiny cracks, but others were almost three feet across, spewing hot gasses from within their depths into the fleeing masses, the intense heat searing their lungs with a single breath.

Just when Cayden began to believe the burning feeling in his lungs and side would overcome him, he came upon the servants' quarters that lay southeast of the city, near the sheer cliffs leading down to the sea. He thought he might stop to catch his breath, but he kept moving. There were stairs that zigzagged down the side of the cliffs. Cayden hoped to find a vessel in which he could move away from the destruction and out to sea until the quakes ended.

Cayden stopped once again to catch his breath. The fishermen and stone masons whose livelihoods came from the quarries and seas to the south stood amongst the rubble of their shanties, watching the great city fall. Their mouths hung open in disbelief of what they were witnessing. Mothers covered their distressed children's ears so they could not hear the cries of agony that echoed from the north.

"The whole world is running toward us, Mommy!" one of the children cried just as one of those fleeing ran into his mother and knocked her to the ground. Cayden started toward her, but one of the men grabbed her and helped her to her feet. The fleeing mob was forcing them closer and closer to the sheer cliffs of Rion's southern border.

"You've got to get out of here!" Cayden yelled.

"But our masters . . ." one began.

"Wait no more!" Cayden interrupted. "I've come from the city. All is lost!" They themselves looked lost at his saying this, and Cayden grabbed the man closest to him. "To the docks! It is their only hope!"

The man appeared to regain his senses and called out to the others, "Flee! Flee to the docks!" Several others took the cue and surrounded the women and children, walking, and then grabbing up their children and running to the cliff stairs.

Cayden reached the staircase landing and looked over the railing. The sea itself seemed tossed in the turmoil. He could see the Rionese galleons straining against their moorings in the docks some three hundred feet below.

There are so few boats, he thought. He looked back toward Rion and saw a seemingly endless flow of people evacuating the city, and then he bolted down the stairs.

He rounded the second turn in the long staircase that cut into Rion's sheer cliffs and glanced up. Above him, the stairs were flooded with all walks of life—the rich, the poor, laborer, and gentleman—all rushing down in hopes of boarding the ships below. Some stumbled on the narrow stairs and fell past him to their deaths, others collapsed on the stairs in exhaustion. Cayden ran with every ounce of energy that he had left into the third, and final, turn and managed to make his way to the head of the pack.

With each rumble of the earth, the staircase cracked and split, and he heard the collective screams of the crowds in response. Crumbling pieces of stonework were falling all around them, but the crowd choked the steps, and now some of those caught up in the knots of fleeing people screamed against the crushing weight of the vastly overcrowded staircase.

When Cayden finally reached the docks, he ran down the long central pier, away from cliff walls. Several of the ships had already moved out to sea.

There was suddenly a strong aftershock, and Cayden again heard loud screams from behind him. He turned back toward the cliffs in time to see the upper section of the crowded stone stairs tearing away from the cliffs, the volume of screams increasing with its descent toward him. The massive upper section of steps struck the next lower section and that rubble caught the center of the lower third. Bodies fell into the sea or burst upon the wooden decks of the harbor, and debris buried the four ships closest to the staircase. The decking broke loose from the shoreline in several places, but Cayden managed to leap onto the rope ladder thrown over the side of the nearest ship. He pulled himself over the side as a second wall of stone collapsed into the sea.

"Come on!" Cayden yelled, waving the terrified people toward one of the boats. "We have room for more here!" The throng scrambled into the boat, falling over each other in their panic. "Hurry, we must clear the harbor!" he yelled. "Move to the front! More can get in!"

Cayden could see a young woman on the dock scanning the expanse of the staircase, her panicked eyes dancing back and forth, up and down their length. Her baby was crying, screaming even. They met eyes, but she looked at the thickening throng attempting to board the larger ship Cayden occupied, and she hesitated.

"Come on, lady!" he yelled to her, but her face appeared as if she thought that she'd no chance of getting on it. She turned and moved toward a second boat across the docks, where a small group was throwing off the moorings in preparation to leave.

Cayden continued pulling others into the boat when he heard a man in the opposite boat shriek, "Get back!"

He turned to see the woman fall back upon the dock, her child screaming in her arms. The quakes rippled the docks beneath her, several boards ripping loose with the great strain of the sea's surge.

"Get out of the way!" he heard someone yell from behind him, and several men were pushing long wooden beams into a capstan in the middle of ship.

"Warp her!" another yelled and several of the men began straining against the horizontal beams, turning the capstan ever so slowly, pulling tight a heavy rope that ran along the deck and out the rear of the boat.

"Wait!" Cayden yelled, but the boat had already started back from the dock, and the deck was jammed with people. He scanned the deck for another way across and saw that there was a longboat suspended on ropes just over the railing. He jumped upon the railing and tip-toed across it before jumping into the longboat, but he couldn't figure out how to lower it.

Her shrill scream made him look over the side. She held the baby at arm's length toward the man. "Please, sir, take my child!" she begged.

"Get back!" the man yelled again. He and three others used oars to push against the dock, and their small ship drifted away from her. The woman drew her child to her chest, and she fell back upon the sea-smoothed wooden slats that made up the dock, trying to comfort her screaming child. People were jumping over her into the ocean in chase of the departing boats.

Cayden was still fumbling with the wenches to lower his boat, when he and the man in the other boat met eyes. The man dropped his gaze in shame. Cayden was looking right at him when a great piece of stone fell from the cliff walls and struck them amidships, dragging the wreckage to the bottom of the harbor.

The crash of the stone surged the waters of the harbor, tearing away the dock, carrying the woman and child away from the shore with a great wave.

Three other men jumped from the deck into Cayden's longboat and began helping him work the wenches to lower it. The section of the dock turned slightly and Cayden could see her face for a moment. She had closed her eyes, and it appeared to him that she had exhausted her will to live, but the sound of her son's choking on the water snapped her back into action. She rolled over and pushed his head above the water, and her own face sank beneath the waves. She grasped him beneath his armpit, and he writhed in her hands, his tiny fingers pinching the skin of her arm with all their tiny might.

"Come up!" he yelled, but the woman's arm continued to sink, until the baby's feet splashed the water furiously. Cayden's longboat had just reached them when the hand relaxed and the baby eased under the waves.

Cayden thrust his hand into the water, and though he worried that his strong grip would break the child's arm, he grabbed him and pulled him above the stirring waves. "Help me!" Cayden yelled.

One of the other men sprang to his side. Cayden thrust the crying baby toward him. "Take him!" he cried, and then he turned to the frothy ocean.

The child's mother had disappeared in the darkness of the depths, and without thinking, Cayden leapt overboard. He was not a swimmer, but the urgency of saving her overcame his fear for his own life.

The stormy sounds of Rion's destruction left his ears for the deep hum of the ocean's weighty water. He opened his eyes to their salty sting and caught the wispy movement of her dress descending into the darkness. He kicked with all his might, pulling the water toward him with the sweep of his arms. His boots and clothing seemed to fight his movement toward her, his exertions forcing the air in his lungs to bubble from his nose. His eyes widened with the thought that he was descending beyond his ability to return, and his kicks shortened. He was sure he was going to gasp, going to fill his lungs full of water.

Suddenly he saw her kick spasmodically. Her body turned in the water, bringing one of her legs just within reach. He grasped it, and the weight of her body made him continue to descend against his efforts to pull her to the surface. The pressure of the water pushed some of the air from his lungs, and panic gripped him. Only the outline of the boat's hull stood out against the bright surface of the water above, its ghostly shadow leading back to his salvation.

He looked at the distant hull and resolved that his strength was no match to its distance, and he stopped struggling and pulled her toward him, wanting to look at her face before darkness overcame them.

He brought her upright, and a *thunk* vibrated the water. The longboat's anchor came rushing toward them, narrowly missing them and disappearing past them in the darkness below.

The anchor rope snapped taut before him. He grabbed it and struggled with all his remaining strength to pull them upward, when suddenly it began to move in his hand, burning even his rough palm with its gnarly fibers. In response, he clutched it even tighter, a death grip on life itself, and he zoomed toward the surface with the ascending rope. He could almost make out the men, their broken image dancing in the rippling waves, but he could take it no longer, and the gasp he had fought so hard came involuntarily. The sensation of water filling his lungs made him convulse, and his own survival instinct overwhelmed him again. He lost his grip on the rope. Three or four splashes and bursts of bubbles appeared in the water, and then everything went black.

* * *

Cayden awoke on the deck of the ship. He coughed the seawater from his lungs and choked on the air that replaced it. There was a blur of faces over him.

"It's a miracle!" someone said.

"Stand back! Stand back! Let the air come to him!" another yelled. They turned their attention to the woman, still lifelessly sprawled on the rough deck of the ship.

Cayden rolled to his side, his focus returned just in time to see water issue from the woman's nose and mouth. She too gasped for air.

"The Creator be praised!" one woman said, but attention instantly shifted away from them. Her voice was drowned out by the needs of the boat itself.

"Man the sails!" the sailors cried.

"The kedging anchor is up, captain!" one of the men yelled.

"Secure the capstan! Out to sea!" another responded. "Away from the cliffs!"

Cayden watched the young mother's face roll toward the deck. Her nose crumpled against the hard planks. He coughed again, and remnants of the seawater water burned his nose and throat. Through his bloodshot eyes, he could see that she was alive, her chest rising and falling sporadically. It was enough, he thought, and he rolled to his back and watched the sails blossom against the stormy clouds, and the makeshift crew blurring past him in all directions.

Cayden's head bobbed with the snap of the sails. He could actually feel the boat's lurch forward, straining timbers connected to the mast beside him. Faintly, he could hear the slap of water against the bow. The cool breeze rushing over him brought the strong smell of fish and sea. He didn't have the energy to turn his head toward Rion, but he could still hear its loud explosions over the orders being shouted by the seafarers among them.

Another young woman sat down cross-legged on the deck between him and the rescued mother. Her simple tunic told him that she was likely a servant in the temples, but she tucked one side of her long brown hair behind her ear, exposing her rosy cheeks and comforting smile. Cayden thought her face shone. She carried with her the small child Cayden had rescued. The baby was sound asleep in her arms, and she was focused on his every movement.

"Is the baby, alright?" Cayden managed.

As if noticing Cayden only then, she adjusted her skirt to cover her legs and smiled. "Yes, thanks to you." He struggled to sit up, but she placed a hand gently on his chest. "You must rest."

He laid his head back against the deck. "I'll be fine," he said.

"What's your name?" she asked.

"Cayden." He folded his hands behind his head, but he found no comfort in them, so he rolled over on his side and wiped the water from his face with one hand.

"I am Nara," she said. "You're from Rion?"

"Yes. I am . . ." he began. "I *was* a mason there." He looked toward the cliffs of Rion. Smoke and ash could still be seen rising into the air, though they were now miles from shore. "I'm afraid there will not be a Rion to which we may return. Even if there were, my father's fathers spent many years carving out the stairs to the ocean. Without them, there is no way to ascend the steep cliff walls."

"The captain says that we must round all of Etharath in the west, where the cliffs turn to shores," Nara said, looking west. Her face suddenly stretched tight with anxiety. "I've never been on a sailing ship before." She pulled the swaddling cloth tightly around the child.

The rescued woman stirred, and Cayden attempted to prop himself up on one elbow. "You gave us quite a scare," he said.

The woman's eyes closed slowly and then shot open. She struggled to rise. "Where's Ronan?" she asked. "My baby!"

Nara moved closer and lowered the sleeping child by her side. "The baby is fine. He sleeps."

The woman sighed deeply and pulled Ronan tight to her bosom, and then suddenly, burst into tears. Nara stroked her fine, blond hair, its wet braids slowly unraveling to her shoulders. She had a thin, gold chain around her neck that the baby was toying with in his sleep.

"Everything's going to be fine," Nara said. She nodded to Cayden. "Your baby's safe and you as well, thanks to . . . Cayden," she said.

"I give thanks to the Creator for sparing our lives," Cayden added. He smiled and looked to the sky. "I should not want to test his mercy in that way again," he said. He rolled his head back to face her, and their eyes met. Cayden smiled. "Now Nara and I know your *child's* name, but not yours."

She did her best to stop her tears. "I'm Jalin," she said.

With a sudden, girlish giddiness, Nara called out, "The boat's leaving the cliffs. We're heading for the western coast!"

Jalin's eyes sprang to life. "I can't leave Rion!" she cried. She attempted to stand up, but her legs were still too weak. "My husband—wait! I have to wait!"

Cayden looked at Nara. "Oh, no," he uttered before he had realized it.

Jalin saw the strange look on Cayden's face. "What?" she asked.

Cayden couldn't lie to her. "There's nothing left of the stairs in the southern cliffs. There's no way back to Rion that way. We are going west, where the cliffs end."

Jalin stared at him, speechless. She glanced from Cayden to Nara, shaking her head in denial. He reached out a hand to comfort her.

She pulled away. "No!" she screamed. "My husband works off our debt north of Rion. How will he find us now?"

Cayden let his hand drop. "I don't know. I'm sorry."

Jalin doubled over as if she'd been punched in the stomach. Her mouth opened, but made no sound, and then deep within her, a moan worked its way to some volume, loud enough that several of the sailors paused to see what was happening.

Nara picked up the baby and rocked him, but the sound of his mother's voice stirred the child to crying himself.

"Oh, Jalin!" Nara said. "I'm so sorry."

Though Nara was able to calm Ronan after a short time, Jalin cried for nearly a solid hour. An hour more, and Jalin became quiet. She stared into the distance, watching the horizon rise and fall just over the port rail. "My actions shame me. When the water covered me, I just gave up. I always thought I would struggle until the very end, but I just gave up."

"Feel no shame," Cayden interjected. "Even the bravest warriors ran for their lives today."

"Thank you for saving us," Jalin responded. "Saying it is not enough. I've no words to tell you how thankful I am."

"I'm glad that you both are safe. Forget about it. Anyone would have done the same."

"I wish that were true," Jalin said. "But you saw that madness at the docks. Even with a child in my arms, I was turned away."

"They paid for their cruelty," said Cayden.

"Some have said the evil of men has brought the Creator's wrath upon us," Jalin said. "That we have brought all this upon ourselves."

"I don't believe that," Cayden said. "Evil and good alike died today."

"Enough talk then," one of the men said, and then he rose from the deck's hatch and crossed the deck toward them. "Your philosophizing won't bring us to the Western Shore."

"Leave 'em be, Tadhra," another responded. "We've enough men to raise the sails—that's good enough for now. Captain's got to shoot the stars."

"Well, he'd better be about it," Tadhra replied. "There's little food on board, and sailing or no, this bunch will want to eat."

"Yeah, yeah, why don't you tell the captain to 'urry then. But call me first—I want to be there when he beats the fool outta ya," the man said. He laughed deep and hearty, much to Tadhra's chagrin. The sailors among them laughed loudly, but Cayden, Nara, and Jalin remained silent.

"Drag the nets as we go!" the captain yelled from the stern, and the sailors pulled the nets from the stowage chests.

"Drag the nets as we run!" the order repeated round the ship.

"These nets are only big enough to slow us down!" Tadhra complained.

"Watch yourself!" one of the other sailors yelled, ignoring Tadhra.

Tadhra drew the nets up on the short starboard mast that swung out over the side, watching the bubble mounted on the downside of the bow upper deck. "Get the port mast out! Keep the bubble!" he yelled. The bubble slid starboard with the movement of the nets and the starboard mast.

"Aye!" came the response, and the port mast swung into position and the bubble slowly recentered.

"Let 'em down!" the first officer yelled and the nets were released. The winches whined and spun. "Not too deep!" the officer yelled and two of the sailors applied the winch brakes. The officer watched the bubble. "A little deeper on the port side!" he cried, and the sailors hand-cranked the port winch in response. Again, the bubble came to the center. The first officer raised his hand. "Lock 'em down!" he yelled.

The officer moved past Cayden. "Ever been on a ship?" he shouted to him.

"No, sir, but I'm willing to help," Cayden responded.

He pointed the bubble out to Cayden. "Watch the bubble—that there," he said. "If that changes, you yell out!" he said gruffly, and then he paused to check for Cayden's understanding.

"I can do that," Cayden responded. The first officer said nothing in reply, but walked quickly toward the stern. Just as quickly, he ascended the three stairs rising from the amidships deck to the stern deck and approached the captain. Jalin and Nara sat with Ro against the port railing, and Cayden watched the bubble intently as he had promised, but their position amidships put them right in the middle of the action, listening intently to the sailors around them in an attempt to understand what all was happening.

"Nets are running, captain," the first officer reported.

"Very well, Markston," the captain said, and then he turned to a young lad at his side. "Fetch me my sextant, boy."

The young one scrambled. "Yes, sir!" he said, practically jumping down the stern deck stairs and bolting into the cabin below.

"We make our way round the cliffs, Markston," the captain said, pointing to the west. The boy reappeared with his sextant, his small chest huffing the air.

"Thank you, lad," the captain said, and then he scanned the sky. "Give them nets an hour and bring 'em up. Perhaps the women can make themselves useful with the catch," he said. "Don't leave much to the land dwellers and my bubble."

"Aye, captain," Markston replied.

"And watch the tension on those nets' masts. Snap one off, and we go hungry."

"Aye, captain," Markston replied. He made his way back toward the bow and Cayden's intent watch of the bubble. "I've got this. Help the women until the nets come in."

"Of course," Cayden responded, and he, Nara, and Jalin made their own way back amidships, joining the group of townspeople standing there. Jalin was struggling with Ro, and Cayden thought that she was not looking very well. She was taking on a green color.

He placed one hand on Jalin's shoulder. "Feeling any better?" he asked.

"This is madness." She smiled weakly. "The baby is doing fine, and I feel as if I'm going to be sick."

"Let me hold him," Cayden said. He nodded to Nara. "Perhaps Nara can help you?" he asked. "I think there's some privacy on the bow of the ship, behind the mermaid."

"Mermaid?" asked Nara.

"That wood carving—on the front of the ship."

"Yes, of course. Come, Jalin," Nara said. She took her hand, and they made their way forward, around the starboard side to the wooden trellis that wrapped around the bow.

Cayden sat on the deck with Ronan in his arms, admiring how the rocking motion of the boat did not seem to bother him in the least. There had been times when Cayden had felt a bit of dizziness, especially when the sea kicked up and sloshed the boat about, but it had passed.

He touched the baby's cheek and marveled at his tiny fingers. Suddenly the little hand grasped Cayden's finger tightly, even though the baby was still fast asleep.

A smile formed on Cayden's face. "You're a strong one," he said. Out of the corner of his eye, he saw Nara helping Jalin back across the deck toward him. Jalin held one hand out in front of her. She carefully made her way back to Cayden and sat down.

"Any better?" he asked.

"No," Jalin said. "I feel awful."

"You're all wet," Cayden said.

"We stepped on the slats, and water shot up through the trellis."

"The rocking motion got the better of me, and I got very sick," said Jalin. "Thank you for holding my dress back."

"Of course," Nara replied.

A belch slipped out of Jalin's mouth, the taste of which looked to be terrible. "I'm sorry," she said. "Oh, this is awful. I've nothing more in my stomach, and I still feel as if I must retch."

"Sea sickness—they say it's the worst of all," Nara said.

"See if you can sleep. Nara and I can watch the boy," said Cayden.

"Well . . ." she said almost cautiously.

"It's okay, really," Nara added. "We'll be fine."

Jalin looked at the baby cuddled tightly in Cayden's arms. "Well, maybe for just a little while."

"Sure, then, just for a little while," Nara said.

The first officer walked back by them and pointed to the deck hatch. "Why don't you take the women below?" he asked. "There are hammocks in the galley area. The missus looks a little under the weather, and there'll be fish on the deck soon. I'll need you out of the way for the catch to come in."

"Yes, sir," Cayden answered, and then he moved to the deck hatch with Ro and nodded Nara and Jalin over. "Hold him, Nara," he said. He handed over the baby and lifted the heavy hatch, holding it open for the women and the child. They descended into the depths of the boat, and Cayden let the heavy deck hatch fall back into place.

The first officer squatted down to look through the deck hatch lattice. "Latch it and stand back," he added. "Lest you want to get wet. All men will be on deck to bring in the nets, and the captain will expect all the women to work the fish. The missus with the child and her friend can take turns below with the child. Don't bring him on the deck then—too much going on then, you know."

"Yes, sir," they responded.

The cargo hatch let a little light around the middle of the galley, and it took a minute for their eyes to adjust to the dim light. Cayden noticed the hammocks piled in the floor next to the Healer's quarters. He grabbed one up and hooked the ropes' eyes to two hooks in the ceiling.

Jalin climbed in the hammock and closed her eyes. The hammock gently resisted the motion of the ship. "Yes, that's much better already," she said. Cayden and Nara sat down at a small table bolted to the floor of the galley. She glanced at Ronan once or twice as if confirming Nara was attentive to him, and within minutes, Jalin and Ro were asleep.

Cayden's curiosity got the better of him, and he began looking around the galley. "You'd think with all the water I just ingested, thirst would be the last thing on my mind, but to tell you the truth, I'm parched." He meandered over to a barrel next to the iron stove in the center of the ship's galley, opened it, and the smell of hops filled his nose. "Well, here's something," he said. He eyed a ladle and scooped up a bit of the fermentation. He found a mug along the side of the mess area oven, filled it with the ladle, and took a long gulp. He grimaced and let the remainder of his mouthful spill back into the mug.

Nara giggled at his expression.

"This is nasty!" he exclaimed, and then he looked for a place to throw it out, but seeing none, made his way to the Healer's quarters, a small room on the port side of the ship.

The small quarters smelled rank indeed, but there was a small porthole. He thought to unlatch it and pour out the ale—or whatever they called the concoction—but when he entered the cabin, his eyes adjusted to the even dimmer lighting within. He saw implements of the Healer—saws and clamps and a leather-covered mallet. He noticed a darkly stained bench along the wall and conjured up images of the gruesome medical attention provided there. He quickly opened the small porthole and tossed out the remainder of his mug.

Through the porthole, Cayden could see a number of boats with people scattered throughout the rigging. They were apparently clueless of its operation, and their ships were drifting dangerously close to the rocks that lined the Rionese cliffs. Ropes connected two of the boats, and there appeared to be an all-out fight occurring on their decks. He could faintly hear the men shouting and the women screaming. He closed the small porthole and returned to the galley.

"Stay here," Cayden told Nara and Jalin, and then he made his way up the stairs back to the deck. Upon emerging topside, he called out to the first officer. He pointed to the warring boats in the distance. "Sir, those people are in trouble!" he said.

"Best that you go below," the first officer said firmly.

"But sir, we should help—"

"You see the size of that boat, sir?" the first officer retorted. "Do you see that their men outnumber our own?" he asked. "What would you do? Would you be willing to lose our ship to them as well? I'm sorry, sir, but these are desperate times. We'll not be moving off our course for the western shores. This is a fishing vessel and no warship—we've no weapons, save the few we carry ourselves. We run fast, as fast as we can to the western shores."

"I should speak to the captain," said Cayden.

The first officer looked him in the eye. "I'll not be bothering the captain," he said. "He's fully aware of what is transpiring around us. If he wanted us to board her, the order'd been given before now. So I'll be asking you again to go below, sir." With this, his face hardened and his open palm pointed the way back to the galley hatch.

"Very well," Cayden said, wishing no more quarrel. He looked around once again at the mad scene of the ragtag Rionese flotilla with its infighting, sinking boats, and general insanity. Feeling absolutely overwhelmed, he descended the stairs into the ship's galley without so much as a glance back.

Chapter Three

BOUNDLAND

Amphileph had taken more time than he would have liked to lock down the temple and direct the Camonra to stand guard. The slave, Galbard, had been gone for near half the day, and Amphileph's patience was waning. Amphileph wanted to join with the other Spellmakers in the catacombs below the temple, where the coven had combined forces in the altar room constructed directly below the temple floor.

The smell of the catacombs nauseated Amphileph, but he had ordered the Spellmakers' coven deep within their walls so they could focus on casting the spells of *Ponto Lethargus* and *Absconditus* on Evliit. His head was pounding from the long hours of intense concentration. Not paying attention to where he was walking, he stepped in what he could only hope was water, soaking the leather of the sandal on his left foot before he could jerk it back out of the puddle. He cursed. Looking around to take out his frustrations on the nearest slave he could find, the entire temple suddenly began to shake violently. Rubble and mortar trickled from practically every joint in the stonework. Dust filled the air in the catacombs.

Amphileph held up his hand to shift the micro currents in the air and the polarity of the particles, repulsing the dust around him. His view cleared of the load-bearing arches in the crisscrossing halls. The massive stones appeared to be faring well enough, so he held his ground. He could hear other Spellmakers yelling, but before he could make his way to the room they occupied, the quakes' crescendo suddenly ended.

He stood perfectly still.

Something very significant had taken place—the shift in spiritual energy was unlike anything he had felt before. He could no longer focus on Evliit's life force. It was as if he could feel only the *absence* of Evliit.

Surely the great quakes signaled Amphileph's victory! Now the great city of Rion—the patron city of the Elders, those human ingrates who dared challenge his right to determine the future of humanity—yes, Rion would also fall. The Rion Guard had risen against his creation of the Camonra, and for this, he would destroy them.

Amphileph hurried to the other Spellmakers, whom he was sure were still huddled in the altar room, frightened for their lives. They had barely the stomach to do the real work required to correct the course of Etharath's history.

He passed one of the alchemy laboratories where several of the Camon jailers were attempting to put out a fire, apparently caused by some glass tubing and beakers shattering during the quake. Slaves were screaming for release from their cages before the fires consumed them, but he had no time to deal with that either. He could rebuild the lab, and there were always enough slaves to go around.

He arrived at last at the conjuring room in the innermost section of the catacombs. The Spellmakers were scattered among its ornate wooden kneeling rails and prayer rails, most of them wearing their white prayer robes. Some had collapsed across the rails, but most still knelt at them, elbows up and hands clasped, head lowered to the image of a sword etched into a large stone altar at the far end of the room.

"Do you feel it, brothers?" Amphileph asked, entering the room, smiling from ear to ear. "What we have accomplished in the darkness will soon be known by all! Soon we'll have the Sword of the Watch!"

Amphileph grabbed Clogren, his trusted student, by the shoulders. "Rise, my brothers!" Amphileph said. "This is a glorious day!" He thought Clogren looked especially weak, for the conjuring that had overcome Evliit had been strong magic indeed, and Clogren was committed to him to the death.

Clogren struggled to his feet, pulling up the oversized sleeves of his prayer robes. "Master, you have shown them once and for all that your power knows no limits. The evil of men shall pass away! Now we create the world that should have been." Clogren looked around at his brethren Spellmakers, and then his gleeful look faded. Many of them looked confused and terrified. "Soon everyone will know of our great sacrifice, brothers! The new Erathe will give great honor to the Creator!"

"Yes, yes, of course," Amphileph replied. He reached down to help another to his feet. "Come, let us go to Rion. Let us wear the six colors of tartan and our bespeckled robes! We will watch our Camonra destroy the Rion Guard and carry us to the steps of the Elders' temple." Amphileph turned and exited the altar room, Clogren close on his heels.

They made their way through the twisted catacombs deftly, and quickly entered a laboratory, pushing aside everything in the way on a table there. Amphileph poured water into a brass basin. He pointed Clogren to stand near the end of the table. "Watch and learn," he insisted. Clogren hurried to his assigned spot and leaned over a bit to see the basin.

"*Aperio*," Amphileph said, waving his hand over the basin. The torchlight seemed to dance in the water for a moment, but then the water began to change shape. Figures rose from its surface and slowly took on the forms of the Spellmakers, who one by one lifted their heads and looked at each other, and then the basin sprang to life, showing Amphileph everything that was happening in the altar room.

"What have we done?" Ardidhus asked them. "The slave was only to take the sword while Evliit slept. I have seen a vision of the slave poised to kill Evliit with the Sword of the Watch, and now I do not sense Evliit at all! What have we done?"

"Master . . ." Clogren whispered, but then quickly covered his mouth, fearing the basin might somehow allow the other Spellmakers to hear him.

"Quiet!" Amphileph replied. He leaned in slightly closer to the basin.

The whole lot of other Spellmakers looked away from Ardidhus, moving to one side of the basin and leaving Ardidhus on the other side alone, but he would not stop. "I know that mankind has fallen away from the Creator, but I did not agree to kill Evliit. My mind is clear that I did not speak that spell," Ardidhus said.

With each word, Amphileph could feel his blood pressure rising.

The tiny figure of Ardidhus turned in the basin. "We may have agreed to help Amphileph end the evil of man, but we did not intend for Evliit to be injured. His stubbornness notwithstanding, Evliit has not wronged us." Ardidhus pleaded with his comrades. He hung his head and spoke softly. Amphileph thought he saw the image wipe away a tear. "Our intent was to prove to Evliit the great good we can do with our alchemy and conjuring," Ardidhus said. "The Creator has given us this knowledge. He intended it for us . . ." His voice trailed off, and he looked away from them.

"Enough!" Amphileph said, and the figures fell back under the surface of the water with a splash just before he swatted the basin across the room.

"Come with me!" he said, grabbing Clogren's clothes and hurriedly exiting the laboratory. "The others are coming."

Amphileph and Clogren quickly made their way through the catacombs and exited the temple, squinting their eyes in the bright sun. To the south, in the direction of Rion, Amphileph saw the other Spellmakers exiting the temple. They looked back at him and then began to talk among themselves. They had done the same after the previous attempt at stealing Evliit's Sword, when Citanth, their fellow Spellmaker, was drained of his powers by merely touching it. The skin of his hand had bubbled and fallen off like hot cheese, leaving it useless, and Citanth had barely survived the encounter.

They knew that this time he had sent the slave to *kill* Evliit. They were talking about him, he was sure. And they were gathering against him, Ardidhus at the forefront.

Amphileph breathed in. "Even after the vast majority of the Camonra have left for Rion, I cannot stand that smell," he said. He looked back at the group and thought to himself how they had always envied his abilities. "I ordered all but the temple guard to move to the northern camp near the Black Mountains. Let Citanth bathe in their stench."

"Our brother is delirious with pain, master, he worries not for any smell," said Clogren with a chuckle.

"He has failed me!" Amphileph shouted back. "Let the Camonra females care for him! I don't even want to see his face! Let him tend to the fires with the old and the pregnant!"

A Camon runner approaching from the north interrupted them. "Father!" the runner said, bowing at Amphileph's feet.

"What is it?" Clogren retorted. "The master cannot be bothered now!"

"Forgive me, but you must come toward the northern camp!" the runner said.

"I should strike you dead!" Clogren yelled. "You do not say what we must do!"

"Calm yourself, Clogren. What is it?" Amphileph interrupted.

"Father, there is no path to the northern camp!"

"What is that you say?" Clogren asked.

"I have no words for what happens, Father, I can only show," the Camon replied, shielding his face from the wrath of Amphileph.

"Show me now!" Amphileph commanded.

"Yes, Father!" the Camon responded and immediately turned and headed toward the northern camp.

"The other Spellmakers have noted the commotion," said Amphileph, nodding toward Ardidhus and the others. Other Camon runners appeared as if with news, but stopped to clear a path for Amphileph and the other fathers.

About a hundred yards from the temple, the Camonra camp came into view. A second group had formed on the southern side of the camp. They looked perplexed, pacing back and forth across the path.

Clogren and Amphileph suddenly slowed to a stop some ten feet across from them.

"Father, we cannot pass!" one of the Camonra cried out to Amphileph. Stepping back and taking a knee with his comrades, the lot of them lowered their heads. Amphileph paid them no mind, and moved toward the northern camp with purpose. In mid-step, Amphileph stopped and put his hands out before him, and then he stepped back. "What is this?" he asked.

"Master?" Clogren inquired.

Amphileph's hands began to glow red, and he thrust them forward before his body, but it was as if his hands hit an invisible wall, the red glow of his hands dissipating in its vertical plane.

"No!" Amphileph shouted.

Ardidhus and the other Spellmakers stopped behind him, giving him some space. Amphileph stepped back and paced parallel to the barrier. "No!" he repeated, and then he suddenly thrust his hands against the barrier. The aura around his hands burst forth bright red light that spread throughout the barrier, momentarily giving it some opacity and form. He could see the energy crawling along its surface, arching upward and back over them some fifty feet in the air.

"So Evliit's followers mean to bind us, do they?" Amphileph asked with a grating laugh. "Fools!" he said. He summoned one of the Camonra. "Have your soldiers determine the extent of this barrier," Amphileph ordered, and then he stormed off toward the temple, almost colliding with Ardidhus and the other Spellmakers.

"Amphileph, we need to speak with you," Ardidhus said.

"This is not the time—" Clogren began.

Ardidhus cut him off. "This *is* the time!" He stared menacingly at Clogren, and the latter moved back. "Can you not see that the Watchers have gathered against us? Can you not see the irony in it? They that we could not convince to make spells have cast a spell of Binding upon us!" he began breaking into a nervous laughter. "They have bound us in our own temple!"

"What do you need, Ardidhus?" Amphileph asked.

"What do I need?" Ardidhus demanded. "Let us begin with this question, Amphileph: where is the Sword of the Watch?" The group of Watchers slowly moved in behind him. "Where is this man, this slave, Galbard, and where is the Sword?"

Amphileph's jaw tightened. "Are you questioning the path you've chosen, brother?"

"It is true that we chose to join with you, to end this haggard race of men, and it was we who stood beside you when Evliit caused the distortion of the Camonra. We were the ones that believed we could bring honor to the Creator with the purity of a new race. We *all* agreed that it was time to bring about that new beginning, but . . ."

"But?" Amphileph moved in closer to Ardidhus.

Ardidhus pulled at his clothing as if he began to feel heat rising around the collar of his cloak. He glanced back at the other Spellmakers to renew his confidence. "We have seen the man Galbard standing over Evliit with the sword poised over him—ready to kill him, Amphileph! Why would we see such a vision? We never agreed to any violence against our own."

Amphileph almost smiled at how terrified Ardidhus looked.

"'Against our *own*?'" he shouted. "'Oh, what have we done? I can no longer sense the spiritual forces of the Watchers!'" said Amphileph, mocking them. "Step back, Ardidhus!"

Ardidhus held his ground. "Not 'What have *we* done,' Amphileph, it's what have *you* done?"

"He would never have joined us!" Amphileph shouted, causing the group of Spellmakers to jump at the sound of him. "Evliit has forfeited his right to command me by his siding with this heresy called *men*!"

Ardidhus stepped back. "This causes me great sadness. We've all been wrong. Here is no great prophet, but merely a man consumed by his own desire for power. Amphileph . . . brother, we were wrong to do this," he said. "We must pray for forgiveness from Evliit and the Creator!" Ardidhus turned away from Amphileph to seek a response from the other Spellmakers, never seeing the bright glow that erupted from Amphileph's hands.

"Wrong?" Amphileph screamed. A burst of energy shot Ardidhus through the air at incredible velocity. In horror, his fellow Spellmakers watched his body smack against the temple stone almost a hundred yards away. He slid down the temple dome and off onto the ground, crumpling into a pile.

The other Watchers gasped in unison. "No, Amphileph!" they yelled.

"I knew you would turn on me!" Amphileph shrieked.

A blue aura formed before the other Spellmakers just before a second blast of Amphileph's fury struck it in an explosive mix of greenish red plasma, the splatter of it blackening the dirt it touched. They struggled to maintain their footing and the protective aura with their combined energies, but Amphileph's onslaught began pushing the lot of them back.

"Amphileph, please stop!" one yelled from behind the aura. He thrust his hands downward, raising them with a grasping motion. Roots exploded from the ground and wrapped around Amphileph's arms and waist, squeezing him.

"You will not stop me!" he shouted, but fear began to well up in him when the branches curled around his arms and neck, slowing his furious pounding against the aura and then stopping it altogether. Root after root sprang from the ground and latched onto Amphileph until the knotting foliage engulfed him.

In the darkness, Amphileph could still hear the muffled sounds of shouting over the closer creaking of the tightening vines. It was becoming harder and harder to breathe. He imagined that the Spellmakers were sighing in relief, their fast, heavy breathing telling of their struggle. He could not move at all, but he imagined that several of them were bent over, placing their hands on their knees and resting, allowing their protective aura to dissipate. Panic was rising in his throat. He had to think. *Where was Clogren?* He concentrated his thoughts on his closest disciple.

"Master!" he thought he heard Clogren yell, and then the thumping sound of an impact. He was sure Clogren was crying for him. There was more shouting, and Amphileph felt the roots stop their squeezing action. Amphileph moved his arm and the embrittled roots broke free.

The roots stretched and snapped, and suddenly, Amphileph burst forth, sending Clogren flying.

"You would kill *me*?" he screamed at his associates.

Five of the Spellmakers scrambled back together, re-forming the aura with their combined strength, but a sixth stopped short. Amphileph's energy shot through his body.

"He's gone mad!" the Spellmaker cried, grabbing his chest. His face broke out in a cold sweat as he looked at the others, expressing his remorse that he'd failed them. Then he collapsed to the ground.

"You will join him soon enough!" Amphileph cackled at the cluster of Spellmakers, a burst of energy almost causing them to lose control of their aural shield.

Amphileph saw movement out of the corner of his eye. A group of Camonra paced nervously against the outer wall of the Binding. "Father!" they cried repeatedly. One of them trumpeted a call to battle.

"They summon the other creatures in the eastern camp!" another of the Spellmakers shouted.

"Do what you can!" another cried. "We can't hold this defense much longer." Two of the Spellmakers stepped back and kneeled in prayer, attempting to ignore Amphileph's unending attack.

The dirt at Amphileph's feet began to rise up and take form. With a wave of his hand, a chunk of the mass at its base splattered into the binding spell's force field. Its velocity slowed to a stop before being expelled back out of the field and onto the ground.

The mound of earth formed appendages and lashed out at Amphileph.

"You've improved, brothers!" Amphileph shouted. He jumped aside, and the golem's massive arm burst the tree trunk just beyond the place where he stood.

A second golem rose up from the dirt, and it seemed the two together would neutralize Amphileph's attack, but the Camonra from the eastern camp ran to his aid. They pounced upon the golems without hesitation, stabbing and slicing, clawing and tearing at their earthen bodies. The golems seemed impervious to their attacks, wading through the Camonra in an effort to reach Amphileph, crushing them and batting their lifeless bodies in every direction. Amphileph rolled away from them and yelled to the Camonra. "Fools! Destroy *them*!" he said, pointing to the small remaining group of Spellmakers. A blast of energy removed the upper half of one of the golems, and then the Camonra turned on the Spellmakers themselves.

In terror, the Spellmakers commanded their golems to protect them.

Amphileph brushed off his clothes and watched the onslaught. The Camonra swarmed the Spellmakers, jumping back and forth to avoid the golems' attacks. Their scimitars hacked into the Spellmakers' aura, cutting deeper and deeper.

"I cannot hold them!" one of the Spellmakers cried.

"Enough of this!" Amphileph said. He closed his eyes and held his palms together at his chest. The energy engulfed his hands, tinting his face red with its glow. He pushed the energy away from his body with a scream, and a huge energy wave struck the aura, shattering it in a colossal explosion. The Camonra quickly closed on the defenseless Spellmakers, their golems disintegrating with their final screams for mercy.

As the commotion ended, Amphileph heard a whimpering sound. "Master!" cried a gurgling voice from Amphileph's left. Amphileph pushed aside the Camonra to find Clogren sprawled upon the ground, fragments of the exploded roots stuck in his face and chest. A large sliver was stuck into his neck like a stake. He was bleeding profusely. "Master, help me!" he said, his wide eyes staring intently at Amphileph.

Amphileph suddenly felt numb. His ears were ringing. In an afternoon, his plan to dominate the Watchers had not only gone awry, but now he, Clogren, and Citanth alone remained in their pact, and Citanth was in the northern camp, *outside* the Binding.

"I am here, Clogren, I will save you," Amphileph responded. He closed his eyes and rubbed his hands together, trying desperately to remember the incantation for healing, but the words eluded him. He turned around and looked at the bloody streak down the temple dome. "Ardidhus?" he called out, and then he turned away from the sight of it, only to recoil from the bloody mess that was once his beloved followers piled among the dead Camonra. "They challenged *me*, Clogren. I had no choice. I cannot allow such insurrection. Insurrection cannot be tolerated." He began pulling on his hair. "Clogren?"

Amphileph turned back to see that Clogren struggled for life no longer.

The grunts of the Camonra brought the stench of their breath to Amphileph's nostrils. "Leave me!" he shouted, but when they moved toward him in concern, he screamed again. "Leave me!" The remaining Camonra ran from him then, heading back toward the eastern camp. Within seconds, he was alone, and he sat down on the ground beside Clogren.

Clogren's lifeless eyes gave Amphileph their full attention, and Amphileph continued to talk with him until the sunlight faded from the sky.

Chapter Four

Discovery

Black soot blotted out the sun at times, choking the oxygen from the air, making Galbard's frantic run to the west that much more unbearable. His side burned, and he could not produce enough saliva to keep his tongue from sticking to the inside of his mouth. The pounding rhythm of his running droned on, each step vibrating his frame. His joints ached, and the skin on his face and lips had gone numb. Galbard tried to think of anything but the running.

Stopping only to keep his footing during the aftershocks, Galbard had descended the mountain's western face with all the speed he had dared attempt, dodging falling stone and dirt that slid off the mountain in whole sections.

When he reached the western foothills of the Black Mountains, he kept running. Sheer exhaustion would have dropped him, but every noise, every cracking of a branch, every movement in his peripheral vision drove him onward, fearing that the Camonra were on his heels. Slowing only as he came upon a clearing, he would pause to look this way and that for his pursuers, but then dashed across to the safety of the jungle on the other side. If they discovered him, he was done for.

When he did stop, his legs wobbled or just gave out, and he often fell to the ground. Once, he rolled to his back to try to catch his breath, but the soot fell like snow, and it made him choke to breathe. He was sure he heard the Camonra yelling in the near distance, and he was terrified that any noise might alert his would-be captors. Galbard wiped away the black mud that had formed from the tears in his eyes, and he blew black soot from his nose and cleared his throat as quietly as he could. He looked around for any kind of reaction to the noise, but thick, dark smoke hung close to the ground, and his visibility was limited to a very short distance.

After about six hours heading due west, he turned southward, hoping to find some relief from the smoke and ash, but found none. *Creator, help me,* he thought. Everything looked so different than he remembered, and he felt so completely lost. Despair was about to get the better of him, but he heard movement in the high grass. Panic quickly replaced despair, and he frantically looked around for cover, ducking behind an ancient live oak.

Blackened figures emerged from the foliage. They moved closer, and Galbard could see the dazed look in their bloodshot eyes. Ash muddied their faces; they walked without purpose, barely seeming to notice anything but the larger aftershocks that upset their footing. When they were nearly upon him, he slowly came out from behind the tree and called out to them, hoping not to startle them.

"I mean you no harm," he said. "I am Galbard, from Rion." One of them came to an abrupt stop, while the others appeared to completely ignore Galbard and continued north.

"I am Jaradh," said the one who registered Galbard's presence. He stared into the distance in a way that reminded Galbard of the faces of soldiers he had seen returning from war. "You cannot go that way. The world has opened up and its boiling blood meets with Blue Water—there are great explosions and the land gives way without warning."

"No!" Galbard shouted. His desire to return to Rion had kept him alive when he lived as a slave of Amphileph, and now to learn that he was yet denied his return took his breath away for a moment. He stopped and stood there, staring at the billowing smoke that blocked his view of Rion.

A young woman stopped beside them. "It is as he says," she announced. Tears streaked her cheeks. "We've no way of returning home," she said. "I will never again see my children."

"Have hope," the man said, as if her sadness triggered his senses, breaking some of shock's grip on him. "You don't know that," he encouraged. "We must find shelter now, and then we'll find a way around them."

"Around them?" Galbard inquired.

"The Inferiors—they were everywhere. The Rion Guard had marched from Rion to meet them in battle north of the city, and then the sky grew red and Erathe shook and ripped apart! It was if the land fell away and . . ." The woman broke down in tears before she could finish.

"You're from Rion then?" Galbard asked the man. He had not heard the term "Inferior" in some time. It had been coined by the Rion Elders to describe the Camonra when they first learned of Amphileph's plan to replace humankind. It was not a term of endearment.

"Yes, yes, a fisherman," the man replied. He pointed to the ever-growing number of Rionese that were appearing out of the haze. "Most were servants to the Rion Guard," he said.

Galbard was just beginning to realize the sheer number of people that had fled the city.

The fisherman's eyes grew wide. He seemed to blink with every other word. "The Elders sent large numbers of us to the west and north out of the city before the battle began. Another larger group left about eighteen days before us. They were told to head to the mountains far to the north. We were to hide in the wood far to the northwest—'Highwood,' it is called—where a clear river splits the ancient forest. But just as we left the city, the Inferiors attacked, and we ran for our lives."

"Erathe split open and swallowed them all!" the woman said, and she burst into tears again.

The man tried to console her. "I am afraid that nothing is as it was," he said to Galbard.

"It is a dark day upon us," Galbard said, wishing he had not said it in the next instant. "It is important for us to keep moving." Even here in the clearing, Galbard felt the searing heat from the ruptured earth in the South. "We need to do as the others—go northwest to Highwood."

"Yes, of course," the man answered, and he talked to the others, very few of whom were armed. They decided it was prudent to follow Galbard, and they set out together in a northwest direction.

The thunderous boiling of Erathe and the thick black smoke lessened, but the rain had done anything but that. It beat down on them, and after they had walked about twelve leagues, Galbard noticed that their group was trailing off with fatigue.

"Let us rest!" Galbard called out to them, taking a seat beneath an enormous live oak tree to block the stinging rain. He rested his head against the moss-covered trunk of the tree and closed his eyes, listening to the raindrops tapping on the leaves.

The group said nothing, but each stopped and made their way to cover from the rain, some sitting in the protection of the interwoven ferns and maples in the understory, some leaning against a stand of bamboo. The exhaustion had stolen their speech. For a few minutes, there was just the rain and their heavy breathing, and then nothing but the rain for almost an hour more.

After too little rest, the group struggled to their feet and proceeded northwest, but upon arriving at what should have been the lakes, they found that the waters had gathered to overflowing, leaving a singular land bridge a little further southwest.

Galbard didn't like the thought of moving further south in the least. Closer to the Camonra was not a direction he wanted to take. "Where is the fisherman?" Galbard asked.

"Here!" the man answered.

"How far is it around the lakes to the north?"

The man held his hand over his eyes and studied the horizon. "It looks so different," he said. "The northern lake was the largest of the group. If it has overflowed, then it has likely engulfed the smaller lakes and streams. The higher ground here would be much closer."

"Let us be about it," Galbard said. He did not like this one bit.

They made their way southwest for another hour and the pounding rain began to slow. This alone was heartening. They continued west until nightfall, setting watches for the Camonra.

Galbard had not slept in almost three days. His ears were starting to ring with the intense pain in his eyes and temples. The sheer act of lying down without the rain pouring in his face was all it took to send him into a complete blackness that lasted, dreamlessly, until he was awakened for his turn at watch. He wiped the sleep from his face with one hand, jumped up, and took his place.

They had not chanced firelight giving away their position, so Galbard could do nothing but stare out into the black night and listen to the sounds of the others sleeping against the sounds of the wilderness. Though he felt somewhat renewed after the short sleep, the deep darkness reminded him of his old cell, and it turned his thoughts inward.

He would not tell his fellow travelers that even now, the great good of Erathe, the Watchers, had likely departed. It would break them, and they already stood little if any chance of surviving the Camonra who sought to destroy them. He would keep them moving and keep their hope alive.

The sun's pre-dawn reflection crept across the night sky from the eastern horizon and began its slow illumination of the darkness from deep purple and red to golden yellow. Galbard was hoping to see the green landscape, but the sunlight instead brought nothing but grays and blacks. As he scanned the brightening panorama from this highpoint, though, it became clearer that the worst of their travels was behind them to the southeast.

"Two or three days, I figure, to make it to Highwood," one of the refugees said. The fisherman was there, too, smiling and cheerful. Galbard wanted to share his sentiments, but that would not happen until they were safely tucked away in the woods with their kinsmen.

"We should take advantage of our good fortune," Galbard said, holding his palm up to the sky.

"No rain is good fortune indeed," said the fisherman. "And the wind picks up at our backs. We should make good time today." He began rustling the weary travelers one by one.

Galbard looked to the east and thought he saw a sudden movement in the far distance. "Wait here," he said to the fisherman, and he walked south. When he had separated himself from the others, he drew Evliit's sword and continued south for a few minutes more, but he saw nothing.

As he turned around, Galbard noticed the Sword's blade. On its length, the inscription read: "Fear not, for your Creator is with you always. He will send his Warriors of Light to protect you!"

Courage filled him. "Give me a powerful hand that I might wield your mighty sword," he said quietly. He held the Sword tightly to his body. *I would welcome the Warriors of Light right now,* he thought.

Galbard felt a warm sensation run through his body, its traversing energy making him quiver.

What was that? he thought. He stared at the blade intently. "Camonra na Flodh," he whispered in the old tongue and the energy wave passed over his body again, emanating from the Sword through his hands and passing up his arms into his chest, and then outward to the top of his head and the bottom of his feet. His eyes stretched open wider, locked upon the Sword.

The energy that passed through his body was purifying. He felt energized, revived. *What mysteries have ethereal blacksmiths folded into this blade of Evliit?*

He looked at the dark sky to the southeast and consciously turned his gaze northwest, where a small patch of blue sky still fought against the creeping darkness. It was a sign, he thought, a sign to him that they needed to move northwest to rejoin the remaining Rionese refugees.

He made his way back into the clearing and walked through the group, making sure that the lot of them had caught up, and then they all heard a horn in the distance. Galbard recognized it immediately.

"I know all of you are tired, but we must move with all speed to find the remaining refugees from Rion. I don't think that the Inferiors will follow us into Highwood," he said pointing to the forest in the distance. "We need to move farther north of the fault, and we need to do it now."

"What was that sound?" a woman asked.

"We need to move," he said. "Now."

Galbard turned and walked briskly away from them toward Highwood.

The group assisted each other in rising to their feet, following Galbard in single file or small clusters of two or three, each falling in line behind him. They managed to make it across the open plains of the second quarter, but Galbard kept a close eye on the jungles to the south.

The overflowing banks of the small tributaries made the grasslands a muddy bog, and the footing only improved after they had traveled the remainder of the second day. Sleep was still a luxury they could afford only in shifts, and twice, Galbard was convinced he saw lights in the distant jungle. He didn't want to panic his fellow travelers, but he was sure someone was watching them.

On the third day, a rider approached from the west. He wore the armor of the Rion Guard, and he rode up to them with abandon.

"You must hurry. We've spotted the Inferiors' scouts to the south!" the rider said. "You've the better part of a day to reach the woods, but many of us are hiding there. We've food and sanctuary."

"We give thanks to the Creator for you!" one of the refugees shouted.

"Thank him later!" the rider said. He looked to the south. "Get your people to the woods!" he shouted, and then he turned his horse and rode south of them.

There was a general frenzy of activity amongst the group, but Galbard tried to keep them moving toward the wooded area ahead of them.

"Men, let the women and children move to the front!" Galbard shouted. "We'll bring up the rear, those with weapons in the very back!" The group's fear picked their pace up substantially. "Look sharp!" Galbard yelled to the men at the rear.

About four hours later, the rider they had seen previously topped the rolling hill just behind them and flew toward them, yelling. "Run!" he said flying past them. The rider had one hand grasping an arrow just behind the tip, which had passed through his right side. "Inferiors!" he screamed between gasps for air. The rider shot toward Highwood without looking back.

The refugees looked back at Galbard, their faces stretched with panic. Galbard assumed that the majority of them had only heard the hair-raising stories of Camonra from the Rion warriors. Those from the city had likely never actually seen a Camon, but the stories were terrifying enough, and when there was a roar from just behind them, it jolted them all. The entire group, without saying anything, burst into a dead run for the woods.

Galbard jumped through the high grass toward Highwood, and one of the women fell. "Get up! Keep moving!" he yelled. He was sure he heard at least three distinct voices of Camonra closing on them, and he knew they would make swift work of the weary travelers. He pulled her up, and she took off running.

In that moment, Galbard stopped and looked at her turning back in her panic and seeing the Camonra. His mind began to race so quickly that she seemed to be running in slow motion. He could see her wide-eyed expression and her blanched face with sublime clarity. He turned then and looked in her eyes' direction. There were three of them for sure, coming toward them. They bound toward the fleeing refugees, their heads bobbing above the grass.

"I am your slave no more!" Galbard shouted. He drew Evliit's sword. "I will stand firm, here and now!"

The Sword suddenly felt almost weightless, and light seemed to converge for a moment on the blade and travel its length.

One of the Camonra screamed his sighting of Galbard to his fellow warriors. Galbard saw them take notice, and he just had time to flinch before an arrow zipped past his head.

A second arrow sprang from the Camon's bow and sped directly toward Galbard's left eye. He turned the blade out from his body and the arrow's trajectory curved around the Sword and whizzed by in a long, looping arc behind him, gathering speed. It turned back toward the archer, its speed increasing until it became fire.

Galbard swung the tip of the sword around toward the Camon. The bolt of fire shot through the soldier's midsection effortlessly. The Camon fell to his knees, and his leather undergarment caught fire around the hole.

The other two Camonra stopped, yelling something in ancient Rionese. They moved slowly around the smoldering flames coming from their downed comrade, and they split up. The first circled to his left and the second to his right. The first Camon jumped through the air and swung down upon Galbard's head, the arc of his sword bending around the Sword to Galbard's left, slicing into the ground with incredible force. The surprised Camon quickly pulled it from the ground, and then Galbard attacked. The Camon raised his sword laterally in front of his face to parry. Galbard's sword arced downward, its glow intensifying, and then passed through the metal of the Camon's sword without even slowing, parting his face and jaw and halfway down the front of his chest armor. Galbard pulled back on the Sword, and the Camon fell away from him into the grass.

The third and last Camon shrieked and closed on Galbard, but Galbard pivoted around the attacker like a trained swordsman and swung, opening the Camon's chest diagonally. The Camon stopped instantly and fell. Galbard heard him moan and then his life exhaling from his body.

It was suddenly very quiet. He could hear the distant sound of the Rionese refugees still crying out for help. He waited for a moment more, but seeing no other Camonra, he slowly slid the Sword back into its scabbard.

The wind blew the grass around the dead's motionless bodies. Had it not been for the moments leading up to this, Galbard would have thought the gentle breeze was peaceful. He bent down and looked closely at the last attacker's face. His eyes were wide open. His face almost looked surprised. Clearly, they too were not expecting the ferocity of the Sword's power.

Galbard made a quick look around and then started running toward Highwood.

He caught up to the group about a hundred yards from Highwood, his breathing heavy. Four of the Guard's cavalry galloped out from the tree line and moved between the last of Galbard's group and the high grass to the East.

"Did you see them?" someone asked.

"Yes," Galbard responded, still debating what to say . . . or whether to say anything.

"How many of them?" a soldier asked pulling his horse back toward Galbard.

"I saw three."

"You saw them?" the soldier inquired.

"Yes," Galbard said, but the soldier's anxiousness made him stop at that.

"You're to stay here until the captain arrives. Your companions can go."

"He's with us," said the fisherman called Jaradh. "Let him go with us to the forest. We are all exhausted."

"He stays here."

"I'm fine," Galbard said to the fisherman. "I'm right behind you."

The fisherman looked at the soldier's face and conceded. "We'll see what accommodations we can put together in your absence." The fisherman pursed his lips with dissatisfaction. "Take good care, Galbard," he said, and then he joined the others going into Highwood.

The group looked back at their accosted friend. Their hushed conversation faded from earshot. Galbard waved them on and turned his gaze back to the East.

Shortly, several other horsemen rode out of Highwood with their long spears. They and their horses also wore the battle gear of Rion. The soldier that had stopped Galbard yelled to the others, "This one says that at least three are coming!" His fellow soldiers stopped just a few yards from Galbard and shuffled nervously on their horses. They spread out in a short line, and Galbard was thankful that the focus had moved off him and onto another rider that strode toward the group.

"Any sign of them?" the approaching rider asked. Galbard recognized him as a ranking officer, his horse's braided mane visible beneath the horse's faceplate armor.

"No, nothing," the first rider responded.

"Where did you see them?" the officer asked Galbard.

"They were there," Galbard said, pointing to the exact area where in fact they lay dead in the high grass. However, the riders could not see them.

"Ready, men!" the officer said. "Assemble and charge. Keep your spears down and in front. Use the weight of the horse and keep moving," he said. Galbard noticed some of them practice the maneuver when the officer wasn't looking, and Galbard thought they did not look too sure of themselves.

"If they will not come to us, we will go to them!" the officer shouted. His voice caused the other riders to tighten up their line and press ahead slowly. "You had better leave now," he shouted to Galbard. "Best if you made your way to Highwood."

"Sir, I have to tell you—" Galbard began.

"No time for that now," the officer interrupted. "On to Highwood now, if you know what's good for you." The riders pushed into the higher grass, and he turned his horse and rode into position at the rear of the group.

Galbard started to run after them to tell the officer about the Sword and his encounter with the Camonra, but then something stopped him. What would he say?

He had drawn enough attention to himself. As much as he wanted to find some comfort with his kinsmen, his primary objective had to remain clear and unwavering: escape with the Sword of the Watch. It was crystal clear to him that Amphileph had meant for him to kill Evliit and return the enchanted weapon to him. It was also clear that, in Amphileph's hands, this weapon would change their world forever.

He hoped for the Rionese warriors' sake that these Camon scouts were alone, but Galbard decided it would be best to take the officer's advice. He turned and ran toward Highwood.

After covering a little over half the distance to the tree line, Galbard could see people emerging from Highwood and joining the other Rionese refugees. Many embraced them, and then they moved the newcomers quickly into the protection of the forest.

Galbard was within ten yards of the tree line when the soldiers on horseback returned from the field.

"Stop!" the officer yelled. He leapt down from his horse, moving quickly toward Galbard. "I must speak with you!" Galbard noticed that the other soldiers brought their horses between him and the woods.

Galbard looked around at the other refugees who were staring at him. "Yes, of course," he said. The officer took him by the arm and led him into Highwood with an escort of three soldiers, who dismounted to follow them.

"Please come with me to my quarters," he said.

They walked along a path of patchy grass and flat stone that ran between the massive trees of Highwood, some of which Galbard estimated to have trunks that were fifty feet in circumference. Patches of moss crept through the cracks in the stone paths where the trees had spread their roots, and on either side of the path, there were twenty-foot thick hunks of granite jutting upward at various angles between the trees. The canopy of tree cover started at about seventy-five feet in the air, and he couldn't really see how high the treetops rose. The underbrush was a mixture of ferns and oaks, with a sprinkling of slender maples. Where paths did split the foliage, the depth of the forest was lost in the misty haze that hung in the air.

There were refugees working everywhere, carving and cutting, sawing and shaping the woods. Many of them stopped what they were doing and talked amongst themselves as Galbard passed.

Galbard followed the officer up a short grade toward the base of one of the trees. The bark had been cut laterally, and it was pushed upward and outward with posts and rails, forming a covered porch. The moss along the porch "roof" gave it an appearance of shingles painted green, and elaborate carvings decorated the entryway and windows. They proceeded up a short set of wooden steps and onto the deck of the porch, which cut into the tree's huge girth. Galbard saw what looked like a thousand rings of growth in the porch floor, circling outward from the doorway carved into the side of the tree. The officer turned and signaled the soldiers, who stopped at the foot of the porch steps. Galbard noticed that they were eyeing him with a fair degree of interest that quite honestly broke a sweat upon his brow.

"Where are we going?" Galbard asked.

"We need to speak in private," the officer responded. "Please follow me." He turned and followed the curvature of the porch around the tree trunk. Galbard continued behind him.

At one end of the porch, a wooden staircase spiraled upward around the great tree's girth. It led to a platform that bridged to another wooden structure intertwined with three great trees rising high off the forest floor. From there, Galbard could see the entire forest floor beneath them. The wind whispered in the leaves. The breeze slowly rocked the branches at some distance from the trunk, but the massive trunk itself was motionlessly rooted some sixty feet below.

The officer removed his helmet. "I am Ariden, captain of the Guard," he said.

"Galbard," the escaped slave replied.

"You must know why I have sought you out," Ariden said, staring intently at Galbard. "I must know what happened out there."

"I was attacked, and I defended myself," Galbard began, somewhat concerned about where things were headed. This was no time to draw attention to the Sword.

"Defended yourself?" the captain questioned, nodding. "I see. My good friend, am I to understand that you, alone, fought off three of the Camonra? You parted their weapons and armor as without effort? They look as if they were killed where they stood. I mean no offense, friend, but you don't have the appearance of a warrior. This is what my soldiers are questioning."

"Yes, I understand, and I assure you that your first impression is correct, I am no warrior," said Galbard. "I was once a mason, but even that was some time ago."

"A mason, you say?" probed Ariden. "Why would a mason have the prisoner's mark?"

Galbard looked down at his arm. He hurried to pull his sleeve down over the tattoo on his outer forearm. "None too lucky with masonry," he said. "I borrowed for my tools, but I wasn't very good at the trade, and I couldn't pay my debts. Debtor's prison was my reward. I served my masters in Rion for six seasons, but in the seventh season, I sought to pay my debt by harvesting the Soru bush near the Black Mountains. En route, the Camonra killed my owner and took me as a slave."

"You've been to the Black Mountains in the east?" the captain queried suspiciously.

Galbard's jaw tightened. "Terrible fates awaited those whom the Camonra took as slaves. A more meager existence you cannot imagine. I'll ask you to forgive me, but I don't wish to speak of those things."

"Of course, of course," said Ariden.

Ariden moved closer to Galbard, eyeing Evliit's sword for a moment and then looking directly into Galbard's eyes. Ariden gestured at the surrounding buildings. "But might I ask, what brings you to our small sanctuary in the forest of Highwood?" he asked. "I've done as the Guard has asked of me. I've brought the people to Highwood, while my fellow soldiers have faced the Inferiors, and now? Now the earth has opened up and swallowed them, my friends, my brothers, while I but watched from a distance."

Galbard begin to feel uncomfortable with the tone of things. "These are difficult times . . ."

"Has the Guard sent you?" Ariden interrupted.

"No, sir," answered Galbard. "The Guard?"

"I know the people are worried about all that they have seen," Ariden said, ignoring Galbard's perplexed face. "I have occupied them for now with building these structures, but this is not their home, and I fear these tasks will not sustain them for long. They grow restless and ask of news of Rion."

"I have no news of Rion or the Guard," said Galbard. "I have been in the east, right up until the great quakes."

"The east, yes," said Ariden. He stared back at Galbard as if he expected him to say more.

Galbard changed the subject. He pointed to the series of bridges and homes, intricately interlaced among the trees themselves. "I am amazed by what I see. The Rionese are incredible builders, that is sure," he said. Galbard put a step between himself and Ariden and leaned on his elbows against the wooden railing.

"Wood, bah! 'Tis a pity that this material will never last like stone. One would have to truly love to work with such stuff as this, for after but a few seasons, so much will have to be replaced. Stone and steel are for the craftsmen of Rion."

"Stone and steel, indeed," echoed Galbard, but he noticed that Ariden was looking at his sword again. Suddenly, Ariden turned to some soldiers waiting attentively on the deck just across the rope bridge from them. They moved toward him with a look of concern, but he raised his hand to wave them off. "Leave us," Ariden said, and the soldiers removed their hands from their swords, bowed, and descended the spiral staircase, disappearing around the tree's trunk.

"Walk with me, Galbard," Ariden said. He led Galbard away from the main encampment crossing three other rope bridges until they neared the northern edge of forest.

"I supposed you didn't want to talk in front of the other men," said Ariden.

"I don't know what you mean," Galbard responded.

"This weapon, how did you acquire it?" he asked.

Galbard thought Ariden's eyes appeared to be slightly bulging, but the look on his own face must have made some impression, because the captain regained his composure and looked away.

He looked down at two soldiers sitting beside a campfire, far below them on the forest floor. "This is the last outpost of our little village. There is no one out here, but us and those two soldiers, and they do not even recognize it," he said.

"Recognize it?" Galbard replied.

"Did you not think that I would notice what you carried with you?" Ariden asked. "Did you not know that an old soldier of the Guard would recognize the Sword of the Watch? These young ones are ignorant of the lore, but in my day, the Rionese teachers taught these things."

"Of course," Galbard answered. "I'm sorry; I didn't want to deceive you."

"No, I thought not. Though I am curious how any man could acquire Evliit's sword," Ariden said. "This is it, is it not?"

Galbard drew a deep breath. "Yes, this is Evliit's sword," he said. He instinctively tightened his grip on the Sword's pommel. "I would not bore you with the full tale of my acquiring it, but suffice it to say that I have been tasked with keeping it from the hands of Amphileph himself."

Ariden's eyes grew a bit wider. He wiped his mouth with his sleeve.

"What is it like to draw that weapon?" he asked.

"I have drawn it but once, and you have seen the result."

"The Sword defends its bearer," Ariden said. He looked around at the forest floor and then back to Galbard. "Come this way," he said, leading Galbard around the deck surrounding the largest dwelling. Galbard noticed that the dwelling blocked the view of the soldiers below.

"This weapon could save Rion," said Ariden. "With this weapon, a great warrior could destroy the Inferiors once and for all!"

Ariden reached out to place his hand on the Sword, but Galbard moved away from him.

"What are you doing?" Galbard asked.

Ariden stood up straight and looked away. "Forgive my forwardness, but you must know what it would mean to Rion to end this war, Galbard."

"Yes, yes, of course," Galbard responded.

"Then you must know that the Sword of the Watch must be given to a great warrior, to someone who can wield it with might against our enemies!"

Galbard moved back a bit more. "What are you saying?"

Ariden suddenly drew his sword. "You are not that warrior, Galbard. Evliit's sword requires someone of strength to carry it rightly."

Galbard held up his hands and backed away again. "Ariden, I have no quarrel with you. Put away your sword."

Ariden raised his sword with one hand and held out the other. "Give me the Sword, Galbard, I do not wish to hurt you!"

"I'm warning you! Let me leave this place in peace!" Galbard yelled. He turned to run, but Ariden swung at him, narrowly missing him but cutting one of the guides on the rope bridge. The boards of the bridge fell away, but Galbard held on to the remaining rope. Ariden dropped his sword and grabbed for the remaining rope as well, and the two of them hung precariously over the forest floor. Ariden swung up his foot and kicked Galbard in his side, causing him to drop one hand. He quickly grabbed the rope again and began to move toward the opposite tree structure, hand over hand. Ariden gave chase, and almost two-thirds of the way across, caught up to him, kicking him again.

Galbard stopped to defend himself, and Ariden reached over him to grasp the Sword's tang, but his fingers extended away reflexively as if from heat. His fingers burst into flames that consumed his hand and wrist and crawled up his arm. He beat the flames frantically, but they crawled up his chest and face, catching the remaining rope on fire. Ariden screamed and fell, but the flames completely consumed his body before hitting the ground, a rain of ash falling amongst the leaves.

Galbard tried to move quickly, but the rope suddenly broke, and he swung across the forest floor toward a gigantic live oak's trunk, letting go in time to tumble hard upon the dead fir needles, leaves, twigs, and fallen branches that littered the ground. Had it not been for the thick carpet of mosses, leaves, and a patch of huckleberry shrubs, he would surely have broken something. He lay there smarting and felt for the sword, but it was gone. He heard soldiers shouting.

Fighting through the pain, he rolled to his knees, frantically raking the leaves with his hands in search of the sword. A horn sounded.

Suddenly, he felt something. It was the Sword's tang. He sheathed it and listened, rising to his feet slowly. A clamor arose from the direction of the main camp. It was hard to breath—he realized Ariden's vicious kicks might have cracked a rib—but he pushed on, limping, walking, and then running, stopping only when a random opening in the trees revealed the mountains in the distance to the north.

Chapter Five

Journey to the Western Coast

Moonlight was a welcome sight to Cayden, for sailing all these days on the *Nurium* had felt eerie in the swallowing darkness of moonless nights. The ocean had a way of seeming completely dimensionless in the absence of the moonlight, revealing nothing across the horizon for as far as the eye could see except the torches of the larger ships. Cayden thought they danced on the horizon like fireflies in the fields of Rion.

He had developed a bad habit of waking up around the third hour, an anxiousness growing in him with each passing day on the sea. He missed the land more than he could say. Long gone was the uneasy feeling of the ocean moving beneath him, but it had been replaced with an insatiable desire to step foot on dry land again.

On those nights that the anxiousness got the better of him, he would ease out of his hammock so as not to wake anyone and make his way up from berthing and onto the deck. Out there in the dead of the night, he'd noticed that the sailors tended to clump tightly together, smoking and talking in low voices, interrupted at times with a quieted chuckle or muted belly laugh. He had never felt comfortable enough to enter their circle, but he had become addicted to the smell of the tobacco's smoke drifting by on the night air.

The ship moved almost imperceptibly forward. Even in the dim moonlight, the sea's vastness refused good calculation of distances without star and sextant, and though he'd watched the captain on several occasions shooting the stars, he'd no faith he could do it himself.

Maybe it was that feeling of utter reliance on them that spurred his intense desire to get off their ship and back to land, but the gentle murmur of the sailors and the tart smell of their pipes was somehow reassuring. Cayden would sometimes stand the remainder of the night with them until the first mate or captain would appear, usually just before or after dawn. They would walk down the *Nurium*, inspecting the ship's activities on their way to the helm. When they passed amidships, Cayden always felt like he was in the way, no matter where he was standing, and he had made note of the fact that the sailors generally always found something to be busy with at that time.

Cayden started to go below. One of the older sailors looked at him and winked. He was deeply tanned and weathered, belying a cheerful nature. "You learn quick that it's better to find something to do than 'ave it found *for you*," the sailor smiled.

"You're right there," Cayden laughed.

"I heard the woman with the child call you Cayden, 'sthat right?"

"Yes. Cayden."

"Salmos," the sailor said, extending his calloused hand. Cayden shook it. "Rough hands, I see. Not a sailor . . . so I'm thinking you're a stoney."

Cayden laughed. "A mason, you mean?"

"Sure, yeah, a stoney," Salmos replied, and then he grabbed a bucket and started cleaning the portside railing, never realizing how Cayden's pride had benefited from having someone in the sailors' ranks speak to him. With a big smile on his face, Cayden descended the stairs to see what the girls were doing.

Berthing converted to the galley shortly after dawn, with the cook stoking a small fire in a small, brick-hearth stove. Nara was folding the hammocks and placing them on hooks on the wall. Jalin was sitting on a barrel, breastfeeding Ronan.

"Beautiful day outside," Cayden said.

"Up early again?" Jalin asked.

"Yes," Cayden responded.

"We are beginning to worry about you, Cayden," said Jalin, repositioning herself and Ronan's head. He seemed determined to roll away from her.

"Yes," Nara reinforced. She finished with the last of the hammocks.

"Don't worry for me," Cayden said.

"Who'll worry if we don't?" Nara quipped. "You?"

"Now don't start with me," said Cayden with a smile. "Come and see the day. It *is* beautiful."

Jalin adjusted her clothes and brought Ronan to her shoulder in one practiced motion. "Yes, Nara, don't waste your time with this one," she laughed. "Ronan could use the fresh air."

"Oh very well, you're right of course," Nara laughed in return. "Can I carry Ronan for you?"

"No, no, just make sure Cayden catches the hatch!" said Jalin.

"I was raised well, ladies, I assure you," said Cayden. He pushed the hatch open for the three of them to go topside. "After you."

The clear day was remarkable, and Cayden noticed that many of the ships were closer than usual. The seas were calm, and the water and sky met on the horizon in beautiful shades of blue. There were the soothing sounds of gulls overhead and canvas sails billowing in the gentle breeze. The sailors were busying themselves in the rope ladders, letting down the three largest sails.

"Let us gain a little wind at our back and then steady as she goes, Mr. Markston," the captain called out.

"Aye, sir!" the first mate called back to him.

By midmorning, smoke was rising from the galley, and there was the smell of beans boiling. Word had it that the cook was going to break out some dried bread in honor of coming to the end of the cliffs, and the thought of food had Cayden's stomach growling. He saw one of the closer boat's deck was dotted with emaciated, weary-faced passengers that seemed to be staring back at the three of them. "They look like they're starving," he said.

"Yes, that's a bit scary, I'm afraid," Nara said. "I hope that we find port soon."

"Surely soon," Jalin responded, but the nervousness in her voice made her unconvincing.

"I overheard the captain and the first mate," said Cayden. "They spoke of being close to our destination."

The girls perked up, which was much more to Cayden's liking. "Did he say *when* we might arrive?" Nara asked.

"Oh, please, please say that he did!" said Jalin.

Cayden looked around them. "They kept saying to 'watch the starboard bow for land,' so it should be soon."

Salmos came down the deck toward them "They watch for the Witch of Southwood," he revealed. "To the north there." He quickly added, "Sorry. Didn't mean to butt in, but cleaning this here rail for the four-hundredth time isn't really keeping my interest."

"A witch?" Cayden asked. "Why do they think a witch lives there?"

"They're not thinking it, sir, they're knowing it. Been known to attack anything comes near to her, sailors say."

Cayden looked northward but could see nothing.

"We've given her a bit of distance," Salmos said. "But as for land, should be seeing it today," he said with a smile, and then he picked up his bucket and threw the water overboard.

The girls looked at each other, and Cayden thought they were ready to squeal with delight.

"I want no part of any witch, but the land—just to see it!" Nara said. "Oh, that would be a fine sight indeed."

"I'd second that," said Jalin.

Salmos stowed away the bucket and rag and moved on to checking the knots on the mizzenmast tie-downs.

"Have you ever been this far west?" Cayden asked him.

"Oh yes, sir," Salmos said. "Great fish wander in this part of Blue Water. Sometimes we would come this far out to find large schools of them, fill the hold, and return to Rion. Good money to be made."

"But have you been round the cape, to the western shores?"

"No, sir, I'm not thinking there are many that 'ave been to the west coast of Etharath, at least not that I'm knowing of. The old sailors' maps say the coast turns north ahead there," said Salmos. "But the maps I've seen 'ave nothing but blank canvas when it comes to the western shores," he added. "Right then . . . I've got to be about me duties." He turned and proceeded up the rope ladders to help with the sails.

About three hours later, they finally heard it, what they had been anxiously waiting for. "Land! Land, ho!" one of the sailors shouted from the crow's nest. Everyone on board turned to see the great cliffs of southern Etharath just becoming visible in the distance. The sheer cliffs came better into view, and the call echoed in the surrounding ships as well. The ruddy face of the southern shoreline rose far above the crashing spray that pounded the outcropping of jagged stone at its base.

"No getting near that," one of the sailors said. "Break up your boat like a child's toy."

About an hour later, Cayden could see the captain and first mate talking. Then the captain turned the ship's wheel about a quarter turn to the right.

"We're moving in a bit," the sailor said. "We'll follow the coastline around."

They spent the remainder of the day watching the coastline, growing closer each hour, until by nightfall, the rhythmic crashing of waves against it finally took their toll on the excited travelers. Jalin and Nara's wide eyes eventually tired, and the two of them went below. Cayden watched until sleep tugged at his eyelids, and then he too went below, slipped into his hammock, and fell fast asleep.

* * *

Around the second hour, Cayden awoke to footsteps scurrying on the deck above. There was suddenly a loud thud above him, so loud that he instinctively sat up. He moved toward the galley door, when Salmos half fell down the galley stairway at his feet.

Cayden reached for his friend. "Salmos!" he exclaimed.

"They've killed me," Salmos said. His shaking hand tried to hold back his intestine that pushed out from a large gash in his stomach. He grabbed Cayden's shoulder. "They killed me!" he cried. There was a stirring in the hammocks behind him.

"Cayden?" Jalin whispered.

Salmos handed Cayden his bloodied sword. "Take this!" he said. "Don't know—how many . . ." He sputtered, and then Salmos gave up a great sigh and died.

"Salmos!" Cayden whispered desperately. He could hear voices growing louder, and he readied for their entrance. The footsteps stopped at the entrance to berthing. There was a short burst of whispers, and Cayden's heart beat wildly until he thought it would jump out of his chest.

He started to call out to the others, but out of the corner of his eye, he saw the hatch swing open. Two men forced their way into the hatchway, one jumping down the stairs, catching the tip of Cayden's sword under his chin. Everything happened so fast, and before Cayden realized it, he heard the sound of his blade tearing through skin, startling him. The attacker's scream drowned in his own blood.

Jalin's scream, however, rang out loudly. Everyone in berthing rose with a start.

Cayden pulled back his weapon, and the man frantically grasped at the wound in his neck, collapsing backwards on the stairs. The second man tripped over him, falling face-first onto the galley floor. One of the sailors who was off-watch tore the sword from the man's hands and struck him full in the face with his huge fist. The man moaned in pain, his head bouncing off the floor with the impact of the blow. The sailor raised the sword above his head. Nara screamed again, and the sailor swung the cutlass for the intruder's neck.

Cayden's sword stopped the sailor's deadly blow inches from its mark, sparks flying, interrupting the darkness of the galley.

"Wait!" Cayden yelled. "Wait! Someone grab some fire from the hearth and light a lantern!"

"You don't order me!" the sailor said, and then he backhanded Cayden to the ground. "This one dies!" he cried.

A lantern was lit toward the back of berthing, and the attacker's frail body could be seen stretched across the galley floor, the position of the light creating odd shadows that appeared to amplify his sharp, bony features.

"Please," the attacker's weak voice proclaimed. "They made us do it! We didn't want to hurt no one, but we couldn't take it no more! My family, my kids—we was starving!"

"Tell that to Salmos!" the sailor yelled, and he thrust the sword into the man's chest, killing him.

"No!" Cayden yelled. "He could have told us how many others are on the ship!"

"Shut your trap!" the sailor replied. "You men grab up those swords and follow me! And put out that light! You!" he shouted at Cayden. "You and Tadhra stay with the women!" There were more footsteps on the deck above them, scrambling in different directions like rats, and then suddenly . . . nothing.

"I'm coming with you!" protested Cayden. "Salmos was my friend."

"Don't make me tell you twice," answered the sailor. "They'll kill the women same as him—or worse!"

Everything went dark again. Cayden's eyes adjusted to the darkness, and then he could see the sailor looking through the galley hatch. The starlight was bright, and the sailor signaled that all was clear and proceeded up the stairs. He exited the hatch with two of the other men.

Cayden moved to the middle of the galley and looked up through the grate over the galley stove, trying to see anyone topside. After a few seconds, he could hear shouting. "I am going above," Cayden told the others, and then he made his way to the galley stairs.

Two of the men moved to follow him, but they were unarmed. "We'll come with you," one said.

"Go with him, and you're on your own!" said Tadhra.

"No, stay here and protect the women and children. There's a mallet and saw in the Healer's quarters. Look for anything else that could be a weapon and give it to the women."

"Very well," he replied.

"Cayden, no!" Nara said, but Cayden held his hand up to stop her.

"Stay here!" he replied, and then he moved slowly up the stairs.

He tried his best to open the hatch silently, and he cracked it open enough to look for movement, but the bright moonlight revealed nothing across the width of the ship. Crates blocked his view of the stern, but he could hear men fighting.

He moved out onto the deck, trying to let the hatch down slowly and silently. He jumped behind the crates, and looked between them just in time to see someone swinging toward him. Cayden attempted to duck, but the force of the man's swing kicked the crates into him, and he flew across the deck, dropping his sword.

"Get him!" someone yelled, and several other voices sounded out around him.

He jumped to his feet and scrambled for his sword. It had slid into one of the port drains, tip first, but had hung up on the tang. He bent over to grab it, but his assailant's yell made him look up to see a sword blade swinging down at his face. Cayden flinched, ducking, and the blade stopped just shy of his brow, sticking almost a third of the breadth of the attacker's sword into the deck railing. The assailant put his boot on the railing to free his blade, but Cayden grabbed his first. Jumping back, Cayden cut him across his right hamstring, dropping him. He howled out in pain.

The deck hatch jumped with attempts to open it, but the crates were too heavy.

"Another one! Here!" a yell came from above him. Two acknowledgments sounded from the bow behind him, and Cayden ran toward the stern.

A big bear of a man jumped down from the wheel deck, and another ran up from behind him. The burly man thrust his sword at Cayden's chest, but he slid to the ground. The one behind him could not stop, and tripped over him, the tip of the larger man's sword passed through his shoulder. He quickly pulled the blade out of him, the injured man screaming in pain. Cayden swung with all his might, but the large attacker deflected his blow, the force of it nearly knocking the sword from Cayden's hand. When his attacker raised his sword to strike, Cayden kicked downward upon his knee, hyperextending it. The large man fell to the ground, shouting curses.

Cayden jumped upon the ladder to the wheel deck, but when his face cleared the level of the deck, he saw nothing but the bottom of a boot. The blow to his forehead caused a bright flash of white behind his eyes, and he flew backward off the ladder, striking the deck with enough force to knock the wind from him.

He rolled to his side and saw the captain lying face down on the deck. He was not moving. The sailor from the galley was dead, lying in a pool of his own blood. There were grappling hooks and a boarding plank leading to a second larger ship that had the name *Merrius* painted upon the bow.

Cayden could then see the other ship's passengers clearly. They were a frightened, ragtag bunch, thin and desperate, eyes bulging. He could just see their thin faces moving behind crates of pottery on the *Merrius*. Cayden thought they looked like they could die of starvation at any moment, and it filled him with a strange mixture of anger and pity.

That was not the case for the pirates that stood over him and the captain. These fellows were stout and well fed. He could see the man standing over him had the mark of Rion on his clothing.

"We are from Rion!" Cayden said. "We are your kinsmen!"

"Shut up!" another said. He kicked Cayden in the face with the top of his boot, catching him in the upper lip and nose. Tears filled his eyes, and he grabbed his face, fingers searching to see if the gristle of his nose was loose.

"Grab up the women and anything you can carry! Kill the rest!" one yelled. "Drop the anchor! We'll come back for 'er later!"

A line of pirates ran across the plank and onto the deck of the *Nurium*. Cayden cleared his eyes just in time to see the pirate standing over him raise his sword over his head and point the tip at Cayden's heart, and then the pirate placed both his hands on the tang, as if to drive the sword through his chest.

Just over the pirate's shoulder, Cayden thought he saw a star cross the sky, but to his amazement, it arced around and came toward them. A blue light began to color everything, and Cayden's attacker turned to look at what was happening. Cayden pushed the flat of the blade away from his chest and it stuck into the deck. He grabbed his attacker's clothing and pulled him down, trying to keep him from dislodging the sword tip, and then punched him twice in the face.

The star fell upon the ship with a huge crunch of wood decking, its blue flames converging into human form. The impact rocked the ship, and a concentric ring of energy burst forth from its landing, casting men into the dark waters on either side before it dissipated. Cayden and his attacker were thrown against the wheel deck wall next to the entrance to the captain's quarters. The pirate pulled a dagger and stabbed at his face, but Cayden moved just in the nick of time.

They wrestled to their feet, and Cayden tore the dagger away from his hand with his sheer strength. The pirate lunged for the sword, but Cayden jumped in front of him, knocking Cayden back against the door of the captain's room. He shook the impact from his head and looked back to see his assailant grab the sword's tang. He pulled the sword from the deck and turned, and Cayden saw the dagger sticking out of his chest. He raised the sword to swing, but then stumbled and collapsed.

The ghostly figure slowly arose from a crouch and moved toward the stern of the ship with purpose.

"The Witch!" one yelled, and the pirates regrouped and turned all attention to her. They tried to attack her wispy cloak, but it seemed to drift around their blades in the night air. Cayden saw the apparition reach toward them, pulling ether from their bodies. They fell, instantly lifeless, to the deck.

Each and all they fell, until only the captain and he remained on the deck, and then the ghostly apparition turned about and drifted in their direction, reaching out her hand.

Cayden lay against the door, motionless. It was if he saw Death itself had come to take him, but inexplicably, she stopped suddenly and backed away. Her head cocked to one side, she flipped her black hair over her shoulder, moving her face close to his. There was sadness in her dark brown eyes, and Cayden felt that sadness wash over him in a wave.

She broke her silent stare, snapping Cayden out of a dreamlike trance with a start. "Cayden of Rion! You must help the man Galbard in his quest," she said. Her voice was distant, though she was just before him, its volume rising and falling in waves that washed over him. "Go to the western shores. There you will find the bearer of the Sword!" She moved back from him slowly, her face fading again into the wispy blue aura that moved around her like a flowing robe. The apparition lifted into the air and then shot into the sky, its glowing light fading with its ascent.

Cayden lay in the darkness, his mouth standing open. He watched the creature's trail of light turn toward the northeast and then descend over the coast of Etharath, disappearing behind the ship's hand railing. In the silence that followed, he thought he heard the captain's labored breathing. Then there was the sound of the others pushing open the hatch, and footsteps. A group of men appeared from below decks, followed cautiously by several of the women, including Nara.

"Thieves! Murderers!" one yelled, seeing the body of one of the assailants.

"Check the captain's quarters! Find the captain and the first mate!" another cried, and they fanned out around the deck. Markston appeared out of the doorway to the captain's quarters, his head bleeding.

"Here!" Cayden said breathlessly, but he saw that they spotted him. The group ran to Cayden and the ship's captain, and they saw the *Merrius*, the ramp, and the grappling hooks.

A girl child stepped out from the shadows of the *Merrius*. "Help!" she cried. She jumped when she noticed the men approaching, and then she burst into tears. "Please don't hurt me!" she said.

"Get the girl!" Markston yelled. "Board the ship! Now!"

They stormed the *Merrius*, returning shortly with men, women, and children they found in the holds below.

"They were malnourished and hunkering in the darkness," the sailors said as they brought them aboard. "They are well stocked. We weren't the first of their conquests."

"We were their slaves!" one cried out. "We didn't visit this evil upon you!"

Cayden gathered his strength and stood up at the railing. He called out to the sailors that remained on the *Nurium*, pleading. "Those that have wronged us have paid their penance. Let there be no more of this killing. Have we not enough misery in our lives?"

There was a moment when everyone seemed to stop and hear his words.

"We could help them reach the western shores. We have plenty of food to make it that far!" Cayden said. "Surely, some of you could command this ship?"

The sailors talked among themselves. "Two ships and plenty of stores. It's a smart move."

"Light a lantern on the stern!" Markston ordered, and then he turned to the sailors boarding the *Merrius*. "Follow our light! Give us a ship's length and follow us in to shore."

Nara burst through the crowd that had gathered amidships and ran to his side. "Cayden!" she cried. "Are you alright?"

Cayden thought again of the apparition, and he sat down with Nara's help.

"Yes, I'm fine," he said. "Just give me a moment."

The ship's Healer pushed by them, and the sailors lifted the captain up. A clump of them began to move him below decks. "Gently men, to my quarters!" the Healer shouted.

The remaining sailors scrambled about the deck, shifting the sailcloth and the boat's direction toward the Western Shore.

"Jalin is fine?" Cayden asked.

"Yes, she's with Ro down below."

"Good."

Nara suddenly put her arms around Cayden's neck. "I was so worried about you when you left us, and when that awful sound shook the entire ship, I feared you dead. Oh, Cayden, when I thought something had happened to you, I was beside myself."

Cayden's squirm was reflexive. Her affection caught him off-guard. The Rionese masonry trade allowed little time for families, and it had made him more than a little rusty when it came to such affairs of the heart. He cautiously moved his face closer, and she quickly closed the distance and kissed him, pushing him back against the ship's railing.

He pressed his lips to hers, and the sensation consumed him, but suddenly, the face of the Witch flashed across his mind's eye, and he recalled the apparition's words and pulled back from Nara.

"Nara!" Cayden said.

"What is it?" she asked. Cayden thought she looked a little surprised by his abrupt ending of their embrace.

"I'm sorry, Nara," he said. "But I *must* tell you something." He leaned close to her ear. "The great crashing sound you heard—it was a creature that fell from the skies." He pointed to the circular burn mark on the deck. "The pirates scrambled about to attack it, but they were helpless against it. I heard one of them call it the Witch of Southwood."

"The Witch of Southwood? The demon-woman the sailors spoke about?" she replied in a hushed whisper.

"What's more—she spoke to me."

"The creature spoke to you?"

"Yes, it was like a ghost—*she* was like a ghost—drifting across the ship, striking down all who got in her way, but then, when she came to me, she spoke of me helping someone when we arrived at the western coast."

Nara searched Cayden's eyes.

"She said to 'help the man Galbard,'" he said. "She told me to protect him."

"Protect him?" Nara replied. Saying the words curled her face into a funny look. "Protect him from what? Who is Galbard?"

"I have no idea," said Cayden. "The entire thing seems a bit—surreal."

As they spoke, Jalin appeared with Ro and several others.

"I thank the Creator that you're alright," Jalin said. Ro awoke hungry and fidgety, and she prepared to feed him.

"What happened up here?" Jalin inquired.

Cayden and Nara looked at each other. "Come closer," said Nara, and Cayden recounted the night's events to Jalin.

"What can this mean?" Jalin asked. She looked confounded.

"I'm not sure," Cayden began, but then he noticed Jalin's expression. "What's the matter?"

"My husband's name is Galbard," she replied. "It's an unusual name, you know. Don't you think it's strange that she said you needed to protect Galbard?"

Cayden and Nara looked at each other. "Yes, that's very strange. I thought you'd said that he had gone north of Rion to pay a debt," said Cayden.

Jalin looked down at the ship's deck. Her face blushed. "He was indentured," she said.

"Your husband was a slave?" said Nara.

Jalin nodded, and a tear ran down her cheek. "It had taken over a year, but he'd worked off most of our debt. His master said that he could pay the last of the debt much faster if he could harvest the Soru bush that grew in the northern fields, but the Inferiors had been seen there, and I told Galbard not to go there anymore, that it wasn't worth it. He said he was going, even after I begged him not to, and I—well, I panicked, I guess. I was so afraid that something might happen to him. I didn't know it, but I was pregnant with Ro, and I was very emotional. We had a huge fight, and I told him that he cared more about the money than me. I told him that if he left, I never wanted to see him again, and then he left and never came back. I've waited for him every day since then, hoping and praying he'd return, hoping for a chance to tell him that I hadn't meant what I'd said, that I wished it had never happened, but he never returned. He's never even seen his son." Jalin began to cry openly.

Nara held her. "Oh, Jalin, I'm so sorry."

"We have no way of knowing if it's even the same person, this Galbard," said Cayden.

Jalin sniffled. "You're right, of course," she acknowledged, and she did her best to put on a happier face. They talked of other things until dawn approached.

Nurium's deck remained alive with action. Cayden had to compete with the shouts of the sailors intermixed with the rustling of the sails, the creaking of the deck planks, and squeaking of ropes under the strain of *Nurium's* turn northeast toward the sloping line of the shore. The new light brought a few ships into view in the distance, with the *Merrius* just off their stern.

Jalin and Ro were standing near the bow. "Cayden! Nara! Look!" She pointed excitedly to the shores, hopping and swinging the child firmly planted on her hip.

"I don't think that I've ever wanted to see a shoreline more than I do at this very moment!" said Nara.

"I couldn't agree more!" added Jalin. Even Ro giggled his approval.

"Coming through!" shouted Markston, and Cayden moved to the side. In the captain's absence, Markston had performed double-duty directing the two ships. "The cliffs end," Markston said. "We should make landfall somewhere over there. Notify the captain. Signal the *Merrius*." He hurried toward the helm.

"Are these other ships to follow us?" Nara asked.

"They seem scattered to the four winds," Cayden replied. The ships did indeed appear to be crisscrossing the ocean before them. Some appeared to be continuing north along the coast.

"But they will follow us, won't they?" Nara repeated.

"I expect some will, Nara." Cayden said. He noticed the look on Nara's face while the vast wilderness passed before them. "Something troubles you?"

"This land, to be sure. The journey that we would need to make to return to Rion—well, through a wilderness like this, numbers would be in our favor. We could gather all of our food and make for Highwood or the mountains, surely . . ."

Cayden had stopped listening. The deep foreboding wilderness had made him think of the Witch. *What of this man Galbard?* he thought.

"Cayden? Have you heard *anything* I was saying?" inquired Nara. She smiled and hit him on the shoulder.

"I'm sorry. I still struggle with the night's events. I'd think that all of the ships would soon be on the western shores. From the looks of the people on the *Merrius*, they'll be more willing than we to escape the confines of their ships."

The sun was low in the western sky when the *Nurium* slid into the sands of the western coast of Etharath, followed shortly by the *Merrius*. Cayden had picked up a few things about sailing from Salmos, and he pitched in to help the sailors. They could see several of the *Merrius's* passengers jumping overboard and rushing onto the shore with abandon. The sailors that had been tying off the *Nurium* growled under their breath.

"Awful thankful, to be sure," one of the sailors said.

"Don't you worry your pretty little heads, we'll take care of the ships," mocked Tadhra.

"Be about your business," said Markston. "Secure the ships, and let's get an inventory of our supplies. Let down the rope ladder so these fools don't break a leg."

Cayden and Nara helped Jalin and Ro get their things together, and then Cayden helped the sailors toss over the rope ladder into the neck-deep water. Tadhra climbed over the side, and people began to storm the rope ladder almost immediately.

"Wait a blasted minute!" Tadhra shouted.

"Let's give them room," Cayden said, picking up the bags and moving away from the starboard hand railing toward the portside of the *Nurium*.

He set the bags down and turned to say something to Nara. He noticed she had stopped when she crossed the bent and burnt deck planks where the Witch of Southwood had landed.

"I feel strange," Nara said. She lifted her hands, and Cayden could see they were shaking. "I've got a tingling sensation in my fingers."

There was a sudden change in the skies. A swirling blackness above the *Nurium* rustled the canvas of the two ships.

"Nara?" asked Cayden.

Nara looked at him. He could see she was frightened, but then her head flew back and light shot from her eyes and mouth. Several people jumped over the side of the ship's hand railing, and the rest doubled their efforts to climb over, screaming and shouting. The crowd pushed Cayden back toward the bow side of the railing.

"Nara!" Cayden cried, attempting to get to her. He forced his way toward her, but she suddenly rose into the air above the ship's sails. Blue bolts of energy shot out from around her body, causing small areas of the ocean water to vaporize and sand to rise up in twisted patterns of glass.

"Hear me!" a voice boomed from Nara's mouth.

People were dragging themselves onto the beach and running inland in a panic.

"The Witch!" Tadhra yelled and started back toward the ship, but he stopped and threw up his hands before his face. A large bolt of energy sprouted glass from the sands at his feet.

Nara raised her hand, and Cayden lifted into the air. He tried to grab the ship's railing, but failed to get a handhold, and he drifted slowly toward the crowd. "Arise!" said the voice. It echoed up and down the beach. "This one is to build a temple to Evliit and the bearer of the Sword of the Watch! See that you help him in every way. Do as he says, or I will visit vengeance upon you!"

"Get back from us, you witch!" Tadhra screamed, pulling a knife from his belt. "Come a little closer, why don't you? I'll gut you like a fish!"

Nara moved toward Tadhra. The unseen forces that lifted Cayden from the ground suddenly released him, and he fell with a good deal of force to the sandy beach. He rolled over, winded, and saw Nara's shape change momentarily into the wispy form he had seen upon the ship, the form of the Witch of Southwood. She pointed to Tadhra and a great burst of blue energy shot from her hands, blinding everyone.

"Protect the Sword!" Her voice boomed in all directions, amplified by their blindness. The echo of it resounded in the surrounding hills.

Cayden heard Nara's body fall to the ground next to him. "Nara!" he cried, feeling around himself in the darkness to find her. His eyes began to adjust, and then he saw her unconscious on the ground. He scrambled to her side and rolled her over.

"Nara?" he whispered into her ear. "Nara, are you all right?"

"I think so," Nara muttered. "What is happening?"

"I'm not sure," he began, but stopped when he noticed the remaining sailors and passengers closing in on them.

"Look," one said. Cayden realized that they were pointing past him.

Cayden adjusted Nara's arm over his shoulder and turned. Tadhra was behind him, still pointing to the sky, his wide-eyed stare frozen within the glass that sprung from the beach sands to encase him.

"We'll do whatever you ask!" the group said, sheepishly looking to Cayden, not knowing that he had no more idea than they did of what they were to do next.

Chapter Six

The Northern Fields

Tobor, the Camon General, surveyed the remnants of his once great army strewn across what had been the northern entrance to Rion. The battle in the Northern Fields was to be the deciding victory over the Rion Guard, the final obstacle in his conquest of Rion, but everywhere the land roared defiantly, making it nearly impossible for his captains to hear his orders. He had never once seriously considered retreating from an enemy, but this—this tearing open of the land and the accompanying storm of fire and smoke—it appeared as if the land itself had turned on them, and it had become obvious to him that moving forward toward the rift's edge was mere suicide.

"Retreat!" he cried, hoping desperately that the chain of command could hear him over the chaos.

The very mouth of the underworld appeared to have opened up beneath their feet, and a vast chasm now separated them from the Rion Guard. There were gas jets exploding upward through the stony ground ahead of them, jettisoning three and four of the Camonra into the air at a time. Their bodies combusted in the intense heat, and what remained of them swirled upward like ash from a campfire.

Tobor looked at the place on the horizon where only moments before he had seen the Rion Guard—columns of archers and infantry—but the massive column of soot rising out of the fissure blocked out everything. His army scrambled back from the smoke, fire, and molten rock in sheer terror, and Tobor soon realized that his own army might trample him if he stood his ground.

He pulled upon the reins of his mount, an Azrodh, and the great lizard reared and turned. Its front legs crashed down and nearly crushed two of their own Camonra running by, but then it bound forward and lumbered northward away from the fissure. Accelerating, its tail swept back and forth, knocking several more of the Camonra to the ground.

The remaining captains saw the general's retreat and attempted to do likewise, but the entire concept was foreign to the Camonra. Amphileph had created them for war and domination, and the retreat's execution was an exercise in confusion.

The Azrodh brayed at one of the Camonra, whose movements stuttered ahead of them unable to interpret the Azrodh's direction. "Out of the way!" Tobor yelled, but then a large chunk of molten rock fell on the Camon, removing fully half of his body. A splattering of lava seared the neck and face of his lizard mount, spurring it instinctively to jump away.

The sudden turn sent Tobor flying. He hit the ground and skipped on one shoulder, rolling face down in the dust and ash, the force of the impact knocking him senseless. Years of battle taught his body to get up quickly in such situations, and reflexively he rolled over and attempted to gather his footing.

He did so at his own loss. The more recent war wounds burned and bruises ached anew, and the crudely stitched wound on his shoulder popped its thick thread and bled freely. He screamed his defiance of it all, rising to his feet and drawing his great sword.

"This way!" Tobor cried, waving them on. He turned and ran through his exhaustion, looking ahead until he outpaced the nearest soldier, and then he pulled ahead, looking only at the ground before him. He ran what seemed like a full league before he looked back again, and then fell like the others to the ground. His eyes closed. Fatigue consumed him.

* * *

Tobor awoke to a gray world. A heavy rain fell, and the majority of his men lay in the thickening mud of the ash and rain mixture. A gray mud was everywhere, and a puddle of milky water submerged half his face.

He pushed himself up with some effort, and then looked to the skies to get his bearings, but the gray ash blotted out the sky. After some time, he got a feel for the light and dark of it, and determined that they had generally run north. Turning to the south, he could see the ash's origin, still actively spewing great mounds of lava into the air with thunderous noise.

It was hard to breath, and the taste of the ashen water bit his tongue.

"Captain!" Tobor yelled, but there was no reply. "Captain?" he called again.

There was some movement to his left. Tobor thought he heard Idhoran cough.

"Captain!" he called a third time.

Idhoran's upper body shot up from the ground, shouting, "Yes, my liege!" Idhoran kept his head shaved high above his ears, and Tobor could see a decent-sized cut starting in the stubbled scalp over his left ear and running into the short hair covering the crown of his head. The captain seemed to struggle to maintain his balance.

"Rally the Camonra!" the general shouted. "Count heads!"

"Yes, my liege!" said Idhoran. He placed his hands on either side of himself on the earth, forced himself to his feet with a quick thrust of his mighty arms, and found his helmet among the bodies. "Camonra, ready!" Idhoran shouted, the gruffness of his voice being enough to roust all but the dead.

His subordinates found their feet in similar ways, the order rippling through them.

Tobor walked back from them to higher ground some hundred paces north, hoping that he might rise above the storm of ash that hovered over the plains, but to no avail. He coughed, spat, and blew muddy ash from his nose, but he could not get the taste of it out of his mouth.

Amphileph's fury will be great, he thought.

Idhoran approached him. "My lord, eighteen companies of the Camonra remain. We have forty slaves and some supplies, but few of the Azrodh remain."

Tobor winced and nodded Idhoran to come near. The two of them turned away from the other Camonra, ascended a small hill, and Tobor waited until Idhoran came around him, so that Tobor faced away from his warriors. "I have failed," he said.

"No, my lord," Idhoran interjected.

"Look around you, Idhoran! Little remains of Amphileph's great army—*my* great army!"

"My lord, reinforcements come. Amphileph will know of these things and send our brothers to our aid. The great kingdom of Rion will still fall."

Tobor pointed to the south. "The men of Rion have fared no better than we."

"We need of water, my liege," said Idhoran. "The water in this place assaults the tongue and turns back out the meal. The Camonra despise it. Let scouts determine the fate of the Guard while we move north. We will determine the fate of Rion and report it to our master."

Our master, Tobor thought. *Amphileph will not care that Tobor could have never known the land would tear apart; he will be furious.*

"You are right," Tobor said instead. "We must have water and clear our nostrils of this air. No Camon can breathe this air for long."

"Yes, my liege."

Idhoran moved back down the hill and crossed the short distance to the soldiers, shouting the order to march north. "We march north, Camonra, out of Etharath's sickness that spills upon our heads!" he screamed to them.

Tobor watched them pass by, the rhythm of their sloshing feet helping him organize his thoughts on the best way to proceed. With Rion possibly crippled by the great quakes, he would need to find a way around these new fire gates to the city's entrance.

Idhoran drove the Camonra northeast until the rain fell clear or not at all. The winds carried away the ash from the great chasm in a north-by-northwest direction.

"We will make camp here!" announced Tobor. "Sound the drum. We must recapture the Azrodh that have scattered to the winds."

* * *

That night, Tobor summoned Idhoran and waited for him at his tent. He looked at the moonlight through the holes in the entrance fabric, and he remembered their reckless escape from the rain of molten rock.

Idhoran pulled back the entrance sash and entered. "My liege?"

"Please, at ease, my friend," Tobor said, and Idhoran removed his helmet. "I have need of your consul."

"I am your servant, lord, but what help could this old, scarred head lend to your wisdom? I'm afraid I'm good to you only as a warrior."

"Sit . . . sit," Tobor said gesturing to the crudely hewn chair. "A warrior's head is clear of many meaningless things, Idhoran. Life and death is never clearer than it is when swords ring."

"Battle alone makes our eyes see," Idhoran said.

"Yes, my friend. Battle is the fire that cleanses the soul. Let us drink to this!" Tobor grabbed a goblet and threw it to Idhoran, and then he picked up a flask and a second goblet, filled them both, and they struck them together.

"To the end of men!" Tobor said, and then he turned up the goblet.

"To the end of men!" Idhoran echoed and drank as well, but his face became stoic. He put down the cup. "My liege, if you have heard complaints from the ranks, I will kill them myself."

Tobor grunted. "They know who to challenge if they wish to lead!" he said. "It's not the troops, Idhoran."

"What troubles you, my lord?"

Tobor looked around, ensuring no one was within earshot. "Amphileph sees the future; he created us," Tobor began. "Why would his lordship wish to challenge our loyalty this way?"

Idhoran looked confused. "As I said, my lord, I am a Camon. I don't know of such things."

Tobor looked him in the eye. "Why would Amphileph lead us to our deaths? Have we not done whatever he has commanded of us, whenever he commanded it?"

"Without question," Idhoran answered.

Tobor rose and paced around the tent. "Let me ask another way, Idhoran: When does a general lead his men to certain death?" Tobor asked.

"When all is lost, my lord," Idhoran responded. "A Camon general will lead his men into certain death so that they may take as many of the enemy to the Underworld as they can."

Tobor moved close to Idhoran. "There is another time, Idhoran."

"Yes, my lord?"

Tobor hesitated, drinking again from his goblet. "A general will lead his army to certain death when he does not know that it awaits him."

Idhoran stood up suddenly and looked around the tent, checking for anyone that might be listening, and then saying in a hushed whisper, "To say our master, our Father, Amphileph did not know these things—my liege, forgive me, but this is wickedness! Amphileph is all knowing!" Tobor had been in many battles with Idhoran, but it was the first time he had ever seen Idhoran genuinely troubled. "I beg of you, my lord, speak no more of this!"

Tobor poured the remainder of the goblet's contents down his throat and slammed the goblet down upon the table. "That will be all, Idhoran!" he shouted.

"My lord?" Idhoran probed, a look of pain crossing his face.

"That will be all!" Tobor repeated.

"Yes, my liege," Idhoran said, slamming his fist on his chest and then turning to leave.

"Tomorrow we begin sending scouts to find a new passage to the men of Rion," Tobor said.

Idhoran stopped and turned to his general. "As you wish, my lord," he said and then turned again. Pushing the thick cloth of the tent aside, he exited.

Tobor felt a mixture of excited abandon and guilt. He waited for the waving of the tent folds to slow to a standstill behind Idhoran's exit before he turned to the small wooden cabinet from what remained of his personal effects. The adorned case his attendants once so carefully marched behind his army had been crudely reassembled after being partially crushed in the frantic dash from Rion. He opened the small doors that protected the even smaller likeness of Amphileph. Like he had a thousand times before, Tobor lowered his head to pray for guidance. He began with the prayer Citanth had taught him long ago before he had entered the vicious training of the Camon.

But this night, something was different. Before Tobor had grunted out even that first word, he stopped and slowly raised his head, opening his eyes to focus on the idol. "You should have known," Tobor said, and then he carefully closed the small cabinet doors and rose. He stood there, and his guts twisted, suddenly doubting everything he had come to believe about the world around him.

* * *

Tobor rose the following morning still cross with himself. Idhoran was waiting just outside his tent.

"My liege," Idhoran greeted him.

"A new day, Idhoran," Tobor replied. "Make ready the scouts. If a path exists for us to pierce these fiery gates of Rion, we must find it before reinforcements arrive."

"More of our great army comes any day," Idhoran grunted. "The humans will find no comfort in their city soon, my liege."

"Send forth the scouts!" Tobor shouted.

"Yes, my liege," Idhoran responded.

Tobor watched the scouts ride their Azrodh mounts to the forefront of the remainder of the Camon army.

"Search them out!" Tobor cried. "Find a way into the temples of Rion!"

There was the collective roar of the Azrodh and the howls of the scouts. They rumbled away south toward Rion.

For weeks, the scouts came and went from the deadly chasm, twice returning with fewer members of their party. Though Idhoran implored them to find the path to their victory, it was not to be, and the expanse of the chasm prevented them from discerning the state of the city beyond. Disgusted, Idhoran met with Tobor in private once again.

"The great chasm ruins our approach, my liege," Idhoran told Tobor. "We have searched its length, but no way is found around it."

"You are sure of this?" Tobor asked.

"Under threat of death, the scouts have found nothing," Idhoran emphasized. "There is no passage, my liege."

Tobor looked at the map Amphileph had given him, in silence, and then he pushed over the table on which it lay. "This makes no sense, Idhoran! How can it be that we are given the honor of being the ones to destroy the Guard's stronghold, yet we cannot take the battle to them? And why have no reinforcements arrived?"

"Something is wrong, my liege," Idhoran answered. "Father should have arrived by now." Idhoran referred to Amphileph's declaration that he would stand in the ruined temples of Rion in three days, but now it had been nearly five weeks and there was no sign of him. "We must send a runner to him, my liege," Idhoran said.

"And report what?" Tobor retorted. "That our army is destroyed, that we have found no way to carry our master's banner into Rion?"

"My liege, something is wrong," Idhoran said again, the exacerbation clear in his voice.

Tobor, too, was beyond frustration. This latest round of bad news was shaking him to his core. *How can this be Amphileph's will?* he thought. *Do you test me, my master?*

"Send the runners to Amphileph, Idhoran, but know that the master may require our deaths for this failure," said Tobor.

Chapter Seven

Power Revealed

Galbard ran through the seemingly never-ending trees in the northern part of Highwood with breakneck abandon. Branches slashed him repeatedly, he tripped up twice, and he fell a third time so hard that it took him several minutes to rise, even in his panic. He was sure he heard the people of Highwood just behind him to the south, but whenever he looked back, they were nowhere to be seen.

Galbard was a slave and a stoneworker. He was no stranger to enduring mental and physical pain, but even Galbard's stout constitution was no match for these days of running, sleepless nights, and the intense anxiety that was making him jump at the slightest sound. Fatigue found him, and it rested squarely upon his frame until his knees gave way and he slept the silent, black sleep of exhaustion where he fell.

He woke with a jolt in the darkness, thinking a Camon had found him. He frantically felt about for the Sword until he placed his hands on it and squeezed its scabbard and tang tightly. Galbard was not sure how long he had been out, and he steeled himself for another run. For a moment, he thought it was too quiet, and he strained to listen to every sound. He opened his eyes wide, trying to clear the sleep from them, and then he closed them again to listen even harder.

There was no sound but the wind and the birds. He took note of his own heartbeat pounding in his chest, and he gave thanks to the Creator for smiling on him another day. His heartbeat slowed, and he sat back against the rough wood of a tree stump as if it were a pillow of feathers.

* * *

For three days, he marched north, and the last stand of the great trees of Highwood parted, revealing a deep, cold stream and the foothills of another mountain range to the west. In the distance, Galbard could see a hundred foot waterfall pouring over the eastern end, its misty droplets lifting to the winds and drawing his eyes to another great mountain range to the north. The nearer range was much more inviting, but much too close to Highwood. He would have to move further north, to the cold gray stone that shot into the clouds in the distance. They looked barren and bleak, but it was another chance to reunite with people, and his supplies were all but gone. "The mountains, then," he said aloud, and he left the cover of Highwood to head north.

The plains were wide open and tough going. The wind seemed to throw off his balance with its strength. He was hungry, and the pain in his stomach rolled around under his ribs ferociously. Fatigue was omnipresent, always tempting him to stop and turn back. *Remember*, he thought, and the images of the dungeons of Amphileph's city snapped back into his mind. *Remember the silence of true despair. Remember reaching for the scattering of food scraps the Camon jailers had tossed into your cell only to hear the rattle of your own chains and the scurrying of tiny feet all around you. Remember the dank smell of the dungeon, its musty odor broken only by the acidic smell of excrement and the choking smell of death.*

These memories gave him clarity. The Camonra meant to search him out, to kill him, and retake the Sword. He didn't need to understand everything—just that one thing. He had accepted the charge of Evliit, and he meant to make good on this second chance at life outside those dungeon's walls.

He rose then, renewed, and refocused. The far mountain's ominous look seemed to change, its shear stone now appearing as a new refuge from those that meant to snare him. It would give them pause to follow him into the crevices of its jutting rock, and that pause might be his saving grace.

Galbard made his way toward the Faceless Mountains, as he named them. The ever-decreasing distance and sharpening angle brought more hope to him for their crossing, revealing pathways he might take in ascending its jagged rock.

The slow rise of the northern plains to the mountain foothills had given him some appreciation of the destruction that had occurred in the south. He could clearly see a tear in the earth crossing from the Black

Mountains to the sea. The ash and smoke flowed into the atmosphere with unending fury, causing huge storm clouds that came in from the sea and spread their lightning throughout the debris. Large white plumes of steam rose far to the southwest and southeast, on either side of Rion, and rumbling thunderheads continued to pour down rain and lightning upon what had been Rion's beautiful northern fields. He could only turn away from such a sad and terrible sight, for he knew that it served only to discourage him.

That night, he lay his back in a crevice and pulled his long coat tightly around him, trying desperately to seal out the frigid wind that raced over the mountainside. He could see fires burning in the plains to the south. Some were obviously large wildfires struck up by the lightning, but others were more ominous, smaller and gathered too symmetrically. These, he was convinced, were his pursuers.

In the solitude of his climb, Galbard had devoted more and more time to controlling the power that seemed to emanate from the Sword. He sensed something when the blade was drawn, something like a quiet voice, and he could feel the energy coursing through his body intensifying. The link between him and the Sword was growing stronger. He pulled down his hood, and clutching the Sword tightly, he closed his eyes and slept.

He woke the next morning to a dusting of snow. He shook it off and started up the mountain, but something caught his eye in the distance. He dropped low to the ground and cautiously closed the distance between himself and the place he thought he had seen some movement.

For several moments more he waited, thinking he heard whispers on the wind, and then one head slowly appeared, followed by another and another. The foothills of the mountains suddenly revealed many men and boys hiding in the rocks.

"I am Galbard of Rion!" he shouted, rising slowly. "I am alone, and I mean you no harm."

They closed on him in a wide circle, and then one of them stepped forward. "I am Illian, also of Rion! Have you news of Rion, brother?" one asked, his voice betraying a near-desperate sadness on the subject.

"No, my friend, I have not set foot in my beloved city in over a year," Galbard answered.

"It has been months for us," another said. "We were in the third wave that the council sent away in preparation for the war. We've been hiding in the ca—"

"Silence!" yelled one of the elder men of their party. "We do not know this man!"

"Does he look like an Inferior to you?" retorted the younger.

"The Spellmakers do not look like Inferiors either, you simpleton! They look like you and me, but they could kill us all with a wave of their hand."

Several squatted back behind their rock hiding places with the mention of Spellmakers, keeping a watchful eye on Galbard.

"I assure you, I'm no Spellmaker," said Galbard.

"Show us your hands!" cried another.

"Of course," answered Galbard, raising them both.

"Have you seen our brethren?" asked one of the boys. The tone in his voice tugged at Galbard's heart.

"Yes, there were others that fled just before the attack. I met them on their way north from the city. They've gone in hiding in the woods near the mountain range southwest of here."

Galbard did not see fit to share more of his adventure there. He parted his long coat, allowing the sword's tang to be visible. He looked closely at their faces, looking to see if they recognized it as the Sword, not wanting to repeat the events of Highwood, but no one seemed to give it a second glance. They appeared to be peasants, not soldiers, and Galbard let down his guard.

"What of the Inferiors, then?" one asked. "Has the Guard defeated them?"

"I don't know, my friend, but I've seen them in fields north of Rion, so I don't think that is the case."

Questions came at him in a flurry then. They crowded around him, hungry for news of Rion.

"Friends! Friends!" shouted Illian, "Give the man a chance!" A hush slowly fell upon them then. The speaker slung his bow across his body and put out a hand, which Galbard grasped, grateful to see a friendly face. Illian had a fur collar and a leather shirt covered with chainmail, a leather long coat over that. The light peppering of snow blended with his graying hair and beard.

Galbard told them of meeting the refugees in the northern fields. But of his encounter with the Camonra, he said only that they had all run for their lives, and he had wandered as far away from them as possible, and ended up here.

"Many Rionese people were sent to the woods west of the northern fields," Illian said. "We were to find our hiding place within the mountains. There are caves beneath the highest peak of this mountain range. We've taken refuge within them."

"There are many of you?" Galbard asked.

"Around four thousand. It's been difficult, but the mountain's kept us safe for these many months. Now that the battle has ended, we'll make our way home. Rion awaits our return."

Galbard looked at the ground.

"What is it, my friend?" Illian asked.

Galbard hesitated. "There's no passage back to our fair city, friend. The people I met in the northern fields coming from Rion—they said a great chasm had opened in the northern fields, cutting off passage to the city."

A collective cry came from the group.

"We'd seen the fire and smoke in the distance, but hoped for the best," said Illian.

"I'm afraid for the time being, we're separated from our people, exiled to this great mountain." Galbard saw their spirits die, the brightness of their eyes fading with the realization. Many of the men hid tears from Galbard's searching eyes, and Galbard thought to give them new purpose. "If the Inferiors' army has not been destroyed, then we cannot spare time for such sadness, my friends. We must prepare for the battle to come." Galbard saw the fear that replaced the sadness in their faces, and oddly, he took some comfort from it. At least fear could serve them well.

"Yes, yes," they answered. "You're right."

"If Amphileph's temple still stands, then the Camonra will come from that direction," Galbard said, pointing southeast. "But take heart! Do you not remember? We are men of Rion! The builders of the great temples! We have worked the fields and the oceans to feed tens of thousands! Surely, we can make a stand in the protection of these mountains!" The hand Galbard rested on the Sword's tang felt warmth beneath it. Its energy seemed to charge him. *Perhaps the Sword counsels me* he thought, and the sensation increased, driving the volume and strength of Galbard's voice. "You must accept that we will remain in exile for but a short time, and you must do what is necessary to protect the children of Rion!"

Again, all eyes focused on Galbard, and the truth of his words changed them. Galbard saw a flicker of hope and a steely determination.

"Yes!" they shouted. "May the Creator sustain us in our time of need!"

"He is doing so even now," Galbard responded. "Be good stewards of this good fortune he has bestowed. Make ready the mountain! Build a stronghold against whatever evil Amphileph might shower upon you!"

One of the men stepped forward. "Would you not eat with us? You look famished."

"Yes, of course, let us break bread together, brothers. I am indeed travel weary."

The men led Galbard through the paths in the foothills of the mountain toward the caves they had made their home. The sheer size of the rising wall of stone, its snowy peak rising into the clouds continually amazed him. He caressed its surface. "This is good stone," he said. "This stone will stand against even the Inferiors' army."

"Yes, my friend," Illian responded. "And we have just the tools to mold it," he added. "A true stone mason never leaves the tools of trade behind, even when fleeing the very city he builds," laughed Illian.

Galbard laughed as well. "I do remember the cost of a good hammer and chisel!"

Illian waved Galbard forward into the opening in the mountain. "Watch your head," he said. "Keep a good eye," he remarked to the others in his party, and they fanned out to keep watch on the entrance.

Galbard's eyes tried to adjust to the darkness of the entrance to the cave. It was tight for a man to fit, but he squeezed in behind Illian.

"Tight for us, but impossible for Inferiors," Illian remarked. "We are blessed to have found such a place."

"Indeed," Galbard responded.

Illian lit a torch, and the spark's sudden flash in the darkness made Galbard flinch. His eyes adjusted to the light, and he turned his eyes up slightly, looking away from the flame. He could see that the brown stone above them was blackened by torch smoke where others had also raised their torches to fit through the opening, and they worked their way through the passage's varying widths for some time. Galbard thought he heard voices ahead.

Illian turned his head carefully in the narrow space and shouted back. "Almost there."

The voices grew louder, and suddenly the passage opened to a great cave, its flat ceiling at least sixty feet high. "Watch your footing," he added.

Galbard noticed the ground was nothing like the smooth ceiling, but covered in various sizes of pebbles and rocks. The floor began dropping away, its grade increasing with each step, and the voices quieted with each step they took deeper into the mountain.

"It is I, Illian!" the group leader yelled. The torchlight revealed an even more expansive room.

"Who is with you?" a voice replied.

"A brother from Rion, a man named Galbard," he yelled.

There was a sound of voices again, and Galbard saw hundreds appear from around the columns of rock that stood upon what looked like piles of mud, but were hard as the stone he felt outside. It was an eerie place, and the folds of stone hanging from the ceiling danced in the firelight, appearing almost like moving wings or flaps of stony skin. He had never seen anything else like it.

Here the masons had chiseled out a walkway of sorts, and the group gathered on the far side of a crevice, connected to the area where Galbard and Illian walked by, a natural bridge. Galbard could see steps and elaborate rooms cut into the surrounding stone, torches and candles by the thousands revealing an expansive cavern whose size could not be judged in the dim light.

Illian noticed the look of amazement on Galbard's face. "It is not Rion, but we have made do."

"Impressive, brother," Galbard said. "You bring honor to the very name of Rion with this effort!"

Illian placed one hand on Galbard's shoulder. "We must inform the council of your arrival," he said. "Follow me." They moved past the crowds and deeper into the cave, where the stone changed color and texture. Here it appeared as if the stone was softer, smoothed by running water. They passed through yet another opening where a shaft of light illuminated their surroundings, and Illian extinguished his torch. They entered, and a group of men in long white robes came up to greet them.

"Greetings," one of them said. "We are the Council of Moonledge Peak," he said. "I am Caratacus, and I was assigned by the Rion Guard to oversee our time in this place."

"My name is Galbard, son of Gulbrand. I, too, was a citizen of Rion."

"I know the name of Gulbrand—he was of my time," Caratacus said. "Did your father make the journey?"

"No, my lord. My father has returned to the Creator, eight winters past."

"I rejoice in his return," Caratacus said. "My friends, the right good members of this council, wish to know what fortune has brought you to us. Would you endeavor to endure our questions?"

"But of course, my lord," Galbard responded. "Please, ask what you wish."

Galbard found that Caratacus and his companions had many questions, for they were very curious of the progress of the war. Galbard apologized yet again that he had very little news of the war, and recounted once again his journey to the mountains, but beyond that, Galbard said little.

"You are a mystery," Caratacus said. "A man alone in this wilderness is a curiosity to the council, but we can find no harm in your staying here with us."

"I assure my lord that I will bring no harm to the good people of Rion," Galbard answered. He felt his face tighten and redden, though he tried to will it from happening. *The presence of the Sword may bring just that,* he thought to himself.

"Food is scarce, but enough for one more," Caratacus announced to the group. "Illian, show Galbard where he might find food and drink."

"Yes, my lord," Illian responded, motioning Galbard to follow.

Galbard turned to follow him, and he noticed that the council moved close together, their low voices echoing unintelligibly in the corridor Galbard and Illian used to return to the main dwelling place.

"I hope I have not intruded," Galbard said.

"You would have known it at this first meeting if they thought as much," Illian said. "The council has no issue with letting their feelings be known."

"That is good," said Galbard. "I can work for the food you offer."

"That you will," Illian responded. He waited for Galbard's face to change to something akin to concern, and then he could not contain himself, letting his hearty laughter bounce off the cave walls. "That you will!"

Illian led Galbard to a small dwelling where several women were pounding thick strips of meat with stones and hanging them in a small leather tent, smoking them. One of the women handed him a small stone platter of the smoked meat and a cup of clear, cool water from a trickle that passed through their dwelling. Galbard sipped it from a polished stone cup, and he eagerly ate some of the dried meat. He marveled at its wonderful taste so much so that he had to consciously slow his chewing, and when he commented that it was very tasty, they giggled and fed him until he could eat no more.

Galbard thanked the women profusely, and then Illian led him to yet another cave, where several men were winding cord to make or mend nets. The room had many torches.

"There are fish," Illian said, pointing to a dark pool of water at the lower end of the cave, its surface looking almost like pitch in the torchlight.

"Fish?" Galbard asked.

Illian pointed to a strange, pale white creature the men pulled from their nets. "Yes, my friend, there is a great cavern beneath us, filled with all manner of sightless fish. Had it not been for a small boy falling into this opening, we might never have found it. When we pulled him from its clutches, he said that he felt something all around him, touching his hands, feet, and face. He had nearly drowned from panic in the darkness. We have since mounted these torches and ventured with a lanyard into the depths. In the light that the torches provide, we have found neither the bottom nor the sides, and though it is fairly still now, when the rains come, the currents can be quite dangerous."

"Amazing," Galbard said.

"You mentioned that you once fished the northern lake?"

"As a child, I mended nets for my father."

"I was hoping that you could help the men."

"Yes, of course. I'm glad to earn my keep."

Galbard stayed at this task for several days, and his weaving of the nets was considerably helpful to the other stonemasons, whose experience with such things was lacking. It was the first time that Galbard felt at ease, and though he kept mostly to himself, he became fast friends with Illian and the men who worked the nets. His welcome ease brought sleep that he had not enjoyed in years, deep and restful, and Galbard thought that he might at last have some peaceful place to lay his head. However, on the fourth day, his deep sleep brought a dream that changed everything.

In this dream, he walked through the caverns alone, seeing the rooms empty where once the refugees of Rion had been. The silence was menacing, and a chilling breeze moved through the passages, one by one extinguishing the torches that lit his way. Suddenly, there was naught but darkness, and Galbard stumbled and fell, fighting back his rising fear that he would never find his way out from the immense darkness that swallowed him up. He felt a firm hand upon his arm that made him instinctively grab for the Sword, but it was not at his side.

"You must leave this place!" a gravelly voice said, and Galbard thrashed about from hearing it, but he could not break away from the iron grip.

"Who . . . who are you?" Galbard managed.

"I am Tophian, Watcher of the Mountains!" the voice responded, and the grip released. A magical light suddenly illuminated their surroundings. The man before him had his chest-length white hair combed back, with the exception of a single tuft of hair that curled to the side of his light blue eyes. He stood there with his walking stick, its curved handle caught up in one of his fingerless leather gloves, dark crystal studs adorning their long cuffs. He turned the other palm up, and an orb of light floated above it, revealing a beard neatly trimmed around his chin, and a blue cloak that partially covered a breastplate bearing a yellow, triangular pattern and numerous belts and pouches. There was something in ancient Rionese embroidered with brown thread around the forearm-length sleeves of his white tunic. "This is what is to come if you remain amongst these people, Galbard! The Sword draws the Camonra to you even now! Take it from this place, or ruin will come to you all!"

Galbard awoke with a start, striking his head on the ceiling over his bedding so hard that it dazed him. He looked about frantically for the Sword and his pack, and having put his hands on them both, he drew a deep, calming breath and exhaled slowly. He looked out of the window-like opening carved in the humble abode Illian had so kindly shared with him, and he saw the rock walls surrounding him flickered with candlelight. The panic of the dream subsided. Galbard thought with sadness about leaving what little comfort he had found on his journeys. The thick stone walls of Moonledge had become protective, peaceful, where the still of the night was broken only by the faint sound of snoring or the occasional child's stirring. He took that moment to take it all in for what would likely be the last time.

Illian woke to find Galbard stuffing his pack with some of the dried fish and goat meat.

"Galbard?" Illian inquired. "What are you doing?"

Galbard stopped and looked at the pack. "I must leave you," he said, and then he resumed his packing.

"Leave?" Illian asked. "What do you mean?"

"It's not safe for me to be here," Galbard began.

"Not safe? Why Galbard, you're our brother! What possible harm would be done to you?"

Galbard stopped packing again, trying to think of the right words to explain his vision.

"Galbard?" Illian asked. His face was a mixture of confusion and hurt.

"My brothers, indeed," Galbard responded. "It's not what you would do to me, but what evil I might bring upon you."

"What evil you would bring upon us? I don't understand," Illian replied.

"I have had a vision," Galbard began. "A vision given to me by a Watcher named Tophian. He has told me that the Inferiors search me out, and staying here will only mean that I endanger everyone."

"Galbard," Illian chuckled nervously. "It is a nightmare. It means nothing. Stop what you are doing and let us talk of this."

"This was no child's nightmare. I must leave you," Galbard said, his tone causing Illian to straighten up in his bedroll.

Illian stared at him, not knowing what to say. Galbard finished packing, and he rose to leave, but Illian rose to his feet and grabbed his arm.

"Surely, you can explain yourself a bit better, Galbard. Do I not deserve that much?"

Galbard stopped and looked at the floor of the room.

"Yes, Illian," Galbard said. "You do, indeed. If I tell you something, will you swear to the Creator that you will speak of it to no other?"

"I swear it," answered Illian.

Then Galbard told Illian everything. He told him of his capture, of the vision of Evliit, and his receiving of the Sword. He told him what had happened at Highwood, and then he stopped, trying to judge Illian's somber face.

"This is much to take in at one sitting," Illian said. "I am beyond words."

"You have done well by me, Illian. I am forever grateful. What little comfort I have had in my journey, you have provided me, provided by the hand of the Creator himself it seems. Please forgive my leaving so abruptly, but know that I leave because of the very fondness for my brethren that would have me stay."

Illian turned from him and rummaged around in the darkness of their quarters near his bedroll. He produced two loaves of bread and pushed them out to him.

"Here, take this. You will need them more than I," Illian said.

"I cannot take any more from you, my friend," Galbard responded.

"Take them," Illian insisted, reaching across Galbard and pushing them into his pack. "May the Creator watch over you and keep you safe."

Galbard wrapped his arms around Illian, squeezing him tightly.

Illian brought him to arm's length. "Where will you go?" he asked.

"I don't know," Galbard answered. "I really don't know what I'm to do." He turned his face from Illian and moved to the doorway. "I suppose I'll follow the mountains northeast."

"Then take this as well," Illian said, offering Galbard his animal skin coat. "I stitched a hood into it when we first arrived; it was so cold here compared to Rion. I was sure I was going to freeze," he said with a soft smile. "Take care of yourself, Galbard."

"And you as well, my friend," Galbard said. He exited the doorway for a moment, and then poked his head back in. "The Camonra live on. They are not destroyed. Prepare the people for their coming, and I pray that this Tophian, this Watcher of Mountains, may come to your aid when that day arrives."

Galbard looked one last time into Illian's face, searching his eyes for understanding. Illian's nod was enough. He turned and made his way through the caves and out upon the northern plains, and then he pulled the coat over his shoulders and pulled on his pack, looking one last time at the cave opening in the moonlight before venturing east.

Chapter Eight

Shintower

Days after the incident on the beach, Cayden was still trying to deal with the aftermath of fear and distrust that resulted from Nara's possession by the Witch of Southwood. It had scared the life out of everyone involved, and those days passed with little discussion between the other refugees and Cayden, Nara, or by association, Jalin. There were often whispers from the others, and Cayden truly began to worry about Nara's safety, so he had pitched two tents for them away from the shore, away from the other refugees.

Jalin had just put Ro down for a nap, and she and Nara were talking. Nara was complaining of the muscles in her arm twitching. Cayden was building a fire, and suddenly, Nara fell on her back, writhing in pain. She was convulsing, making a choking sound.

Cayden scrambled about and found a wooden dowel that they used for pinning stone among some masonry tools. He wiped it off on his pants, thinking of using it for her to bite down on.

"Hurry, Cayden!" Jalin said.

Cayden pushed the stick toward her face, but she grabbed it from his hands, rolled over, and jabbed the stick into the dirt beside the campfire. She swept her hand wildly across its surface, but something about it made Cayden think it was more than random shapes.

"She's trying to draw something!" he said. "Stay with her. I'll be back!" He turned and headed toward the main refugee camp.

"Where are you going?" Jalin asked. "Don't leave us here alone!"

"I'm going to find something for her to write with," he answered. "Stay with her. I'll be right back." Jalin looked back at him with eyes wide. "It's going to be all right."

"Please hurry," she added. She crossed her arms and then brought one hand to her mouth, biting her lip and swaying back and forth.

"I'll hurry," he replied, and then he ran toward the main camp. The others had offloaded a stash of all kinds of things from the *Merrius*, and he was sure he had seen a wooden pen, ink, and paper among them.

When he arrived at the main camp, people were preparing to eat the evening meal. They had formed a line to a large soup pot that he recognized from the *Nurium's* galley. He moved around them to a broad tent pitched for the supplies. The person posted at the entrance recognized him from a distance, made eye contact, but then looked away. For once, their fear worked to his advantage, and the post moved to the side from the entrance without saying a word.

He quickly rummaged through the supplies and found several pieces of paper, a pen, and ink, and he bolted right back out again, ignoring the looks and murmurs of the few who had noticed his coming and going.

He ran as fast as he could back to Nara's side, removing the paper from the protection of his shirt, and producing the pen and ink well from his trousers. He dipped the pen into the ink and carefully unfolded the largest piece of paper that he had, laying it on a smooth chunk of wood they had used as a chopping block, doing his best to press out the wrinkles with his hands.

"Nara?" he asked. He set the pen and paper before her on the block, and she rolled up to a squatting position and threw down the dowel. She grabbed the pen and began scribbling madly on the paper. At one point, she knocked over the ink, splashing a corner of the paper with blackness. Then she ran the pen through it and across the paper, her mad lines flying out from the splash of indigo, instantly incorporating it into whatever she was drawing.

"I worry for her," Jalin replied. She looked over Nara's automatic drawing. "I pray to the Creator that these spirits will leave her."

"Soon," Cayden said, turning around and sitting beside her to look at the frantic drawing she was creating. He barely had time to replace one scrap of paper with another as she filled them.

"It's a building of some type," he said. "Some kind of tower, I think."

After a few minutes more, Nara suddenly lurched backward onto the ground, dropping the pen from her hand.

Nara's eyes closed. "Ah!" she shouted. Then the strain in her face calmed. She opened her eyes and focused on Cayden.

"Cayden?" she asked. "Is it over, Cayden?"

"Yes, darling," Cayden responded. He noticed the look on Jalin's face when she caught his use of the word *darling*. It was a hint of a smile.

"It's okay, you're with us," said Jalin. "I believe he's quite madly in love with you," she added, leaning down, wiping the sweat from Nara's face, and gently stroking her hair. "No matter what this thing is that haunts you, Nara, you will overcome it."

"Look what you have drawn," said Cayden. The two of them helped Nara sit up.

"I feel strangely relieved," Nara said.

"You were drawing this, Nara," Jalin said. "Can you remember anything?"

"No," Nara replied. "Well, I remember talking with you both, and then the uncontrollable shaking in my arm, but then nothing until now."

There was the sound of Ro's crying from their tent. "Oh, my darling," Jalin said. "Let me check on him."

"I am fine," Nara said.

"Yes, of course," Jalin responded, this time openly smiling at Nara. She glanced at Cayden and entered their small tent where Ro had been sleeping.

"Let me look at this," said Cayden, reaching for the largest parchment.

"Of course," Nara responded.

Cayden took that parchment and studied it. It was a drawing of a tower-like structure, and a scrawl across the bottom gave instructions to the stonemasons of Rion to cut the stone from the massive rocks by the sea. It even delineated where the tower was to be built.

Cayden studied the drawings. "These stones are to be cut thirty hands across and sixteen hands deep and wide!" he exclaimed. "And this tower is nearly two leagues away from the shore! We have no animal of burden to move such massive stones that great distance. Even the great masons of Rion could not do this!"

"It is to be done," Nara responded. "Of that I'm sure, Cayden."

Jalin returned from their small tent carrying Ro. "What have you found?" she asked. "Is there anything more . . . about Galbard?"

"No, Jalin, I'm sorry. It's a map of sorts and a floor plan. This part tells of the quarry, and this . . ." Cayden began. "Wait, look at this," he said.

"What is it?" both women asked.

"This says that we are to cut the stone and move it no further than what is needed for us to cut the next. Cut it and leave it where it lies, so that we may know the power of the Creator."

"What?" the women repeated, but Cayden was oblivious. He grabbed up the drawing. "Wait here," he said. "I must let the masons of Rion see these."

"But," Nara began, reaching out to him. "Are you sure?"

Cayden looked deeply into her eyes. He wanted her to be able to trust him and for him to succeed at being trusted. "I believe in my heart that this is best, Nara. I would never hurt you."

"Yes, of course," said Nara, looking a bit embarrassed at first. "The others have already shunned us, and I must admit I'm a bit afraid that this might only make things worse. I don't want to be alone anymore."

Cayden could see that her lip was beginning to quiver. "Never alone, Nara," he said. "Not as long as I breathe."

Nara nodded. "Of course. Do what you will with it, but I don't want to be there. I'll stay here with Jalin and Ro."

"Surely. Come now, that's enough of this," Jalin interjected. "Ro would love the company." Jalin took her by the hand.

Cayden waited for them to enter the tent, and he walked back toward the main camp, holding the papers open and apart, ensuring that they were drying properly. It was getting dark, and Cayden steadily picked up his pace toward the main camp, for he felt a sense of purpose. He was sure that these drawings held the secret to be how he was to "protect the bearer of the Sword."

When he came upon the edge of the encampment, he stopped and held the drawings over his head. "Men of Rion!" he shouted. "I bring news!"

His excitement quickly faded. The women and children moved away from him behind the men, and Cayden noticed that the men were standing their ground as if they expected to defend themselves. He lowered the drawings.

"What is it you command of us?" someone shouted from the crowd.

"Command of you?" Cayden answered. "*I* command nothing. It is the Witch of Southwood for whom I speak. I bring a message, a way for us to satisfy our oath."

The father of a young family stepped forward. "If your message will end this curse, we want to hear it," he said. "The darkness of these days must end."

An old woman stepped toward Cayden with the assistance of her staff, and then she turned around to face the crowd. "What are you waiting for? Come let us judge for ourselves what message this one brings!"

The young family moved to join her, and then others appeared from the crowd and joined them. Someone shouted to bring a table, and when they did, Cayden spread all the drawings upon it, so all could see.

"It is a tower fit for the likes of Rionese masons," Cayden began. "It has seven floors that rise above the wilderness." He soon realized that the crowd was too large to see the drawings on the table, so he stood upon the table and held them up to show them. "We are to cut gears and wheels of stone, large flat plates like the segments of a circle, and there is work for the blacksmith and the carpenter, for there are great rods of steel, wooden rings, and timbers for floors and bracing."

"What are these?" one of the masons asked, pointing to trenches and pits around the structure.

"There appears to be an intricate labyrinth of square holes and ditches all around the main structure. "Maybe they are for water? A garden? I don't know," answered Cayden. "There are pipes and levers and all manner of gadgetry set in the stone."

"Show us again the drawing of the tower itself," said another.

Cayden shuffled the pages. "The top floor has an altar of sorts, open to the air, and the floors are connected by steps that spiral around a central column of stone." Cayden showed them the drawings of intricate stone and metalwork. Many of the components Cayden could neither name nor describe their purposes, but he was sure of one thing: the Witch of Southwood wanted them to build it.

"Only a Rionese mason can grasp the magnitude of such a project," Cayden said. "Look here." He held up a drawing of three quarries between the beach and the nearby fields. The plan laid out the locations of thousands of stones, though it provided little in the way of how the masons would lay them.

"We'll use plugs and feathers to separate the stones, and then leave them where they lay for the apprentices to put the cock's comb to them. The next day we will do the same, and the day after that, until every stone that is required has been cut and shaped."

"But how do we move the stones?" asked another. "We could acquire the wood for the ramps we'll need to build to get the stone that high, but I have seen only six head of cattle on the boats that are still arriving, and we may be hard-pressed to keep the villagers from turning those into steak."

Cayden sorted through the drawings again. "The tower's location itself appears to be one of the quarries, so that's not an issue." There were arrows from the other quarries to the tower's final location. "Here, brother," Cayden said. He pointed to the words under the arrow. "It says 'Bhre-Nora,'" he smiled nervously.

"What is Bhre-Nora?" another asked.

Cayden stared at the drawing, but nothing came to him. "I don't know, but it is not the oxen. There is a trail marked for the oxen to use to bring iron ore from here," he said pointing to the map.

There were murmurs again, and then another of the masons spoke up. "How do we know that the Witch of Southwood does not mean to use this altar for some great evil?"

Cayden knew that this would come up, but he was not about to let them turn Nara into some harbinger of evil. "I have seen no instruction to build an image of a deity of any kind, nor credit taken by any foul names that we might recognize. There is no reference to anything but the Sword of the Evliit. I fear not the Creator's wrath so much for building it as for *not* doing so. You witnessed what happened on the beach, same as me, and for anyone that doesn't remember, Tadhra still bears witness within the glass."

The murmurs ceased, and one of the master masons spoke up. "We are masons of Rion. This is what we do. What must be done to satisfy the witch must be done, but know that we will hold you accountable for any evil that comes to us."

"I understand," replied Cayden.

* * *

Work began immediately, and though Cayden was very much in the middle of things, Nara did not go to the quarries, but busied herself with Ro and Jalin, away from the central encampment.

After two months of backbreaking labor, the blacksmiths had poured the iron and hammered out the metalwork, the masons had etched the last of the stones into each of the three quarries, and they all laid down their tools. Cayden had dreaded this moment, for no matter how much he looked through all the scraps of drawing, he could find nothing about what to do next. There was only the reference to the "Bhre-Nora," which gave him little more to say to the masons.

"What shall we do now, Cayden?" one asked. "We have laid the metalwork into the pits, and the stone has been cut."

"Rest, friends, let me see what more I can find within the drawings," he said. "We have finished the work we have been given," Cayden announced. "Leave the stone where it lay."

There was a small amount of talk among the masons, none of it sounding too positive, but nothing akin to revolt either. "Leave it where it lay?" they asked.

"Yes. You may return to your camps."

For the remainder of the day, Cayden sat at the northern quarry with Nara's drawings, watching the motionless stone. The sun slowly fell over the ocean behind him. He rolled them up, and decided he had done what could be done.

Cayden approached their small camp, and Nara walked out to meet him.

"Come, eat, and rest, Cayden," Nara said. "One of the snares has netted us a rabbit!"

"Excellent!" exclaimed Cayden, but as he approached her, he could see that something was wrong. "Something bothering you?" he probed.

"That obvious, huh?" Nara replied. "Jalin has had a tough day. She tried to talk to some of the others about leaving for Rion, but no one would talk with her. I think it would be good for her to have a decent meal and hear what all was accomplished today."

"Yes, of course," Cayden replied.

Cayden got a cook fire going, and he laid out two blankets beside it. They had a pleasant meal of rabbit, and afterward, Cayden tried to reassure Jalin.

"You should stay here with us," he urged. "We've cut the stone required by the drawings. I feel like we'll know so much more about the tower very soon, and when its purpose comes to light, you should be here with us."

She seemed about to acquiesce, but Ro became fussy, and when it seemed that he might wake, she got up with him. "Time for me and the little one to retire for the night," she said, and then she heaved him upon her shoulder. "You're getting so big," she said. Ro lay his head against his mother's neck, his thumb just managing to stay in his mouth. Jalin looked at Cayden and Nara, and she smiled. "Thank you," she said. "Thank you for being so good to us. I owe you so much, but . . . this tower will take many years to build, and I don't know if I have the faith to wait that long. I *must* find my husband. Ro needs his father. I hope you can understand."

"Of course," replied Nara, but the disappointment in her voice was obvious.

"Of course," echoed Cayden. "Nara and I will see to the fire; get yourself some rest."

"Goodnight," said Jalin, and then she and the baby slipped into their tent.

The night sky filled with a scattering of stars. Cayden picked up the blankets and checked the fire, and then he and Nara, too, made their way to bed.

* * *

"Cayden?" Nara whispered.

Cayden rolled over, trying to rouse himself from the dead sleep of a hard day's labor. "What is it, Nara?" he responded.

"Sounds like a good wind's stirring up, and I'm not sure the tents are staked well enough to wait it out. Could you look them over? I would hate to lose the tents if the rain follows."

Cayden was a little perturbed, but he shook off the sleep and rose. "Yes, of course, I'll check them both," he said, and he pulled on his pants. Fumbling with his belt, he noticed that the wind was picking up quickly, and his rising seemed better timed with each passing moment. He pushed aside the tent flap and stepped out of the tent facing the west, looking out toward the moonlit ocean. Out to sea, there was a huge waterspout raging over the waves, seemingly changing their pattern of movement with the sheer force of the whirling winds. A rumbling sound quickly grew out of the distance, and Cayden threw back the tent flap.

"Nara!" he yelled. "Get up! Get Jalin and the baby!"

Nara saw the look on Cayden's face and rose immediately, moving quickly into Jalin's tent.

Cayden stood and watched the whirlwind's approach and then looked around at the scattered tents of the Rionese refugee camp. The refugees were slowly emerging from their tents at first, but upon realizing they were directly in the path of the storm, they began to run east toward him.

Cayden watched the waterspout turn onto the shore, and the sand drew up into the funnel. Its white color turned dingy, and then the winds moved onto the mainland and turned to a shade of gray.

Following Nara and Jalin, Cayden began moving toward cover when suddenly he noticed something changing about the whirlwind. The cloud ceiling above it seemed to take on the shape of a face, its widening mouth coughing forth what looked like a dark mist. He stood there, frozen in his steps. The swirling mist grew nearer, until Cayden was sure that it was not a mist at all, but thousands of small creatures. Their fluttering wings rode the whirlwinds with ease, moving back and forth between the twirling debris.

He watched the whirlwind pass over the great stones they had cut from the shoreline, its tremendous winds breaking loose the stones from Erathe's grip and hurling them into the air. The small creatures seemed to swarm the rising stones in clumps, their tiny wings making a buzzing noise that added to the cacophony of the storm. Together, the swarm and the whirlwind navigated the stones toward the southern edge of the valley.

"The Bhre-Nora," Cayden muttered in his shock. The winds whipped his hair around his head, but his eyes remained fixed upon them. Repeatedly, the tiny creatures followed the stones' trajectories, wrangling them under control, and then guiding them into a line behind their brethren like a caravan. There was a rumbling of the clouds, the flashes of lightning intensified, and suddenly, with a great clap, the fingers of electricity combined into one great bolt that shot into the ground from the swirling clouds.

Cayden saw the energy boring into the earth like a carpenter's drill, sending great chunks of stone into the stratosphere. The lightning struck the mixture repeatedly, and a slurry of molten stone formed in the air. This mixture began to spin within the whirlwind, elongating into a cylinder much larger than anything Cayden had ever seen used in the columns of the Rionese temples. When the cylinder formed, the clouds began to slow their winds. The great stone column seemed to stall in the air for a moment, and then it began its fall from the skies. The whirlwind appeared to be dissipating.

The creatures were effective in corralling the cut stone, but they wholly ignored the other debris, and the thought crossed Cayden's mind that it would not be good to be anywhere near the base of it when the whirling winds released the debris. "Run!" he yelled, and then he ran to Nara, Jalin, and Ro, grabbing Nara by the arm.

A large stone shot past them overhead. "Run! This way!" Cayden yelled. They ran for the cover of a small ditch and lay down in the cool water. Another stone bounced once near them and crashed into the ground a second time, peeling the turf from the earth and piling up a mound of dirt, shaking them to their core. Several others saw them and joined them in the ditch.

The column accelerated to terminal velocity, and a silence seemed to take hold. Cayden looked up for a last time, just in time to see the column stick into the ground like an arrow shot, sinking at least half its length. He could see the earth rippling with the shockwave that proceeded from its impact, ducking his head at the last moment before a wave of dust and debris passed over them. The concussive force of the shockwave sent anyone standing flying through the air, and the ensuing layer of thick dust that hung in the air blinded anyone within the circumference of the expanding wave, blocking the moonlight and stars.

Cayden tried to get his bearings, rising from the muddy water in which they lay. The top of his head felt like he had been kicked, his organs quivered as if he had been shaken violently. His hearing returned after a short while of muted ringing in his ears, only to be replaced by a humming sound in the distance, whose volume and pitch rose and fell in waves. Sporadically, there were grating and grinding sounds, and thumps that shook the ground.

Cayden could hear Ro gagging for air. One of the tent poles was still standing in Jalin's partially collapsed tent, but his and Nara's tent was still standing. He hurried to help Nara, Jalin, and the baby into it.

"Stay here," he said, but Nara and Jalin just plopped down with Ro, saying nothing in return. He grabbed a shirt from inside the tent, closed the tent flaps behind him, and tied them shut. Then he tied the shirt around his nose and mouth, using one of the sleeves to wipe the mud from his eyes. He drove a stake in the ground just outside the tent and tied a rope to it and then tied the other end to his belt and looked around for people lost in the aftermath of the storm.

He found several of his people still lying on the ground, many of them exhausted from wandering in the wind and dust. "Follow my rope back to our tents and get inside!" he told them.

For three days, the winds blew wildly, and the dust made it nearly impossible to see or travel. The refugees gathered what they could of their belongings and hunkered down in what remained of their tents and lean-tos.

On the fourth day, the winds subsided. Cayden walked back toward the massive column, but there were none of the little creatures in sight. He topped the small knoll behind which he and his group had taken cover. The Rionese artisans were yelling from all directions, a group of them shouting and pointing to the west. A twenty-foot wall of stone surrounded the column at a radius of about fifty paces. Sounds of hammering and voices emanated from behind them.

Cayden walked around the high wall with the other men, but there was no way in. They waited until nightfall for something more to happen, but then the strange sounds coming from within the walls began to spook them. They returned to their camps.

For seven nights, Cayden stepped outside his tent and looked at the stone column. The buzzing sounds were endless, but the moonless nights left him blind to what was happening. Each morning, he woke to find stones disappearing from the quarries and rising around the stone column, until at last, under secrecy of night, the tower had risen.

On the evening of the seventh day, a blast of wind rushed through that place, and a low trumpeting pitch rumbled through the valley. There was the sound of chains and gears, and the mighty wall that surrounded the tower parted. Cayden marveled that it did not swing like a gate, but the two walls slid apart horizontally, almost like the eyelid of a giant who was lying on his side.

Cayden joined some other craftsmen mingling at the opening, watching the tower for some sign of life, but they saw none.

"Should we go in?" one of the masons asked.

"Cayden should go," another piped up.

"Yes, Cayden should go," they all agreed.

"I will go," Cayden responded. "This stonework is of the Creator's doing, there's nothing to fear."

He walked alone through the outer walls to the inner court and looked around, but there was no one in sight. The tower's height seemed to shoot into the sky, and when he moved to the south a bit, it blocked out the sun so that Cayden could see the balconies above him.

His gaze drifted downward. He noticed a doorway where three of the small creatures shot out from its opening, two racing away toward the trees in the south. The third one fluttered to a stop in the grass just before Cayden. It was a little, winged, but man-like creature, about knee-height, whose long hair stuck out from under a tight leather cap with a ridge across the top from which little brass goggles hung before his eyes. He had elbow-length gloves that flared at the top, knee-high boots, and a long coat. Poking out from beneath the long coat was a tiny golden rapier, and leather straps crisscrossed his vest, having strange devices hanging from them. He looked up at Cayden, and his wings twitched once or twice, revealing metallic panels in place of feathers. The wings were jointed in three places, which the little man spread and then folded behind him when Cayden approached.

"The Creator has seen fit to build a temple here," the third little creature said.

Cayden was speechless for a moment. "It is truly amazing," Cayden replied finally. And then, almost as a question, "Thank you."

"My Lady of Southwood has sent us to help you protect the Sword. She has seen the labor you have put forth with the stone and has found favor in you. Prepare for its coming and she may yet find favor in you still."

Cayden stepped forward and reached out to the creature, which zipped away some thirty paces. "But how should we prepare?" he asked.

Looking very pleased, it circled back to him. "There is woodwork and furnishing, of course," he said. "And much more stonework that you should do to make ready the way for the sword! I have left you a list. And look for the man named Galbard to bring the sword, for he has saved it from the clutches of the evil one, Amphileph!" He spun around and quivered upon uttering the Spellmaker's name. "We will make a great battlement to protect the mighty Sword of the Watch from the evil one and his creatures!" he said, with great defiance in his voice. "You must build it mighty indeed!"

The winged artisan suddenly flew within inches of Cayden's face, making him flinch. "Build it in honor of the Creator himself!" The little creature flipped his goggles out of the way and searched Cayden's face for a moment, his tiny head moving back and forth to look into each of Cayden's eyes. Finding something that gave him satisfaction, he said, "Blessings upon your efforts, human." Dropping his goggles back into place, he flew off in a *whoosh* of air that caused Cayden's eyes to flutter with the wing beats.

Cayden tried to shake disbelief from his head, but placing his hand upon the surrounding stone, he found them real enough. It was not a dream.

He walked toward the doorway of the great tower with the same awe that he would a holy temple in the old city of Rion. He looked everywhere around it for some sign that forbade him enter, but found none, and then he knelt on one knee before the entrance and looked up at the sky.

"Mighty Creator!" he yelled. "Please grant me entry!"

After a moment, he stood up, took a deep breath, and then broached its doorway. He entered the threshold and counted three paces to the room within, the tower's massive outer wall being the thickest at its base.

As Cayden's eyes adjusted to the light, he looked around at the massive arches that stretched from the walls to the ceiling, supporting the additional stories within the tower. Set against the far wall was a set of stairs that wrapped around the walls in each direction, just as he had seen them in the Nara's drawings. Six small windows lit the landing. Cayden noticed something in the light above. He passed between the columns that supported the opening and up the stairs, where he found a large scroll tied up with a ribbon. He untied it and unrolled the scroll, turning to see it better in the light.

"Oh my," Cayden whispered. "We've much to do."

Chapter Nine

The Hunt Begins

Amphileph stared at the bloodstain that Ardidhus's body had left on the temple dome. The summer heat had long since changed its reddish hue to brown, but it seemed to Amphileph that the events had transpired but moments ago. He could still see Ardidhus's face just before he'd hurled him through the air.

For the first time in his life, he felt utterly alone. "Creator," he said. "Why have you allowed Evliit to torture me so? I've demanded nothing but reverence for you!" He stood still, awaiting an answer, but his prayers seemed to whisk away in the wind, and silence was the only reply.

The stench of the other Spellmakers' rotting corpses seemed to hang in the air, a constant reminder of his violent coup. He could take it no longer. "Camonra!" he shouted. Within moments, three of the Camonra appeared from the western camp. He thought they smelled of wet dog.

"Yes, master!" one of them said. The three of them stayed low to the ground, diverting their eyes from him.

"Burn the bodies of the other Fathers!" he screamed. "I can't take the smell of them anymore!"

"Yes, my lord," they replied, and immediately they turned to the task.

"You!" Amphileph said. "Bring my beloved Clogren to my study!"

"Yes, master!" he replied.

Amphileph walked to his temple and opened the door to his study with the wave of his hand. He entered and began rummaging through the glass jars on one of the shelves. The Camon carried Clogren in and attempted to set him in the chair, but *rigor mortis* had already set in, and when Amphileph heard the snapping sound of the Camon trying to bend Clogren's legs, he screamed at him.

"Leave me!" he shouted. The Camon turned to leave, but Amphileph cast him out of the doorway and slammed it shut behind him. "Such incompetence!" he said. "I need nothing more from you!"

He gathered several jars and set them on the table. "You, Clogren, are a different matter altogether. You alone have remained faithful." Amphileph opened the jars and arranged them in front of Clogren. "What's that?" he asked. "Yes, of course, my friend. I have much to discuss with you. Please, please, be seated." Amphileph rubbed herbs and oils into Clogren's body, and he soaked his joints until he was able to gently bend them and seat him at the table.

When he finished, Amphileph capped the jars, removed them back to the shelves, and sat down beside Clogren. "We will unravel the mystery of this Binding Spell together." Amphileph rummaged among the books scattered everywhere on the floor around them.

"I have made drawings of the exact shape of the spell's effective area, its height and depth, objects that failed to pass through its force field—any bit of information that might be of potential use."

"Yes, I have punished the Spellmakers that did this to you. Now they wish that they had sided with us rather than with Evliit!" he laughed. "They fully expected to foil everything that we had worked so hard to achieve. The Creator's holiness demanded more than the simpletons of the human race could provide, and I have moved to make things right."

Clogren's mouth hung open, as if in reply.

"You are right. Evliit lacks the discipline to remove these worthless sacks of meat from this world, and in his arrogance, he stands against me, his poison costing us everything, and now—now there is nothing left of the Spellmakers save that impossible Citanth! He will never serve me as you have," Amphileph cried out.

"We see what you are," said a voice.

"What?" Amphileph replied. Instead of Clogren, Ardidhus's battered body sat in Clogren's chair. "We see what you are," Ardidhus repeated, though the crumpled left side of his face lagged behind the right side.

Amphileph stood up and screamed aloud; his heart felt like it would burst. He instinctively cursed, and the energy of it blew the chair apart. Clogren's body scattered about the room while pieces of the chair's stuffing slowly drifted down around him, but Ardidhus had disappeared. He bent over and picked up Clogren's arm, looking around at the splattered mess.

"No!" he cried. "Clogren!" He dropped the arm, and tears welled in his eyes. "Ardidhus! Show yourself!" Amphileph screamed again. "I will . . . I will . . ." he stuttered. The volume of his voice quickly fell to nothing, but the thoughts screamed inside his head: *Ardidhus is dead! Ardidhus is dead!*

He tossed Clogren's arm to the ground with disgust as if he just realized what it was. *The Camonra watch me, looking for my weakness. They would not hesitate to usurp me in my weakness.* Amphileph looked toward the courtyard, expecting to see them crowded at the entrance with blades drawn, but there was no one there.

"Citanth!" Amphileph screamed, its high pitch revealing his terror. He waited for a moment, but no one answered. "Citanth!"

Amphileph stormed out of the library and walked toward the northern fields. He approached the stones marking the Binding's edge, and he yelled again, red faced and huffing, "Citanth!"

Amphileph noticed movement through the windows of the small mud hut at the Camon's post just north of the Binding. A Camon appeared and then groveled before him. "Find Citanth!" Amphileph cried.

The warrior scampered away from him toward the larger tents that were pitched some sixty or seventy paces north yet. A man exited the tents and looked toward Amphileph. It was Citanth.

He was almost seven hundred years old, but Citanth looked to be in his forties, with a sturdy, muscular physique. He tilted his head back with disdain, looking down his nose, his pursed lips causing his soul patch to protrude from his chin. With his left hand, he tossed his long black hair over the high shoulders of his brigandine. He had a bloodstained rag wrapped around his right hand. He was favoring it, holding it against his midsection.

Evliit had chosen Citanth among the last of those he called to be Watchers. Citanth had immediately migrated toward Amphileph, and he had been instrumental in convincing many other Watchers to take up the study of Spellmaking. When ties with Rion began to unravel over Amphileph's condemnation of mankind, he had fiercely defended Amphileph's methods, insisting spellmaking alone could advance man at the pace necessary to stem the tide of man's wickedness. When the Elders of Rion called upon Evliit to intercede in Amphileph's creation of the Camonra, Amphileph called upon Citanth to steal the Sword of the Watch. The attempt had been disastrous. "Ci-tanth!" Amphileph screamed at the top of his voice, at which point Citanth feigned attentiveness, stepping into a jog toward the Binding's edge.

He stopped just in front of Amphileph, but he did not look him in the eye. "What is it that you require?" Citanth asked.

"Move quickly when I call!" Amphileph said. "You have lain around for months, doing nothing!"

"You fail to remember what you have done to me," Citanth said. He held up his hand, a mass of twisted and charred flesh and bone. "Because of you, my powers are gone! The brothers told you that we could not take the Sword from Evliit! But you, in your *infinite wisdom,* you said your spells would protect me! Look at me! One touch of the Sword, and I am all but ruined."

"You are nothing!" Amphileph repeated. "You are but a little man, a little man whose bravery depends solely on this spell that separates us!"

"I, too, am a Spellmaker!" Citanth shouted. "I too was called by the Creator. You have long lost respect for that!"

Amphileph instinctively thrust his hands forward and the energy blast that erupted from them was so incredible that even Citanth jumped back. The energy spread through the Binding like ink poured into a basin, momentarily giving the Binding visible shape between them. But then it dissipated.

Citanth looked indignant. "You would kill me, too?" he asked. "The Creator has caged you up for your maleficence! You have brought this upon yourself!"

Amphileph screamed his defiance, and energy from his hand ripped open the ground between them right up to the Binding's edge. A blackness poured out of his body, spreading outward like paint rolling down a lamppost, withering the grass around him. He reached out his hands toward a nearby tree, and its leaves withered and died from some unseen force that ripped it from its roots. It rose above Amphileph's head with the movement of his arm, and he smashed the tree against the Binding until nothing but fragments remained. Amphileph's labored breathing brought him to his knees.

The dust cleared, and he could see Citanth on the opposite side of the Binding, but for the first time, Amphileph noticed Citanth was not cowering. In fact, he had barely changed the stance he had taken moments before the rampage began.

"Honestly, Amphileph, you waste your energies," Citanth said.

Amphileph stood up and brushed off his clothes. "Be aware, my brother, that sooner or later, I will find a way to break this binding spell. I will not have forgotten your insolence."

"When that day comes, my *dear lord* Amphileph, you will have much bigger issues than me to deal with," Citanth sneered, checking the dirt in his fingernails of his good hand. "While you have been studying your incarceration, I have been doing a little thinking of my own. Surely, you can see that this Binding is quite grandly made. Undoing it might have been possible with the help of our brethren, but your murderous rage has denied you their cooperation. What is *in there* will remain for now—it is what remains out *here*," Citanth said, pointing to the ground. "That's what we must focus on."

"What are you saying?" Amphileph asked.

"I'm merely pointing out that I am capable of executing your plans while you are . . . well, incapacitated."

Amphileph gritted his teeth. "What is it that you want, Citanth?"

"You will make me the commander of the legions that have not been ensnared by the Binding's power, and when I return with the man Galbard, you will restore my hand and my powers!" He let his demand hang between them for a heartbeat or two as if it too could spark along the invisible plane that kept them apart, never taking his eyes from Amphileph's. "Swear it!"

Amphileph clenched his teeth and fist. "It will be as you wish."

"You will swear it!" Citanth demanded.

He felt his left eye twitching. "I swear it!" Amphileph shouted.

Citanth could barely contain his giddiness. "I will gather the Camonra and return. You will tell them as much!"

Amphileph did not answer, straining his last shred of patience.

When Citanth returned with the leaders of the Camonra, they bowed down before Amphileph. "Tell them," said Citanth.

"Citanth now commands you!" Amphileph said. "Do as he wishes, or you will deal with me!"

The warriors bowed before Citanth, an act that clearly pleased their new commander. Citanth dismissed them and walked close to the edge of the Binding directly across from Amphileph.

"I will find the Sword, Amphileph," Citanth said. "The slave, Galbard, could not have traveled beyond the reach of our great warriors. He is on foot, with nothing more than the clothes on his back. If we find the man, we find the Sword. It will grant us the power to break the Binding Spell of Evliit."

Citanth removed his charred hand again from its wrappings, reached out to Amphileph, and placed it against the Binding. "And when I find him, how do you propose that I bring the Sword to you? I'll not touch it again."

Amphileph looked over the atrophied limb and back into Citanth's eyes.

"Capture this Galbard alive and bring him to me! He will give me the Sword!"

"And what of our war with Rion?"

"Tobor knows what I expect of him. Send him word that we have given chase to the Sword's thief."

Citanth placed his hand back in its wrapping, cleared his throat, and turned to the Camonra.

"Captains!" he shouted. "For my first act as High Commander of the Camonra, I will send the less seasoned warriors to Rion to make contact with Tobor. Make your best warriors ready for travel to the mountains to the north. We go to bring the Sword back to our master!"

Citanth turned back to Amphileph. "If you will excuse me, my lord," he said. He bowed, and then rose and marched away toward the northern camp.

"No excuse will likely come," Amphileph said under his breath.

* * *

Galbard struggled to dress the small caribou he had managed to corner and kill just east of where the Faceless Mountains' elevation died away and the Northern Plains opened up to the northern frontier. The blood dripping down his left cheek from a small cut on the side of his head was purely an annoyance, but the caribou's glancing blow had hit more squarely on his left shoulder before he had driven his mighty blade into the deer's charging heart. The larger part of the impact area was turning a purplish blue, leaving his left hand and arm a little numb. It was difficult to pull the meat back from the ribs, but his short blade made fairly quick work of the animal's hide. He would waste only what he could not dry and store in his pack, and already, several cuts of meat sat squarely over the smoky fire he had built for that purpose.

Galbard kept a constant watch around the horizon. The long, clear view in each direction was the only reason he risked the heavy smoke of the campfire at all. It didn't hurt that he'd done without much protein since leaving the caves and smoked meat was one of his favorite meals, either. Just smelling the slow-cooking meat in the wisps of smoke made Galbard's stomach feel like it was going to burn a hole through his navel.

He was concerned about the top of the Faceless Mountains being lost in the clouds that were moving in from the west, and having the dried meat for the journey northwest around them was an absolute necessity. Though the rough terrain did provide some wild grains, roots, and the occasional chance at small game, this meat would sustain him for what could be a long journey toward solitude with the Sword. He cut off a thin slice of the meat from the spit with his knife, and then put away the blade to free his hands, swapping the meat between his fingers and then his hands; it was almost too hot to touch. When the meat was just cool enough to eat, he tore off a piece of it with his teeth, savoring the flavor.

Drawing the sword from its scabbard, he marveled again at its perfect edge and balance. He rolled his wrist over, and watched how the Sword's blade caught the sunlight. Galbard's mind wandered around the memory of Evliit's entrusting him with it, and then the sun's reflection flashed across his eyes and broke the trance.

If only he could move farther north, he thought he could make himself disappear with the Sword until Evliit returned for it. To the northwest, a vast tree line looked like just the place in which to disappear. He was sure that the Camonra's confusion over their Rion strategy would soon be resolved, and they would quickly turn their attentions to him. When that time came, he wanted to be as far away as possible. If there was only more time to master the mysterious power of the Sword—or at least some small part of its power—then if it came down to it, he could stand against them.

The Sword's power was a very difficult thing to put his finger on, but he had begun a morning ritual of drawing it and clearing his mind, channeling its energy through his body. It was then he could feel the warmth in the Sword's tang slowly creeping down his arms. He tried to remain focused. "I do your will," he said aloud. "I command this power!"

Suddenly, it was if everything around him began to slow down and a sense of calm poured over him. The heat in the tang of the sword surged to an almost painful level, but he held on tight. The intensity grew until his chest was burning.

He carefully allowed his mind to think of the tree just in front of him. The intensity dropped with the slightest change in his focus, but he felt a distinct difference between this attempt to control the Sword and the previous attempts. He stepped forward and swung laterally across the width of the mighty tree and the resultant burst of wood fragments startled him.

A small piece struck his face next to his right eye. His flinch made him look away, and before he could open his eyes, he heard the moaning sound of the great oak tree, followed by the snapping sound of wood under strain. He opened his eyes to see that most of the tree's circumference was missing on the side nearest to him and the tree was slowly falling toward him. He looked up its length and fell on his back, pushing his hand from his body reflexively as if to deflect its fall. The massive tree's deadly path toward him suddenly slowed and reversed, falling away to the side with an awful crash.

Galbard felt the hairs on his arm stand up. The unseen energy coursed from the pit of his stomach to the palm of his hand at the moment the tree stopped its fall. The energy seemed to move up and out of him, pushing the tree to the side. Galbard thought it almost felt like a physical element—like water—was moving inside him, and then it passed through his hands. The energy left him, and then new energy from the Sword seemed to flow into his body to replace it.

Days passed, and Galbard's proficiency with this newfound power improved dramatically. The experience with the tree had been a watershed point to his realizing greater control over the energy's telekinetic use. He had moved through the valley and toward the stand of trees northwest, but each time he stopped, he had worked to learn more about controlling the energy. He found that it was becoming easier and easier to gather the energy inside himself and push it away from him with some degree of directional control.

Now, he could actually see the wave of energy moving through the waist-high grass around him. He concentrated for a moment, filling the building momentum of the energy within him. He held it back until his skin was crawling on his frame, and then he threw his arms outward and released it. The clouds overhead moved apart, and the energy spread outward from his body, pressing the grass down around him for thirty paces with such force that it did not stand back up.

* * *

Amphileph cried out, "Citanth! Did you feel it?"

Citanth stopped his discussions with the Camonra and slowly closed his eyes. "Yes!" he yelled, springing to action. "The fool thinks he can control the power of Evliit's Sword!" he yelled to Amphileph.

"Find him! Find him now!" Amphileph screamed and then stormed into his temple.

There was a flurry of action in the camp. The commander rallied the Camonra to make ready to ride. Their scaly beasts of burden, the giant Azrodh lizards, eyed their riders with a kind of contempt. Tamed just enough to allow the Camon soldiers to climb upon their backs, their small brains were trained into submission by the fierce discipline of their riders. The Camon captains mounted the Azrodh and shouted orders to their foot soldiers, and the lot of them made for the north in double time.

Several of the human slaves carried Citanth behind the main column of soldiers in what would have been Amphileph's victory carriage for his triumphant return to Rion. The commander parted the silk curtain of the carriage and called to his head slave. "Aldor, inform the captain that I will be indisposed until we reach the valley. I will expect a report of progress in the morning."

"Yes, my lord," the slave responded without making eye contact. "At once!"

As the slaves lifted the carriage, held it on their shoulders, and moved forward in lock step to ensure their rider's comfort, Citanth glanced back at Amphileph's temple, and then he pulled the silken curtains closed and slept to the gentle rhythmic rocking of the carriage.

* * *

Galbard had reached the Calarphian Wood by early fall when the trees were at their most majestic. He stood at the edge of the great wood and looked back to the snowy peaks of the Faceless Mountains.

As he looked down the ridge to the west, he heard something behind him, and Galbard instantly drew the Sword. He pressed his back against a tree and looked around it into the forest.

There before him stood an elderly man, doing the best he could to stand with the aid of his staff. His long white hair and beard tossed in the wind, but his eyes remained focused on Galbard. His sleeves billowed under his animal-skin vest, and Galbard could see that he wore a number of necklaces, some with talismans of the earth and animals, and one with some type of pouch embroidered with a symbol of a tree. He wore a wide leather belt around his ankle-length tunic, and other tiny pouches and an ornate horn of an ox danced from loops around its circumference when he moved.

"They are alerted to your presence," the old man managed.

"What?" Galbard responded.

"Your efforts to control the Sword's power alert them to your presence," the old man explained. "They're coming for you." He supported himself on his staff and closed the distance between them.

"Who are you?" Galbard asked. "Have you been watching me?"

"My name is Mategaladh. You've nothing to fear from me, I assure you."

Galbard studied him for a moment more. The old man attempted to move toward him, but he stumbled and nearly fell. "You appear to be injured," Galbard said.

Mategaladh tried to laugh. "Don't mind yourself with my ailments. It's you that is in great peril."

Galbard moved closer. "Why do you say that?"

"You've channeled the Sword's energy," Mategaladh said. "And movement of that kind of energy ripples through our world like a wind."

"Only a Watcher could know these things," Galbard said. "Or a Spellmaker," he said, placing his hand on his weapon.

"Would a follower of Amphileph give the bearer of the Sword the courtesy of an introduction?" he asked. "When Evliit gave you the Sword, fully ten Watchers stood against the Spellmakers' evil and forced our greater will upon them. This taxed some beyond their strength; their very spiritual energy was used up, and they were carried into the Third Domain before my very eyes."

"Let them come for it now, and I will show them its awesome power."

Mategaladh shook his head. "My friend, you play as if you had a toy! You bring the enemy to you like you were shouting in the town square!" Mategaladh grimaced and slumped over.

Galbard looked around, bending over to glance out between the trees to the Calarphian Plains north of the Faceless Mountains. He could not see anyone approaching from the south, but his heart rate was steadily increasing. He thought of his practicing to control the Sword. "How long?" he asked. "How long until they find me?"

Galbard looked at Mategaladh's face. He needed answers, but the old man was pale and motionless. Galbard drew the Sword of the Watch before him in both his hands, closed his eyes, and concentrated on reviving him. When he opened his eyes, his hands were glowing brightly. He placed one of them on Mategaladh.

"Be well!" he shouted, and the glowing light moved into Mategaladh's chest. The old man gasped and his eyes shot open.

"Ah!" he cried. Galbard moved his hand to support Mategaladh in reclining to the nearest tree trunk.

"Careful," Galbard said. "You must rest. If what you say is true, my use of the Sword has likely given away our position."

Mategaladh caught his breath. "We must not tarry." He struggled to take his feet again, but could not. "Give me but a moment, and then I will be well enough to ride. We can likely intercept them in the valley east of here. I—"

"You are in no shape to leave this forest, nor certainly could you stand against the Camonra, much less the Spellmakers!"

"Evliit was sure that Citanth was the only one who was not with Amphileph when the Binding spell was created, but it is no matter. He has touched the Sword with evil in his heart. That alone will have drained what power he had. It's a wonder that he lives at all! I can stand with you! Others have remained here by the sheer strength of their will. We will come to your aid!"

Galbard shook his head. "This thing—this Binding—has sapped you. Recover your strength, for we men may need the strength of the Watchers to win the day. You must be healed and whole! I will hide the Sword as Evliit commanded, and you must gather your strength and your brethren to fight another day."

"Galbard," Mategaladh began his retort, but stopped. He reached for his staff and leaned back against the tree. "You must hurry. Go down this path," he pointed to their left. "There is a rare Ampura tree with very dark wood and roots that are exposed along a spring. Use your dagger and cut those roots that are no bigger than your finger. Keep them, Galbard. They can sustain you when your other food will not. There is also small blue fruit in that tree. This fruit grows in bunches like grapes, but looks more like a large strawberry. Pick all you can carry. Their sweetness belies their ferocity for healing. You can eat them for any ailment, and their paste can heal a nasty wound."

Galbard did as Mategaladh instructed, but the best of them he brought back to Mategaladh.

"If they're healing is as you say, then you can use some of your own medicine," Galbard jested.

"There is truth in that," Mategaladh said, forcing a smile.

Galbard talked with him until he had eaten three of the Ampura tree's fruits, and indeed Mategaladh's color and manner did seem much better.

"You do not need to sit with me, my friend. It will take some time for the herb to do its work, and you have little of that. Go now," Mategaladh said. "A day's ride west, up the slow grade, there you will find a plateau, and the mountains will grow high indeed. There you will find a boulder with a bright red bird upon it—I will see to it. When you see that bird, Galbard, go due south. It is the only passage through those sheer peaks. Go south and flee Calarph. Past this mountain range is another, but it is the lesser of the two to cross. Further still is a valley, and beyond that is Southwood. There was a woman there, and if things are as I pray they will be, she will aid you further. For now though, you must make what distance you can between yourself and the Camonra."

"I am sorry if I have brought them upon you," Galbard said.

"They will not trouble me," Mategaladh said. "The forest will protect me. But you—you must go now, and ride like the wind!"

Galbard couldn't help but flash a confused look: *Ride?*

Mategaladh gathered his strength and whistled. "I have a new Calarphian stallion who can take you to flight!" Mategaladh pointed down another path that led deeper into the wood.

Galbard thought he saw several horses in the mist, and then there was a loud neighing. A strong, young stallion, bridled and saddled, burst through the mist into a small clearing down that path.

"Take this path, Galbard. Take it and this good Calarphian horse. Take them and good care, but hurry now, hurry!"

"My thanks to you, good prophet, may the Creator smile upon you. May you see Rion in this lifetime and the Third Domain in the next."

Galbard climbed upon the stallion and turned him with ease. He was a young horse, but very well trained. "I have heard tales of Calarphian horses in my youth—oh, that they live up to their stories!" Galbard exclaimed.

"His name is Pladus, he will carry you well," Mategaladh said. "You will also find some interesting items in his saddle bags. Use them wisely." Mategaladh waved Galbard away, and Galbard raised a hand in return, and then he turned Pladus back down the path and into the mist, parting it with a *swoosh*. Galbard practically lay across the horse's neck, wide-eyed, watching for branches. They sped north and then west with abandon.

Chapter Ten

Missing Scouts

One of General Tobor's wives interrupted his reading.

"My lord, a runner to see you," she said bowing.

"Send them in," Tobor replied and returned to his reading. The runner entered the room, still winded, as Tobor would have expected. That at least was a good sign.

"My liege," the runner began, waiting for Tobor's acknowledgement.

"What news have you?" Tobor responded.

"My liege, my master Citanth wishes you to know that Lord Amphileph is unavailable to command you, and even now has made *my* master the High Commander of the Camonra—"

Tobor set his reading aside at the mention of Citanth as his *master*. He interrupted. "Your 'master, Citanth?'" Tobor inquired. "You would never utter such words in the presence of Lord Amphileph, young runner. What madness occurs in the Temple of Amphileph?"

The runner was silent for a moment.

"May I speak freely, my liege?"

"Answer," responded Tobor.

"Th . . . things are not right, my lord," the runner said. "Lord Amphileph and many of the Camonra have been . . . captured . . . in some kind of wizardry."

Tobor moved to the edge of his chair. "Go on."

"Lord Amphileph was beside himself. He has killed the other fathers, *his* very own brothers!" The runner looked at the ground in dismay.

"He has killed our makers?"

"All but Citanth, for he was in the northern camp when the wizardry came upon the others, and he was not caught up in it."

No! Not the fathers! Tobor thought. He could barely hold back his anger. He had long thought Amphileph was becoming unstable, like a fire fed too much wood so that no one could stand near it, and now the news of his murdering the other fathers!

"Lord Amphileph will escape this spell," Tobor said.

"Begging your pardon, my liege, but I *must* tell you—Lord Amphileph has been trying since the moon of Denf was full in the west. He has not broken the spell, and he has killed hundreds of our kind in his rage."

Tobor stood up. It was more than he could stand. "That will be all, runner. Stay here in our camp. I will consult with my captain, and we may have further need of you."

"Yes, my liege," the runner said, and then he bowed and exited.

Tobor's thoughts were whizzing in his head. These feelings he had been feeling, his mixed emotions in his worship of Lord Amphileph—these things ran around in his head like two dogs fighting in a pit. It all suddenly came to make sense, and it riveted him—the simple truth of it was that Amphileph, powerful as he was, was less powerful than *something*. If he could be caged like the pit dogs, then the simple logic of a warrior such as Tobor said that Amphileph could not be lord of all.

Now something more raged in the pit of his stomach. Tobor had killed for Amphileph without reservation all his life, and now *this?* He felt a sickness in the pit of his stomach.

A second wave came over him then, one of anger. Tobor had been fool enough to worship him like a god. This stuck in his craw like the bone of some small animal. Amphileph's deceit would require blood payment, for you can do many things to the Camonra—starve them, beat them—but they would not be made into fools. Tobor snorted as if to get the smell of it from his nostrils.

If Amphileph was but a created thing, then he had a vulnerability to exploit. It might take one hundred of his brothers, it might take one thousand, but the Camonra could swarm him, even possibly destroy him. The level of arrogance he had to think himself a god—this would be his downfall, Tobor was sure of it. Such an arrogant man would do well to die quickly, but to be ignored, to be made insignificant, Tobor could think of no greater insult. He threw back the tent sash and walked to the assembly of captains waiting outside.

"News, captains!" Tobor shouted. "Amphileph no longer commands these armies! I alone lead us now! The Watchers war amongst themselves;

they have bound Amphileph up in the east, like a caged dog. Citanth and he are the only survivors! Citanth thinks himself our master, which can only mean that Amphileph is powerless to escape his cage." Tobor looked at his captains. "Have the runner return to the northern camp. Bring our women! We make our camp here!"

Tobor spread the Camonra camp across the north-south trail they had taken from Amphileph's temple to the outskirts of Rion, but after Tobor had personally ridden to the edge of the fault and seen the seawater surging up from the lava below in violent spasms, they had migrated a bit more to the northwest. The cooler ocean air drove north across the fault line, and the steamy mixture created what was an almost constant rainfall. It mixed to create rivers and lakes of water that the vegetation of the Rionese fields could not abide, and everywhere north of the gates of Rion, the high grass and trees died away, replaced by marsh grasses and leafless, twisted tree trunks braved by only the occasional waterfowl.

With the fault keeping his Rionese enemies at bay to the south, and reports from his scouts that the Rionese refugees remained hidden in the trees to the west, the wide-open spaces of the northern plains presented Tobor with a unique opportunity for peace. Two weeks after sending him, the runner returned to Tobor with a great host of young Camonra, their females, and their children. Though witnesses confirmed that Amphileph was unable to escape the area surrounding his temple, the Camonra had still fled the northern camps during the night in fear of him.

It was the first time that the Camonra had reunited with their families without the fear of Amphileph's heavy hand upon them, and the celebrations of this brought a happiness to Tobor that he had never known. The females cooked, the males wrestled with each other for sport, and their offspring ran around in the common square between the mud huts and larger timber structures without fear of Amphileph's wrath—it was life altering.

Their camp had grown into a large clump of structures almost overnight, and the only thing that gave Tobor pause was the possibility of Citanth's return, though he was convinced that he could turn the Camonra against him with little effort. He had no real fear of the humans, though a run-in with them was becoming ever more likely as they expanded their hunting and gathering. He wanted war no more, so he constantly kept a flow of scouts searching their camp's ever-growing perimeter, diligently overseeing that the delicate peace of isolation remained.

And so it did, through the rest of that summer and through the time when leaves began to change their colors. The cooler air came down from the north, and the Camonra prepared for their first winter. The sunlight was slowly fading in the west, and Tobor walked through their camp, looking at the warm firelight that was just beginning to pour from the crude windows of their humble homes.

He saw Idhoran at the northern end of the camp and stopped to talk with him as he often did when the scouts checked in for the day, but this night Idhoran looked unusually tense.

"What bothers you, old friend?" Tobor asked.

"The headcount of scouts reporting in was short," Idhoran answered.

"The scouts from the plains east of the forest?" Tobor inquired.

"Yes, my lord," he said. "I'll look into it at once!"

"Very well," said Tobor.

Idhoran bowed to him and entered the small barracks used by the scouts.

Tobor knew that the humans had sought sanctuary in the distant forest to their west. It was tall and dense, and that kind of forest could provide them both height and stealth, eliminating most of the advantage of his warrior's size and strength. It was only a matter of time before they had fortified their position and concentrated their numbers there.

Idhoran raced back and took one knee.

"What say you?" Tobor inquired.

"Three of our scouts from the west have not returned!"

"Is that so?" Tobor responded. "Much is reported by their absence. Ready a hundred of our best. We march on the high wood."

News of Tobor's orders spread like wildfire. The Camonra seemed extremely emboldened by their newfound freedoms, and they stirred rambunctiously for war. Tobor rode out before them to meet with his captains.

"The Camonra are excited to find the enemy, General," one said. "What are your orders?"

"We'll march through the night so that we may look upon the forest with the light at our back," Tobor began. "If they've killed our scouts, then we'll take blood from them as payment, something that will have them know we'll not have humans dictating where we go or what we do."

"Are we not to kill them all?" another captain asked.

"No," Tobor responded. "What threat do these humans make for the Camonra?" He noticed their disciplined faces giving a hint of confusion with the order. "Are not the Camonra superior in every way to these humans? We need no war with them."

A general grunt of acknowledgement quickly came in answer.

"Ready the march!" Tobor instructed them, and they each returned to their mounts and rode back to their respective charges. Having only a hundred or so soldiers in their company meant the Camonra carried along little of the pageantry exhibited during the preparation for the attack on Rion. There were no banners, war drums, or catapults. This company would move quickly and silently upon the men of Highwood.

They crossed the distance under cover of darkness, careful to use the rolling hills to hide from the watchful eyes of the Rion Guard. In the fields across from Highwood, they found blood in the high grass. The sword of one of their brethren lie close by. No Camon would have ever given up his sword.

"Then they have killed our brothers," Tobor said. "Let us bring swift and terrible vengeance upon them!"

They hid in the high grass through the night, until Tobor could just see the faint glow of dawn over the horizon behind them. He ordered the Camonra to stop. Dawn's light pierced the trees at nearly a right angle, and he could see that the men of Rion had placed archers in the highest limbs, and that height advantage was problematic.

The last hundred yards or so to the tree line was fairly flat, so Tobor knew they would have to cross that distance at a dead run. It was hard to tell just how many archers filled the trees closest to their position, but if he could only draw the humans out of their hiding places, the Camonra strength could easily overwhelm them, but before they could charge in among them, Tobor saw a group of riders broaching the cover of the trees.

"Ready!" Tobor said in a hushed yell. The captains relayed the order and moved to their mounts; the foot soldiers readied behind them. Tobor spurred the Azrodh's ribcage. It hissed in acknowledgement, and then they raced out from the long shadows in which they hid.

It seemed that the instant Tobor's large frame appeared in the morning light, a horn blew a long tone that echoed through the hillside.

Tobor rode toward the riders. "Now! Follow me!" he bellowed. The Camonra battle cry boiled out from the foot soldiers, and they fell behind the captains in double time.

The Rionese cavalry shuffled in disbelief. "Inferiors!" they cried. Their riders formed two rough lines, the first of which lowered their long pikes alongside the polished armor that protected their horses' faces and chests.

The Camonra weaponry varied greatly, some with clubs and axes, and some with nothing more than their bare hands. Arrows whistled by them much more quickly than Tobor had hoped, one striking his mount in the shoulder, another striking it in the lower left leg. A third, he deflected with his shield, skipping it over his head but striking one of the foot soldiers behind him in the eye. The soldier's body folded in on itself. The other foot soldiers parted around him or leapt over him. The Camonra battle cry was deafening, and the Rionese horses appeared as if they would bolt at any moment.

Charge!" the order rang out from down their lines, and bolt they did, directly into the charging Camonra.

Tobor's heart pounded in his chest with the thrill of war. His great reptilian mount flew into their midst, its head passing just to the left of one rider's pike and directly into the path of another. They crashed together in a thunderous clap of armor and the crack of splintering wood. Tobor's mount slowed but a little, and the Rionese rider slammed into his shield and bounced away. His horse stumbled backward and fell on its side, its stiff legs pointing skyward. The second rider that Tobor had narrowly missed tried to pull up his pike, but it rammed into the ground with great force and pushed him backward off his horse. His helmet flew from his head with the concussion of his fall and bounced off the shoulder of one of Tobor's captains who was coming just behind him.

Suddenly four arrows hit the bugler in the neck and chest, and the Camonra battle horn ceased. He fell from his mount, and his limp body skipped into the legs of the oncoming horses. Two horses toppled forward to the ground, and their riders plowed face forward, eating their share of grass. Tobor jumped down from his mount and slashed at two other horses, crippling one with a hobbling cut and cutting across the upper leg of the others' rider and across its ribcage. The Rionese rider screamed out. A spray of blood from his leg temporarily blinded Tobor in the right eye. The horse spun away from Tobor in pain, and Tobor ducked beneath his rider's clumsy thrust.

Tobor raised his hand to wipe the rider's blood from his face, and he felt a tugging sensation below his ribs. Another of the rider's pikes pierced his side. The tip barely protruded through his thick skin, and Tobor spun away from it before the serrated edge tore him open, his own sweeping blade catching his attacker in the chest. His foot soldiers flew upon the riders then, and one of his captains called for Tobor to fall back.

"Kill them!" Tobor cried in return and another arrow struck the chain mail on his chest. He skillfully moved to keep the riders' horses between him and the archers. Arrows rained down around them, and his foot soldiers sprang upon the remaining riders.

"My liege, they prepare another attack!" his captain yelled again, this time pointing toward the wood. Other humans were moving to mount their horses.

He surveyed the tremendous price they had inflicted on the humans. "Back my brothers!" he said. "Back!"

Tobor grabbed his Azrodh by the saddle horn and struck its rump with the flat of his blade, turning the creature toward the south. He held on tightly, and it sprang to a gallop with the sting of Tobor's prompting, lifting Tobor off his feet. Arrows struck its side twice, and it slowed, but Tobor used these lulls to throw one leg over its girth, breaking the arrow shafts off with his shin. He mercilessly spurred it onward, turning southeast toward their camp, the foot soldiers and riders rushing in behind him. They flew back across the marshy plains eastward and moved beyond the range of the archers.

Evening fell before they were welcomed back at the encampment. The females had a large fire burning. The wounded dismounted with their help, and the others rested at the fires, waiting for the females to bring them food and drink.

Tobor surveyed his wounded troops and took count of the lost mounts. His guerilla tactics had been only moderately successful, killing around twenty of the Rionese. He had lost four of his own soldiers, and though it was a good five to one, he was dissatisfied with the outcome.

One of the females stitched his side, and he thought about how to give the humans more than the little sting they had felt this day at their next meeting.

Chapter Eleven

Irreconcilable Differences

Mordher had seen every battle of the Watchers' War from the frontlines, and the battle for Rion had been no different. His father, Mordhonar, had been in the Rion Guard before him, and when his son was seven years of age, he had sent him to be trained in the family business—the art of war—under the tutelage of the Elders of the Guard. Twenty-one years later, Mordher was battle-hardened like steel to the flame and quench, but the Battle for Rion had tested the Guard's training unlike any battle before it.

Mordher sat down upon what had been the cornerstone of the Temple of Evliit and pulled his old, scarred helmet from his head, letting his hair fall around his muscular shoulders. He dropped the helmet and stared at its red plume, singed almost completely away. He loosened the strap holding his shoulder armor, removed the pin holding his draping, red cloak, and lifted the molded iron chestplate over his head, flipping it over before him. He ran his fingers over the gashes in the dark brown paint and the golden symbol of Rion, and then he tossed it on the ground before him. He leaned over, his practiced fingers making short work of the straps on his greaves, and freed his shins from their armor. Then he just sat there in his skirt and tunic, looking at his sandals, feeling the breeze blowing across his sweat-saturated body.

Mordher looked over the rubble of the small homes that once surrounded the great temple, and his hard expression softened. Before he could even come to grips with his feelings, a single tear fell spontaneously, a feeling strangely unfamiliar to a warrior of his mettle. He lowered his head for a moment and ran his callused palm down his face to scrape the tear away, and when he closed his eyes, the images of the battle returned to him.

He had been on the frontlines once again, and the massive eruption of land beneath the Rion Guard and the Camonra had shot them all in every direction. The stampede of warriors fleeing the bedlam had crushed many a comrade; the underworld that opened up burned others alive. The eruption had thrown Mordher high into the air, backward toward Rion, where several of his fellow soldiers had broken his fall. They had recovered their senses only to feel the intense heat pouring out of Erathe itself and singeing their hair. He remembered the smell of it. They had run for their very lives to escape it, and the memory of the screams and chaos snapped him back to the present with a jolt.

He lifted his head to watch what remained of the Guard as they returned from the northern front. They were distant and speechless for the most part, shuffling in no particular groups or order through the city streets. One of the Elders stood in the main square in his full regalia, his purple robes dingy and torn. He was attempting to corral the soldiers back toward the main temple to prevent the inevitable looting and pillaging that comes when desperate men roam the streets, but his voice had little impact on them, and he seemed oblivious to a small child that clung to his robes with one hand, crying at the top of his lungs.

Mordher looked around the horizon, his head pounding. The destruction of Rion's temples was nearly total. The massive temple at the southeastern wall, the heart of the Rion Guard, was one of the few exceptions. *How had the Creator allowed such destruction?* The very ground beneath their feet had consumed nearly two-thirds of the armies of Rion *and* Amphileph.

It was like some kind of cruel joke. The Guard had dedicated their very lives to the defense of the Creator's teachings. What unbalanced fate to die in equal or greater numbers to the very ones who declared their contempt for the Creator's holy army? The Guard had proven beyond the shadow of any doubt that they were willing to die for their cause, but the Creator had chosen to destroy their great city, to take his brothers into the abyss of lava and flames—these things were impossible for Mordher to fathom.

When he could stand to look at it no more, he rose and walked toward the small adobe home he had built for his family in an alleyway off the main thoroughfare. People everywhere were digging through the remnants of their homes, and Mordher found himself picking up his pace with the realization of the true depth of the destruction in the city. In short order, he was running down the alleyway toward his own dwelling, pushing aside rubble and debris, jumping over and around bodies and mourners. He cried out for his wife and daughter. A sinking feeling in the pit of his stomach began to grow telling him something terrible had happened to them.

He found their bodies trampled in the streets just outside their home, and the sight of their dirty, broken, and bloody faces dropped him to his knees. Memories of them flooded his every thought, flashes of events that had formed all his happiness in this world.

Something inside him snapped. *He would have protected them if he had been there.* A high-pitched noise burned his ears, numbing his body with its droning whine. It seemed he was outside his body. It seemed that none of this was happening. It wasn't real. He looked down again through his brimming eyes at their gray faces, hoping against hope that he would not see them, but they were still there, motionless save for the hot breeze that gently stirred their hair.

He drew his sword instinctively; his body flexed tightly, veins bulging in his face, neck, and arms. A scream flowed from deep within him, a scream that terrified the remaining townspeople even through their shock. Several stopped in their places to look at him, his body slowly relaxing, and his sword falling from his hand. He made no effort to pick it up, but reached instead for a shovel that lay next to a fresh grave and walked toward their bodies with new purpose.

When he had buried them near their home, he returned to the place where his sword had fallen and picked it up, squeezing the tang with his mighty hand. He pushed the sword into its scabbard and lowered his head slightly. He fixed his eyes upon the temple of the Elders in the southeast part of the city, and he moved then with another purpose: to kill the ones that had sent him away from his family. Nothing else mattered anymore. There were no gods, no devils, no afterlife, and no theology. There was only the cold vengeance that flowed through his veins and calloused his heart.

He made his way down the city streets toward the temple. The destruction was gradually less apparent, but everywhere there was crying and shouting, people trying to pull personal belongings from their leveled homes, many of them creating little piles of dishes or clothing that they might still salvage. They passed through his peripheral vision without a second glance.

When at last he reached the steps of the great temple, his foot fell upon the first step, and he stopped suddenly. "Elders!" he shouted. "Elders of the Guard!"

Several of the young warriors made their way to the temple entrance, looking down upon him with fear and respect. Others slowly formed a wide circle around him at the foot of the temple.

"Elders of the Guard!" he screamed again. A lone, robed figure stepped from between two of the young warriors.

"Great warrior, Guardian of Rion, what brings you to the temple in anger?" the acolyte asked.

"I seek answers from the Elders!" Mordher yelled.

"The Elders are seeking the face of the Creator in prayer, brother. May I be of assistance?"

Mordher drew his sword and there was a ripple of movement in the encircling warriors, and they ever-so-slightly tightened their ranks around him.

"*You* cannot," Mordher responded. "Tell the Elders that I will speak to them now!"

The young acolyte shrugged his shoulders, and his tone changed. "You do not command the Elders, great warrior."

Mordher flew into a rage and bounded up the stairs toward the acolyte.

"Stop him!" the acolyte commanded the others. He slowly moved backward to stand behind the closing line of warriors.

Mordher's sword rang off two or three of theirs, and then a dozen of his brethren tackled him to the ground. In his struggle, another dozen still fell upon him, and they pried the sword from his hands. Even with three of them holding his arm, he managed to break free and strike the nearest one in the side of the head, instantly robbing him of consciousness. Before he could manage to break free, one of them stood over him on the steps and repeatedly struck him in the face with the pommel of a sword, bouncing his head off the stone steps with each blow. They slowed his struggles very little with the first two or three blows, but the pommel must have begun to cut him on the third or fourth blow, for he could feel the warm flow of blood down his face and neck. His left eye swelled shut. Mordher could still see his clutched fists outstretched before him with his other eye, but the sound of his attackers seemed to be moving further and further into the distance, and then everything went black.

Mordher awoke in a small, low-ceilinged cell that was little more than a cage under the rear of the temple, a place where the Rion Guard once kenneled their war dogs. The old bars were rusty red, partitioning ten or so cages that faced the ocean, exposed to the elements. The wind off the ocean gave him a regular diet of dust, but he was soon regaining the strength that his attackers had beaten out of him.

"You're the one that threatened the Elders, eh?" a voice chuckled from somewhere around him.

Mordher attempted to stand up, but he hit his head on the marble ceiling. He buckled over to his hands.

The chuckle increased. "Too big for that, warrior—sit or squat's about your only options," the voice said. Mordher's eyes were squinted from the bump on the head, but one eye managed its way open to scan the cages around him. Two cages over was another warrior of the guard, dirty and thin, his forehead resting on the bars with a hand on either side. He was smiling broadly.

"Who are you?" Mordher asked.

"Ardhios, at your service my friend," he replied. "It is good to meet someone else who is brave enough—or foolish enough, one might say—to threaten the Elders."

"My motivation will not change the cut I make," Mordher said. "They can ponder such things while they bleed."

"Still hostile, I see," Ardhios said. "Good. You'll need that."

Mordher opened the other eye to get a better look around.

"Yes, they've nine of us caged like dogs. A fitting end for dedicated servants of Rion, wouldn't you say?" There was laughter from the other cages, and Mordher saw them spread out across the breadth of their cages to get a look at him.

"You are Mordher," another said. "We know of your great deeds battling the Inferiors."

"Mordher?" asked another. "Mordher of the Guard?"

Mordher sat down and set his back against the rusty bars. "I fight no more for the Guard," he responded.

"Neither shall my friends and I," Ardhios chuckled. "Our crime is sedition, same as yours. They mean to put us all on the tree."

"I don't want to hear that," said the man in the cage to Mordher's right. "They'll not nail me up! They will have to kill me first."

"They will bring one more than is required to put you on the tree, Borian!" another laughed from down the line.

Mordher had heard enough. He crawled toward the cell door and pushed against the lock.

"Save your strength, Mordher," Ardhios said. "They may not feed you for days, and we've all tried the locks."

Mordher's face was quickly turning red. He worked his hands across the bars until something caught his eye, and then he rolled to his side and grasped the bars closest to Ardhios. With one kick, he snapped a rusted bar in the front of the cage and then rolled to his knees. He held the bar next to it with one hand for leverage and bent the broken bar up and outward with the other hand. The lower portion of the bar was a sharp break and too short to bend away from the cross member that strengthened it, but Mordher put his back against the cage and pushed with all his strength, bending the upper portion of the bar up and out.

"Impressive!" Ardhios said. "You'd better be about getting out of there now. The Guard won't be too thrilled with your attempting to escape."

Mordher ignored him and sat on his knees, grabbing the two bars to either side of the broken one and shaking them furiously. For nearly five minutes, Mordher pushed and pulled with no effect, when suddenly a tiny bit of stone fell upon his forearm from where the ceiling anchored one of the bars. Mordher smiled, and then he began pulling back and forth with even greater energy on the bar that had signaled the slightest weakness. A crack began to form in the stone, and granules of dust fell in Mordher's face. There was suddenly some movement in the bar, and Mordher placed both hands on it, straining with all his might. The marble capstone broke free and the bar jumped outward. Mordher pushed it down beside the other bar and turned sideways. He attempted to squeeze his oversized torso through the tight opening.

"Well," Ardhios exclaimed. The other captives began a quiet encouragement of Mordher's efforts. Mordher pushed against the bars, and his ribcage hung on the sharp metal of the lower broken bar, sticking him repeatedly.

"You've got a nasty cut there," Ardhios commented. He sat back against his own cage's bars to watch the spectacle of the large man struggling to escape. Mordher simply grunted each time the jagged bar stuck his chest, and blood now freely dripped down side, his pants, and leg. With one last effort, Mordher squeezed through, cutting his upper thigh on the same stubborn bar. He stood up, looked each way for the guard, and then turned to run.

"Mordher!" Ardhios shouted. "Take us with you."

Mordher neared the cage. "What advantage are you to me?" he asked.

"I have means of escape," Ardhios said. "You won't get far without such knowledge and the Guard won't make such a mistake twice that you'll ever escape again."

"I'll take my chances," Mordher replied.

"I have a boat," Ardhios gambled. "Let me and my brothers go with you, and we will leave this place together."

Mordher considered his offer. He had seen what had become of the land north of Rion. There was no escaping that way. He had lived in Rion his entire life, and he knew the docks afforded the only way out of the city.

"I will find my own boat," he replied, and he turned toward the southern cliffs.

"The stairs are gone, Mordher," Ardhios said, and Mordher stopped.

"What did you say?"

"The cliff stairs were destroyed by the quakes," Ardhios elaborated. "But I know another way. Take us with you, and we will sail away from this place."

Mordher looked a little perplexed, and then he came close to Ardhios's cell and leaned in. "Lie to me, and I will wring your neck like I did those bars—except with less effort." Mordher grabbed the bar that was bent outward and pushed it back and forth, snapping it off in his hand.

"I have no problem believing that," Ardhios replied. "Behind you!" he said, and he pointed to a guard rounding the temple base. For a moment, the guard seemed not to notice something wrong with Mordher being outside his cage, but then his eyes widened, and he drew his sword. He turned his head slightly in preparation to shout his discovery to his comrades, but he exhausted only a deep sigh instead. Mordher had thrown the piece of bar hard enough to pierce his chest.

"Quick! The keys!" Ardhios yelled, but Mordher had already pounced upon the dying soldier, taking his shield and sword and extracting the keys from his belt. He struggled helplessly, and Mordher seemed oblivious to his dying gasp. He pushed him aside and tossed the keys into Ardhios' cell, who quickly unlocked the gates of all the cells.

"Follow me," Ardhios said. He and the other men moved toward the southern cliffs.

"I follow no one," Mordher responded.

"Come *with* us," Ardhios rephrased, and the eight of them echoed his urging. "Come with us!" they cried. They all waved Mordher in their direction. Mordher grumbled something and fell in behind the others.

They made their way to the southern cliffs, and Mordher saw that the stairs that once made their way to the sea below were indeed gone.

"This way!" Ardhios yelled. He ran west along the cliff's edge and then led them north, where they arrived at the servants' watering well. There was the loud ringing of the alarm from the temple behind them.

"They will not be long behind us, now," Ardhios said. He picked up a stone and threw it into the well. "Quiet!" he yelled, and then he listened for the splash in the well below. There was the *g-dunk* of the stone entering the water, and Ardhios was satisfied that the well was low enough. "We've but one way out. We jump in here," he said, pointing them down into the well.

"What?" one of them inquired.

"Trust me!" Ardhios said. "About ten feet below the surface there is a tunnel that opens to an underground cave. The caves go to the sea."

Ardhios looked to the west, the evening sun turning the sea golden south of them. "Yes!" he said. "We are in luck! The sun is just at the right point to light the cave. Listen to me, listen closely: dive into the waters of the well and feel for the walls. There's a narrowing of the walls just after the last well stone and just before the cave entrance. Before you jump, breathe like this," he said, and then he intentionally hyperventilated. "You'll need to hold your breath for some time before you make it to the cave. Below the last of the stones in the wall of the well, you'll turn through the darkness. Pull yourself forward—keep moving, and don't panic! The cave will open to our escape!"

Mordher looked at the others. They all looked at Ardhios like he was mad.

"This is your plan?" another asked.

"My cousin drowned here when I was a child. I and several of my kinsmen dove into the well to retrieve his body. I am telling you, there is a cave below the surface to the west!"

The Rion Guardsmen were approaching from the east.

"Do you see them?" Ardhios cried. "They outnumber us ten to one. Even Mordher cannot fight them all!"

"All right! All right! I'm going!" one yelled.

"Wait, the best swimmers first!" Ardhios responded. "We all drown if anyone blocks the way!"

Suddenly, an arrow struck one of their companions through the chest, and he fell forward on the side of the well, pulling on the stones, still trying to make the jump, but falling dead to the ground before he was able to pull his body weight over the edge. Other arrows began to fall around them.

"Now!" Ardhios screamed. "If you can swim, now would be the time to prove it!" They all began hyperventilating their breathing.

"To the south, right?" one asked.

"Yes, the south, the south!" Ardhios cried.

Two of them dove over the side, and the rest waited impatiently. The Guard grew ever closer. Mordher used his sword, barely deflecting an arrow that came dangerously close to hitting him in the face.

"Now!" Ardhios screamed, and the others continued to dive into the well one after another, until only Mordher and Ardhios remained.

"Go, Ardhios!" Mordher said. "I'll hold them off!"

"You cannot hold them off, Mordher!" Ardhios replied. "Jump now!"

"I cannot swim!" Mordher growled.

Ardhios looked a little stunned. "What?" he asked.

"I cannot swim!" Mordher yelled. "You must go now! I release you from your promise to lead me from this place. Go now!"

Ardhios continued breathing rapidly. "Look out!" he yelled, and Mordher turned to look behind him. Mordher felt the impact of Ardhios' shoulder striking him in the side, and the two of them went over the well's edge.

Mordher just managed to hold onto the grip on his sword, falling through the light and then into the darkness with Ardhios. Mordher's huge body burst through the surface and then rose back again, the panicked look on his face unseen in the darkness. Mordher's sword struck the stone of the well's wall causing a short spark of light that revealed Ardhios beside him.

"Put that sword away!" Ardhios yelled, and Mordher raised it as if to strike him, but felt himself sinking beneath the surface. He wanted to curse Ardhios, but the water entered his mouth and fear won out over all other emotion.

"If you want to live," Ardhios began, but paused to spit water. "If you want to live, put away the sword, and I'll help you through the caves!"

Mordher began flailing the water, sinking repeatedly. His free hand fought to find some hold on the smooth stones of the well wall. He fumbled to put his sword in his belt. "Help me!" he cried. Above them, he could see the outline of several soldiers, their voices echoing in the well.

"Take a deep breath!" Ardhios yelled.

"Yes!" Mordher replied, and he gasped loudly.

"Now!" Ardhios yelled, and Mordher heard the *thwap, thwap, thwap* of several arrows striking the water around them.

Mordher dove beneath the surface of the water and clumsily felt around for Ardhios in the dark, cold water. He felt Ardhios grabbing his shirt, trying to pull him deeper into the well's blackness. With his free hand, Mordher felt the wall of the well, and when he felt the mud where the well stones ended, Ardhios suddenly jerked him deeper.

Mordher was beyond panic when he first saw the faint light of the underwater cave. He tried to claw his way back toward the light, but struck his head on the well wall stone, causing him to gulp water into his lungs. He lost all hope of reaching the caves when something pulled on him again.

He could just make out the forms of the other men in the dim light of the cave when the water burst from his lungs, and he coughed face down in the soft dirt of the cave.

"Which way?" one of them screamed in their panic. There was the strange sound of muted voices on the water.

"Toward . . . the . . . light!" Ardhios managed to say.

Mordher struggled to his feet and joined the motley group as they made their way through the twisting cave's smooth walls and rich, red mud, moving toward the faint light of the evening sun that signaled their escape. When at last they reached the cave's exit, it was nearly dark, and the men drank in the dank air of the cave in great gasps from their difficult navigation of the cave's winding, slippery, and often erosion-sharpened stone. The old cave had taken them up and down through the bowels of the stone cliffs of Rion, and from the exit in the cliff walls, they saw that the ocean was still some sixty feet below.

"Jump as far away from the cliff as possible!" Ardhios said. "And wait until the wave is going out to jump!"

"Going out?" Mordher probed.

"All of you, watch!' Ardhios said. He broke away a chunk of stone from the cliff wall. He watched the waves crashing upon the cliff walls below for a moment, and then Ardhios dropped the stone when the wave had ebbed. It fell toward the exposed, jagged rocks at the foot of the cliffs. They all watched without blinking, and the ocean surged over the jagged rocks just before the stone struck.

"Going out!" Ardhios said. "You must swim away from the rocks as quickly as possible!"

They all looked at Ardhios like he was insane, but that quickly gave way to a somber realization that there was little choice.

"Wait for each other!" Ardhios shouted. "Wait until the person before you has cleared the tide and the rocks and swum clear!" Ardhios looked at their faces once more, seeing a mixture of fear on some and near contempt on others.

Then he looked down in time to see the water falling away and jumped.

The group watched his descent intently. They could see the large coral and stone exposed below him, and there was a moment of bated breath, but the sea swelled ahead of him, and the tide rushed in beneath him, flooding the rocky shoreline. Ardhios's body plunged a white arc into the deep blue water and surfaced in the wake of the outgoing wave. He rushed to swim with it, to make all the distance he could from the rocks before the swell returned. Then he moved parallel to the shoreline where it shallowed, and the current pushed him roughly upon the sandy shore with a crash of frothy water and seaweed. Ardhios stumbled around to his feet, squeezed the water from his face with his hand, and inhaled his first full breath after the jump.

"Come! You can do it!" he yelled, and no sooner than he had said it, they followed, one by one crashing into the sea and mimicking his pattern to the shore. Even Mordher, with his fear of the water, managed to dog paddle into position for the tide to drop him on the shore.

"Follow me!" Ardhios said. Several of them rested their hands on their knees, and they were all winded. "Come on, now!" he said to them.

The lot of them rounded the short beach before sighting the dock. They ran as fast as they could toward it. The waves crashed in, and the warm knee-high water gently pushed the sand around their feet, sapping the speed from their escape.

When they neared the docks, they could see several archers on the broken staircase above, descending down as close to them as the sturdier rock would allow. The distance allowed them to watch the archers' arrows for what seemed like several seconds, the last of their travel blurring before the arrowheads sunk into the beach around them.

They scrambled for a single-sailed cog that they thought they could manage, with the sound of the arrows striking the wood all around them. They manned the capstan, kedging off into the southern sky. When the boat finally caught the rising tide, the open sea claimed it, and the cliffs of Rion faded into the distance.

* * *

Like the *Nurium* and the *Merrius*, the boat carrying the seven warriors from Rion followed the shoreline around the western end of Etharath, but a storm that blew up suddenly sent them sailing farther out to sea to avoid it. After eleven days at sea, the seven warriors came ashore some thirty leagues north of the refugees that were tending to the building of Shintower.

Having found nothing on their stolen ship but some hardtack and a little fresh water, they abandoned the boat both starving and dehydrated, and moved inland in search of food and water. They found themselves just south of a mountain range that separated the plains in the north from a beautiful valley that the soldiers thought exuded the peace that ancient Rion had once provided them. They happened upon a little stream and drank, but they were all still very hungry.

"Those leaving Rion were to hide in the woods to the east or in the mountains to the north," said Ardhios.

"There are soldiers of the Guard accompanying them," Mordher grunted. "I will never bow down to the Elders again."

"The world has changed, my brother," Ardhios responded. "The Elders will never leave the Temples, and the land between us is no more. The words of the Elders will fast fade from their ears."

"My sword is closer than the words of the Elders," Mordher said. "Let us see which they choose to follow."

"Now, now, my friend," said Ardhios. "We are free of the Elders. What is there in Highwood that interests us?"

Mordher looked toward Highwood and frowned. "I am done with Rion and the Guard. There is nothing in Highwood that I wish to take from farmers and slaves. Let them wait on the Elders to close up the great fault so they can go home. Let them wait on that."

"Then it is done," Ardhios said. "We make our camp here."

As the evening fell, they could see fires in the valley below them, and Mordher refused to sleep until he had seen who warmed themselves so close to their camp. Six warriors followed him into the valley, moving around the base of the mountain that lay to their north. Ardhios called the peak "Candra," meaning *haven* in the ancient Rionese, for it seemed to him that they had found a new home, and the days of the Guard were truly far behind them.

They made their way close to the fires, and Mordher could see that the people around them were haggard and weak, their dress giving them away as refugees from Rion. He made his way into the light at the edge of the encampment.

"Who goes there?" one of the men asked.

"I am Mordher," he replied, his immense form stepping into their midst and taking them aback with his sheer size. "You then are from Rion?"

"Yes, of course," the man said, and Mordher could see a little calm come across the faces of the crowd that moved him. "You have news of Rion?"

They examined his clothing. "You are a warrior of the Guard," one of them said. Though keeping her distance, she pointed to a pin Mordher used to secure his cloak. "You carry the mark of the Guard."

"I am marked by the Guard, that is right," Mordher said. "But not by this pin," he said. He pulled the pin from his cloak and threw it into the fire. "This pin pierced only my cloak—the Guard has pierced my soul."

For a moment, there was only an awkward silence.

"Have you heard news of the Inferiors? Do they attack Rion?" another asked.

"Some say they are coming for us!" one of the women said.

"If they are coming for you," Mordher replied, grabbing the staff away from one of them with ease. "Then they will take you!" he said, smiling and tossing the staff back to its owner. "You cannot fight the Inferiors with staves and rocks."

"What do we do then?" another asked.

"We will protect you!" Ardhios said. "But to do so will require our strength, and we are famished from the trip here. Pray, have you something to eat that we might recover?"

"Yes, yes of course," they responded, and they hurried to round them up what appeared to be the best of the food that they had. Mordher and the others tore it from their hands and ate until they were completely stuffed.

Each of the seven warriors in turn took their helping of the food, building their own fire some twenty paces away from all the rest of the townspeople. As Mordher and the others finished, Ardhios sat beside him, picking over a plate of food.

"We could have taken what we wanted!" Mordher said.

"Oh, yes, my friend, you could have done just that. You could even have killed a few of them in the process!" Ardhios smirked, looking over at the watchful refugees.

"I can do what is necessary," Mordher responded, and the other warriors appeared to stop their talking and began watching the banter between him and Ardhios with some interest.

"I am sure you can do pretty much whatever you put your mind to, Mordher," Ardhios said. "But why kill them when they can feed you, follow you—fight for you?" There was a low rumble of agreement from the group.

Mordher did not answer, but this idea met with his approval. These townspeople were no more warriors than he was a cook, and their food *should* be divided amongst the warriors. *In fact*, Mordher thought, *they might just be willing to part with so much more.*

Chapter Twelve

Witch of Southwood

Rendaya landed just outside the deep Southwood forest. Her face was taut with regret for the lives she had taken on the *Nurium* moments before, but her resolve remained unshaken. Nothing must stop the Swordbearer from finding sanctuary in the west. To do less might mean the end of humankind, and it was a chance she was unwilling to take.

She walked for about a league into the darkness of the forest, finally seeing the familiar glow of a fire through the bubbled window glass her husband had made with his own hands for a wedding present. He had used no conjuring, mind you (though he had been an incredibly gifted conjurer and alchemist), but had intentionally made it with the sweat of his brow in the heat of a makeshift glass furnace. Winter or summer, sun or rain, the old window glass always reminded her of him and the great effort he had put into providing her with some level of luxury that Rion once had.

She could see the shifting shadow of her cat, Bellows, moving dimly through the more translucent than transparent panes. Bellows moved to greet her entry, and when she opened the cottage door, Bellows was right under her feet, his tail brushing her leg with each step she took.

"Bellows! Out from under my feet!" she said, more worried she would step on him than angry. He looked at her with those eyes of his, and she melted. "Oh, come here. I bet you're hungry!" she offered. She checked the stew pot on the small fire in the fireplace, and then she ladled up a small bowl for Bellows and one for herself, and plopped down in the old rocker.

"My bones hurt, Bellows," she reported, but Bellows gave her only the slightest look before returning to his soup.

"That good?" she asked, feeling a faint smile forcing its way onto her face. Bellows listened intently to every word. He slurped the soup bowl dry in record time and then jumped into her lap. She set aside her own bowl, half eaten. He turned on her lap twice and, finding a comfortable direction, fell into a clump, placing one paw on her hand. Then he looked at her with his big black eyes. She gently rubbed his head just behind his ears, and he let out a loud purr, flipping on his back and playfully biting and swatting at her hand. She took the look on his face as absolute devotion.

"I needed that, Bellows," she said. "It's been a very long day."

A long day indeed. She had come to grips with the fact that the Camonra were here to stay. They had camped near the great fault that now separated Rion from the rest of Etharath, and the Creator only knew how long it was until the Camonra declared all-out war with the refugees of Rion that had moved into Highwood northeast of her. Combine this with the fact that a slave named Galbard was carrying Evliit's mighty Sword of the Watch somewhere to the north—it had all the makings of a catastrophe of proportions that no one could imagine.

"What will we do with them?" Rendaya asked her cat.

Bellows answered with a flick of his right ear and a quick pass of his paw across his face.

"You are right, of course," Rendaya responded. "We will do whatever is necessary to protect the Sword, won't we?"

Bellows stopped, perfectly still and locked his eyes with hers.

"You know what I'm saying, don't you, Bellows? They will *never* have the Sword." Her serious tone prompted Bellows to spring from her lap onto the floor in front of the fireplace. He turned and glanced back at her, slowly arched his back, and then darted across the room and up onto Rendaya's quilted bed.

"Yes, of course; we must rest," Rendaya said. She pushed herself from the rocker and checked the fire once more. Its tamped coals would do fine to keep the soup, so she removed the large wooden cook spoon and carefully seated the pot lid. Then she threw herself upon the bed and watched the warm red glow of the fireplace dance on the ceiling until sleep overtook her.

For the next few weeks, she and Bellows worked the garden in the clearing just down the path from the house. Rendaya often used that time to reflect, while Bellows loved exploring the woods surrounding the garden. There was a large assortment of herbs and vegetables, and out of no necessity other than her own pleasure, she had planted a nice flower garden where she would often sit for hours when the sun was not too hot, thinking of simpler times, before she knew of Watchers or Spellmakers.

Today, she was in that flower garden, and the sweet perfume of the flowers faintly scented the air all around her. She enjoyed the smell of them so much that she produced a small vial from her garden apron and spoke the word *Captus*. A mixture of the flowers' scents visibly raced into the vial, concentrating into a golden liquid, which she immediately corked and put back away in her apron pocket. Now when the cold of winter gripped Southwood, it would take no more than a drop of golden liquid to remember the warmth of summer and her beautiful garden.

She wiped away a bit of dirt from her face and noticed the distinct smell of tomato vines still on her fingers. She looked back over the basket of tomatoes, okra, and peppers that she had picked and thought of a soup recipe that she hadn't made in some time. She was fairly sure there were still some cloves of garlic in the pantry. The coming of fall meant no more tomatoes for some time, and she really wanted to make that great tomato and okra soup recipe one more time before the long winter in Southwood.

The next morning, Rendaya left the cottage early, much to the chagrin of Bellows, who sat in the window and stared at her, motionless except for the occasional swish of his tail.

Rendaya saw her breath on the crisp cold air. She pulled her wrap across her head and walked northwest. With the ever-increasing size of the Camonra camp, it was time to ensure the Bhre-Nora's construction plans for the tower were coming to fruition. Though it was a long walk, she wanted to conserve the energy required to take flight.

She made the walk across the Fields of Hannington and into the rolling hills that preceded the site for the tower, but even before she had crossed the last of Hannington, she looked up toward the setting sun and stopped. They had done it! And now it was if the sun rested upon the top of the great tower, its blazing light like a fireball atop a torch stand.

"Shintower," Rendaya said under her breath. "Stand strong, great tower, preserve the hopes of mankind." She stood there for several minutes, a prayer of thankfulness somewhere between her heart, her head, and her lips, and a peaceful feeling washed over her. *We will reclaim this land for the Creator*, she thought. *There will be a new beginning, a Third Age.*

Rendaya carried that peaceful feeling with her across what remained of the distance to the tower and moved closer to the people working in the land around it.

* * *

In the two months since Cayden had returned from the tower, the people had taken the message to heart that the Witch of Southwood was pleased with their efforts. When he had presented the Bhre-Nora's list to them, it had been life changing. The list had set an end in sight for fulfilling their oaths, and urgency had taken the place of fear. When the list had dwindled to a few items, there had even been an air of victory among the Rionese refugees. It was as if there was a level of *certainty* growing—a feeling that the worst might actually be behind them. Being the messenger had finally worked in Cayden's favor, for as the news turned good, the refugees' opinions of him had quickly changed, and they welcomed him, Nara, Jalin, and Ro back into the fold. He took down their tents in the eastern fields, and they moved back into the main encampment. In celebration of the turn of events, he had asked Nara to marry him, and she had accepted.

The rise of the tower had also been a tipping point for Jalin. Galbard had not appeared as she had hoped, and it seemed to break Jalin's spirit. He and Nara had both pleaded with her to stay and help with the wedding, and that pleading might have been the only thing that had kept her from taking Ro and heading east. She had reluctantly stayed, and she seemed to drop the conversation about her husband altogether. Maybe that had been best.

The small refugee encampment, once nothing more than the passengers, tents, and cargo from the *Merrius* and *Nurium*, had grown almost overnight. Builders who completed their work in the tower turned to buildings around the encampment, and working together, they raised a combination tavern and store in the first few weeks. Everyone pitched in on raising the structures, and modest homes steadily began to replace tents in the hills and valleys that rippled eastward from Shintower's higher, flatter terrain.

Scouts from Highwood had seen the tower from leagues away, and eventually traders found their way to the flourishing little village. With the Highborne River separating it from the east, traders considered the village somewhat of a safe haven, giving it the name "the Dales," a name that had stuck with the locals. The sheer number of construction projects kept the Dales lively, and a trickle of traffic began to flow from Highwood and as far away as Moonledge Peak.

Cayden was working with several other men on the massive oak door for the entrance to the tower's base. They had rigged some eyelets with several ropes and were straining to set the door on its hinges. The door swung into place with a great rumble that echoed through the glassless windows above them, and they could just hear the men inside attempting to set the pins. They waited expectantly, and then the muffled hammering stopped, and the door slowly swung open to the large smiles of the men inside.

The sweat poured from their faces. "It is set!" they yelled, slapping backs. In the midst of the celebration, Cayden suddenly felt a cold shiver run down his spine, and he suddenly recalled that fateful night on the *Nurium*.

"A draught! A draught for all!" the men shouted. They started toward the Dales.

"I'll catch up!" Cayden shouted.

"No, you won't!" one of them answered, laughing. "Unless you've got a drink in each hand!"

Cayden pretended to look over the tower doors. They walked away, and when he was sure that the happy celebrants were gone, he strained his eyes to see a dark figure, her silhouette almost lost against some trees to the southeast. It merged with the long shadows of the ending day that stretched across the rolling hills.

The Witch! he thought, and the urge to yell out caused him to cough and clear his throat, but he did no more than that, for he was mysteriously drawn to her, as if his fate had become somehow inexplicably intertwined with her own.

Except for the gentle movement of her hair and her long coat, her dark-hooded figure was motionless against the tree limbs that stirred in the sudden cool breeze.

He looked around for others watching, and seeing no one, he approached her, stopping just across from her as the last light passed below the horizon. The darkness engulfed them, and he could see her eyes glowing within the recesses of her hood.

"Are we not doing as you have said?" Cayden inquired. "See? The tower rises as you have commanded."

"Yes, you do as I have commanded," Rendaya responded, "but I have come to show you what must be done next."

Rendaya bent down and touched the ground with one finger. A golden glow appeared to flow from it and travel across the ground, etching the ground with an intricate design that encircled the tower. "You have until spring to build another curtain wall that rings the base of the tower. On the eastern side, you will build a great gate. When the wall has been constructed, close the outer gates and lock them, and tell no one to enter until La and Sapath cross in the northern sky, for in this time, the Bhre-Nora will do a mighty work."

"It will be done," Cayden replied.

"You must protect the Sword," she said. "Do not think that you have escaped the wrath of Amphileph."

"It will be done," Cayden responded.

"Be about it then," she replied. "I will return again." Rendaya turned from him and walked back toward Southwood. Cayden's resolve reminded her of her late husband. That memory brought back her anger with Amphileph, and she suddenly just wanted to be home. When she was some distance from Cayden, she shot into the night sky toward Southwood to be with Bellows and those surroundings that gave her comfort.

She quickly came closer to Southwood, but thoughts of Amphileph began to cloud her mind with anger. Her flight began to fail. Had she not refocused in the last instant on her landing, she surely would have crashed—and with enough energy to do herself great harm. As it was, the landing was bad enough, and she tumbled through the high grass just outside the trees, rolling to a bruised and battered stop. She cried out with the pain, and after lying there for some time, she managed to pick herself up. Her left wrist was obviously broken, and she had a nasty cut above her right eye. She squinted to look at her right shoulder where a hole in her clothing revealed raw meat, which began to bleed profusely.

"Creator, let me be strong," she managed, and she pushed herself to limp home. With a great deal of effort, she opened the latch on the door and entered the house. Bellows moved around her frantically.

"Not now, Bellows," she begged. But Rendaya's obvious pain made the cat circle her repeatedly, his ears standing straight up and his eyes wide with concern.

"Bellows! Stop!" Rendaya cried.

Bellows's ears fell back. He quietly curled up in a large pillow on the loveseat by the window. Rendaya saw him look away from her and lick his paw, and she felt a twinge of guilt.

"I just . . . need . . . a minute, Bellows," she said. Though he appeared to be ignoring her.

Rendaya lowered her head in prayer. She raised her one good hand to the heavens, her palm open as if to receive the gift. She raised her head then; her eyes remained closed. Her palm began growing hotter, spreading across the hand, and then up her arm. She silently gave thanks to the Creator, placed the heated palm upon her wrist, and winced, feeling the bones moving back into place. When the last of the carpals had popped back into place, she moved the palm down and across her fingers. She raised her hand to her eye, cupping the bleeding cut, and it immediately stopped bleeding. No sooner had Rendaya removed her hand than the skin had mended, leaving only the dried blood to hint at the injury there had been.

Rendaya placed her hands together for a moment and then gingerly placed her left hand on the torn shoulder. It also stopped bleeding in an instant, and the lump on her collarbone slowly disappeared. She opened her eyes and carefully crawled into bed.

"Now, you," she said to Bellows, whose head popped up at the welcoming tone in his mistress's voice. Rendaya groaned and blew out her lantern, curling up with her blanket. Bellows gathered in a knot at the small of Rendaya's back, and in no time, they were both fast asleep.

Chapter Thirteen

The Faceless Mountains

Citanth had rounded the Faceless Mountains and tracked Galbard to Calarph forest, but the thick, dark forest hid too many unknowns and there were horse tracks leading to the west, so Citanth chose not to venture deep inside. He was unsure if the Watcher Mategaladh had survived the Binding Spell, but he knew if the old man was somewhere in this forest, the brush would provide far too great an advantage to his foe—he would surely unleash his fury on their company, even if it required the last of his life force.

"Move along, commander. My old *friend* Mategaladh—if he is even alive—is in no shape to ride, so the man we seek rides west," Citanth replied when the commander told him of their findings. "Send your fastest riders west!"

Far in the distance, Galbard pushed Pladus, his new horse, relentlessly. He had to draw the Camonra away from Mategaladh and distance himself from his pursuers.

The speed of the horse was frightful—it ran like no horse Galbard had ever seen. He held on with white knuckles, and the horse shot across the Calarphian plains north of the mountain range where Galbard had once huddled in the deep caves with Illian and his kinsmen.

When he looked to the south, the peaks of the mountain range appeared to go on forever into the west, and the thought occurred to him that he might be trapped. As far as the eye could see, there was only the tundra to the north.

They were streaking by the mountains, when Galbard suddenly pulled back against the reins. "There, Pladus," he shouted, and he pulled the reins toward what appeared to be a goat trail up the mountain's side. They galloped along the trail until the narrowing of the passage caused Galbard's leg to scrape the rock wall, nearly knocking him from his mount and sending him tumbling down the slope. He pulled Pladus' reins until he recovered his seat in the saddle, and then they crept along the trail, finally finding a small landing, where he dismounted and began leading Pladus up the ever-steepening trail by the reins. After hours of struggling, there was a break in the steep grade, the trail widened, and Galbard decided to ride again. He stepped into the stirrup and threw his leg over Pladus, but then he thought he heard voices in the distance. He leaned forward to whisper into Pladus's ear.

"Hold, Pladus," he said, stepping back down. Galbard wrapped the reins around an outcropping of stone and squatted to look back over the terrain they had managed to cover in that afternoon. He watched and listened for several minutes, but there was no sign of his pursuers.

A light powdering of snowflakes evaporated in the air, but higher up, Galbard could see the small flakes were sticking, and eventually, where the long upward path climbed to the ridges high above, there was deeper snow still. The cold was clearly something that would affect him more than the Camonra, and if he could not find a crossing, they could easily wait him out until he starved or froze to death.

Galbard's stomach reminded him of Mategaladh's saddlebags. He stood back up and walked around to Pladus's side.

He worked the aged, soft leather through the buckle with worn ease and opened the saddlebag flap. There Galbard found small packages and vials within, some unlabeled. One, however, was labeled with the single word, "Traveler." There was smaller print that read, "Use sparingly." He opened it, thinking to assess its taste, and instinctively sniffed its contents. His nose burned from the intense fragrance, and he quickly eased the cork stopper back into the vial. A feeling of lightheadedness struck him, but he had the presence of mind to replace the vial in the saddlebag and work his way around Pladus back up the trail before he had to sit down.

Struggling with a bout of nausea, he felt a wave of blood flow passing front to back across his brain, and with what might have been a momentary loss of consciousness, his surroundings changed. He lifted away from his own body, the clouds raced across the sky with the sun, and then everything came to a sudden standstill.

He could see himself, frozen in time, a mixed look of concentration and anger on his face, hiding behind a large outcropping of stone.

Suspended in mid-leap, the scouts were making their way up the hill in front of him.

"It looks pretty dire, doesn't it?" a voice said.

Galbard jumped, startled. "Mategaladh?" Galbard could barely make out the old Watcher's face in the strong light that seemed to surround his body.

"I see you have found the Traveler potion that I put in the bag," Mategaladh said.

"What's happening to me?" asked Galbard.

"You're seeing the future," Mategaladh answered. "Be quick and take note of their attack, for the effects will not last long."

"Are you here with me?"

Mategaladh let out a little laugh. "That's a little Connection tincture that I mixed in—my own special blend. We can talk but a short time, so be quick."

Galbard shook his head. This whole experience was surreal. He looked again at the scene before him. Below him, at the far end of the valley, he could see an army of Camonra approaching. "I am completely outnumbered."

"Yes, it looks so, but it is said that the righteous warrior is always outnumbered," answered Mategaladh.

Galbard crinkled his nose, and then his face gathered a look of calm.

"If I am not to be, then I go to the feast of my ancestors in glory. They will see that the son of a mason has done great things, and they will be proud of my brave passing."

Mategaladh's image appeared to shift on the wind for a moment.

"What's happening?" Galbard asked.

"The connection is ending," Mategaladh replied. "What will you do?"

Galbard turned his back to Mategaladh, and drawing the Sword, he held it high. "Let them come for me!" he shouted, and then closed his eyes and listened to the echo of his words ringing throughout the mountainside below. "If I must, I will die in the service of my oath! I have given my word to Evliit!"

There was a second rush of blood across the top of Galbard's brain. He snapped back into the present, sure that he heard the echo of his defiant shout in the valley below. He drew a deep breath, sat up, and tried to get his bearings on the time of day, but it seemed as though no time had passed at all. Pladus dipped his head and shook his mane, displaying his boredom with his being tied off to the mountain.

Galbard moved on his belly to the edge of the vantage point of the stone ledge, and just as he had seen in the vision, three scouts were closing on him. They were hunters, the skulls of *men* hanging from their belts. One of the Camon scouts saw him then, and he shouted up to him.

"We have seen you, little man!" the younger scout barked. He suddenly changed direction and moved quickly upon Galbard's position. "You are surrounded by the Camonra!"

Galbard moved back from the edge and rolled to his back. He held the Sword tightly in both hands, the sweat on his palms making the leather-covered tang feel slippery. He stood up then and looked over the edge at them. "Come to me, bastards of Amphileph! I will end you!" He felt the temperature rising in the tang of the Sword, and a blue flame engulfed it.

"I am Pras!" The elder Camon bristled. "*You* would challenge *me*?" he screamed. The other Camonra appeared from behind their cover. The one called Pras turned to the younger scouts and growled, "He is very brave hiding on that ledge. Let him come down from there and say such things to me!"

"Your master could not take this Sword from Evliit! What makes you think his lowly servants could?" taunted Galbard.

One of the younger Camonra had heard enough. He came up from beside Pras up the hill, but Pras knocked him aside with a wave of his great shield. "Hold your ground, Dahran, and wait for Citanth! This one is going nowhere!"

"Enough of this talk!" the younger Camon said. "We can kill this little fool of a man!" He burst forward and Pras moved to stop him, narrowly missing his leap to a thin perch of stone.

"I'm coming for you, little man!" Dahran shouted. He leapt again to a second perch.

Pras put his horn to his lips and blew loudly, sounding to all that the bearer of the Sword had been found.

Galbard was amazed how quickly the Camon moved up the face of the rocky mountainside. He stepped back from the ledge just as Dahran leapt over it.

The Camon pulled his large scimitar from its scabbard and walked toward Galbard with something akin to a smile on his face. "Time for you to die, little one!" he screamed and leapt at Galbard, bringing his sword over his head in a death strike. Dahran's blade descended with enough force to knock the Sword from Galbard's hands, but instead, the attacker's blade parted where it touched the Sword, the last six inches or so whizzing by Galbard's right ear.

Instead of recoiling from the impact, Galbard's parry continued upward and collided with the chin of his opponent's unchecked forward motion, effortlessly passing through his jaw and out the back of his head, leaving the two halves of his helmet to clang to the ground. The scout fell forward upon Galbard in a lifeless, bloody heap, knocking him from his feet.

He stared in disbelief at the blue flames that danced around Dahran's parted skull and the red molten half of the great scimitar he still held in his hand. The Camon's weight pinned Galbard down.

"Get off me!" Galbard yelled, and Dahran's body flew away from him over the ledge as effortlessly as tossing the last of the ale out of a cup. It burst into blue, and then yellow-red flames for a brief moment, arcing through the Calarphian skies, and disappearing over the mountainside.

Galbard jumped to his feet. He could hardly control the power that surged through his body. "Leave now if you want to live!" he cried. He forced a deep breath, and a wave of energy emanated from deeper in his gut. The blue plasma began to radiate from his body, lifting him off the ground.

As the second Camon scout topped the ledge in chase of his zealous brother, Galbard pushed the plasma toward him, incinerating the scout in a flash of yellow and red flames. Galbard topped the mountainside and looked down for the remaining Camonra. He could not see the one called Pras at first, but then he poked his head out from around the mountainside, his eyes growing large at the sight of Galbard, and then he fumbled for his horn and ducked back behind the stone.

Galbard heard the horn's signal, and he cried out again. "Come if you dare!" A wave of blue energy passed down the mountainside, and the horn's note just stopped. He raised the sword and jumped down to engage the Camon, when he saw that he was motionless, still holding his horn in the air. The Camon's ashen form held for but a moment more before the winds of the Faceless Mountains swirled him skyward.

At the foot of the mountain, Citanth's warriors heard the familiar battle horn's long tone cut short, and they knew that could only mean one thing. The human was within their grasps!

"Master Citanth!" an acolyte yelled. "The alert is sounded! The human has been found!"

Citanth peeked out from the curtain of his carriage to see what the ruckus was. News of the man Galbard was a welcome sound to his ears.

"Master Citanth, the scout's horn sounded just up there," the acolyte repeated. He pointed just up the mountainside ahead of them.

"We stand ready to do your bidding, lord!" one of the captains shouted.

"Take your men and bring me the man called Galbard," commanded Citanth. "Leave only the slaves—take all the rest. Capture this man Galbard at all costs! Capture him and bring me his weapon!"

"Yes, my lord!" the captain responded. He pulled his battle horn to his lips and blew it loudly. The other captains surrounded him within seconds.

"Bring our High Commander the man Galbard and his sword! Even now, our scouts have found him out. Capture the sword at all costs!"

The resulting rumble of warriors was deafening. The Azrodh riders led the way, and the foot soldiers followed behind them, creating a dust trail that remained in the air for minutes after their departure.

Galbard heard the second horn from the valley below, and readied for their assault. "I will not fear you," he told himself. A peace came to him then, and Galbard looked back at Pladus for a moment and then moved over the edge of the ridge, falling directly toward the oncoming horde in the valley below. The blue plasma hugged the terrain, descending rapidly down the mountainside.

When he reached the base of the mountain, the plasma set him gently on the ground. Galbard could feel the ground shaking at their approach, but he kneeled before them.

"Creator, grant me your grace once again. Help me to destroy my enemies."

The Sword seemed almost white hot, and fingers of blue plasma licked the air around him, illuminating his body like a blacksmith's bellows stokes the coals. He rose to his feet, and the Camonra moved to within moments of crashing down upon him. He pointed the Sword in the direction of the oncoming wall of warriors, and there was the sound of air drawing in toward him, followed by a burst of energy so great that the sound lagged behind its fast-moving wave. It devastated the Camonra ranks, vaporizing the vast majority of them in wisps of flame and ash, while the remainder flew through the air away from him.

Silence hung in the air like the ash. The grass around him was blackened or burning, and the bodies of the Camonra were scattered across the valley before him. His attack struck terror in the hearts of the few Camon survivors, and those that could not walk clawed the ground to escape from him. Those that could run did so without looking back.

Galbard felt drained. The plasma disappeared, and he fell forward to his knees, just catching himself with one hand to prevent falling upon his face. He lifted the sword with great effort and pushed it into its scabbard, and he turned and struggled to ascend the mountainside toward Pladus.

When he arrived at the ledge where Pladus stood waiting impatiently, Galbard climbed upon Pladus and spurred him with enough force to bring about a flight that Galbard could almost not control.

Pladus bolted past the snow line, and still showed no sign of slowing. They had nearly topped the mountain before Galbard knew it. He saw an opening up a steep grade.

The angle of the terrain had him nearly lying on Pladus's neck. The great horse dug in his hooves in his attempt to ascend, but slid repeatedly, dangerously tempting the edge more than once.

When at last Pladus neared the mountaintop, they came upon a large patch of ice on the plateau. Galbard pulled on the reins, trying to stop Pladus's forward momentum. Pladus straightened his legs, sliding across the ice-covered plateau until his front hooves caught some traction, but his rear footing slipped out from under him, and the reins slipped through Galbard's cold hands. He fell to the frozen ground with a loud thud, knocking the air out of his lungs.

Galbard tried to regain his wind. He slowly rolled to his side and watched Pladus struggle back to his feet, and then Galbard lay on his back and let the snow land gently on his wind-burned face.

Out of the corner of his eye, he saw a tiny red bird flittering across the snow, jumping and turning this way and that. It twitched its head and looked at Galbard, and then it darted away. Galbard's eyes followed it through a passage in the mountainside. He stood up and struggled along the little bird's path until he saw the southern valley below through the snow-filled winds held at bay by the passage walls.

"To the south then," Galbard said. "We are saved, Pladus."

He had found a passage that he could use to put some real distance between him and whatever remained of the Camonra. Galbard called to Pladus and struggled to gain his mount again, both of their breathing strained by the altitude. They made their way down the twisting path of the mountainside toward the smaller mountain range to the south.

* * *

Citanth shifted nervously in his coach. He had heard the booming noise from the mountainside and felt the wave of energy dissipating around him.

"Master!" one of his slaves said. "Master, the Camonra return!"

Citanth bolted from his coach with great anticipation, stepping down upon the slaves' shoulders and backs. There were no more than handful of the Camonra left, and even those seemed startled and confused.

"Where are the others?" Citanth inquired.

"They are . . . gone, my liege," one of the Camonra announced. He dragged what remained of one of his comrades and dropped him at Citanth's feet. It folded in a heap upon the ground, spilling the organs from the half that remained.

"I do not know what happened, master," the Camon replied. "I was at the rear of the column when the order came to attack the man-creature. I heard a shout from in front of me and then a push, like a great wind, master. Then the dust blinded me."

"Stop!" Citanth yelled, looking over the dead soldier. "Speak no more of it!" he cried, raising a hand to strike the soldier's face. He turned and attempted to climb back into his coach. Stumbling slightly, he managed the steps and entered what privacy the curtained coach provided. He put his arm to his face, muffling his gasp with the sleeve of his coat. Everything was gone, erased by this man, Galbard.

"I will have my vengeance," he muttered and then sprang to the curtain and pulled it back. "Back to the Temple!" he screamed, and then he threw the sash closed again. The slaves looked at each other.

"We cannot return to Amphileph in defeat!" one of them whimpered. "He will kill us all!"

"Shut up! Grab up your part!" another yelled, and they each grabbed the horizontal supports and lifted the coach into the air. "To the Temple!" yelled the slave, groaning under the weight of the coach.

Chapter Fourteen

Autonomy

A corps of twenty or so of Camon soldiers had gathered outside Tobor's tent to celebrate their victory over the humans in the raid on Highwood. The females had prepared a feast in honor of the warriors, a Camon favorite, Rudh-Oric, a spiced roast of less-than-agile Azrodh lizard, the animals the Camonra preferred to ride into battle.

Tobor had coined the phrase "less than agile" after watching the female Camonra that very afternoon running in amongst the Azrodh's pen with their mallets ready. The Azrodh had been quite aware of why the Camonra were in the pen, and they were scrambling in all directions. Tobor never failed to note the ruthlessness of the attack, either. When the females had cornered the animal, one of them moved before it, distracting it from the real threat, and another often struck it down with a single swift blow, attacking from outside its peripheral vision. *Never let them swarm you, Azrodh!* he thought to himself, and the image it conjured made him shake with laughter.

One of the females tried to pull his parted side together with her stitch work. "Be still, master, please," she said. A slicing wound ran horizontally along his ribs, and she had stopped her business in mid-stitch, the skin stretched to a point on the thick thread.

"Of course," Tobor replied. He tolerated a certain amount of backtalk from the concubines that traveled with him. Many times he had returned from battle a mess of injuries, the sum total of which would have infected and killed him had it not been for the females' nursing him back to health within the secrecy of his tent. Hidden away from the eyes of the other soldiers—they remained within the confines of his tent's inner quarters at all times—they had seen him at his best and worst. They had never once shared the secrets of his inner sanctuary with even his most trusted captains, even when, in his weakness, his rivals might have torn control of the clan from his grasp. Not even then had they betrayed him, and Tobor valued their loyalty highly.

The ripping open of the land before Rion and the binding of Amphileph had changed everything; now the exodus from the Third Quarter was almost complete, save only for those completely faithful to Amphileph. The Camon females had never been so close to the battlefield, but now they settled in with the males on what could only be called a "new frontier" of their own making.

The great rift to the south had prevented the Rion War from continuing, and the Binding of Amphileph had taken away the terror that seemed to drive his people. Tobor could only feel good about these changes, even if Rionese were scattered to the west and north. Humans didn't seem to want this land of rumbling rain clouds and quakes, and for the first time in his memory, there was a small spot of land that the Camonra could call their own. So tonight would be different, for Tobor had announced to his concubines that they would be allowed to venture outside during more than just the preparation of the feast or its service, and they were obviously excited by the proposition.

The afternoon had been quiet, interrupted only by the chatter of the Camonra females. They sorted the largest Awira insects to crisp in a pit of coals. The scent of the slow-roasting Azrodh wafted among the tents, mixing with the strong odor of the baking Awira, an insect that the Camonra prized for the juices in their lower thorax. The heat of the coals made the sac-shaped stingers swell like they would burst, and when a clear liquid began to ooze from the tip of the tail, the cooks would take them from the heat of the pit and throw them across a special stone made just for rolling out the juicy insides. The juice from the Awira's tail made a potent drink that the Camonra would fight for—well worth the hard efforts the females might spend making it. Since squeezing Awira tails was normally a morning duty and they had started the process later in the day, the constant chatter seemed a requirement for speeding the process along.

Tobor removed the high-back chair from his tent that he reserved for such occasions and sat back in the afternoon sun, watching the clouds pass overhead. The misty warm air from the southern storm clouds seemed to soothe his nasal passages. Several soldiers were working on a table for the feast, using their short blades to plane planks for the top. The noise of the woodwork combined with the females' chatter was relaxing in an odd way, and Tobor dozed off.

As night fell, Tobor sat outside his tent with a mug of Awira and a plate piled high with Rudh-Oric. The celebration was in full swing.

"Rudh-Oric! More Rudh-Oric!" one of the Camonra yelled. "The only animal you can ride into battle or eat if you have to wait for the fight!" A roar of grunting laughter followed his pronouncement.

A bonfire blazed light that danced upon the soldiers' happy faces, lit as much by the drink as by the flame's luminescence.

Tobor listened to the loud carrying-on by the soldiers with little comment. For him, there had been many battles, and many celebrations had followed. Over the years, the memories that seemed to follow the drink were those of fallen friends who once shared their stories with him, as did these younger ones. He could almost see them again, charismatic and brazen, shouting at him from another time. He watched the young Camonra retelling the day's events. *A rite of passage*, he thought, this retelling of the battle. His eyes panned the crowd, and he noticed the other older soldiers also quietly eating, smiling occasionally at one story or another.

Tobor reached for his cup and felt the stitches in his side pull. It made him wince a bit. He silently raised the cup to one of the older soldiers, who nodded ever-so-slightly in response but in whose eyes Tobor saw the stare that countless years of war had darkened forever. Deep within his being, a sadness welled with the realization that this had been their lives.

His mind raced with thoughts he had never dared before. Had they ever known anything but war and death, and the ever-pressing demands of Amphileph? When would there be a time to raise the young, to grow old and die?

Tobor could remember only a handful of warriors who had seen the number of winters he had seen. Was it beyond their hopes to live out their lives in peace? Hadn't they sacrificed enough for Amphileph's seemingly never-ending conquests?

Tobor moved his hand to touch the coarse thread that held his wound closed. It was still tender to the touch, but a bruised sensation around the entire area had replaced the sting of the cut. He was thinking of turning in early.

"The humans will not challenge us again!" one of the Camonra shouted. He raised a cup into the air, undeterred by the sloshing of the drink down his arm and across the table.

Another Camon jumped upon the table. "We should kill them all!"

"What say you, General Tobor? Should we ride back and finish them off?"

There was a roaring response to this suggestion. The cheer had just began to settle, when another rose out of that one, the soldiers yelling, "To-bor! To-bor! To-bor! To-bor!"

Tobor could see that the drunken soldiers were not going to let it go. He could see the wild look in their eyes, and he recognized the frenzied release of pent-up emotions that can overcome soldiers after a battle. With the drink and the camaraderie, it had fallen over the lot of them like a spell. He stood up, and they went crazy with shouts and grunts.

"Settle down, young ones!" Tobor said. The crowd took a moment, but did just that after a few more slaps on the back and individual roars of fierceness. "I too celebrate avenging the death of our brothers," he began. There was another roar from the group, and his mind wandered back to the statuette of Amphileph that he kept in the prayer case in his chest, the very chest he had carried with him from his hut in the village that had sprung up around Amphileph's temple. His mind wandered to the old warrior and the years of war already past. "Amphileph would be proud . . ." Tobor began, but he could not find the words to finish the sentence. He looked at his soldiers, and again his words failed him. The group seemed poised to hear him revel in the moment, but Tobor did not deliver the expected goading for drink and blood. Instead, he put his cup back down on the table and took a serious tone that passed through the room like a cold wind.

"I have thought long about how the Camonra should deal with the humans," he started again. "I have fought many battles against them, and as many of you have also found, what they lack in stature they add in determination. I have looked hard at the human 'threat' we have been assigned to eliminate, but I have found little threat at all."

There was a surprised look forming on the faces of several of the drunken soldiers. Many struggled with what they heard.

"No one will go into the forest again. We will not war with the humans unless they bring it upon themselves. Let us have no more of the humans, for what have they that the Camonra require?"

"Lord Amphileph would have them all killed!" one of the warriors yelled.

Tobor did not flinch. "Lord Amphileph would sacrifice every warrior among us if it suited his purpose."

There was a sudden silence. All eyes were upon him.

"This is blasphemy!" one of the Camonra burst out. He jumped upon the table and drew his sword. The cups and bowls flew across the table, and the Camon's upward swing lopped off the tip of one the general's dreadlocks hanging from his chin. He recovered quickly while Tobor drew his own sword, swinging downward a second time. Tobor leaned to the left, and the attacker's sword narrowly missed his head, removing the upper corner of Tobor's high-backed chair. Tobor's swing however, was unaffected by the drink, and his blade crashed into the side of the helmet of the young Camon, crushing the side of his helmet with the force. Blood sprayed from his nose, and the would-be insurgent flew from the table to the floor.

A second attacker stepped over the body and leapt at Tobor's retreat from the table. Tobor moved back toward his tent, and the circle of troops widened. This attacker was joined by a second and a third, and Tobor's back touched upon his shield hanging from one of the tent's outer supports.

"Our lives for Amphileph!" they shouted and moved in on him.

"If that is your choice, then I will oblige you!" Tobor shouted back at them. He grabbed up his shield in one hand and blocked the first thrust with his mighty sword in the other. He swung around, striking the one at his right with the edge of the shield just at the bridge of his nose, the sound of it ringing through his shield. That one crumpled instantly. Tobor reversed his hips and flipped his blade in his hand, running through the second attacker with the familiar sound of punctured leather and the thump of his tang stopping against the attacker's chest. The stitches in his side broke loose with his exertion, but Tobor was oblivious to it, allowing nothing to detract from the movement of his sword and the sounds of battle.

As the last of the attackers struggled to pull away, he tried to cry out, but no sound came out of his mouth, and his struggle slowly ended. He slid backward off Tobor's sword and collapsed to the floor. Tobor looked around the room for any other challengers. No one moved.

"Challenge me now, if you dare!" Tobor screamed at them and then drew in a great breath and bellowed. "*I command you!*"

Several of the elder soldiers dropped to one knee, lowering their heads, and a ripple effect passed over the entire group of soldiers.

Tobor's labored breathing was more from the excitement of the battle than his exertion, and it quickly subsided.

"Go not into Highwood! I command it!" Tobor shouted. "Find your wives! Build your dwellings! If the men of that place wish for war, the Camonra will show them no mercy! They are not welcome here, nor us there, so will we keep our distance. If men have brains enough to leave us be, then we shall do likewise!"

There was what seemed to Tobor a long silence before the grunt of acknowledgement rumbled back from the group.

"Throw these rebels on the fire!" he yelled, and several of the soldiers moved to carry away the dead.

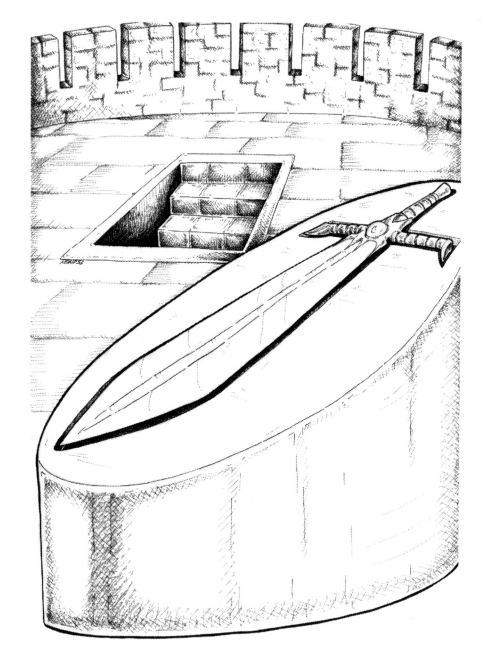

Chapter Fifteen

Altar for the Sword

For two months, Galbard wandered the wide-open plains north of the second mountain range that he had seen from the top of the Faceless Mountains, moving first to the west toward the beaches of the Western Shore. He longed for the warm air that blew in from the sea there, the warmer temperatures helping to thaw the Faceless Mountains' chill from his bones. Galbard's prayers were one-minded: asking his Creator to remove the threat that had stalked him since the day he set foot outside Rion.

It had seemed to him that his prayers had been answered, for he had not seen a soul since the encounter with the Camonra in the mountains to his north.

He wandered along the shore letting the ocean's waves crash upon his pant legs, their baggy leather saturated and sagging. He stood on the beach and looked to the sea, allowing the sand to trickle between his toes with the tide. He threw the thick boots that he had received from the refugees in the Faceless Mountains over his left shoulder; the thick wool coat, he had tied on top of the pack Mategaladh had given him. It had doubled as a bedroll quite nicely.

He had made his way around the second mountain range that lay south of the Faceless Mountains, and after most of another day, he came upon an abandoned sailboat big enough for ten or fifteen men. He glanced over the contents, and immediately recognized the tattered flag of Rion that snapped about in the strong winds blowing in from the ocean, and that alone was enough to spur him onward. He wanted no more encounters like Highwood, no more chances to tempt the Rionese with the power of the Sword. There had been so much death surrounding it, that at times he thought it might be best to cast it into the sea, and had it not been for his strong belief in Evliit's return, he would have done it.

Half a day more along the beaches, and he saw it—a structure that towered over the hillside. It was a structure like that of the oldest in Rion, and no matter its age, the architecture was unmistakable—Rionese hands must have certainly built it.

The tower's magnificent height must also have taken many years to construct, even with the latest techniques of the greatest builders in all of Erathe. How it could have been built without all of Rion knowing of it? He could not imagine. More importantly, a Rionese temple would likely have a contingent of Elders, and surely they would take the Sword of the Watch for safekeeping until Evliit returned for it. This thought made Galbard immediately begin a march in that direction.

* * *

In the fields east of Shintower, Cayden stood on a flat, circular stone about ten feet in diameter at the center of a little amphitheater. The stone was set upon two similar stones, each larger than the previous, forming a slightly raised platform in the concave excavation of the hillside. Jalin was trying to finish weaving flowers in a wrought iron arch beside him.

The amphitheater had stone seats surrounding it, and flowers lined four paths leading from the center platform. Pillars stood on either side of the four paths leading out from the circle, and there was an oil basin on top of each of the pillars. Jalin had made a hanger with wooden dowels and some string, and she had hung some silky white fabric from each of them. It tossed lazily in the gentle breeze of that beautiful day.

"Sometimes I can't believe how much this place has grown," said Cayden. From the little bit of elevation the platform afforded, he could see a line of fifty or sixty people coming toward the wedding circle from the Dales. "And this wedding circle—it's really nice. Your decorations are beautiful, Jalin. I can't thank you enough." He stood on his tiptoes and craned his neck, but he couldn't quite see the oil level in the basins atop the eight-foot high pillars, even with the added elevation of the platform. "They're bringing some oil for the basins, right?" asked Cayden. "I'm expecting the celebration to go into the night."

Jalin stopped what she was doing and looked toward the coming crowd. "I'm pretty sure some of those girls are carrying jars of oil," she said.

"I hope we have enough food," said Cayden. "That's a lot of people."

"To think we could even have a wedding in the Dales," she said. She used the back of her hand to wipe her forehead. "People are so fickle. One day they hate you, the next, they're dancing at your wedding."

Cayden looked down at the ground. He had worried his wedding to Nara might strike a nerve with Jalin. The closer the date had become, the more she had talked about moving on, getting past the loss of her husband, but the drive to reconnect with him had been replaced by more than a tinge of bitterness. He hated that.

"What can I do to help?" Cayden asked.

"Ro's exploring is making me crazy," Jalin said. "I keep thinking he's going to fall on the steps or run headlong into one of those benches."

"Ro!" Cayden said. "You need to settle down, little one." Ro stopped and looked at him. "Into the grass with you!" he said, grabbing him up off the stone steps and patting him on the backside in that general direction. Ro chuckled and ran into the grass.

"Thank you, Cayden," Jalin said, sighing.

"Oh, when they learn to walk!" Cayden laughed. Ro started back up the steps, and Cayden grabbed him up, tossing him up in the air. The funny face turned to a brief instant of panic until Cayden's strong hands caught him up, and then a giggle bubbled from Ro's lips.

"I've got you, little man!" Cayden laughed. He turned his gaze to Jalin, and his smile faded. She was fighting back tears.

"Men and boys," she said, batting her eyelids. She caught a tear falling from the corner of her eye with one shaking finger. "I miss his father so much, you know, I . . . ." She stopped and shook her head. "No, no, I'm sorry. I refuse to let anything spoil this wonderful day."

"Hey, it's okay," Cayden said. He looked at Ro and back to her. "Keep your faith, Jalin."

Jalin forced a smile. "Come here, Ro!" she said, reaching for him, and then admonished Cayden, "If you don't stop all this excitement, he'll never sit still during the ceremony!"

"That will make two of us," Cayden replied, but his laughter was cut short when the crowd coming from the Dales neared the wedding circle. They were abuzz with laughter and talking. Some carried stools and tables; others brought baskets of food and instruments.

Two young men walked around the stone benches and placed a table just outside the wedding circle on the hill closest to Shintower. The musicians roosted upon one of the benches, tinkering with their instruments, while the clergy in their hooded garb stood along the edge of the circle and watched the procession, talking quietly among themselves. Some of the men began pitching two wedding tents, one on either side of the circle along the paths that lead to the platform.

Two young girls approached him and Jalin. Cayden was amused how seriously they took themselves and their baskets of summer sausage and crackers and cheese. "Excuse us, please," one of them said.

"Excuse *me*, ladies," Cayden responded. He watched them skillfully weave among all the others that were busily decorating.

"It's time to go!" Jalin said, grabbing him by the arm. "Nara doesn't want you to see her before the wedding!"

* * *

Galbard had slipped behind the pillar marking the path from the wedding circle to Shintower. He had seen the crowd of people coming from the village, and the sounds of celebration drew him in. It had been so long since he had heard laughter. In the chaotic jubilee, he had moved toward the wedding circle unnoticed, but when he saw Jalin, he was overwhelmed with emotion. She carried a child and was arm in arm with another man. He was confused, furious, and crushed, and he could think of nothing else but getting away from there, away from them. He pushed off from the pillar and headed directly for the tower.

She's gone on with her life, had a child, and settled down, he thought, wrestling with the revelation.

For over two years, he'd thought about the day he left her for the Soru plant harvest, how sure he'd been that the money he'd make would save their marriage, and how sure he was that she would recant her rebuke of him. It had been the very hope that had driven him to survive his enslavement by the Camonra, to survive his journey to return the sword to Evliit. Now that hope was shattered, and he struggled with the meaning of it all. He had been convinced that delivering the sword would tip the scales of fate for him at last, and this one great feat of bravery would somehow bring him back to the one he loved. Now he was sure of nothing. *Perhaps the sword's commission was but a penance, and the journey to return it not but a time to savor its sting.*

"No!" he shouted, stopping in mid-stride and looking up at the sky. "Give me strength!" *This is beyond my relationship with Jalin. Amphileph must be stopped from destroying all that I have ever known. The sword must be returned to the Elders, to Evliit.*

He tried to clear his mind and focus. A Rionese wedding might easily go on for a couple of days, and with the Rionese custom of inviting everyone in the village for food and drink, music and dancing, the tower would be as unguarded as it would ever be. It might be his only real chance to take the Sword into the tower in secrecy.

Galbard moved around the southern side of the tower's outer wall and confirmed that indeed, the guards were few. Several of them had moved to the eastern side of the walled courtyard to see the procession. He slipped silently into the courtyard through the western entrance and moved to the massive first floor door.

He was contemplating how he might enter, when suddenly the door creaked open. Two of the guards pushed open the great doors of the tower. This was his chance.

"The wedding's today?" he heard one of them ask.

"Yes, yes," said the other excitedly. "Lots of food, and I heard that Isha will be there."

"That's all for you, then," the first laughed. "How can you be expected to stand your post when Isha sings?"

"We could stand watch at the eastern gate—you could give me your horn, and I could watch while you go for a bit, and then I could go when you come back."

"Yes, that could work," said the other. "First one to the eastern gate gets to go first to the party!" he said, laughing as he took off running.

The second guard quickly gave chase toward the eastern exit of the courtyard. The great doors slowly began to close, and Galbard waited until the last possible moment for them to get the farthest away, and then he slipped inside just before the doors closed.

The Swordbearer moved his back to the wall and listened, looking upward at the vaulting that crisscrossed the tower's first floor ceiling with its skyward-leaping walls. There was a large stone column in the center of the room, and a spiral stair wrapped around the outer wall that led upward, its flight so incredibly high that Galbard could not see its end.

Scattered about were mason and carpentry tools of all types, apparently supporting any number of projects in various stages of completion. He could see what appeared to be a prayer room off the main wing, and across the way beside a six-inch-thick locked door, he could see a weapons armory through metal bars.

There were alcoves with slotted windows along the rising central tower and outer walls, allowing light to fall lattice-like on the structures within. Galbard held the sword and its scabbard with his left hand as he proceeded, to prevent any noise as he ran across the main floor to the staircase.

He thumped his back against the wall—the lack of sound from his impact hinted at the massive thickness of the walls themselves. Galbard had seen the newer structures of Rion rise up, their construction requiring the resources of the entire city for half a decade.

How could they have built this just since the quake?

Galbard was rounding the staircase quietly. The tower door moved again. The two guards returned inside, followed by another soldier, who was shouting a reprimand of some sort.

"We're sorry, sergeant," one of the guards responded. "We wasn't trying to do no harm."

"You stand your watch!" the sergeant barked. "You stand it *here!*"

"Yes, sir!" they answered, and when the sergeant exited, Galbard could hear them still bickering.

He moved with swift stealth up the steps that spiraled around the stone column of the tower, branching off to landings with floors and rooms upon each. He searched several rooms, but he found no Elders anywhere. In fact, most of the rooms had no furnishings at all.

At times, Galbard could hear singing and clapping, and when he neared a window slit, there was music in the distance, the faint sounds of fife and fiddle, drum and tambourine—he could even make out the melodic percussion of a hammered dulcimer.

Finally, Galbard reached the top floor. The wind whistled through the slanted opening to the sky. Cautiously he poked his head up at the upper deck level, looking for another guard post. He saw nothing but some sculptor's chisels and stone in a neatly swept pile aside.

He chanced a look upward, but the tower's height gave him a little vertigo. The sky was deep, the heavens' thick black canvas broken only by the stars' tiny points of light showing through like needle pricks.

Galbard stepped out onto the tower's roof. He could see the top of the large column that ran the height of the tower. It protruded from the upper deck, the crown cut at an angle and highly polished. At its center, the shape of a sword was etched in its face. Instantly, he recognized the shape as that of Evliit's Sword.

This must be it! Galbard thought. *This must be the place that I was destined to find.*

This was no coincidence. There was no mistaking the painstaking detail. The sculptured stone was a perfect match. Surely this was the Sword's final resting place, this high perch where Evliit himself might reach down and pick it up.

He drew the Sword, and held it before the perfectly etched outline, and then he turned away, daring himself to test the fit. He walked to the edge of the steps leading back into the tower, and hearing nothing, he walked again to the edge of the deck and looked over. He could see the wedding party and a crowd of onlookers far below, and then he walked back and examined the stone cradle again. Gently, he placed the Sword into its marble top. It fit perfectly.

"I've made it," he said. He placed his hands on either side of the Sword on the marble surface and called upon the power of the Sword to signal Evliit of its return.

The stone's face began to glow, and a heat began to be generated from below the surface of the stone, forcing Galbard to step back. Inside itself, the very tower rumbled, the structures' vibrations making him lean over the Sword and steady himself on the altar. Air rushed all around him. Galbard tried again to look to the heavens, fully expecting to see Evliit as before, but the movement of the tower beneath him made looking up even more unsettling.

* * *

"How can this be?" Aleris, the leader of the Bhre-Nora, demanded. "Someone's activated the tower's defenses!" He adjusted his goggles and flew around the stone column that ran the height of the cavernous room from the bedrock far below, up through the cavern's center, through a hundred feet of stone and rising through the tower to the very altar Galbard had placed the sword upon.

Here, deep beneath the tower, a flurry of activity filled the airspace of the cavern. Here is where the Bhre-Nora lived, tending a monstrosity of copper piping, connecting valves and tanks of every shape and fed seemingly from every direction by a coil of piping wrapped around the stone column that had begun glowing.

Off the central cavern was a labyrinth of arch-ceilinged tunnels, stairwells, and catacomb-like anterooms opening into other rooms. The Bhre-Nora's simple dugout dwellings lined the walls of the cavern, where frequently the busy sprites buzzed back and forth between rest and work, regaled in their goggles and leather caps, their long, leather coats, elbow-length gloves and tall boots that protected them from the frequent jets of steam or scalding water. They were an exceptionally nimble race of beings, zipping between the twisting piping in coordinated groups like birds in a flock, working together to tackle valves, chains, and levers that required their combined strength.

The stone's heat radiated through the coil, and the temperature in the room rose almost instantly. Movement began to occur seemingly everywhere at once. Counterweights, slides, and pistons sprang to life, turning a series of gears and belts of a myriad of sizes. The pipes banged and jumped, squealed and screamed. Steam spurted out sporadically around the valves and all along the piping at almost every other connection.

The Bhre-Nora dispersed through the tunnels by foot and by wing, tightening bolts and connections with tiny tools wherever they could.

Aleris launched himself into the air and through the piping with unparalleled grace. He sighted a group of his kin madly trying to open several valves on a group of pipes. The piping began to rattle so badly that they were having great difficulty holding on to the handles with their wrenches.

He passed three others working on a small tank at the intersection of several tunnels. "Blow down that line! Watch the pressure!" he yelled. "Be sure that—"

He was cut short by the shrill banshee of escaping steam, punctuated by the *pop—pop—pop* of rivets flying from a seam. With an explosion of scalding vapor, a plug blew off the tank and ricocheted around the room, damaging several other pipes, but narrowly missing all of his workers, most of whom had hit the ground and covered their heads. The billowing steam completely engulfed Aleris and the other sprites. A deafening roar issued from the open hole in the tank, ending only after Aleris and the others managed to close the valve to the pipes coming from the stone core. They had been lucky, Aleris thought, that only the plug had ruptured and not the tank, for that surely would have killed them all.

"Find that plug!" he screamed. "And get it back in that tank! Riveters!"

The workers immediately began helping each other to their feet, searching about the room while a team of riveters began working on the seam, beating the two pieces back into alignment. Three of them threw back the hatch into the tank, flew inside, and worked the red-hot rivets with their counterparts on the outside, mushrooming the heads of the rivets with their hammers.

Unaware of the chaos occurring beneath his feet, Cayden stood on the circular platform under the flower-lined arches in the sacred circle of his and Nara's hand fastening. Two of the women had donned robes and, to the music of a tambourine and a lute, were spreading sea salt around the wedding circle. Following them around the circle, one of the young men walked with a sword drawn, a hint back to the pagan days before the Elders forbade such rituals of white magic. Cayden did not care much for the ritual, but it seemed harmless enough, and the women making the food for the wedding celebration seemed adamant about performing it to ward off evil, so he just let them have their way. But all he wanted was to see Nara. When they had chanted and circled him three times, they sat down on the stone benches, and finally, the moment had arrived.

He watched Nara emerge from her wedding tent, and his heart began pumping wildly. He thought she had never looked so beautiful. Her eyes lit up, and a broad smile crossed her face. She walked slowly toward Cayden and reached out her hand to him. "You look absolutely incredible," he whispered.

"I thought that *you* looked a bit frightened," she said, letting out a giggle. "It was beyond my wildest dreams that the love I feel for you could grow even more, but when I saw your face, it grew even more in that very moment."

Cayden lifted her hand and kissed it. He opened his mouth to say something, but the loud grinding and groaning of gears turning startled them all. Behind them, the tower suddenly roared to life. A rumbling of chains and machinery launching into gear completely stopped the progression of the wedding. Steam shot into the sky from the upper deck of the tower.

"What is happening?" Nara yelled above the din. Cayden thought her face was a combination of fear, anger, and disappointment.

"I . . . I don't know!" Cayden stammered.

The ground suddenly quaked beneath them, and she fell into his arms. Chaos overtook the grounds around the tower, and guards were running in every direction. The walls of the outer court began to quake. A grinding noise of stone on stone shook the air, and the inner wall's ring shifted, closing the gaps between the wall segments and forming a solid wall of stone.

On the roof of the tower, Galbard was just as taken aback. He tried to gain his feet, but the tower shook and growled with activity. Dust puffed around the perimeter of the column where it passed through the tower's top deck, and then there was a clattering of what sounded to Galbard like stone gears.

Galbard fell forward and looked back over the deck's edge. He could see dust stirring on the grounds below him, and the sounds of whooshing air, ratcheting chains, and stones colliding rocked the tower to its core. He struggled to regain his feet and grabbed the Sword from its resting place, its link of mysterious energy visibly breaking into feathery wisps like a dissipating gas.

The tower's altar stone suddenly dimmed.

Deep in the bowels below the tower, the Bhre-Nora leader smacked the side of his head, perplexed. "Now what's this then?" Aleris yelled. "Stop everything! You know what to do!" The workers scrambled about, turning hundreds of valves to reroute the rapidly building steam pressure to the outside vents. The order to stop repeated throughout the tunnels beneath the tower, unheard by human ears far above them.

Three hundred feet above Aleris, Galbard could see steam shooting into the air from exhaust ports around the tower's courtyard and the upper deck's perimeter. As inexplicably as it had begun, the activity slowed to a stop and things returned to their places.

The tower's violent vibration ended with its internal grumblings, and Galbard placed the Sword back into its scabbard. He made for the stairwell, but he heard the sounds of shouting and running feet within the tower. Trying to stop, he slipped onto his haunches, scooting back from the stairs until his back was against the still warm altar stone at the deck's center.

"Evliit, why do you not claim the Sword?" Galbard questioned.

Several armed guards sprang out of the stairwell and surrounded him. "Hold!" he yelled at them, but they drew their swords and lowered their spears to his chest level. "I am not your enemy!" he said. "I only mean to return the Sword to its rightful owner!"

The man he had seen arm in arm with Jalin sprang through the stairwell onto the tower's upper deck and burst into the group. "Stand down!" he yelled, trying to catch his breath. "Stand down!"

The man moved to the front of the soldiers and stood within the circle between them and Galbard. "I am called Cayden," the man said, and he looked as if he was searching Galbard's expression for some clue to his intentions. Galbard saw Cayden's eyes drift to the Sword, and then Cayden's jaw fell open. "Are you Galbard?" he asked.

Galbard was speechless for a moment. "How do you know my name?"

"In the name of the Creator!" Cayden shouted, unable to take his eyes off the sword. "You are the one we have been waiting for!" He turned his attention to the guards. "Lower your weapons! Lower your weapons at once!" He looked around for the guards to comply. "This is the one we have waited for! This is the bearer of the Sword of the Watch!"

"What is the meaning of this?" a tiny, high-pitched, and obviously annoyed voice rang out.

"Aleris!" Cayden said.

Aleris removed his goggles. He buzzed in front of Cayden's face, and Galbard saw the tiny creature's face squeeze together in a scowl.

"You cannot just call upon the tower's defenses without—" Aleris began, and then he saw the Sword of the Watch in Galbard's hand. "My lord, forgive me. I have not shown my place!" Aleris immediately flew to the ground at Galbard's feet and bowed on one knee.

Cayden and the other men followed suit, leaving the stunned Galbard leaning against the stone altar looking at them in disbelief.

"I meant no harm!" Galbard announced.

Aleris's head popped up, and he sprang into the air and bobbed before Galbard. "My lord, you are among friends of the Sword. We are at your service!"

Galbard was still stunned. "I'm not sure what is happening."

"It is no mistake, sire, your being here," Aleris said.

"We've been waiting for you for many months," Cayden said.

"Here indeed is the bearer of the Sword!" Aleris accented his words with a quick circling in the air. "But why has the bearer of the Sword initiated its defense?"

"I am sorry to have caused such turmoil, and at a wedding no less," Galbard said. "It looked surely as if the Sword belonged in this place, on that altar. I thought for a moment that I might lay it there and Evliit might return for it. I thought I might do so undiscovered and take my leave in peace. I flee the Camonra, and I had hoped my journey had ended."

"Camonra!" Aleris said. He shot up a few feet above them so that he might see over the edge of the upper deck to the grounds below.

"No, no," Galbard said. "I left them in the farthest mountain range to the north. I've been running from the Camonra ever since I was given the Sword," he said. "There seems no safe place for a weapon such as this."

Aleris returned to their eye level. "You have found sanctuary here, sire," he said. "This is Shintower, an altar for the mighty sword. You are safe here."

Galbard let out a deep breath. "Safe?" he asked. "I have not felt safe in a very long time. You could not have said more good to me than words such as that."

"Come with me, sire," said Aleris. "We have much to discuss."

"Discuss all you will later," Cayden offered. "But for now, you and I must speak to the swordbearer alone."

Aleris looked at Cayden and then to the soldiers. "But of course," he said.

"That will be all," Cayden said, signaling the soldiers, who nodded and immediately marched down the stairwell.

Galbard came to his feet, and the three of them stood silent in the steady northwest breeze. Galbard spoke first. "I have seen you with Jalin, but I have no quarrel with you."

It was obviously Cayden's turn to be stunned. "I was struggling to think of how to tell you about Jalin, but now I'm even more confused. I don't know what you mean."

"In the wedding circle—I saw that she was with you."

Cayden's stunned look turned puzzled, and then his eyes opened wide. "No, sire, not *with* me," Cayden chuckled nervously. "Your wife was decorating for my wedding day."

"*Your* wedding day? But I saw you with Jalin and a boy . . . ." mumbled Galbard, his voice trailing off. He took a deep breath and sat back against the altar.

Cayden approached him and put his hand on his shoulder. "This must be a great deal to fathom. Jalin has told Nara and I many times of your last day together, of your argument and the harsh words that were spoken. It's by the grace of the Creator that they are here, it can be nothing else. They should have died in Rion like so many others, but they are here with us, and the Creator has brought you here as well. I can only imagine what you must feel, but you must know that she misses you very much. The boy's name is Ronan, and he is *your* child."

"A son," Galbard said. He was silent for another moment, and then he looked up at Cayden and cleared his throat. "Could you tell them that I would like to see them?"

"Come then, my friend, you can tell them yourself," said Cayden. He took Galbard by the hand and lifted him to his feet. "Won't you honor Nara and I with your presence?"

Aleris flew in front of them, hovering at head height. "Wait!" he said. "The Creator has brought you here to Shintower for your own protection. You can't just carry the Sword of the Watch around in the open. Surely, you realize by now that Amphileph and all his minions will not sleep until they possess it."

"What are you saying?" asked Cayden. "Are you trying to say that he can't even see them?"

"I'm saying that Amphileph would not hesitate to use them to get to him. He will only endanger his wife and child by bringing them into this." Aleris moved closer to Galbard's face. "No one should know of your relationship to them, for their own protection."

"I'm sorry, Aleris, but you ask too much. I've not seen my wife for two years, and I've never seen my son before today," Galbard said.

"I can see that you care for them very much, and it's for that reason that I warn you. Meet them only in secret, at least until we've completed Shintower's defenses and the escape tunnels for the catacombs. Then you can judge for yourself whether they're safer here with you, or if they should be far away from here."

Galbard's face tightened. "If she will come, please ask her to come and bring the child with her. I must see them," he said.

Cayden looked at him. "I can tell you without doubt, she longs to see you. Tonight, after the wedding, I will tell her to come to Shintower."

"It will be done in secret?" asked Aleris looking at Galbard, then Cayden.

Galbard nodded.

"In secret then," said Cayden.

* * *

In the distance, Rendaya stood at the edge of Southwood, looking upon the great tower. She had felt an urgent desire to take the walk from her home in the deeper wood that afternoon, and she had arrived in plenty of time to watch the tower roar to life on the horizon and then grow silent once more. She somehow knew that it was a good sign, and she was confident Aleris would quickly report to her the events of the night.

The past few months had been unreal, even for one that had looked deeply into the inner workings of their universe. For weeks after the arrival of the Rionese refugees, she had prayed for the whirlwind to come, often fasting, often feeling as if she might have misread the signs about the coming of the bearer of the Sword. Doubt had encircled her, and she had been unable to see what the Creator intended for her to do. The arrival of the Bhre-Nora completely revitalized her spiritually and gave her peace of mind that her vigil had altered the course of events, but it had taken a heavy physical toll.

Until she had regained her strength, Aleris had been kind enough to update her regularly in every possible aspect of the project, first at her bedside, and then daily in her garden.

She must have been deep in thought, for she had not even heard Aleris's approach. He flew upon a branch at about her eye level and sat down, looking quite winded.

"Aleris! You startled me!" Rendaya reacted.

"I'm sorry, my lady," said Aleris. "But I could not wait to give you the news! The Sword of the Watch resides in Shintower!"

Aleris spoke on excitedly, but Rendaya's mind drifted. While she had rested for months, the Bhre-Nora had toiled beneath the tower, fashioning defenses that only they might build. Physical rest had barely quieted her feelings of anxiousness, but for the first time in a long time, she realized the sword was safely tucked away with the Bhre-Nora in Shintower. A thin smile came to her face.

"You have done well, my friend," Rendaya said.

"How well I've done remains to be seen, my lady."

Rendaya's smile faded slightly. "That it does, Aleris. That it does."

* * *

Galbard watched the wedding from the height of the tower's upper deck, anxiously awaiting the time when he might see Jalin and his son. It had grown very late before the wedding celebrants began to disband for the night, but he was not tired. In fact, the closer he thought he was to seeing them, the faster his pulse seemed to race.

Sometime after midnight, Galbard heard someone coming up the stairwell, and then Cayden appeared with Nara on the upper deck. Jalin walked behind them. She was carrying the sleeping child, and she looked frightened.

"Let me hold Ro for a minute," Nara said. She leaned into Jalin and lifted him away.

"Why are we here?" Jalin asked. "To tell you the truth, I don't like this place."

Galbard moved out of the darkness toward them. "Jalin?" he asked before Cayden or Nara could say a word more.

Jalin saw Galbard then, and her knees buckled.

"Whoa!" exclaimed Cayden. He caught her arm and held on to her. "Steady."

"Galbard?" she asked. She looked at him as if she still couldn't believe it. "Is it really you?" Tears welled in her eyes.

"Yes, my love," he replied. "I'm here."

"We'll take Ro downstairs for a moment," Cayden suggested. Galbard and Jalin nodded, and Cayden and Nara turned and descended the staircase.

Jalin waited no longer. She ran to him and threw her arms around him. Her emotion rocked him, but then he wrapped his arms around her and laid his head upon hers. He stroked her hair and lifted her chin to look into her eyes. They kissed passionately, and then Jalin looked into his eyes.

"I'm so sorry," she said. "I . . . ."

"Don't say another word, I just want to hold you," he said. "I've missed you more than you'll ever know."

They stood there in the cool of the deep night, her crying and thanking the Creator for his return, and him retelling the story of his capture by the Camonra, his receiving the sword from Evliit, and his incredible journey to the upper deck of Shintower.

Shortly afterward, Cayden and Nara returned. Jalin went to Nara and took Ro, and she held the sleeping baby up to Galbard.

"This is your son," she said.

Galbard took him and held him in his arms. He kissed the child on the cheek, unable to take his eyes off him. "He's beautiful."

"May we never again be apart," Jalin said.

Cayden shuffled nervously. "We must talk about that."

"What?" asked Jalin. She turned to Galbard. "What does he mean by that?"

"The tower's defenses and escape tunnels are not complete," Galbard answered. "You and Ro would be in great danger staying here until we can finish what we have started."

"No!" exclaimed Jalin. "We will not leave you again."

Galbard pulled her into him. "Jalin, listen to me," he said. "Amphileph himself is looking for this sword. If word arrives that Amphileph is making his way to Shintower, and our preparations are not complete, you must flee. Go to the Western Shores and then north to the second mountain range. You can follow the mountains east to Moonledge Peak. Many of our people are there." He looked at Ro again. The boy's face was peaceful. He arched his back and raised the knuckles of one hand to his mouth, and then he snuggled his face against Galbard's chest. "We must not tell anyone of our relationship. If Amphileph knew of you, he would come for you to get to me."

"You can't leave us! We'll take our chances here with you!" Jalin exclaimed.

It was silent for a moment. Galbard handed the baby back to Jalin. "Listen to what you're saying. I could never do what must be done to protect the sword as long as I knew you were in danger."

"Then we're a distraction?" asked Jalin. "Is that what we are?"

Galbard let out a deep sigh. He could see the deeply pained expression in her face. "No, Jalin," he answered. "How can I explain this to you? The hope of seeing you again was the reason that I survived my time in

Amphileph's dungeons. You and Ro are my life. No matter what happens, I want to protect you. If the situation made me choose, I would choose you, and many people could die."

"Jalin, you know that Nara and I want nothing but the best for you," said Cayden, looking rather hesitant at jumping into the conversation. "The Bhre-Nora are amazing. They'll complete their preparations quickly, and then you and Ro can be here with Galbard. Let them complete their work so that you and Ro are safe."

"You will be close, Jalin," said Galbard. "Cayden and I have arranged a place for you and Ro. Cayden and Nara will be there also, right across the road from you."

"In the Dales, Jalin. We'll be just over there," he said pointing toward the little village.

Galbard wrapped his arms around her and the sleeping child. "We've made it this far. We can get past this."

Jalin attempted to smile. "I want to be with you now, but I understand," she said. "You're only concerned for us." She moved from his arms, and looked at Cayden and Nara. "We should probably go."

Galbard tried not to show his disappointment, but when Jalin looked at him, he couldn't help it. "I love you, Jalin," he said, reaching out to her, but she turned away. Fighting back tears, she hurried down the stairs. Cayden nodded, and he and Nara followed behind her.

Galbard turned away from them and looked east. The burden of the sword seemed greatest in that very moment.

Chapter Sixteen

Imperfect Cage

Citanth's carriage stopped to the north of the Binding. There remained but a few of the warriors that had avoided Galbard's summoning of the power of the Sword of the Watch in the Faceless Mountains. Most had died after its powerful blast of energy had shaken the very foundations of the mountainside, and most of the remaining wounded died in transit back to Amphileph's temple.

Citanth had taken the better part of two weeks to return from the mountains, chiefly due to his loathing giving such news to Amphileph.

He exited the valley leading to Amphileph's temple, but the situation got no better. Even from a distance, Citanth could see that there was no one remaining in the northern camp, and the villages within the Binding seemed scarcely alive. Furniture blocked the windows of the small huts as if the occupants were trying to keep something out.

Citanth exited his carriage and moved to the northern edge of the Binding Spell, stopping just short of the markers that outlined the spell's edge. "Wait here," Citanth commanded his attendants, and then he moved toward the Binding Spell. He scanned the area, but there was no sign of life. He moved along the perimeter of the force field, off the path, and east.

"Amphileph!" Citanth cried out.

There was a fire smoldering on the southern side of the Camonra huts, causing a thick white smoke that drifted lazily along the ground. A small dog seemed to appear out of the haze. It stared back at Citanth with sad eyes, but remained perfectly motionless, save for the twitch of its left ear. Its face was bloody and matted, and a yelp from beside it made his head jump suddenly. Another dog scurried out from the smoke and turned toward Citanth, and then sat down and panted, its ears back. There was the outline of what appeared to be a ditch, with the dirt thrown out from it as if something had exploded.

Citanth squatted to look more closely, and his movement caused the little animal to bolt, disappearing once again into the thick smoke. "In the name of the Creator," Citanth said under his breath.

The decomposing bodies of the other Watchers still lay where they had fallen, though the dogs of the Camonra were busily scattering their remains. They nipped at each other, and the pack tore the once holy prophets apart like so much scrap meat. Citanth's nose wrinkled with the smell of death that drifted on the slow-moving smoke.

There was the sound of glass breaking, and Citanth moved back upon the path and forward until the energy field of the Binding pushed against him strongly enough to cause his footing to slide back. It was a strange sensation, repelling him like the forces of magnetism he had studied with such great enthusiasm under Amphileph so very long ago.

There was cursing in the old tongue, and Amphileph appeared at the entrance to his chambers, his head down, scrawling something on a piece of paper.

"Amphileph!" said Citanth.

Amphileph made no sign that he had even heard Citanth, but seemed completely preoccupied with a large set of brass tubing and flasks assembled in the courtyard, interconnecting what appeared to be all the equipment that had once occupied Amphileph's alchemy laboratory. There was a beaten path lying between the equipment and the temple.

"Amphileph!" Citanth yelled again, holding his sleeve up to cover his nose, and for a moment, Amphileph appeared to notice Citanth.

"Could you not retrieve my property, Citanth?" Amphileph asked. "Could you not even retrieve my property from a simple Rionese slave?"

Citanth stiffened. "He has learned of the Sword's powers, my lord. I followed him past the woods of Calarph, into the Faceless Mountains. He was cornered by the soldiers, and we attacked him in force," Citanth said.

"You failed me as I knew you would, you sniveling fool!" Amphileph said. A red glow surrounded Amphileph's hand, and he ran across the courtyard, thrusting his hand into the force field of the Binding Spell, directly at Citanth heart. His hand slowed to a stop in the force field, and energy crackled and dispersed through the force field like bolts of red lightning skipping among clouds. The energy emanating from

Amphileph's hand suddenly stopped, and he fell upon his back and burst into laughter.

Citanth watched Amphileph's reaction and felt like crying. "Do not laugh at me!" he said. "You will not laugh at me!" Citanth stepped toward the spell's edge, pushing against it.

"We had him cornered, ready to destroy him!" he shouted. "We attacked him in force, and he released the power of the Sword upon us, destroying everything around him. I had no choice but to flee!"

The disgust in Amphileph's face was unmistakable. He jerked up to support himself with one hand, pointing the ink-stained finger of the other back at Citanth's face. "You are worthless, Citanth! You are utterly worthless!" he screamed, veins bulging in his neck and eyes. "Wasn't it you who I first sent to take the Sword from Evliit's sleeping hand?" he asked, his sentence wrapping into a laugh that boiled Citanth's blood.

Amphileph stared up at the sky. "How can it be that the most incompetent of us all would be on *that* side of this Binding and I *here*?" he asked the heavens. He looked at the dogs fighting over the remains of the other Spellmakers. A twisted smile crossed his face. The dogs became frenzied, barking and howling and whining. "But of course! They know it, too!"

Amphileph ranted on, and the smile evaporated. "Is there anyone who does not know of your absolute impotence? You who looked upon the Sword for your own taking? How could an imbecile like you even believe for a moment that *you* could lead the Spellmakers?" Amphileph asked. His face became deeply red, and then he burst into laughter again. "I will kill you, Citanth! I will snuff out your life without raising so much as a finger!"

Citanth looked beyond Amphileph, distracted momentarily by the tearing sounds of the dogs ripping apart the corpses' bloody clothing. The look on the dog's faces seemed suddenly horrific, their bloodstained teeth bared, their lips curled up. They snarled with their eyes wide and wild, and they dug in their heels and jerked on the sleeve of a Watcher, his partially rotted hand flailing in the tug of war. The sight made Citanth raise his hand to cover his nose and mouth.

Amphileph's rambling stopped. He rolled up on one elbow, studying Citanth intently. Citanth slowly lowered his hand and looked at it himself, confused by Amphileph's sudden curiosity. He stared at the strips of dirty cloth, saturated in spots with blood. It was like a shoddy veil covering what once had been his right hand. The memories of touching the mighty Sword began to flood his mind.

Amphileph suddenly jumped to his feet and ran back toward the temple, appearing to only half notice a set of intricately placed stones around a map of sorts drawn in the dirt. He plowed through the middle of it and disappeared in the smoke. There were again the sounds of glass breaking in the lab and Amphileph shouting. The master Spellmaker seemed thoroughly mad.

Moments later, Amphileph appeared again in a dead run, smiling like Citanth had not seen in some time. He looked strangely happy, Citanth thought, and he came to a stop right in front of him, waving the smoke along with him with his arms, and then seemingly cupping it in his upturned hand. It feathered around him in the micro-currents of air that followed in his path.

"Amphileph?" Citanth queried.

"Gases are amazing, are they not?" Amphileph asked. "Do you remember when we spent a whole season boiling water, trying desperately to understand its properties? Do you remember when I forced the water through the cloth? How we'd purified the water of Rion for the sacraments?" he asked almost giddy with excitement. "Must make a note of that," Amphileph said, and he returned to scrawling something on the paper. Citanth could see that there was little left of the tattered parchment, and Amphileph's palm was black with ink. Amphileph noticed Citanth's interest in it, and he quickly stuffed the parchment in a pocket and turned away, mumbling to himself.

"My lord, the Sword Bearer has disappeared in the mountains," Citanth began again, attempting to regain his composure. "He is likely—"

Amphileph snapped around to Citanth, a sudden intensity taking control of his face. "You covered your nose, Citanth!" he shouted back at him, and then he burst out in laughter.

"Yes, my lord, I was overcome by the stench," Citanth responded. "This whole place smells of death."

"You miss my point, Citanth," said Amphileph.

The joyous look on Amphileph's face was indeed distracting Citanth from seeing any point at all.

Amphileph moved closer to him, to the edge of the Binding. "The bodies are in here; you're out there, yes?"

Before Citanth could answer, Amphileph carefully removed a small vile from his cloak. Citanth watched Amphileph gingerly remove the intricately carved glass cap from the bottle, and the red liquid within the bottle vaporized almost instantly. Amazed, Citanth watched the vapor began to swirl slowly in the air. When it made contact with the Binding, it dispersed.

"Watch! Watch!" shouted Amphileph. After a moment, it appeared that the vapor was recombining in the air just outside the Binding.

"My lord?" Citanth began, but the dark red vapor suddenly crossed the distance between them and struck him the chest, throwing him some thirty paces back across the temple grounds.

Amphileph laughed hysterically. The vapor raced across the courtyard, lifted the carriage out of the hands of the servants and raised it some twenty feet off the ground. It hovered effortlessly, and then it fell to the ground, the force snapping off its front wooden struts and collapsing the covered frame for its once royal rider. The servants witnessed little of it, for they ran toward the western valley the very instant it had lifted out of their hands, never looking back.

Citanth lay on the ground beside the broken carriage. He lifted his head just in time to see Amphileph wave his hands, and then the red vapor moved through the grass in waves toward him. His body flew again through the air.

"Not all my spell-making fails!" Amphileph screamed with delight. "I can make use of this!" he said, turning back to his laboratory. The vapor dissipated, and Citanth crashed back down upon the ground.

Chapter Seventeen

Uneasy Peace

Two winters had passed since Galbard's arrival at Shintower. Two winters without a sign of the Camonra; two winters without war or any communication from Rion. Ever vigilant, Galbard stood his post with Evliit's sword, watching over his son and wife from a distance. He had been sure the Camonra would come for him, challenging Aleris daily on the progress of the tower's defenses and tunnels. The pressure had taken its toll, and Galbard was weary.

The former artisans of Rion had done anything but stand still in that time. Small shops had sprung up throughout the Dales, and a sense of normalcy had returned to their daily lives. With the days of the Witch of Southwood apparently behind them, they seemed oblivious to further danger.

Galbard listened to Cayden's regular updates about life for Jalin and his son. She was forging a new identity separate from that of his wife, and though that separation tore at Galbard's heart, he remained steadfast to his duty. The entire experience made them somewhat distant, and even when she had come to him in secret, the distance between them remained, and Galbard worried for a love lost. For two winters, Galbard had kept to himself, locked away in the upper two floors of Shintower.

Today, a beautiful blue sky stretched across the southern part of Etharath, and once again, Galbard had made his way to the upper deck of the tower. He was surveying those scurrying below him with such great interest that he did not hear Cayden ascend the stairs behind him.

"I thought I might find you here," said Cayden.

"As if it had ever been difficult to find me," Galbard laughed.

Cayden smiled. "It is that difficulty I wanted to talk about," Cayden began. Galbard noticed that Cayden was stalling.

"Well, spit it out," Galbard said. "You know how much I hate to see you worried!"

Cayden laughed aloud at that. "Yes, I know." He moved to sit on one of the stone seats that surrounded the Sword's altar and looked around at the other empty seats. "We have discussed many things here, my friend: important matters about the future of our people, the workings of our great temple, even times when we pondered a war that never came." Cayden paused, and Galbard turned to look at him. Cayden closed his eyes and lifted his face to the cool touch of the wind.

"Something is bothering you, friend?" probed Galbard. "Was it not you that said to me, 'you are among friends' on this very site—there is nothing we cannot speak about."

"Jalin needs you," Cayden blurted out, and Galbard's next words failed him. "She knows that you have provided much for her and Ro, but they need *you*. She spoke of this with Nara, and Nara has asked me—"

Galbard burst out in somewhat nervous laughter. "Nara has told *you* to come to me about Jalin?"

Cayden's face reddened. "Do not make this harder than it has to be, Galbard. Nara and I care for you both very much, and things are different now. Aleris reports that the Bhre-Nora have completed their work in the catacombs below the temple, and many a man from the Dales would swear allegiance to the Sword, if you but call upon them to do so. You don't have to stand this watch alone." Cayden let out a sigh. "You know all these things, Galbard, but you have not brought Jalin and the boy to the tower, and that has Jalin very confused." He glanced away. "There, I've said it."

Galbard moved to the southern side of the upper deck and looked to the tall, proud stand of trees in the south. "I am about to see the leaves fall from Southwood's trees for the third time, Cayden," he said. "I never thought I would live to see her again, you know."

"She is worried that you might not be with her because of the child."

"Ro?" Galbard replied. "Nothing could be further from the truth—she should know that."

"Well, she doesn't, brother," Cayden replied. "It's time for you to make your intentions clear, I think."

Galbard paced back around the circumference of the deck and then turned to look at him. "I have worried so that the Camonra were right behind me, so worried that the darkness of Amphileph would follow me here. My entire focus has remained on protecting the Sword and fulfilling my promise to Evliit."

"But what if Amphileph's attack is in the distant future, Galbard? This tower will stand long after we are no more than dust. Think about this for a moment: What if the Creator never intended that you see that battle? Maybe you have already done what you were tasked to do, for you have brought the Sword *here*."

Galbard opened his mouth to speak, but stopped himself. He sighed deeply. "That could be the truth of it," he said.

"Then if that *could* be the truth of it, Galbard, why should you live through this time alone? I know that you fear for their safety, but push your wife and child away no more."

A faint smile appeared on Galbard's face. "You *should* have been a barrister, Cayden."

"What message should I give her?" Cayden asked.

"No message. I'll talk with her in person," Galbard replied.

"That's excellent!" Cayden said. His face beamed momentarily and then quickly turned serious. "Wait! You're leaving Shintower?"

"You said it yourself, my friend. It's time," said Galbard.

Cayden nodded and turned to leave, but stopped. "Do it soon, Galbard, for both of you," he said and continued on his way.

Galbard watched his friend descend the stairs, and he looked around the horizon until his eyes stopped on the rising ash from the fault line surrounding Rion. "You mourn for us, don't you?" Galbard questioned. "Erathe, mother of us all, I pray for the Creator's healing touch."

As he turned to descend the stairs, lightning jumped from the storm clouds north of Rion down through the billowing cloud of ash that rose out of the glowing tear in the very heart of Etharath. Galbard stopped for a moment and watched the silent flashes' misty glow through the haze until the low booming sound covered the distance between them, and then he descended the stairs into the safety of Shintower's stronghold.

Galbard stopped at a small anteroom off the tower's ground floor, which acted as a prayer room for some of the more faithful followers of the Watchers. Its thick, tomblike walls provided its visitors with a profound silence, and for Galbard, it was strangely peaceful—with one exception. The stoneworkers had created a special tribute to his "calling"—a free-standing sculpture of him standing over the sleeping Evliit, with the Sword positioned precariously over the Watcher's head, Galbard's face looking to the heavens as if pausing in rapture. He had never liked it, though he had graciously accepted it and its placement in Shintower. Over time, he had come to ignore it and the terrifying memories it invoked.

He knelt and closed his eyes, attempting to lose himself in the silence. It was as if his ears became attuned to that silence, and slowly, he began to sense his own breath and heartbeat. He squinted his eyes in concentration, and he could hear the blood flowing into his forehead. He wanted so much to hear the Creator's voice, Evliit, or one of the Watchers, just as he had on the fateful day of his calling and at so many critical times in his life. He loved Jalin, and that love for her vexed him with questions about where he was going with his life. He had known no love like his for her before, and the thought of hurting her or Ro by involving them in his life of Watchers and their war seemed selfish at best.

"Why do you speak to me no more?" he asked aloud. "Will you not tell me what is expected of me now?" Galbard asked.

This time, the silence was not a welcome one. Galbard found himself longing for the days when the Creator had spoken to him aloud through his prophets. He waited patiently to hear that voice, but after almost an hour of prayer, the lack of response shook him somewhat.

"Lord, is it safe to bring Jalin and Ro to the tower?" Galbard spoke up again, "Guide me not to this, if that is your will, Lord, for I know that you wish your servants no ill. Search my heart, oh Lord, that I am ready to be your servant over all else."

There was a fluttering that startled Galbard.

Aleris stopped on the ground at Galbard's side. "I am sorry, master, I did not mean to disturb your prayers," he said.

"You disturb me not nearly so much as the lack of an answer to them," Galbard replied.

"Perhaps you ask for something that has been *answered*, my lord," Aleris said.

"I'm sure I don't know what you mean, Aleris," said Galbard.

Aleris looked at Galbard a little perplexed, and then his expression changed. "I am quite versed in the Book of Time, my lord. I would count it a privilege to help you in any way I might. Perhaps I could help you with the appropriate verses. Rest assured, our discussions would be held in the utmost privacy," Aleris said.

Galbard looked around a moment and back at Aleris. "I am asking the Creator to speak through his prophets, Aleris, in answer to my desire to be with Jalin and Ro."

Aleris looked puzzled for a moment, and then his face brightened. "You need no verses to answer this, Galbard," he said. "Love is an inseparable part of our Creator. If it were possible, the Creator would have no one live without love."

It was not an earth-shattering revelation, but something about Aleris's words rang true to Galbard, and his hope for love seemed to overshadow everything else that he felt.

"Thank you, Aleris," he said.

"You are most welcome," Aleris responded, and then he buzzed from the room with a contented look upon his face.

Galbard left Shintower and for the first time in over two years, he proceeded across the grounds toward the Dales.

"Afternoon!" said a man carrying flour from the little mill on the western end of town.

"Good day to you," Galbard responded. "I'm looking for the *Horses's Ear*."

"You on the right path, straight ahead then," the man answered. "Can't miss it."

Galbard nodded his thanks and made his way on the dirt alleyways between the small shacks that housed their ever-growing population. He rounded the corner and saw the *Horse's Ear*, Jalin's modest bed-and-breakfast that she shared with several older women and two couples.

Ro was with a group of other small children gathered around the doorway. A young man sat at a table in the corner, apparently garnering the attention of everyone.

"I've seen many fires burning in the Inferiors' camps in the east," the young man said. "Their numbers grow even faster than ours!"

Galbard pushed through the group of boys and stood with his back against the wall. There had been a lot of talk lately about the Camonra, and Galbard did not want anyone frightening the young ones.

"I hope Cayden has made it quite clear about the Camonra," Galbard said.

Everyone stopped as if suddenly noticing Galbard leaning against the wall.

"Oh yes, sir, of course!" the young man said. The entire group of young boys and girls listening to him shook their heads in agreement.

"We will keep our distance," Galbard said sternly.

The young man finished his drink, and the group began quickly disbanding, leaving Galbard and the older inhabitants of the inn to themselves. Ro began to follow them out. Galbard stopped him. He smiled and reached out to him, but it was obvious that Ro didn't quite know what to make of him. It cut Galbard to the core. He pulled his hand back down to his side.

"Ro? Where is your mother?"

"She's in the kitchen, sir," he responded.

"You grow up faster by the day," remarked Galbard. "What will you remember?"

"To keep our distance," Ro answered.

"Very good. Take off now!" Galbard said, and Ro scampered away into the alleyway and ran to catch up to the other boys.

Galbard made his way to the kitchen where he found Jalin washing some clothes in a large caldron. Before she saw him, Galbard looked around the room and put a hand upon her shoulder. She jumped and raised the wooden spoon in her right hand as if she would strike.

"I'm sorry! I didn't mean to frighten you," said Galbard.

"Galbard! In the name of the Creator, what are you doing here?" Jalin asked, wiping the sweat from her face and pushing the hair from her eyes. She put down the large wooden spoon that she used to stir the caldron and adjusted her apron.

Galbard touched her arm. "The tower is finished," he said.

She raised her hand to her face and gasped. "Are you telling me . . . ?"

"Yes," he interrupted. "It's time that you and Ro came to live in the tower with me."

She suddenly burst into tears. "I thought you'd lost your love for me." The tears streamed down. He touched her face and wiped the tears from her cheeks.

"Never," said Galbard.

"Not much to look at, eh?" she asked, and then she wrapped her arms around his neck.

"I'll have you know that my tastes are quite refined when it comes to the ladies, and I am quite sure that you are the best-looking one of them all," he quipped.

"Especially right now, eh?" she replied, pursing her lips and blowing the one dangling piece of hair out of her face for a moment before it fell right back again.

"Especially right now," Galbard said. "Pack some things for the two of you. Cayden will have the rest of your things delivered to the tower."

"Yes, all right," she said. She sniffled and grabbed a towel from the clean laundry on the table, wiping her face. She grabbed a bag from the bottom shelf of the pantry and rustled through the clothes, stopping with a small pair of pants.

"That boy of ours," Jalin said. "He'd better be prepared to make quite a living if he continues to run through the clothes like he does." Jalin ran her hand up the leg until her fingers danced from a hole in the knee. Galbard laughed aloud at her gesture.

"Boys are hard on pants' knees," he said.

"Mothers can be harder on the seats of them," Jalin said, her head cocked to one side, eyeing him from under that troublesome bang.

"Indeed," Galbard replied, feigning a worried look. Then they laughed aloud together, and before he knew it, she had closed the distance between them and kissed him passionately. When she pulled back, they looked in each other's eyes, and there was a moment of blissful silence.

Jalin's eyes grew wide. "It really is time, isn't it?"

"Yes," he said, taking a deep breath. "I want to share the remainder of my days with you and Ro. I want to declare publicly what I held secret these past two years: you are my wife and Ro is my son!"

"Oh, Galbard!" she exclaimed. "You've made me so incredibly happy! I'll get Ro, and we'll leave at once!"

* * *

Leagues to the east, Tobor sat next to the stone fireplace in the great room at the center of his adobe home, about a hundred yards from the main camp housing the Camonra families. He often sat facing the thick wooden door, left ajar so he could watch the campfires in the night and smell the food of hundreds of cook pots in the valley below him. Packed away were the tents of the nomadic existence they had always known under the iron fist of Amphileph. The Camonra now built structures to accommodate the new, more settled nature of the lives they had built in the past three years.

Tobor's home was a spacious dwelling even among the oversized adobe homes that the Camonra often built due to their inherently colossal size. It sat upon an outcropping of rock that had apparently jutted up during the great upheaval of the land. The Camonra jokingly called it *Bern na Stydhra* after the Hill of Kings in Rion, the mount upon which the Rion Temple sat, the spot that was to be their ultimate conquest in the battle of Rion. The fault that tore the land apart between themselves and the Rionese now made this ridge of stone in the middle of what had been Rion's northern fields their "final conquest." It had become the inside joke among the workers who had carved the sweeping curve of stone steps that led up the edge of the ridge to the entrance of Tobor's home.

In the passing of three springs, Tobor had seen two attempts on his life for control of the Camonra, but his experience and cunning remained outmatched by the would-be usurpers' youth and strength. There were times in the harsh, icy winters that Tobor had laughed ruefully with his wives that the assassins' success might simply have brought sweet relief from the ever-growing tension in his people.

There were often torrential rains, and they were laden with volcanic ash and seawater from the fissure. The rain's high acidity began a systematic mutation of animal and plant life in the area north of Rion, now simply called The Rainland. Strange creatures and flora began to multiply and expand at a surprising rate, so that now the populace felt the effects here, a camp that once had been a good deal of distance west of it all.

Water was slowly becoming less potable, and there were strange sounds in the darkness. War-dogs began to go missing in the night.

A storm was brewing to the southeast. It was often the case nowadays, as the hot ash and dust from the rift in the land mixed with cool northerly winds blowing in from the ocean. It had been true for most of that day. Tobor always liked to watch this spectacle of nature, where lightning jumped from the storm clouds through the heavy ash and into the ground with spectacular explosions. He liked to grab the razor-sharp knife from his belt and a sizable stick of wood and sit upon a short stool on the porch, whittling curled-up wood shavings into a pile. He never really made anything, but he found it relaxing to whittle away a hefty piece of wood into nothing. He just sat and whittled, watching the lightning crash upon the surrounding lands, lighting trees ablaze or blowing a chunk of earth into the air.

Both of the attempts on his life had happened on a night such as this, so Tobor liked the front porch, for it afforded him a panoramic view of the only pathway to his home along the curved steps leading up the hill. It had been a flash of lightning that had alerted him each time to the presence of assassins. So now, whenever the lightning came, it always made his mind wander back to killing them; those thoughts always brought him back to the stool on the porch, even in the middle of the night.

As Tobor eyed the surrounding area, he saw movement on the stairs, and his heart rate jumped up a beat or two. The figure stopped in the middle of the flight of stairs and spoke. "It is I, Idhoran."

"Good thing that you chose to call out to me," Tobor smiled. "I would hate to kill my best commander." Tobor released the tension on his cross bow and sat it back down by his side. He removed his knife from its scabbard and began whittling again, satisfied that Idhoran's face showed his obvious relief at being recognized rather than shot.

"You do not sleep, my liege?" Idhoran asked.

"Things to think about," Tobor said. "And I like to watch the fire fall from the sky."

Idhoran stepped upon the porch and leaned against one of the rough wooden posts that supported the porch roof.

"Have you ever wondered why the fire falls from the sky, even though Father—Amphileph—does not command it?" asked Tobor.

Idhoran looked as though he was about to answer, but stopped. "I'm a soldier, my lord, I think not of these things," he said at last.

"I've thought about it many times, Idhoran. I sit upon my porch, carving wood just such as this, and question everything that I have ever known."

Idhoran fidgeted a bit, but kept his silence.

"Soldiers do not think about such things, eh?" asked Tobor.

"No," Idhoran replied.

Tobor rolled the wood in his hand and set the blade against the bark. "As I have sat here, watching the fire fall from the sky, I asked myself, how does the fire fall from the sky when it is not commanded by Amphileph? And do you know what I have discovered?"

"No, my lord."

Tobor cut a large swath of wood from the tree limb that he clutched tightly in his strong hand. "Without so much as a word from Amphileph, the fire falls—day after day, again and again. I tell you that another father lives in the skies, a father greater than Amphileph, and it is *he* that calls down the fire upon the land."

Idhoran's face spoke volumes. His eyes ventured their surroundings like an answer might appear out of thin air. "My lord," he stuttered. "I . . ."

Pricari, the first of Tobor's concubines shot from the doorway of their home, the quick movement causing both Tobor and Idhoran to jerk their eyes to her.

"Master! Come quickly!" she said. She just seemed to notice that Idhoran was also there, and she stopped in front of Tobor, quickly lowering her head in submission. "I am sorry, master; I did not know that you were not alone."

"Speak freely, Pricari," answered Tobor. "What is wrong?"

"Lurenda has borne you a child," she said. "She is asking that you give the child your blessing."

"A male?" Tobor inquired, turning back to Idhoran.

"Yes, master."

At this answer, Tobor rose to his feet. "It's time that I name an heir, Idhoran," Tobor said. "Let's see if the young one is fit for such a claim."

"If he is not, you will make him so, Tobor," Idhoran replied.

"I will make him so or kill him trying," Tobor said, grunting. "Can you stand watch for me while I tend to this?"

"Of course, master," said Idhoran, and then he turned his back on the doorway and fixed his gaze on the grounds in front of Tobor's home.

Tobor made his way through the living area and past his bedroom, up the short stairwell to the upper level of the home where the concubines made their beds. There he found them circled around Lurenda's bed. But when Tobor entered the room, they quickly moved aside.

Tobor looked at Lurenda. Her face was tired, but oddly content. Her gaze never left the tiny swaddling cloth in which the other concubines had wrapped the child. Something about her expression affected Tobor, for it appeared to him to be more like the face of a victorious warrior rather than that of a mere concubine.

A miniscule hand grasped the cloth, and Tobor noticed the fingers of the child were a miniature of his own. Tobor reached for the tiny hand, and Lurenda opened up the cloth so that he could see the baby within.

Tobor was unprepared for the emotions that swept over him, and he instinctively drew in a breath. The boy looked so much like him, the tiny face curled into a cry that sounded to Tobor like a wee battle cry. A rare smile stretched widely across the father's face.

"You've done well, Lurenda," Tobor said. "You've done well, indeed."

"Thank you, master," Lurenda replied. Her voice resonated with the pride that shone in her face. "He'll make a fine member of the Camonra."

"He will be leader of the Camonra!" Tobor barked, handing the infant back. The concubines rushed back around Lurenda, and Tobor turned to leave.

"Tobor?" Lurenda said. "Master?"

Tobor turned back to her.

"He will know the peace that we have never known. He will know the new life we have built here, not the bindings of servitude under Amphileph."

A hush fell upon all the concubines, and they stopped everything.

Tobor drew a deep breath and exhaled, his nostrils flaring. "It shall be so," he replied.

"Master," Lurenda said. "What name will you give your son?"

Tobor looked at the child and raised his hand to his jaw. "I will call this one Adheron, after my father's father."

PART TWO

Chapter Eighteen

New Paths

Sons of warriors, worlds apart—some born in the stormy darkness of the Rainland, others far from their homeland of Rion, exiled by the cause of that same darkness. Theirs seemed two paths divided by choice, their two destinies separate and distinct. The forest and jungles of the Rainland grew thick, while the villages and hideouts of the Rionese refugees became towns and fortresses. Though all prepared for war, few but the Candrians sought it out, and fewer still dared into the Rainland's steamy wilderness. Those who ventured there were thought captured or killed, for they never returned.

Seventeen more years would pass, while Ro and Adheron trained dutifully, one seeking to control the Sword of the Watch, while the other, the hardened steel of the Camonra blade.

* * *

"Again!" Idhoran directed, and Adheron snapped to attention. He carried his father's large frame, and today, he added another of his father's characteristics—battle scars.

Idhoran stood along the rim of the training pit, leaning over the wooden beam that circled it, watching Adheron's tactics carefully. The boy's father had felt it best to have his captain train his son, to make it clear to all that Tobor showed Adheron no favoritism. He would learn the Camonra style of fighting in the training pits, or he would die, like all the other young males who wanted the title of Camon.

He tightened the grip on his shield and sword, trying not to think of the wound above his left eye. It was in the corner of the socket, narrowly missing the eye itself, and each time that he turned his head to the side, the blood ran into it, effectively blinding him to attacks on the left. His opponent noted Adheron's new disability and circled in the direction of his fresh blind spot.

His opponent swung the spiked balls of his flail slowly back and forth, adding a little momentum to them to decrease his reaction time should Adheron challenge. Adheron had garnered a new respect for the flail, a weapon he had not yet mastered. It had certainly fared much better against his sword than he had expected. It was capable of smashing and tearing the flesh from his body with a single strike, and it was obvious from his first close inspection—his now swelling eye—that his opponent meant to do just that.

Adheron knew the Candrian slave had nothing to lose, for captives and Camon convicts served out their days as training partners for the young would-be warriors. It was an interesting mix of punishment and possibility, for more than once, a training slave had ended a young warrior's conquests with a single blow. Victory could earn a slave his freedom or a convict a return to warrior status.

"Watch him!" Idhoran said.

Adheron always listened closely to Idhoran, and his grating voice seemed to ring through the jeers and cheers of the trainees and Camon soldiers that had gathered to watch the son of Tobor for his first bout in the training pit.

The slave jumped suddenly at him with abandon, slashing Adheron across the cheek.

"Just a few stitches, that one!" belted Idhoran's voice. "Did you see his eyes? Watch him!"

Adheron played the attack over in his head. He tracked his opponent's movements with practiced pace. His challenger swung at him again, and this time Adheron clearly saw it: the slight closing of his eyes right before he swung.

Adheron moved to his own left, watching the slave's eyes without flinching. *There it was,* he thought. The slave prepared to swing and feinted with his shield, but Adheron pivoted, deflecting the blow with his shield. Then, with a thrust, a full inch of his blade transected the warrior's side just an inch below his ribs.

The slave's eyes told even more to Adheron then. The realization swept over his face that Adheron had most likely struck a mortal blow. His eyes darted to his side where his skin parted. He pulled his swinging arm into his side and used his elbow and forearm to hold back the flood of red that ran from his wound. The slave's flail fell harmlessly to the ground, and he fell to his knees before Adheron.

Tobor's son ignored the crowd's bloodthirsty calls to add the slave's head to his belt. Instead, he lowered his blade and motioned to the other slaves. "This one is worthy of care," Adheron shouted. "Take him and tend to him so that he may fight another day!"

The other slaves scrambled to him and carried him away.

"Well done, Adheron!" Idhoran said. He dropped his massive hand on the young warrior's shoulder armor with a loud thump. "Well done, indeed!"

"I wonder if there will ever come a day that you will teach me no more, Idhoran?" Adheron asked. "How can it be that you know the fight so well?"

Idhoran laughed. "Why do you think the hair of my beard grows gray? It is the battles themselves that ferret out the weak and unskilled."

Adheron stopped and turned. "Do you think I should have killed the slave when I had beaten him, then?"

Idhoran also stopped and looked him in the eye, and then he looked around at the crowd. "They would have liked that, would they?" he replied. "You did well to decide as you did."

Adheron bobbed his head in appreciation. Idhoran stopped and put his hand on Adheron's head, turning it for a closer look at the cut beside Adheron's eye.

"Come with me," Idhoran said. "I know just the female to stitch that up."

* * *

"We must unify the West," Cayden said. "Your father believes the future of men depends on that unity."

"Yes, I understand," said Ro. He reached behind his head and adjusted the band his mother insisted he use to pull back his long, brown hair, and he pushed his bangs out of his face. He was more than a little anxious to meet the envoy from Moonledge Peak.

With the growth of the west, the Rionese refugees now controlled Highwood and the caves beneath the highest peak in the Faceless Mountain range, which they had named Moonledge Peak. A group of former Guardsmen known as the Seven Warriors held the valley called Candra, north of Shintower, and there was talk of the Seven Warriors claiming the stretch of Highwood that lie on the western bank of the Highborne River. Some had even told his father that the Seven Warriors meant to bring all the lands in the west under their control, but while the Seven Warriors had rejected the Elders, the leaders of Highwood remained faithful to Rion, and tensions were high. His father worried that the aggressive stance of the Seven Warriors might intensify if they discovered that Shintower held the Sword of the Watch. He had written Caratacus, the leader of refugees in the caves of Moonledge Peak, and over the course of several months, they had decided to ally Moonledge and Shintower through marriage. The betrothed would meet at Highborne Falls, approximately halfway between Moonledge Peak and Shintower, just at the eastern end of Candra Valley. He made the secret journey with Cayden by horseback in support of his father's vision of unity.

It was mid-morning in the early fall, and Ro thought that Highborne Falls was absolutely beautiful. The trees were a gorgeous mix of greens and reds and browns. Ro and Cayden dismounted, and the Shintower soldiers that accompanied them waited under the trees next to the falls. Ro and Cayden walked their horses alongside the pool at the base of the falls. The pool was over a hundred feet wide, and its deep, calm waters belied the force of the Highborne River downstream, which flowed from Highborne Falls through Highwood and on to the ocean near Shintower.

"Won't they be on the other side of the pool?" asked Ro. "Isn't Moonledge Peak about there?" He pointed to the high ridge atop the Faceless Mountains to the north.

"Yes, you're right," answered Cayden. "Beneath the peak there, at the base of the mountain."

Ro looked across the deep water of the pool. "But I mean, how do we get over there?"

"No worries," said Cayden. "Follow me." He led Ro along the mountainside where erosion indented the base of mountain beneath the falls. The sound of the water striking the stone edge of the pool was impossible to talk over, but Cayden guided him through the narrow path behind the falls to the eastern side.

"That was incredible!" said Ro.

"Thought you'd like that," replied Cayden. They made their way around the eastern side of the pool and watched the northern plains for riders.

"What do you suppose she'll look like?" The question burst from Ro's mouth.

Cayden started to say something, but continued walking. It was quiet other than the sound of the water falling, and there were yet beautiful flowers this late in summer.

"She is the daughter of the leader of Moonledge Peak. I'm sure that she's well-suited to you."

Ro saw Cayden's brow wrinkle as soon as the words were out of his mouth.

"Well-suited to me, eh?" Ro responded.

"Okay, even I know that sounded absolutely idiotic," said Cayden. "I, too, struggle with the thought of an arranged marriage, but I know the love your father has for you, and I can tell you that it is unquestionable. I have watched you grow up, and I have seen no father love his child more. Your father bestowed a great honor on me when he asked that I escort you to this meeting. I know how much he wanted to be here himself, but the protection of the Sword can be its own kind of prison."

There was the sound of horses to the north. Cayden signaled the Shintower soldiers across the pool.

"I think I see them coming," Cayden said.

Half a dozen soldiers carrying the flag of Moonledge Peak trotted before a young lady and her entourage. They stopped when they spotted Cayden and Ro, and it seemed to Ro that they were motionless for a moment, save the waving of the flags in the gentle wind.

A single rider came out in front of the group and dismounted, walking to Cayden and Ro at the water's edge.

"I am Trestaire, the Lady Tiamphia's escort," the man said, and then he bowed.

"I am Cayden, Master Ronan's escort," Cayden announced and returned the bow.

"Shall we let the two of them have some time together?" Trestaire asked.

"Of course," answered Cayden. "After you," Cayden motioned to Trestaire. "Master, may I take your horse?"

"Yes, please," answered Ro.

"Milady," Trestaire said, giving a hand to her so that she might dismount.

"We will give you some privacy," said Cayden, and he and Trestaire each waved the young betrothed to meet, pulling aside with the entourage to keep them in eyeshot, but not within earshot.

Ro looked at Tiamphia, a ringlet of flowers crowning her waist-length, wavy blond hair. She wore a silken veil across her face, but her light blue eyes drew him in, and the breeze brought the sweet scent of her perfume to his nose, sweeter even than the flowers surrounding the Highborne Falls pool. Her silken dress flowed around her in the wind, hinting at her alluring figure. Ro felt his blood in his cheeks and butterflies in his stomach. He tried to think about what to say to her.

"Hello . . . I am Ronan, son of Galbard and Jalin."

"I am honored," Tiamphia said, looking down. "I am Tiamphia, daughter of Caratacus and Sadhra."

"You're eyes are so beautiful," said Ro. "I think now you can remove your veil."

Tiamphia looked away, and suddenly Ro felt like he had said something wrong. "I don't mean to be too forward," he said. "You can call me Ro . . ."

Tiamphia looked him in the eye again, hers with laughter in them. "No, that's a very nice thing to say . . ." she replied, "Ro." She removed one side of the veil and let it fall away. Her smile enchanted him.

"I kept thinking you might be like the large woman who works in the tavern," he laughed nervously.

"I thought you might be a balding, potbellied fellow," she said, covering a giggle with her hand.

"You're nothing like that, of course," he added quickly.

"Nor you," she replied.

They walked along the edge of Highborne Falls for about an hour, though it seemed like minutes to them. Trestaire and Cayden walked their horses back to them.

"It is time, milady," said Trestaire. "We should return to Moonledge."

Cayden mounted his horse. "Come along, Ronan," he said. Ro helped Tiamphia to her horse and remounted his own.

"And what shall I say to your father?" Trestaire said, his eyes searching her expression.

"Give father my love," she answered. "And let him know that it's a good match."

Trestaire smiled at her; then he turned away and rejoined the Moonledge entourage. "Make ready!" he said. Tiamphia waved to them and watched them head back toward Moonledge and disappear over the horizon. Then she joined Cayden and Ro for the long ride back to Shintower.

When the three riders arrived in Shintower, Tiamphia was welcomed with open arms. Jalin took a special interest in making her comfortable in her new surroundings, and it was she who insisted that Tiamphia have a room to herself, close to her own room. During the coming weeks, she would sit and talk with her on many occasions when the men were attending to their duties. Jalin was thrilled to see that the young bride-to-be completely charmed Ro. Her worries that the girl would not feel likewise were assuaged when she confided in Jalin that she found him "quite handsome."

For Galbard, the romance had been a distraction, and though he wanted love to blossom for his son, the importance of teaching him to control the Sword was paramount. Galbard knew that unless Evliit returned to claim it, one day Ro would bear the responsibility of protecting the Sword, and with that responsibility would be the dangers it would bring. Galbard felt strongly that it was in Ro's best interest to master the Sword, and he brought Ro to the upper deck of Shintower with regularity to show him all that he had learned of the Sword's power. Later in the fall, it had become miserably cold on the upper deck, but Galbard had insisted that the lessons continue. It was on a blustery day such as this when Galbard felt that Ro was ready for a test of his skills.

They stood atop Shintower, and Galbard gently removed the Sword from his scabbard. He walked toward the altar at the center of the tower's upper deck and looked up at the sky. The wind was surprisingly strong, though the sun was clearly visible. Sometimes it felt like a gust of wind might lift him up to the heavens, and the thought of drifting away on the winds to the Third Domain caused a faint smile to cross his face.

He glanced over at his son, Ro, feeling a sense of pride in the way his solemn stare toward the heavens reflected the seriousness with which Ro took his father's faith. It was obvious to Galbard that Ro respected him, and nothing could have honored Galbard more.

A buzzing noise announced Aleris's entrance, capturing Ro and Galbard's attention. He lit upon the deck next to them, struggling a bit with a sudden gust of wind, but quickly recovered his composure. He came to attention, pulling his long coat straight.

"Is he ready, Galbard?" Aleris asked.

Galbard looked down at Aleris for a moment and then back to the skies. His gray hair blew back from the force of the wind.

"As ready as I was," Galbard said.

"I have made a second check of the grounds, master, and all is clear. Cayden has made it clear to the townspeople that they're to be clear of the tower until further notice. The Bhre-Nora stand ready."

"Very well," Galbard said. He thought that it was the first time that he had ever seen Aleris looking nervous. "I'm afraid my charge over the Sword is going to have to end *one* day, Aleris," Galbard encouraged with a bit of a chuckle. "I'm getting no younger. I look to Ronan to carry on this task."

As Aleris looked up at Galbard, his face exuded the friendship that had grown steadily over their years together at Shintower. "Of course, master," replied Aleris, but Galbard thought there was a bit of a pained expression peeking out from his disciplined response.

Galbard breathed in a deep breath and exhaled. He looked at the misty covering on the mountains to the north and marveled afresh at their beauty. "This is the natural order of things with men, Aleris," Galbard smiled. "We come about our power but for a fleeting moment before we realize it was never ours to keep. We beget naught but dust in the end, save the souls of the children that carry on. The Sword will far outlast me, I'm afraid, and it will likely outlast even the Bhre-Nora."

"Yes, lord," replied Aleris. "I have seen this in men, and even my beloved Bhre-Nora must pass into the Third Domain in time."

"Then this is our duty today, Aleris: to lead Ro in the way of the Sword, to teach him these truths of Men and the Bhre-Nora, and to draw him ever closer to the Creator and his creation," said Galbard, motioning to the majestic mountains in the distance.

"May it be done," Aleris answered.

Galbard turned to address Ro. "Come, Ro; it is time."

"Yes, Father," said Ro, and then he moved to the altar of the sword beside his father.

Galbard thought Ro appeared mesmerized by the Sword. Galbard removed it from its scabbard gingerly. "This is the Sword of the Watch, my son, given to me by Evliit himself. The Creator has given it great power, and Evliit himself said that it has the power to control the destiny of all humankind. It has fallen to me to teach you of its power to defend its bearer. The ability to control even a part of its power has saved me on more than one occasion."

Ro listened intently, and his eyes moved down the Sword's length, as if admiring the beautiful inscription on the blade. "I've watched firsthand your devotion to the care of the Sword, Father, and for you to allow me the opportunity to wield its power is a great honor."

"It is a statement of my belief in your worthiness as the future leader of Shintower," answered Galbard. "Kneel, my son!" he shouted.

Galbard held the tang before him with both hands, its tip resting on the stone of the upper deck just in front of the altar.

Galbard shouted to the heavens. "Oh, Creator of everything, grant that Ronan might wield this, your mighty sword! May he stand against evil as your warrior, and let the holy power of the Sword flow through him!"

The clouds began to swirl and darken around the upper deck of Shintower. A hum of electricity filled the air, and small bolts of energy jumped between the swirling mists and the heavy, steel rods that jutted from the stonework of the upper deck's buttresses.

"I am ready, Father!" Ro proclaimed. His eyes were like saucers.

"Good luck," Aleris said.

"It is your time, Ro," said Galbard, echoing Aleris' encouragement. He placed the Sword in Ro's hands, let go of it, and then he stepped back from the Sword for the first time since Evliit's commissioning and took a knee beside Aleris.

Ro's face tightened. "Stay calm," Galbard said. "Let the Sword's fire pass through you."

Ro rose up and placed the Sword into its resting place, and then he placed both hands on the altar. A bluish plasma outlined the Sword and spread to his hands and over his body.

"So begins the test!" Aleris shouted to Galbard.

Galbard said nothing, for fervent prayer completely consumed him. He knew the Sword was searching his son for his worth as a bearer of its power and that his son's life was very literally in the balance of that assessment.

Ro squeezed his eyelids tightly together. "I feel a little nauseous—and dizzy," he said. One of his knees buckled, and he caught his weight on the altar with his hands.

Suddenly the tower quaked with energy. Steam shot from the ports in the tower walls and a slow rumble began deep within.

"Keep your focus!" his father shouted

"Wait, Galbard!" said Aleris. "Something is not right!" Aleris flew to the edge of the upper deck and looked upon the grounds below. "The walls are shifting at too fast a rate!" shouted Aleris. "Steady! Steady!"

The energy of the Sword moved through the stone very quickly until the stone itself began to glow a deep red. Steam blew steadily from the reliefs in the tower. There was a loud crash!

"Two of the courtyard walls have collided!" screamed Aleris. One of the Bhre-Nora shot up from the upper-deck opening in a panic. "We must stop!" he screamed above the din, waving his arms.

Galbard rose to his feet and ran to the altar, grabbing Ro by the waist. The blue plasma separated from Ro as Galbard pulled him away from the altar.

Galbard bent over him. "Ro!" he cried. He searched him for any sign of injury, but there was none. Ro's head slumped over Galbard's arm. He was lifeless. "What have I done?" he shouted to Aleris.

The high-pitched scream of the blowing steam began to slow, and the clouds began to dissipate.

"Ronan!" Galbard said, and then he glanced up. "Creator, please! Have I not done as you have asked? You must spare my son!" he cried. Galbard frantically listened to his heart. "Please!" He turned to Aleris. "Get the Healers!"

Aleris flew down the stairwell, and in moments, the Healers returned with him.

"Will he be okay?" Galbard inquired.

"We do not know, my lord," the Healers replied. "Let us take him to his room where we can treat him." They carried Ro's limp body downstairs, leaving Galbard and Aleris alone on the tower's upper deck. Aleris paced around the altar and sat down at the top of the stairs, attempting to find the words to comfort Galbard.

Galbard was silent. He walked to the tower's edge. "I have done my part!" Galbard shouted to the heavens. "I was willing to sacrifice my son!" He looked out over the countryside. "Why should I follow such a vengeful god? You are no different from Amphileph! I curse your wrath!"

Aleris's jaw dropped open for a moment. "This is only a setback. We—"

"No." Galbard stopped him. He turned to retrieve the sword from the altar, but when he reached for it, a bolt of energy shot from it, striking him in the chest. He skid across the tower deck and slammed into the parapet wall.

"Galbard!" Aleris shouted. He flew to Galbard's side and found him conscious, but in great pain. "Galbard, what have you done?"

Galbard struggled to his feet, holding his chest. His face was a mixture of anger and shame.

"My time with the Sword has ended. The Creator will call another to carry it now. I have brought it here to the Bhre-Nora, and I have ensured that it has remained safe all these years."

"Shintower requires the bearer of the Sword to be present. They are one, inseparable," said Aleris.

Galbard raised his hand in witness. "I have fulfilled my promise."

Aleris flew to the hand railing beside Galbard's head. "We just need to make repairs, my lord. This is only a setback."

"Yes, be about that," Galbard said. "Evliit will return for the Sword in his own time. The Bhre-Nora and the people of the Dales have been most kind to us, Aleris, but my time has passed. I will make room for the next to bear the Sword. I must go and see to my son. I leave the Sword in your care."

Galbard said nothing more, but descended the stairs on the way to Ro's room to check on him.

* * *

"Father calls for you!" the Camon said, beating upon the door of Citanth's shack. Citanth rolled his bruised body in his bed, but before he could rise, the Camon pushed the door open, breaking the latch. "Father wants you now!" he said. The Camon put his massive hand on Citanth's ankle and pulled him out of bed.

"I am coming!" moaned Citanth.

It was raining again, so he pulled his hood around his face and walked to the edge of the Binding. Amphileph stood just on the other side, obviously excited.

"Did you feel it?" he asked. "The thief has used the Sword again!"

"I am injured, my lord, I was sleep—"

"Shut up and listen, you fool!" snapped Amphileph. He raised his hands, and the water running off the Binding began to circle and shift, clinging to the Binding to form the shape of a tower. "The Bhre-Nora meddle in my affairs again. They have built a tower in the southwest to protect the Sword."

The rain and lightning intensified, and the water ran off the Binding again so that Citanth could see Amphileph's face. The excitement was gone, replaced by grim hatred.

"This time, I will destroy them all," said Amphileph.

* * *

Caratacus and the High Council of Moonledge Peak were ending a dedication ceremony deep within the caves of the Faceless Mountains. There had been food, drink, dancing, and music in celebration.

"We honor the stonemasons that have worked so diligently," Caratacus said.

There was loud applause that echoed through the stone chambers.

"Only the Rionese could create such a stone fortress beneath the high peak called Moonledge! You have performed above and beyond what even the High Council could have expected, and we salute you!" Caratacus yelled above the roar.

"All is not to celebrate!" someone in the crowd yelled out.

"What's this?" Caratacus asked. "Who said that?"

There was a great deal of stirring about in the crowd that had gathered.

"'Twas I, my lord!" one of the men said. He stood up, and several in the crowd booed him.

"Quiet!" Caratacus shouted, slamming his gavel upon the council table. "Speak up, man!"

"My lord, rumors are rampant concerning a strange group of creatures hunting in the fields below the entrance to the caves," he said.

"We have seen the creatures of Amphileph, my lord," another of the townspeople cried. "The ones the Elders called the Inferiors."

The room suddenly became very quiet.

"Were you seen by these creatures?" a member of the council asked.

"No, my lord, we remained hidden in the cliffs."

"Describe these creatures," another of the council requested.

"They were brutish creatures, my lord, walking on two feet as if men, but almost twice the height of a man, and they rode upon scaled creatures, like wingless dragons!"

"They were armed and armored as if for war!" another interrupted. "And they ripped apart a deer before our very eyes, my lord, viciously tore it to pieces, and stuffed the bleeding carcass into their packs!"

"They could smell your fear, I am sure of it!" a voice rang out from their midst.

"And who is this?" Caratacus inquired of the voice.

The Watcher of the Mountains parted the crowd and stood before the council. Other than bearing the trappings of a wizard—his herb bags, potion flasks, and his staff—Tophian concealed his true identify from the council. He intended to reason with them, to give them the opportunity to solve this problem themselves. "These creatures could have hunted you down like the deer they savaged," Tophian said. "But they didn't. They killed food for their kind and left you alone to spy upon them."

"What do you mean by that, good sir?"

"Only that they wanted you to see that they hunted only food, not men," Tophian said. "They let you watch them, and they knew well that you would report what you had seen. Be assured, they will do the same."

"It's said that the creatures of Amphileph are soulless, that they roam the land in search of the spirits of men," another of the council exclaimed. "The Guard warned us of their evil."

"The Watchers have given themselves so that you would be saved from their bloodlust," said Tophian. "A new age of men and Camonra has begun."

"A new age?" inquired Caratacus. "You speak in riddles, good wizard."

Tophian walked to the center of the floor before the council's curved table. "The time of Amphileph's power over them has passed," he said. "The Camonra were created and bred to end the time of men, that is true, but we have separated them from Amphileph by binding him in the east. There he will stay until the end of this age. This was done that men might live and prove themselves worthy of the Watchers who perished on their behalf."

A druid rose up from his seat. He was ancient and blind and stood only with the help of his staff.

"The ancient one speaks truth," he said. "I am blind, but even I see as much. This one is a Watcher!"

There was a collective gasp that echoed in the council chamber's stone walls.

"Silence!" Caratacus said, raising one hand. He looked over Tophian with great curiosity at this. "Is this true?"

"It is as the druid has said," Tophian said. "I am Tophian, Watcher of Mountains."

"Why then have you not ascended to the Third Domain?" the druid interrupted. "Has not the time of Watchers come to an end?"

"In many ways, yes, the time of Watchers is no more," Tophian replied. "I have not joined my brothers because I was not completely given to the hope of Evliit, a hope that men could be saved from their own vices. I would not give my life for you, though near enough to it I was."

Again, there was a rumble among the crowd.

"If you've no love for men, Watcher, what are we to make of your presence here today?" another of the council asked.

Tophian's face suddenly reddened. "My brothers cared enough for men to give up their lives!" The cavern began to shake around them. Small pieces of stone and dust fell about the council hall, and all those attending cowered in fear.

Caratacus threw up his hands. "Great Watcher of the Mountains, do not destroy us!" he cried. "We fear the creatures of Amphileph, and this fear consumes us!"

Tophian heard these words and his face calmed. "Yes, councilor, this is the truth of it." The rumblings ceased, and all eyes fell upon Tophian. "You and your people deserve to live without this fear; for it is these fears that will destroy any hope for peace, and Amphileph wins without lifting a finger."

Tophian paced the room, but no one made a sound.

"In honor of my fallen brothers, I will raise up with you a great castle of men, one that even the War of the Watchers might not pierce! When you fear no attack, maybe then, you and the Camonra will war no more."

Caratacus moved from behind the council table and slowly walked in front of Tophian. "We are in your deepest debt, Lord Tophian." He fell to one knee and bowed his head. "All hail, Tophian, Watcher of Mountains!" One by one, the other councilors did likewise, until not a man was standing in the room save Tophian.

* * *

Due west of the council's meeting, Ardhios and the remainder of the Seven Warriors were huddled around a fire with a group of fifty or so villagers and townspeople. Mordher made good on the Candrians' oath of fealty, immediately having them raise a stone house in which the warriors would stay. Several of the men dug a pit and began working a mixture of mud in it while the women thatched roofing from the long, thick bladed grasses that grew in the fields. The outline of the stone wall had been completed by evening, but the Candrians' diviner was upset that the structure was much bigger than the round, stone hut dedicated to their god. There was a great deal of shouting and arguing among those in attendance, though the warriors were themselves silent.

"We do not hold to the traditions of Rion," one of the townspeople said. "We have abandoned the ways of the Guard of Rion, for they have brought us naught but ruin. Fehamina, the spirit of the river, has led us here to this promised land!"

"Fehamina! Fehamina! Fehamina!" The chant's volume rose, calling the name of their god at the top of their lungs.

The heads of the crowd spun about looking for their diviner. "Let us hear from Fehamina what we are to do!" the cry rang out. A part rippled through their midst, and a man made his way toward the fire. He was covered in white ash and oddly painted across his body with handprints and wild slashes of black coal. He had a wooden figure with hands outstretched dangling from a leather strap around his neck, and it had the name Fehamina carved across its chest in the ancient tongue.

Mordher grunted, "Another priest? I thought we had rid ourselves of those fools when we escaped Rion!" The once heroic warrior had never regained his heart after finding his family trampled in the ruins of Rion.

Ardhios smiled at him. "A diviner? He should read your palms, Mordher!"

"He can read my knuckles if he tries," Mordher retorted.

Their diviner cut a branch from a tree, and the chant began to die down. He mumbled a prayer and cut the branches into small sticks that he marked with a short blade.

The crowd gathered around him. "What do the lots say?" one of them asked.

"Quiet!" said another.

The diviner lay a deerskin face up on the ground and pulled four sharp pegs from his waistband, driving each of them into the skin to pull it taut. He threw the sticks upon the skin and read them thrice. The diviner paused between each of the casts and took in deep breaths of smoke from an urn he swung slowly before him. After the third reading, he sat the urn upon a chest-high stone and continued to fan the smoke into his face until his eyes rolled back in his head and he fell upon the ground. When he did this, two of his acolytes cut the throat of a sheep and threw its body upon the fire.

The flames engulfed the carcass, and the diviner jumped to his feet and roared in a great voice. "Thrice the lots so cast were read, and truth itself has Fehamina given me! She speaks to me of conquerors from the south, and of a new kingdom of men."

"She speaks of the strangers," another whispered, pointing to the Seven Warriors. Mordher looked over his shoulder at the villager, and then feinted lunging at him. When the villager jumped back, Mordher laughed heartily.

"Maybe your Fehamina will protect you!"

"Enough, Mordher," urged Ardhios. "We are soldiers for no one, but ourselves. We have done our duty to Rion, sacrificing much with nothing to show for it."

"But we would swear fealty to the Seven Warriors!" the crowd cried in unison. "Protect us as Fehamina guides our paths!"

"That you would fight for us is no consolation," Mordher replied. "What more can you give that might pique our interests?"

"We will build a great hall for you, our Seven Lords! We will grow food and make crafts to give you pleasure."

"Let it be done!" said the Seven Warriors, raising their swords to that pledge. "Build for us a great castle, swearing fealty to us for all time!"

"We swear it!" the crowd cried.

"Then you will need no diviner!" yelled Mordher, and he grabbed the diviner by the arm and stabbed him in the heart with his short sword, killing him instantly. The crowd fell deathly silent, and Mordher raised his body over his head and cast it into the fire. "We are your masters now! Ardhios will oversee the building of our Great Hall, and I and my brothers will search out these creatures and destroy them! Bring us food and wine! Play the lute and harp! Let us celebrate your oath!"

"Yes, my lord!" the crowd responded, and they quickly set about making a great feast for their warriors.

Ardhios watched the body of the diviner burning upon the fire, and he silently prayed to the Creator for forgiveness for the evil he had unleashed upon these frightened souls.

* * *

"You mustn't leave!" Aleris urged, but Galbard did not answer, continuing to gather his things. The Healers had worked on Ro through the night, plying herbs and chanting incantations. Jalin and Tiamphia had prayed for him the entire time, but Galbard would not join them. Even when the morning came, and Ro awoke, his father's face remained drawn and tense while Jalin and Tiamphia gave thanks to the Creator.

"I'll be fine, Father, really," said Ro. He was weak, barely able to sit up.

Jalin looked somewhat panicked. She was busily moving about the room until she sighted something that seemed to pull her toward it, quickly grabbing it and placing it with her other things in the chest, which sat in the middle of the room, and then repeating the process.

"My lord, please don't do this," said Cayden. "The evil one will surely follow you all the days of your life. You can protect your family no better than you can within these walls."

"Then I have built no less than a prison," Galbard replied. "It's the Sword Amphileph wants, and I will bear it no more, but put some distance between it and my family. For you are right: Amphileph will not rest until it is his. I should have cast it into the ocean long ago. Maybe that is my best advice to you now. Rid yourself of it. If the Creator means for it to survive, he will send you another who can control it. I've sacrificed enough." He stuffed the last few items from his room into a chest and signaled one of his attendants to take it away. "Jalin, are you ready?"

"I am coming," Jalin said, struggling to close the stuffed chest.

"I wish you good luck," said Galbard to Cayden.

"I have arranged for you a wagon," said Cayden. "Let me help you with that," he said, forcing the latch closed on Jalin's trunk. He immediately picked up some of their baggage and held the door open with his foot. Several of the Bhre-Nora entered and removed the larger items. The Healers moved Ro to a stretcher and carried him out of the room with Tiamphia close behind.

"We'll see you downstairs," said Jalin. She exited, and Cayden followed, letting the door close behind them. Galbard moved toward the door, but Aleris hovered to a stop in front of him.

"But where will you go?" asked Aleris. "What will you do?"

"Jalin and I have decided to build our home upon the western shores. We've often watched the sunset upon the ocean from Shintower's upper deck, and thought to ourselves how wonderful it would be to spend our remaining years there. I'll learn to fish, and I'll forget about the years lost to the Camonra. I'll make new memories of peace and happiness, and with luck, I'll live to see my children's children prosper."

Aleris acted as if he was going to say something, but then he stopped, changing his mind. "I have said what I can say to you," he said. "It is a great dream, of course. I cannot deny that." He hovered lower until he lit upon a small table next to the door. "I'll wish you well then, and tell you that all Bhre-Nora hope the best for you."

Galbard resettled the weight of his bags and looked at Aleris. His wings were down at his side, and he'd lowered his head. "Come now, my friend, this is hard enough without thinking that I've wronged you."

"No, of course," replied Aleris, forcing a smile. "We are friends until the end. Be well, Galbard."

Cayden and Aleris watched Galbard and family load up the wagon and disappear into the west.

"What do we do now?" asked Cayden.

"We've repairs that must be made," answered Aleris. "Walls and piping can be fixed."

"But what of defending the Sword? With Galbard gone, how then will Shintower's defenses stay an attack?"

"Having twice activated the tower, Amphileph has surely found us out. I must contact Rendaya. She will know what must be done," answered Aleris. "Until then, tell no one of what has transpired."

"No, of course. As you wish," said Cayden.

"I will return within the hour," said Aleris. "Meet me on the upper deck."

Cayden nodded. "I'll be waiting."

Aleris flew toward Southwood, and Cayden ascended Shintower's steps to the upper deck.

Just as promised, Cayden saw Rendaya and Aleris approaching from the southeast. They landed upon the upper deck still speaking of the Sword. Cayden instinctively gave Rendaya a wide berth.

"If Amphileph did not discover us when Galbard activated the Sword's defenses, he surely has felt the Sword's power on Ro's attempt. We must assume that he has found us out. We must move the Sword," said Rendaya. "It is said that the Watcher Tophian is building a fortress in the mountains to the north. It could be hidden there."

"But you could use it to power Shintower," Cayden blurted out.

"No," answered Rendaya. "If you knew my feelings for the Watchers, you would know why I dare not touch it." Her somber stare was fixed upon the altar, but then suddenly, her face lit up. "The Bhre-Nora made Evliit's sword. Though they cannot command it, they are immune to its power." Rendaya leaned down to Aleris. "Do you still have the strongbox that the Sword was stored in before it was given to Evliit?" she asked.

"Yes, of course. It is a holy relic to the Bhre-Nora," answered Aleris.

"Then the Bhre-Nora will return the Sword to its case, and Cayden can take it to the leader of Moonledge. For the safety of his daughter, Caratacus would surely hide it there, and no one should know that it has left Shintower. If Amphileph attacks, perhaps Tophian could wield it, and draw the Camonra to Moonledge Peak."

"I'll bring the chest," Aleris said, and he sped away. Within minutes, Aleris and several of the Bhre-Nora appeared with an adorned case. Aleris flew to the altar and lifted the Sword, placing it in the case and closing the hasp.

"I'll get my horse and meet you in the courtyard," said Cayden.

"No, we'll not chance taking it by land," said Rendaya. "The Bhre-Nora will take you."

"Take me how?" asked Cayden.

"We will carry you," said Aleris. "And you will deal with Caratacus."

Cayden swallowed hard. A flurry of butterflies spun round in his stomach. "As you wish."

"Hold on to the case," Aleris said. "Tightly. Now raise your arms." Two of the Bhre-Nora brought a wide leather strap up under his arms, while two others grabbed his belt on either side, and the last two each grabbed an ankle. "Ready?" asked Aleris.

"As ready as I will ever be," answered Cayden, and suddenly they lifted him off the upper deck. "Oh!" he cried and closed his eyes, leaving the upper deck and hanging precariously in the sky. The buzz of their wings was louder than he imagined.

"Relax, we've got you," Aleris said flying ahead of him. "We are crossing over the Dales."

His eyes had remained closed until Aleris said that, and then curiosity got the better of him. He opened them and saw the most amazing sight that he had ever seen. It was as if he were a bird, flying over the Dales. The wind blew his hair out of his face, and he closed his eyes again, feeling the cool air flowing over him. He opened his eyes again, and smiled at the sight of a flock of birds to their left.

"You see, flying is wonderful," said Aleris.

"Absolutely incredible!" said Cayden. Within minutes, he could see the lights in Highwood and further west of them, the lights in the Candra Valley.

Within four hours, they descended upon the fields before Moonledge Peak. Cayden blew out a deep breath upon touching the ground again. It was the deep of the night.

"We will stay out of sight," said Aleris. "Take the Sword to Caratacus, and when you return here, we will find you."

"Very well," answered Cayden.

When he reached the outposts of Moonledge, soldiers confronted him, but he explained to them that he was an envoy of Shintower and that it was urgent that he see Caratacus. The soldiers led him up the chain of command, where he explained repeatedly that he must see the Moonledge leader. When at last he had been taken to the highest soldier in charge, Cayden was taken to the council chambers. The soldiers' superiors had reluctantly awakened Caratacus.

"What is the meaning of this?" Caratacus asked, entering the council chambers. He was still buttoning his shirt.

"Sir, please forgive my intrusion, but I have urgent news from Shintower."

Caratacus looked mortified. "Is Tiamphia all right?"

"Oh, yes sir," said Cayden. "She is fine, but her well-being is threatened."

"Threatened? What do you mean?"

"Shintower's defenses have been damaged, and the safety of the Sword is at risk," said Cayden.

Caratacus paused and looked at the case. "You mean, you've brought the Sword of Evliit here?"

The look on Caratacus face gave Cayden alarm. "Yes."

"That thing is like a magnet for Amphileph—it cannot stay here!" said Caratacus.

"My lord, please hear me out. It is true that Amphileph's armies seek Evliit's sword, but I have come here in secrecy, sharing with no one that which I carry. My lords ask that you put away the Sword in the safety of your keep only until such time that we have made repairs. At that time, we will come again to retrieve it. Galbard has taken Tiamphia, Ronan, and Jalin into the west, away from Shintower, to make their home upon the western shores."

Cayden felt the heat rising in his face. Telling Caratacus that Galbard had given up the Sword did not seem prudent. "My lord, I beg of you. If the Sword is captured at Shintower, will not Amphileph seek out the fortress of Moonledge on the very next day? And declaring it here could bring the Camonra away from your daughter, could it not?"

"To the very people I have been tasked with defending!" cried Caratacus. "No cast of this die favors me."

"The die favors the brave," answered Cayden. "I'm told that there's no short supply of bravery in the hearts of Moonledge Peak's people," he said. "These are desperate times, my Lord Caratacus. The people of Shintower are calling upon that bravery now."

"I will consult the priests," said Caratacus. "Give me a moment."

"Yes, my lord," Cayden replied. Caratacus left the room, and he placed the Sword's case upon the council table. It was the first time he had taken pause to actually look at the craftsmanship of the case itself. The dark polished wood was adorned with symbols of ancient Rionese, embossed with gold. The hinges were intricately carved with flowers and vines. It was truly a thing of beauty.

Caratacus reentered the room followed by a priest and two acolytes. They looked tired and put out until they sighted the case, and then Cayden could see that they could barely contain their excitement.

"My lord," the priest said. "Is this what I think it is?"

"Quiet," said Caratacus. "Make a safe place for it, and say nothing."

The priest's face immediately turned stoic. "Yes, my lord." He picked up the case and exited the room.

Cayden's anxiety level jumped with its unceremonious exit.

"It will be well guarded," said Caratacus, apparently noticing Cayden's expression.

"Yes, my lord. Then I will ask for your leave and report to Shintower."

"Very well. I expect every effort made to see to Tiamphia's safety."

"Of course, my lord," replied Cayden, bowing and exiting the council chambers.

He made his way back through the keep and out onto the steps with the escort of the soldiers, and when they had left, he continued into the predawn darkness south of the temple steps, his hands extended in front of him in his blindness. He was greatly relieved to hear the familiar buzzing of the Bhre-Nora. Aleris appeared carrying a small lamp, shielding its green light so that it only illuminated his face.

"We must hurry!" said Aleris. "Lift your arms!"

Cayden complied, and his stomach turned over as he soared into the dark night sky.

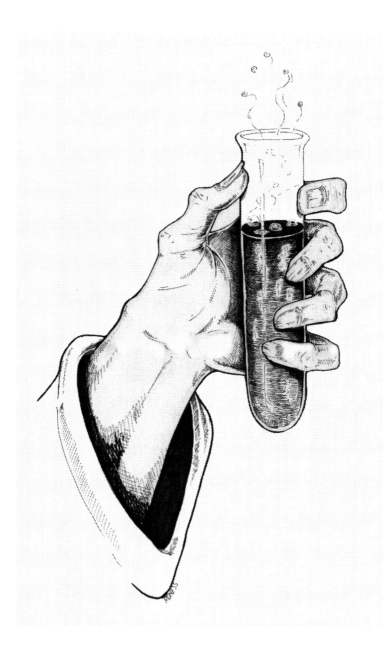

Chapter Nineteen

Amphileph's Revenge

Ardhios was frustrated. He lay in his bed looking at the ceiling.

The woman lying beside him touched his cheek. "My lord, what troubles you?" asked Portina, a woman he had met during his travels to Highwood. His life had been loveless before her, and her decision to ride back with him six winters past had changed his very fiber. With the pressures of kingdom-building and the growing tension among the Seven Warriors, it was his talks with her that helped him maintain his sanity.

She curled up to him, gently stroking his chest. "Is there nothing that gives you pleasure anymore?"

Ardhios moved her dark, flowing hair from her playful smile. "For ten seasons, I have tried repeatedly to talk some sense into Mordher, but it is no use. Mordher refuses to deal with the men of Highwood, or anyone related to the Rion Guard."

"Perhaps, my lord need only find what brings Mordher pleasure," she giggled.

Ardhios sat up. "Mordher and the other warriors care not for the domestic skill required to *build* anything."

Portina sat up as well, pulling the sheet up to her neck. "It is so cold. Will you build us a fire?"

"Of course," he answered. He rolled out of bed, pulled on his pants and his boots, and then he slipped on his shirt, and walked over to the mammoth fireplace across the room. He threw some logs on the glowing coals, poking them with the wrought-iron poker until flames danced around them. He stared at the flames, deep in thought.

"Mordher and the others have opted for war alone," he said. "And if not for that, who could say that the Camonra would *not* have taken this kingdom from us before a single stone was laid? Even now, as we warm ourselves by this fire, Mordher is watching over the eastern edge of the valley. He does not shiver in the cold. He builds an army of warriors with his iron fist, disciplining their ranks to fear him more than the cold. But they do not build—they destroy. He loves nothing else."

"Then it is good that you will show him the great works that you have done," Portina said. She pulled the sheet off the bed and sat with it wrapped around her behind him, leaning her head on his back. "Look at all that has come to pass. You undertook the building of a massive fortress in Candra, and when the small forest to the west could not supply the wood required, you came to the men of Highwood and found them willing and able, and you alone have built a bond with them. It was wise, my lord."

"The wisdom of it may yet be proven," answered Ardhios. "But one thing is true: without the wood from Highwood, we would never have completed the framing, flooring, or ceilings, much less the scaffolding required to raise the structure. Candra may have had hundreds of skilled masons, both cutters and layers, but they would still have only outlined this Great Hall had Highwood not supplied the thousand or so laborers to support them."

"You worry too much, I think," asserted Portina. "Mordher will see."

"You don't know Mordher like I do," responded Ardhios.

Portina wrapped her arms around him and moved to his side, watching the flames with him.

"You alone have garnered the love of the people, my lord, even though you never subscribed to their beliefs in Fehamina or any of the other gods of the moon and stars. They love you, not Mordher, or any of the others."

"Careful how you speak of them," cautioned Ardhios. "Such words would bring wrath from my brothers—a wrath I could not control." She looked down then, and he reached out his hand to lift her chin and placed a kiss on her cheek. "Get dressed; I must be about my business."

* * *

Ardhios came down from his bedroom and walked outside, looking about the courtyard. Craftsmen were building carts and wagons to transport stone and sea coal; they built boats to fish. The quarrymen and smiths were having a friendly game of pins in the early light, smoking their pipes and laughing; carpenters were cutting the joists and floorboards and other necessary supports for some of the outer rooms. Most everything was finished in the main hall and keep, and there had been talk of creating a second set of curtain walls around everything, though he had not approved of a final design.

Maybe he had been too busy to notice, but it suddenly dawned upon him that it was just as Portina had said. By doing these things, by bringing together the crafts and the peoples of Candra and Highwood, he created something more than stone buildings—he managed to recreate the life they had lost in leaving Rion, and that semblance of their old life brought a new sense of belonging and community to all involved. He did take a moment then to truly stop and look around with amazement at what he had managed to raise in the quiet valley next to the Candra Mountains.

It is time, he thought. "Page!" he shouted, and a young boy snapped to his side.

"In celebration of the Great Hall's completion, send messengers to call upon Mordher and the other Warriors to return from the eastern front. Bring me paper, pen, and wax, and I will write it in my own hand and seal it. Be quick, boy!"

Within the hour, the scroll was sealed, and a rider bolted eastward.

* * *

A week after Ardhios dispatched the messenger for Mordher, the first winter's snow fell. Ardhios walked upon the short curtain wall that surrounded the central temple and pondered the beautiful night sky. He made his way down the stairs along the wall and into a domed room in the corner of the curtain walls. The room housed an olive press, and Ardhios often came into that room to think, for the woman that minded the donkey that turned the pressing stone rarely spoke or even seemed to notice him, and oddly enough, the ceaseless sound of the stone wheel crushing the olives was soothing.

She lightly switched the donkey's rump, and then she picked up the bellows to stoke the fire that warmed the room and boiled the oil in a clay jar that hung above it, scooping some of the impurities from the surface without saying a word to Ardhios. He smiled to himself how little mind she paid to his supposed position of authority, so dedicated was she to her craft. She shared the room with him, tolerating him, Ardhios thought, as long as he did not interrupt her work.

When her fire appeared to die down, she stepped out of the room, and a man emerged from the shadows, his hood covering his face.

"Be quick," said Ardhios. "What have you learned?"

The man glanced around and removed his hood. It was one of the acolytes of Moonledge Peak's Elder priest. "The sword of Evliit is at Moonledge Peak," he said.

"Evliit's sword is a myth perpetrated by The Guard," answered Ardhios. "Do not bother me with wives' tales."

"No, sire, I have seen it with my own eyes!" the spy insisted. "The Elder priest has locked it away for protection, and Caratacus tells no one of its existence, not even the high council of Moonledge."

There was a rustling sound outside. Ardhios fished out a small bag of coins from his coat and tossed it to the acolyte. "Keep your ears open. There's more where that came from. Now be gone." The acolyte quickly put away the coins and disappeared up the stairs just as the old woman reentered through the opposite doorway carrying several pieces of wood. She went back to tending her fire, and Ardhios was pondering the meaning of his spy's news when a page burst through the door, rating a short stare from the old woman.

"My liege, the warriors return!" the page said, winded.

"Very well," Ardhios said, and he walked up the winding, wrought iron staircase that took him to the square tower's landing above the valley. A thousand men rumbled to a standstill on the grounds below the Great Hall, and Ardhios had to admit that the sheer number of warriors that followed his six brethren—Mordher in the lead—concerned him. Mordher could be ruthless, but by himself, the damage might be contained. Saddle an army behind him, and Mordher might truly become totally unmanageable.

Ardhios made his way back down the stairs toward the fields east of the castle to meet Mordher and the others coming through the large wooden gates that marked the entrance to the courtyard.

"So *this* has occupied your time?" Mordher inquired in his usual gruff tone.

"Yes, brother," Ardhios replied. "This is it."

"Have the men make camp on the lawn," Mordher said to one of his soldiers, who responded with a fist against his chest.

"Yes, my lord!"

Ardhios led them through the courtyard into the Great Hall, where they removed their helmets and some of their heavier armor. He pointed out the various features of the incredible craftsmanship that had gone into the building of the hall, leading up to a massive table of polished wood. "And here we have our feasting table!" he said, hoping to spread some of his enthusiasm.

"We will drink to this!" Mordher replied. The roar of Mordher's voice set the maidens into action, and they began preparing the long table at the western end of the great room.

The Warriors walked into the hall, and Ardhios noticed them running their hands along the table's polished surface and admiring the eagle-claw carvings on the table legs. The seven high-back chairs were padded and covered with woven upholstery bearing a symbol of seven swords. As they laid down their weapons and were seating themselves, Ardhios started to take the seat at the center.

"I notice you seat yourself at the center of the table, Ardhios," Mordher commented. "Does that mean you have set yourself above us?"

In the two seasons Mordher and the others had been away, Ardhios had forgotten how much Mordher enjoyed stirring things up.

"Sit at the center, brother, there's no rank between us," Ardhios said with a slight nod.

"I wouldn't think of it, my liege," Mordher answered, and the other Warriors laughed. "Keep your seat and whatever power that having carpenters and farmers bowing to you brings. I haven't the stomach for work such as this," Mordher said. Still standing, he grabbed a large piece of meat from the plate before him and ripped the meat from the bone with his teeth, and then he snatched up a cup of ale and washed it down.

"As we rode in, I saw that some of the craftsmen wore the colors of Rion. Were I in need of entertainment, I might have shown them how I spit upon Rion!" he said, hocking up a mouth full of spit and hurling it forward onto the floor with the whole of his upper body to emphasize his point.

"It has taken many able craftsmen, Mordher, to build a hall such as this," Ardhios replied, ignoring Mordher's gesture.

"You have brought them from Highwood, I take it," he said. Mordher plopped down in the chair nearest the end of the table, crossing his legs on the table and letting the mud of his boots drop beside the food plates.

"I've met with the leaders of Highwood, Mordher. They wish to keep the peace between us," he answered. "They have seen the Inferiors to the east of their homes in the wood, and they see us as much less a threat than they are."

"Then they do not know *me*," Mordher said dryly. Again, a hearty laugh rang through the hall from the other warriors.

"Still," Ardhios continued. "The builders have been requested to construct a defensive wall between them and the Inferior encampments, and I have agreed to—"

"What?" Mordher asked. He slammed his cup upon the table with enough force to bend its brass base. "*You* agreed?"

"I've made many agreements for our part, Mordher, this is nothing new. The men of Highwood have seen our strength grow mightily, and they only wish to join with us against our common enemies."

"They'd better," Mordher said. "While you have been busy laying stones, I've built an army that is unmatched in this new country."

"A treaty is wise, Mordher. Many craftsmen have made their home in Highwood. We couldn't have completed so much without them."

"I despise them," Mordher said. "They swear no allegiance to anyone but the Rion Guard, the very ones that brought us the misery we now enjoy."

"Look around you," Ardhios smiled. "You're a lord in your own hall. You command an army that even the Rion Guard would envy. What misery indeed!"

Mordher rose from his seat and walked around the table, looking over the arched ceiling, his eyes tracing the stained beams of wood that crisscrossed the expanse of the hall's stonework. He made his way to where Ardhios sat, and he turned and placed his fists on the table, knuckles down, leaning forward to look into Ardhios' face. "If you think I wouldn't trade all of this for even a moment with my wife and child, you are sadly mistaken. I will build an army that will control the new world, and neither Rion nor any of its charges will stand against us, or I will crush them—mercilessly."

Ardhios leaned into him. "I'm not your enemy, Mordher."

"You would do well to keep it that way," Mordher replied, and then he leaned back from the table, walked over and picked up his cup, and emptied the goblet. "Beautiful hall, Ardhios," he said, tossing the cup into the middle of the floor and walking toward the door. The other warriors rose to follow him.

"Wait!" Ardhios called out. "I've something you'll want to hear."

"That you have women and more drink?" Mordher scoffed. There was a round of laughter.

Ardhios was already regretting saying anything. He didn't want to lay all his cards on the table, but their lack of respect cut more deeply than he wanted to admit.

"The Elder at Moonledge Peak has Evliit's sword," he said.

The laughter stopped.

"What did you say?" asked Mordher.

"I have established a source in Moonledge, and he has informed me that Evliit's sword is under the protection of the Elder there," answered Ardhios.

"There is no Evliit, and there is no Sword of the Watch. These are tools to control the minds of simpletons," said Mordher.

"But if you were to *acquire* such a holy relic of The Guard, would that not shake the very foundation of their faith?" said Borian. "What better way to strike at the heart of Rion?"

Mordher seemed very pleased with that potentiality.

"Careful, Borian. A move such as that could unite all of Erathe against us," said Ardhios. "Wouldn't it be better to convince the followers of The Guard that Candra's strength would best protect their holy relic, and that the time of The Guard has passed? It could be acquired without spilling so much as a drop of blood."

"You and your politics," Mordher sneered. "You do your talking, and I'll build an army of unquestionable strength. We'll see which path is best." Mordher turned and threw open the massive doors leading to the courtyard. He walked outside, leaving the doors open behind him, and snow spiraled across the beautifully etched floor.

The other Warriors followed him out, leaving Ardhios alone with his thoughts.

* * *

"Hold still!" Amphileph yelled. Citanth tried to keep his hands from shaking while he held up a sheet of thick parchment.

Amphileph used his new mastery of kinetics outside the Binding to scrawl a list of items he demanded. The pen lightly dipped into the inkwell and stroked the parchment with grace, making Amphileph's face shine with delight. With a flick of his finger, he tapped the pen upon the paper, making a strong *splat* for punctuation.

"If your idiocy were not to have so severely thinned the ranks of the Camonra, I could send them out into every land, and I would have these ingredients in no time!" Amphileph said. "Fill a clay pot from the well and bring it to me!"

"Yes, master," answered Citanth. He returned to the Bindings edge with the pot, and water sloshed out of it with his sudden stop.

"Come close," said Amphileph. "Lean the lip against the Binding."

Citanth pushed it in as far as he could, and Amphileph pushed his hand out into the Binding's energy field until it would go no further. His ring opened, and tiny granules from a small compartment escaped, sticking to the Binding's wall as if the water pot attracted them. A thin line of them passed through the energy field and into the water; one granule at a time, they passed into the clay jar that Citanth supported on his hip.

"Now, pour the water all around the Binding and out into the field!" commanded Amphileph, and Citanth did so. Covered in pulsating red veins, green vines the size of Citanth's thigh burst from the dirt and spread across the land, leading outward from around the Binding to the edge of Black Mountain Valley. They sprouted up over trees and buildings, bearing sacs all along their length. Opaque at first, the vines' sacs became translucent as they matured, filling with a cloudy yellow liquid, and within them, something was moving. Upon closer inspection, Citanth saw a Camon growing rapidly upon the veins within the sac.

Amphileph watched them closely. "The vine will last but one season, giving me but one chance to rebuild my army, so you will tend them night and day. If any struggle to claw their way through the sacs' thick membranes, cut open the sacs to release them, and mark the weaklings with a brand! Fail me, and I will serve your guts to them."

After weeks of harvesting the Camonra, Citanth felt haggard. The sticky substance from the sacs matted his hair, and many days' growth of beard was on his face. His clothing was dirty and soiled, and he had scratched sores on his forearm until they bled. He had opened hundreds of these sacs, and immediately determined that these Camon were more vicious than their counterparts had been, as well as darker skinned and with much more hair upon their bodies. Citanth had beaten several of them away from him at birth, for they had attacked him almost immediately upon clearing their eyes of the thick mucus-like liquid.

This new breed of Camonra were even more fearlessly obedient to Amphileph, and though they had skin like humans and their Camon brothers before them, their blood red eyes and thicker body hair set them apart. When the sacs burst, they gathered before the Boundland, just outside Citanth's simple home. More than once their chanting had made Citanth mad with loathing, for they would call out Amphileph's name sometimes deep into the night. They tirelessly made weapons and armor, bred war dogs and Azrodh.

When the Camonra numbered in the hundreds, Amphileph began to send the strongest among them into the west, and one by one, they returned to him with the ingredients that he demanded. Amphileph rewarded each of them with dominion over some facet of the meager existence of the Camonra, a greater weapon, or some potion that made them stronger, faster, or healed some ailment.

They gathered his strange list of ingredients from Moonledge and Candra, Calarph and Highwood to the edge of the deadly chasm that separated Rion from the remainder of the world and even east into the Dark Forest of the frontiers. They killed men and Camon alike to find that which their master desired, but return they did, six seasons gone, with everything he had asked.

For nearly two risings of Erathe's moon, Amphileph had stood careful watch over Citanth. He heated and stirred, separated and combined the elements, distilling a sickly black mixture that stank of death. When it was done, Amphileph ordered the Camon females into the huts of the northern camp, and he called the males to himself. They filled the grounds north of the Binding, but when Amphileph stood up to speak, a hush fell over the warriors, and their war dogs were jerked into silence with chain or strap.

"The Creator hath given them life, these men of Rion, but they have done nothing but blaspheme the very name of the Creator whose favor lets them take their next breath! Do they honor him that hath created them?"

"No!" roared the rows of Camonra seated before him.

"All the beauties of proud Erathe have they been given, but do they respect the gift of the world around them?"

"No!" they roared again.

"They considered themselves the very embodiment of the Creator in this world, but will these faithless men reign over all?"

"No! No! No!" the Camonra bellowed.

"You are right and true, my beloved warriors! Your children will be numbered like the leaves of the great forest of Calarph! You will destroy the petulance of men upon this world! You will set right that which men have made contemptible. You will ride into the west—to the castle in the mountains that men call Moonledge, to Highwood, and to the Tower near the sea—you will go and slay every man that makes their homes there! And will you have mercy on their wives and children?"

They beat upon their chest like drums, screaming "No! No! No! No!"

"First, bring me the weak that I might make them strong!" Amphileph demanded. The majority of the Camonra separated themselves from the branded males. "You that do not bear the brand, go forth to the northern camp and join the females! Lock your doors and wait for Citanth to come for you!" When they had left, Amphileph faced the remaining Camonra that bore the brand. "And for the Watchers who have turned against me and for all mankind, I have brought about a destroyer!" Amphileph screamed. "Citanth!"

Citanth emerged from his hut carrying the culmination of Amphileph's alchemy—a single glass vile of black liquid. His face was sallow and emotionless.

The night sky was clear and cold, and Amphileph saw the bright, near planets of La, Sapath, and Denf clearly. He pointed at a line that the shining planets made between the horizon and Erathe's moon.

"They align only once in this age, Citanth! Bring forth the Aramadhi now!" Amphileph cried. His face grew deep red, and his eyes bulged in their sockets.

One of the Camonra stepped forth, and his brethren's grunts took on a rhythm with an increasingly frenetic pace. He was dressed in the ceremonial garb of the Aramadhi, a sacrifice to the Creator, the long, black feathers of the Arama birds fastened to his arm and head with bands of leather. He took the vile in his hands, and the chanting rose to a deafening volume. He uncorked the vile, drank its contents, and screamed his most defiant battle cry. All the Camonra in attendance followed with equally chilling howls and screams.

"Go now, my son! Go with all speed to the west!" shouted Amphileph. The Aramadhi ran then, ran with the abandon of one on a holy mission.

The crowd opened a path to the west, and he sped by them, his skin showing through a pulsating blackness flowing through his veins with the pace of his racing heart. He was still running when his skin tore apart at his back with a gushing sound that opened to the birth of an Angrodha, a fearsome dragon with a near insatiable desire for destruction and the taste of flesh and blood. It shook off the skin of its dead host, trumpeting a violent screech. Citanth thought the sound of it pierced the hearts of even the brave Camonra, who for a moment stood their ground in spite of their brand. Steam rose off the leathery skin of the creature in the cold air that permeated the month of Naap, and when the creature turned its angular head toward the Camonra, they slowly moved back from it until several of them broke for cover.

Their quick movement seemed to attract the creature's attention, and it suddenly struggled to fly toward them, half bounding, half pushing itself with its wrinkled, nubile wings. It pounced upon one of the Camonra and tore him to pieces, looking up from the frayed carcass with quick jerks of its head as if it might catch another of them, and then it quickly fed again with its ripping teeth.

"Good!" Amphileph squealed with laughter. "Feed! Be strong! Grow!"

Citanth backed into the wall of his hut. Then he scrambled inside and slammed the door shut, laughing, then crying, then screaming at the top of his lungs as the horror of the Angrodha was unleashed on the Camonra outside. He could still hear Amphileph shouting, and he raised his head just enough to peer through the wooden slats in his window.

"Taste the flesh of your brothers, Angrodha!" Amphileph shouted, and the creature stopped for a moment as if to acknowledge Amphileph's words. "Go and destroy all that stand in your way!"

The great creature raised his head, threw back an arm of the Camon into its gullet, and then flew into the air, clumsily at first but ever so slowly with gathering skill, disappearing west into the cold night air.

"What have you done, Amphileph?" Citanth questioned from within the security of his small room. Amphileph seemed even more emboldened by the creature, raising his hands and swirling the dark clouds that hung over the Boundland. "Rain down this misery upon all who stand against me, and on all that stand in ignorance of my power!"

Citanth watched the Camonra in horror. They beat upon their chests, the vast majority of them still standing their ground, showing their bravery and devotion. "Run!" Citanth shouted, but they could either not hear him, or did not care.

Slowly, drops of black rain began to fall upon them. Boils rose up on their flesh within seconds of contact, and any that had not made it to cover howled out in pain. Those of the Camonra that could not reach cover fell to the ground and melted into it. A foul stench rose from their blistering bodies. The spines of the fallen Camonra arched up and tore away from their appendages, forming some kind of new creature that emerged from the blackened mud and slithered away.

Citanth covered his ears, but he could still hear shrill cries, and he realized then they were war dogs. He ran to the opposite wall and moved the wooden blinds to look toward the northern camp. Hair fell from the bodies of the dogs that were unlucky enough to be out in the open, down in the fight pits, or in uncovered cages. They writhed in agony, chewing their way through their cages, clawing their way out of their pits, and dragging their mutated bodies into the west.

He could hear Amphileph laughing and then make a choking sound that drew Citanth back to the opposite window. The dark rain began to blot out his view of Amphileph, sizzling on the spherical orb of power that was his cage, but just before the black coating was complete, he saw Amphileph fall to the ground foaming at the mouth, looking near death.

* * *

The Angrodha flew westward, ascending higher and higher into the air, circling in great arcs, drying its birthing from its wings and snorting the cooler air. It encountered the rising ash from the great tear in the land below, and it turned northward, where its coal black eyes caught a herd of deer among the wooded areas north of Tobor's camp. It folded its wings and accelerated into a dive, swooping down upon them, baring its teeth for the kill, saliva spraying from its mouth. It had already grown considerably larger, and the joy it experienced in the hunt caused it to *caw* once, scattering the herd.

It slammed one of the large bucks to the ground with its razor sharp talons. The buck struggled against the pressure of the creature's strong jaws for a moment more, when the still young dragon turned its neck with a jerk, tearing the buck in half. It crunched down the buck, bones, antlers and all, and then it curled up upon the bloody mess and rested, waiting for the darkness of night.

* * *

Tobor was once again whittling on his porch when he heard the strange noise in the night. The piercing cry was like nothing he had heard before, and he laid down his carving block and placed his knife back into his scabbard. Moments later, Idhoran appeared with several warriors in tow.

"My lord, you've heard the sound coming from the north?" he asked.

"I have," Tobor said.

"What creature makes a noise such as this?" Idhoran asked.

"I know not," Tobor responded.

Adheron appeared upon the porch; the concubines in their nightclothes could just be seen behind him in the light of the torches that the soldiers carried.

"What is it, Father?" Adheron asked. "I heard a terrible shriek in the distance."

"Quiet," Tobor said. "Close the door."

Adheron reached behind him to close the heavy oak door. The concubines attempted to look around it until the latch set. For their protection, Tobor did not allow the Camon females and young to venture out at night.

"Do not alarm the women," Tobor said.

Dark clouds began blotting out the moon and stars, and Tobor could hear a murmur beginning among the troops in the camp across from him.

"What's happening, Father?" Adheron asked.

"Go inside, Adheron."

"Father?" Adheron replied, noticeably upset by the command.

"Question me not," Tobor retorted.

"Yes, Father," said Adheron, the door closing behind him to the muffled sound of a litany of questions from the concubines.

No sooner was his son indoors, than different strange sounds starting coming from the east. At first, Tobor thought it sounded like rain, but there was more than that. There was a sizzling sound and animal cries of agony.

"Out of the rain!" Tobor shouted, and Idhoran and the other men shuffled inward under the porch, slowly at first, and then as drops of the black rain fell upon them and the awful boils appeared, rapidly. They pressed with all their might against the others closer to the front wall of Tobor's home, squeezing up under the cover of the porch, crying out in agony themselves. Tobor opened the door to his home, and the group pushed inward, falling inside. Smoke rose from the sizzling pockets in their skin.

"Help them!" he yelled, and his concubines quickly covered their wounds with cloths.

Tobor jumped to his feet and stood back in the doorway. He could see the movement of the rain was westward toward the main encampment. A wave of smoke stirred from the ground as it crossed the open space between them, life sizzling like meat upon the flame, withering every plant that it touched into a black goo.

"Get inside!" he screamed at the top of his lungs, but there was no hearing him over the storm. In desperation, he yelled to Adheron. "Sound the alarm!"

Adheron ran to the second floor and blew his horn from their second-story window. Tobor could see the encampment clearly stirring with the sound of it. Those unfortunate enough to be outside began screaming, and then screams of agony rang out everywhere in the camp.

"I'll go to them!" Idhoran yelled and started out from Tobor's porch, but Tobor caught his arm. Something heavier began falling right in front of them, bouncing off the roof into the yard, bursting on the path and in the grass with a *plop-plop-plop* sound.

"Birds fall from the skies in whole flocks!" cried Tobor. "It is death to go."

Tobor could see his people lighting lanterns in the huts in the main encampment, and much to his alarm, some of the males emerged from their homes to see what was happening.

The Azrodh and war dogs began crying out in agony. One of the war dogs began running toward the Tobor's porch, but it flipped over and writhed on the ground as the black poison that fell from the skies washed the hair from its body. It wiped its forearms over its head, removing its ears in a pile of blackened skin. It tried to run again, but its hind legs withered as if the bones turned to mush, dragging on its belly as quills push out from its spine, one after another, pushing the skin into vanes between them. It clawed the earth in front of it, stretching its front legs to almost twice their original size, shaking its head and craning its neck into a mass of rippling muscles. It howled out then, no longer in pain, but with ferocious anger. It seemed to notice Tobor anew, snapping at him as its claws cut furrows into the stone steps leading to the porch. It stopped for a moment and gagged, coughing up a mass of tissue, and then its jaws grew larger, stretching the skin of its lips away from the gums, its growing canine teeth tearing through the skin of its face. Tobor grabbed his crossbow and fired, and the bolt entered through its open mouth, penetrating its upper soft palette, the arrowhead protruding through the snout next to its left eye. It roared in pain, crushing the bolt with its jaws and slithering away into the darkness.

For two hours, the black rain fell upon the encampment, and all that Tobor and the others could do was watch the misery unfold. When they did finally move down the walkway to the encampment, females and children were crying for their missing mates and fathers, and the males that remained were doing their best just to comfort them.

"Why is this happening?" the females cried. "Why has the father done this?"

Tobor winced at this reference to Amphileph.

"What father does this to his children?" Tobor yelled in desperation. "He has cursed this land! It will no longer sustain us! We move the camp northward!"

Idhoran moved toward Tobor to intercede. "My lord—"

"Today!" Tobor screamed. He turned toward his own home, but then stopped and turned back to Idhoran and the others. He could see his own son and concubines coming toward him, their terrified faces illuminated by the pre-dawn light. It was the only real home they had ever known, and after a lifetime of mastering destruction, its building may have represented the only thing that he had ever *created*. "Get them ready, Idhoran. Whatever it takes! This place will destroy us all! Send out the scouts! I must know where this black death ends."

The Angrodha's call punctuated Tobor's sentence.

"There's little time," Tobor said. "The evil of Amphileph is upon us!"

By mid-morning, the scouts returned. "All manner of strange creatures wander the countryside, my lord, but the black clouds are no more."

"And how far must we go?" asked Tobor.

"This curse poisons all the fields north of Rion and east of Amphileph's temple, but it stops short of the men in the woods."

"The north wind from the fire gates of Rion must have pushed the clouds toward the northern mountains," said Tobor. "Prepare your families to leave at once," he instructed the scouts, and they signaled their respect and made haste to their own huts.

Idhoran looked at him. "What do you command, my lord?"

Tobor felt overwhelmed. "I have lost over thirty of our soldiers to this dark night," he said. "What of the Azrodh?"

"Most of the Azrodh were tied off just outside their masters' huts," answered Idhoran. "What remains of them is twisted flesh. They push around the camp on mangled legs, but all manner of teeth and claws still make them dangerous. I've ordered the soldiers to destroy them," Idhoran said.

Tobor could hear the sorrowful cries of the infected creatures. "Such misery deserves the axe and spear," he said.

His soldiers had cornered one of the mangled creatures in the main walk that split the camp down the center.

"Clear it from the path!" Tobor cried. "We cannot lose any more time with it!"

Two soldiers drew their swords and moved toward it, when suddenly Tobor heard one of the remaining war dogs growling—a sound he knew always signaled a threat to their masters. The growl turned to wild barking and there was a scream from behind him. A rush of wind made him draw his sword.

The Angrodha had landed upon the mutated Azrodh with both claws. The sound of bone snapping signaled the strength of its grip. One of the soldiers was so startled that he fell beside the creature and began pushing himself backward on his hands and feet. The other screamed out and swung at it, his blade glancing off its chin. The Angrodha's head fell away with the swing of the sword and then snapped back, its teeth tearing away most of his attacker's chest cavity. He fell to his knees, and the Angrodha smacked down the quick meal of armor and flesh, and then snapped him up into the air by one shoulder.

"Weapons!" Tobor cried, and the females and children screamed and ran in all directions. A crossbow bolt shot into the dragon's hindquarter, and it jerked back its thigh. It grabbed the bolt with its teeth, pulled it out, and spat out the bolt with a low growling sound. It looked around—eyes narrowing with hatred—and it clawed its way toward the soldier reloading his crossbow and cut him in half with a swipe of its powerful forearms.

A second shot caught it in the thick of its neckline. It roared its defiance, the sound of which was deafening, shaking their guts in their bodies.

"Take cover!" Tobor yelled, and the creature noted his location at the sound of it. He dropped the remains of the Azrodh and moved toward Tobor.

Tobor jumped through the wooden slats of the nearest hut's window. The creature tore away one side of it and pushed his head inside. Tobor tripped over something in the floor and rolled to one of the walls. The Angrodha destroyed the entire wall of the hut, pushing its body through the opening. Its wings caught upon the hut's ceiling, and its teeth snapped the air just in front of Tobor repeatedly. Tobor kicked a chair into its face, which it caught in its teeth and closed its jaws upon it, splintering the chair into pieces. The Camon general attempted to stand, but his sword caught the side of a large pot hanging over the kitchen fire, swinging the pot on the pot-hanger. The Angrodha swung down at him, hitting upon one end of the table and flipping it end over end, where it struck the bottom of the pot. The scalding hot soup pot that had been forgotten over the fire bounced off the ceiling and flew into the Angrodha's face. The winged reptile pulled its head back out of the hole in the wall in reaction to the intense pain. Tobor leapt to his feet and burst through the door on the opposite side of the hut. The creature shook its face and wiped it with its forearm.

The Camonra were yelling from all directions, and the Angrodha looked around at them with intense anger. Two more crossbow bolts struck its body, causing it to jerk back, and scrape one of them away from its side with it claws. It clutched the carcass of the Azrodh with one clawed foot and the soldier with the other and pushed off the ground with a *whoosh,* up into the sky.

Tobor was so winded that he dropped to one knee. Idhoran and Adheron ran to his side.

"Father!" Adheron yelled.

Tobor stood up then and put his hands on his head, still breathing heavily. He made a quick check of himself, somewhat amazed that he had escaped with but a few scratches. The hint of a smile crossed his face, and he patted Adheron on the shoulder. "I live to fight another day," he said, and then he turned to Idhoran and pointed north. "Move them out, Idhoran, immediately."

The tribe began emerging from their hiding places, and Idhoran immediately waved them in that direction. "We move northward! Move quickly!"

"Watch over your mother and the others, Adheron," Tobor said of his concubines. "And keep an eye on the sky."

"Yes, Father," Adheron replied.

Tobor drove them northwest through the swamps of what had once been the battle trails to the men of Highwood. The remaining Azrodhs' loads were heavy, strapped with everything that the Camonra could load upon them, in the fear that there would be no returning to their homes. They were moving much slower than Tobor would have liked. Nightfall was approaching. He opted for the cover of the heavy foliage that grew north of the Lake of Esoria.

The concubines had hauled his battle tent once again, as on previous journeys, but Tobor had not allowed them to pitch it—it would provide too much of a target for their flying adversary to spot. This creature changed everything he had come to know in warfare, for he had never fought with a creature of its size that could pounce upon them from the skies at any moment, rendering them into little more than prey. His years of experience as a predator suddenly felt useless against one such as this.

When the bulk of the females and little ones had curled up among the heavy-leaved plants and slept, Tobor paced carefully among them, trying to think of a strategy for defeating the winged marauder, stepping methodically over the concubines and moving out into a small clearing to see the night sky.

As he gazed at the stars, Idhoran found him.

"My liege, what are you orders?"

"I hear strange sounds in the night again, Idhoran. Have every Camon ready to sound the alert. Tomorrow, we will move northward to the mountains and make ourselves a place there in the caves, as the men have done. At least in the darkness of the stone, we might corner the beast and kill it."

"And what of the men there? Do you mean to make war on them? I count three thousand strong that will follow you and take the mountain as our own."

"The mountains have room for all," Tobor said. "We've lost brothers to this plague from the sky, and there will be more lost if the Angrodha finds us out. Our numbers are our hope of our independence from Amphileph."

"The men will not stand for our presence near them," said Idhoran. "Much of what the father said of them is true; you have seen it yourself."

"They fear us, Idhoran," said Tobor. "We have lived in peace these many years since the Battle of High Wood. The unrest has been stirred by those remaining faithful to Amphileph, for they have chosen to wander into the land of men."

"They do not separate us from Amphileph—in their minds, we are one," said Idhoran.

"The father remains good at war," answered Tobor. "Those attacks break the peace and drive hatred for the Camonra into the hearts of men. He intends this, just as surely as he is behind this creature that follows us now."

"We will follow whatever orders you have given, my lord," Idhoran replied. "You are our leader, and you have proven your place."

"You are my—" Tobor began, but he heard something stirring in the brush. Idhoran drew his sword, and Tobor his own, and they began to move toward the sound.

As they walked slowly around through the underbrush, the rain began to fall again, and they moved undercover of the broad leaves of the nearest Soru bush. To their relief, the rain appeared to no longer carry the black death, but fell harmlessly on the their exposed skin. Still, the damp leather vest that Tobor wore under his chainmail stuck to him, letting off a strong odor of sweat. He hesitated for a moment, and he tried to determine the direction of the wind. He did not want an enemy smelling him coming.

They were easing their way around the Soru bush with great care, when Tobor held up a hand, freezing Idhoran's movement. They could hear chewing and crunching very close to them, and Tobor was convinced that whatever it was lay just on the other side of the Soru bush's large fronds.

He moved one of the leaves back carefully with his sword. The severed foot of one of their war dogs was lying in the mud. He slowly lifted the leaf further, and he saw long fangs pushing through the skin of what remained of the hound, pulling the skin from its side like one of his concubines might lift a bed sheet from his bed. He lowered his head a bit more to see, and he saw the head of the creature. It was like the mutated war dog he had seen from his porch, its body nearly eight feet in length, its gray eyes and white pupils focused on its kill.

Tobor glanced at Idhoran and tilted his head slightly indicating that he had found their foe.

Idhoran moved to circle around the Soru bush in the opposite direction, but his armor scraped a dead branch in the underbrush, making the tiniest sound, stopping Idhoran where he stood.

The creature stopped feeding instantly, remaining motionless except for some holes on the side of its head closest to them opening, one after another, as if straining to listen. It began to growl in a low, grating tone and quills stiffened on its face and back, their fleshy vanes quivering in the rain.

Tobor slowly stepped out from behind the Soru bush into clear sight of his present foe. The creature did not move except to extend the remaining quills on its body and swallow the bloody sheet of skin, hair and all, of the dog. It kept its head low to the ground, one eye focused on Tobor and the other twitching back and forth in the direction of Idhoran.

The creature was obviously sizing him up for the kill, and Tobor knew the time it used to do so would allow Idhoran to position himself for the ambush, for they had performed such a maneuver many times in the past. They needed no words to execute it flawlessly.

As Idhoran disappeared on the other side of the Soru, Tobor slowly raised his second hand to the tang of his sword and prepared for Idhoran's attack. If the creature went toward him, Idhoran would strike from the side, and he would do likewise if the creature chose Idhoran.

Tobor slowly bent into a slight crouch preparing for the ensuing attack, when he saw movement beyond the creature. Four more of them emerged from the brush behind it.

"Idhoran!" Tobor cried out in a strained whisper, but there was no response. This was not good.

"Camonra!" Tobor then shouted, calling for the aid of his fellow warriors.

Idhoran mistook his cry for help and burst through the brush on the creature's left. The creature's head turned quickly toward Idhoran, and its massive front legs dragged the remainder of its body in the direction of Idhoran's attack. Several of the other creatures also closed on him from some ten paces behind it.

Tobor ran toward Idhoran and the creatures. He could hear the battle horn of the Camonra sounding behind them.

Idhoran screamed his own battle cry as the creature snapped at him. He swung his sword, its blade breaking off the lower half of one of the beast's long fangs, causing it to shake its head and back away.

"Behind!" Tobor yelled.

Idhoran looked to his right just as one of the other creatures fangs drove up through his thigh. Tobor's blade swung across the body of the first creature, but the quills were surprisingly strong, stopping his blade from doing any real damage.

Idhoran grabbed one of the teeth that protruded from his right thigh and held on to it, keeping the creature in tow. The creature attempted to bite him repeatedly, but Idhoran bent his knee upon the ground, prying its upper jaw open.

"Aaaah!" Idhoran yelled. He flipped his blade in one hand, drove it into the neck of the creature and tore it downward. He attempted to stand with its decapitated head still hanging from his thigh.

Tobor could see a look of terror on his old friend's face, and he screamed a mighty battle cry and swung at the first creature wildly, its black blood flying through the air.

A third creature moved quickly toward Idhoran and lurched up from its legs grabbing Idhoran by the neck. Idhoran dropped his sword and grabbed the quills on its head pulling on them desperately until his arms fell lifeless by his sides.

"No!" Tobor yelled. The horizontal slice of his blade cut across the creature's back. He raised his blade to make another strike but saw a fourth and then a fifth creature emerging from the brush. They pounced upon Idhoran's body while a sixth and a seventh creature circled in front of it, eyeing Tobor and daring him to move among the pack.

Behind him, several of the Camonra appeared with crossbows. Tobor waded in on the creatures, and the Camonra fired their bolts in a mad panic. Tobor killed two more of the creatures before bolts made quick work of the rest, and he fell on his knees beside Idhoran's mangled remains.

"No, no!" he cried again.

"My lord, let us move back to the camp and protect the tribe!" one of the Camonra said.

Tobor knew that there could be more of these creatures. He wanted to take up his friend's body, to bury it upon the hill beside his home, as it should be done with such a mighty warrior, but instead he screamed again. The warrior hardened himself again as great warriors must, knowing there was no time to give Idhoran the honor he deserved. He stood up then and took one last look at his friend's face, picked up the blood-soaked sword of Idhoran and joined his soldiers in returning to the camp.

The sounds of strange creatures now seemed to fill the night, and Tobor roused everyone to move. Mothers pushed their crying infants to their breasts in attempt to silence them.

"Move quickly and silently. Be sure that none fall behind," Tobor instructed.

It was decided that Adheron, Tobor's son and Idhoran's pupil, would take command under Tobor, though Tobor himself thought that the appointment might have been more in respect for Idhoran's wishes than for Adheron's abilities. The shock of Idhoran's death had cast a shadow of gloom over the entire tribe.

They made their way northeast, passing the last remnants of the Lake of Esoria, into the muddy swamps and marshes that formed there from the repeated overflowing of Esoria's banks and the high amount of rainfall. They encountered an amorphous creature, its waist-high body seemingly a mixture of mud, leeches the size of a Camon's arm, and the black film that formed on the mire itself. They lost more of their Camonra, but they remained on a course due northeast, attempting to keep some distance from Amphileph's lands and the men of Highwood.

The month of Naap passed, and most of Falingsor by the time they reached the base of the Faceless Mountains. Falingsor had brought with it a bone chilling cold, and the entire group was completely exhausted, with little food or fresh water for the last several days of their journey. The toll was terrible, and the young ones cried and slumped in their mothers' arms, incapable of the energy to complain further.

"Send the scouts to find the humans, but keep your distance," Tobor commanded. "We want no war with them."

"Yes, Father," Adheron responded.

"Send hunters to find whatever food can be found, but keep the strongest of the Camonra here to protect the tribe should this . . . this dragon return."

"It will be done, Father, and what of your quarters?" Adheron asked.

The concubines began removing the poles for Tobor's war tent from the back of their Azrodh, but Tobor waved them off. "There is no need for that, we will not be here long," he said.

"Lurenda, bring me my pouch," said Tobor. "I will venture into the mountains to seek out the Watcher there," Tobor said.

"Father," Adheron said. "Do not go into the mountains alone."

"Much has passed between Watcher and Camon. To ask for help from Watchers now may do little more than invoke their wrath, but I will do what I must to protect the Camonra, my son," Tobor answered. "Go now and lead the Camonra in my absence, give them hope that all is not lost."

Adheron straightened. "Yes, Father!" he said. He looked around him, and Tobor knew that he could see the fear in the eyes of his people, a sight that he had never seen before. "I will be strong, Father."

"I've no doubt of that, Adheron," Tobor replied. "Now go."

Tobor left the encampment of the Camonra and traveled on his mount due north through the foothills of the Faceless Mountains until a rumbling could be heard in the mountainside itself.

"You are here," said Tobor. He glanced around for any sign of the Watcher of the Mountain. "I am sure that you move the land beneath me. Show yourself, brother of my father!"

The mountainside shook until a crack began in the stone, which crumbled open wider and wider until the crack swallowed up whole chunks of earth and stone, causing Tobor to step back. The rumble slowed to a standstill, and Tophian appeared from the depths.

"Bastard child of Amphileph, what do you want?" Tophian yelled, lowering his staff toward Tobor.

Tobor bristled in response to this form of welcome. "I am Tobor, leader of the Camonra!" he shouted.

"I know what you are!" said Tophian. "But what do you want from me?"

Tobor stepped back and swallowed his pride. "Our father has created a winged creature with teeth the size of daggers and claws that can rip a Camon in half. Our weapons barely pierce its scaly armor, and I fear that without your help, it will destroy my tribe," Tobor began.

"Your creator is mad, and his magic is as black as it is strong," Tophian said. "He's made good on his threat to unleash doom upon this world, and this Angrodha—this black-hearted dragon—it is only the beginning. The Angrodha makes no distinction between man and Camon. It cares for nothing, lives for nothing but to consume all that is not of Amphileph. It will no sooner destroy the Camonra before it makes its feast upon men."

"And there is more," Tobor said.

"Speak it," Tophian replied.

"The Father has wet the land with black poison," Tobor said. "A terrible plague has been set loose upon us all. We flee the jungles not because we want the lands of men, but to save our wives and children." Tobor looked at the ground. "I beg of you to help us."

Tophian's face softened. He walked around Tobor, looking him over.

"I have often pondered whether a soul resided in you, or if there was any redeemable quality that might warrant the mercy of the Watchers. Amphileph's deceit created you, and with such a beginning, little thought was given to your place among the Creator's creatures."

"I have thought many times of our creation and the Father's place in it," Tobor replied. "Our distance from the Father has opened our eyes to many things. If you could know the wonders we have seen in our struggles to free ourselves from our bondage to Amphileph, then you would know that we have found new meaning to our lives. We follow Amphileph no more."

"What then *is* your destination?" Tophian asked.

Tobor stopped, and his mouth came open as if to answer, but no sound emerged. His brain reeled with thoughts. He looked down almost embarrassed at his loss for words. Then he locked eyes with Tophian, and maybe for the first time in his life, he spoke boldly of a new time for the Camonra.

"Great Watcher, this is a question indeed," Tobor said. "If only answering would make it come to pass."

Tobor placed one foot upon a stone and rested his forearm on his thigh armor. He looked down the mountainside toward the Camonra camp, drawing a deep breath and exhaling as if a great weight rested upon his shoulders.

"I dreamed once that we would be a *people*, without fear of our survival, but having hope for our future. We would work a living from the land, and hunt creatures without malice for our survival. We would live in peace with men and they would live in peace with us. We would have our children have their children and their children's children, and die old in the care of our kind." Tobor looked again at Tophian. "I dreamed we would find the true Father that throws the fire from the sky, and we would know him and he would know us."

Tobor turned his face from Tophian, thinking he might wish too much.

There was a long pause, and then Tophian spoke. "Here is a creature of Amphileph's making, a brute of a being, whose huge, muscular body easily hides a thinking, feeling being! Men seldom find such revelation! Now I see something more than the brute's stern gaze—now I see the weathered face of a creature clutching but a thread of hope for a better life."

Tobor turned and looked directly into Tophian's eyes.

"You have learned much in your short lives, creature," Tophian said. "You have learned much indeed."

"Could you—will you help us escape the wrath of our Father?" Tobor asked.

"Amphileph has done many a great evil. It appears to me now that the Camonra may number among those whose lives were nearly destroyed by his arrogance."

"I ask this not for me, but for all my people, Watcher," Tobor said.

Tophian walked around to Tobor's side and looked down into the valley. "I'll do this thing for you, Tobor, for I see hope in your words. Let me go to the men of Moonledge Peak. They will have to be assured of your intentions."

"Yes," Tobor answered. "A Watcher could convince them. They would know that you speak the truth. We will stay clear of men and wait for your return."

Tobor stood up then and faced Tophian. He towered over Tophian, but the Watcher did not flinch. "It's our way to trade something, but I've brought nothing to trade."

"Remain firm in your word, Tobor," Tophian replied. "Know that this alone will repay your debt to me."

"You have my word, and the Camonra will do as I command," Tobor responded. He turned to go down the mountain, but turned back. "How am I to find you when you return?"

"We'll meet here again in four days' time. Leave your camp, and come to me here. We'll discuss what the men of the west have decided."

Tobor grunted. "It will be done." He lowered to one knee and dropped his gaze as he had done so many times before under the iron fist of Amphileph, but unlike all those times, he felt a strange difference in his heart. This Watcher was very much unlike Amphileph. This one had stood his ground without cruelty or abuse.

"I'll not forget this," Tobor said, and then he returned down the mountain.

Chapter Twenty

War Begins

Making good on his decision, Tophian had proceeded directly to the men of the Moonledge Caves, but they received him with great angst. The people had swarmed the council in a panic.

"Lord Tophian, we cannot do battle with this flying creature! And what of the warriors of Candra? Will they not frown greatly on a pact with the Inferiors? This could lump us with our enemies in the eyes of our allies."

Tophian knew as much to be true. "I'm not suggesting that the Camonra live in your midst. Let the Camonra make their camp far away, in the eastern part of the mountains. I could make great caves for them to stay until the threat of the Angrodha has ended."

"My lord, these are the creatures that brought the wrath of the Creator upon us; these Inferiors destroyed our homeland. It is because of them, we are exiled, and because of them, we may never see our families and kindred again. It is a mighty thing that you call upon us to do!"

"Yes," Tophian replied. "A noble thing for sure. These creatures are but pawns in the Watcher's War—it is Amphileph that merits your hatred."

There was a rumbling from the crowd, and Caratacus adjusted his collar; beads of sweat began to form on his now pasty white face.

"My lord, even if we say these things to be so, that these . . . what do you call them?

"Camonra," replied Tophian with reserve.

"That these . . . Camonra . . . will live in peace with us," Caratacus continued, "we cannot change the minds of the world around us by simply saying that something is decreed to be so! Our people will live in fear, and that fear will be our decree's undoing. And when that day comes, many will die, I'm afraid."

The rumble of the crowd swelled again, enough so that Caratacus rapped his gavel and commanded quiet in the room.

Tophian thought about the logic of the council's words. Though he wanted it not to be true, the Watchers' War had rippled through all humanity. Here, first hand, were its effects. Tophian looked at each of the councilmen's faces, and the fear and anguish was palpable. He knew then that the deep caves of Moonledge were still too close. "Evliit's heart is broken for the despair of men," he said. "I've made my request as I've promised to do."

Tophian turned slowly around, looking each of them over one last time for a change of heart. He did not storm out with flair. No, Tophian walked out from them quietly, letting the next of the arguments begin before a stunned council, who had expected him to demand his way. He moved to the exit, looking at the faces of the crowd. Only the ignorant among them did not notice the eyes of the Watcher. He wandered out from the council chambers, searching their faces for hope, and acknowledging his own responsibility, however small it might be, for their plight.

As Tophian left the High Council's chamber, the crier announced that the Candrians were arriving from the south. Apparently, a contingent of warriors had been set to defend the construction of an additional outer fortress at the Moonledge caves. Tophian moved up against one of the walls just outside the chamber and waited, straining to hear their conversation over the rumble of the chamber.

Mordher and Borian entered, arguing.

"What's needed is a great wall to separate us from the Inferiors," Mordher said. "We would hold the high ground and hold back any against us, and I should control the weapon."

"The creatures that move against us are foul, brother," Borian replied. "We would need a great wall indeed. And of this weapon—this Sword—does Ardhios have other news?"

"Bah! The fool fears its possession!" Mordher laughed. "He would have this lot of politicians keep it! Let him find likeminded fools that will lay stone. Let him build our wall! Let him build it for the rest of his days!"

"He'll do it just to spite you!" said Borian, laughing in return.

Tophian took the opportunity to move to them, and his quick movement into their space caught their attention. Tophian noticed that their hands found the tangs of their swords and their faces lost their smiles.

"I apologize for my intrusion," he said. "My name is Tophian, and I've come to ask for your help."

Mordher and Borian relaxed only slightly. Mordher looked over Tophian's clothing, and he bristled. "What's that to us, wizard?"

Tophian tolerated Mordher. It was necessary, to achieve his objectives. "The Camonra of the east have asked me to intercede on their behalf," Tophian said. "They've come to the land of men to escape the new dangers to the south. They wish to live in peace."

"They've a strange way of showing their intentions," Borian said. "There's word that they terrorize the people in the eastern valley, and we've also heard tell of them attacking here in Moonledge."

"There are apparently factions within their tribe. This Camon goes by the name of Tobor. I've met with him, and he's assured me that his tribe has separated themselves from Amphileph and wishes a peaceful coexistence with men."

"The Camonra? They are *all* but minions of Amphileph!" exclaimed Borian. "Are they not the very ones that attacked Rion?"

"Tobor and his warriors were once deceived by Amphileph, attacking Rion in his name, but that has been years past, warrior. Their situation has changed. They no longer swear allegiance to him."

"Bred to kill, those were," Mordher said. "What kind of peace can you make with such savages?"

"The Camonra are under attack themselves," Tophian interjected. "They have called on me to enlist the assistance of men to defend their tribe against an Angrodha."

"An Angrodha?" Mordher replied. "What matter of creature is this?"

"A winged raptor, a dragon—it is yet another of Amphileph's abominations."

"So their master finds no love left for them?" Mordher laughed. "He has created something to destroy another of his own making? It's either genius or madness—hard to say which."

"Amphileph is the source of this evil, not the Camonra, and the Angrodha represents a threat to men and Camonra alike," answered Tophian.

Mordher eyed Tophian. "Then these . . . Camonra . . . would be indebted to us?"

Tophian did not like the tone of the inquiry, but it represented a break in the ice. "All the people would be indebted to you, warrior. Your names would be heralded far and wide."

"But the *Camonra*—they would be indebted to us, yes?" Mordher repeated.

"Yes, I suppose they would," Tophian acquiesced. Tophian could see the wheels turning in Mordher's head. His desire for power obviously drove his decision-making, and Tophian knew that such a man's loyalties change without warning, but he was resolved to move forward.

"We will kill this creature, this Angrodha, if the Camonra swear allegiance to Candra!" said Mordher.

Tophian did not think that there was much chance of either, but he could present it to Tobor. "I will make your offer known to the Camonra," he replied.

"Let them draw out the creature, and our archers will fill the sky with arrows, and we will hack it to pieces!" Mordher said.

"We'll see if such a creature will stand against the Army of Candra!" echoed Borian.

Their bravado did little to impress Tophian, for the potential danger they so easily accepted told volumes of their understanding of the Angrodha. Nevertheless, their offer represented possibly the only chance he had to stop whatever Amphileph was attempting with the attack on the Camonra.

"When could your warriors be ready to travel east?" Tophian asked.

"We'll gather our supplies and be ready to move tomorrow. Borian, have the captains bring fifty men to carry supplies back to the camp."

Borian nodded. "With your leave," he said.

"Make haste," Mordher said, and Borian marched away.

"I'm going to find a hot bath and love among the wenches of Moonledge, wizard!" Mordher said, with a wily smile. "Would you care to join me?"

"No, warrior," Tophian replied. "I'll join you and your soldiers in the valley tomorrow."

"You don't know what you're missing, wizard," laughed Mordher. "The women of Moonledge could show you some real magic!"

"I go to rest in the cool of the caves, warrior. Tomorrow, then," Tophian said. He made his way up the hill toward the caves of Moonledge.

Mordher walked the opposite path toward the brothel on the western side of Moonledge keep until Tophian had made his way up the long row of steps leading into the darkness of cave entrance; then he turned and hurried to the valley below.

He neared the outer edge of the warriors' encampment. "Soldiers of Candra!" he called out, surprising the two soldiers on watch. They immediately went for their swords, but Mordher raised his blade under the chin of the one closest to him. "If I had been the enemy, you'd be dead!" Mordher said. "Let me get that close again before you question my approach and I'll kill you myself!"

"Yes, my lord!" they replied in loose unison. "Forgive us!"

Mordher dragged the blade under his chin, nicking him, and then put it away. It was a small cut, but it began to bleed, and the soldier pinched the cut together with his fingers.

Mordher squatted and tore a piece of goat from a spit over the small fire. "Get Borian!"

"Yes, my lord!" the lower-ranking soldier said. He pulled a torch from one of the holders and ran toward the encampment.

"Bring me some salt," Mordher commanded. He tore away a steaming chunk of the hindquarter with his teeth, attempting to avoid burning his lips, and then wolfed it down.

"Yes, my lord," the soldier replied. He let go of the clotted cut and pulled a small leather pouch from his belt, handing it to his commander. "And we've ale for you, my lord."

Mordher dipped his fingers into the pouch, sprinkled the meat with salt, and handed it back to the soldier. Then he tore off another chunk. "One can never underestimate the value of salt," he added.

"No, my lord," the soldier replied, handing the commander a wooden mug of ale he poured from a keg sitting upon a small cart that some of the town's wenches had brought down from Moonledge. The black tar-like ale ran slowly from the spigot.

Borian appeared, adjusting his armor as if woken from a sleep. "You called, my lord?" he asked.

"The wizard will take us to the Inferiors tomorrow, so that we might kill this creature that hunts them," Mordher said.

"Yes, my lord," said Borian.

Mordher slugged a gulp of the ale, eyeing Borian as if waiting for him to say more.

"The wizard will take us to the very heart of our enemy, yes?"

"Yes, my lord."

"Maybe the Inferiors have more than one enemy to worry about, eh?"

Borian looked at him for a moment, and then he raised his brows in recognition of where Mordher was leading.

"Have the archers ready their bows, and the fighters their swords," Mordher said. "Surely, the wizard gives us an opportunity to claim the Sword of Evliit for our efforts. I think tomorrow will be a glorious day!" A large smile slowly formed on Mordher's face, mirrored by Borian.

"Glorious indeed!"

* * *

The following morning, Tophian met Mordher and his warriors in their encampment below Moonledge. Mordher insisted that Tophian take one of the horses and ride with them. Tophian agreed, wanting to conserve his spiritual energies for the encounter with the Angrodha, though he really did not care for riding.

He led them around the mountain range east, until on the fourth day, just as Tophian had promised Tobor, they arrived at the foothills near the Camonra encampment.

"I will go alone to the Camonra camp," said Tophian. "With tensions what they are, let me tell them of our plans."

"As you wish," Mordher replied. "We'll wait here for you."

"We'll not tarry," said Tophian. "When the last of the sunlight tips the crest of the Black Mountains, come to the eastern end of this mountain range. The Camonra encampment is just around the bend. We'll group together with their forces, and take the attack to the Angrodha."

"We look forward to it," Mordher said.

As Tophian rode away, Borian leaned in close to Mordher. "What do you make of it, Mordher?"

"The Camonra are weakened, running. This Watcher has their trust. We are at the crossroads of a new era, Borian," Mordher said.

"What are you orders?" asked Borian.

"Gather the captains," Mordher said.

*   *   *

Tophian rode first to the path leading up the little plateau where he and Tobor had met, but Tobor was not there. He waited for a short time, and then he became concerned, so he began his descent into the valley below him further east. The sun was at the point where the Candrian warriors would be on the way.

The last few days had been taxing. The Angrodha was strong and agile, and it would continue to grow in size without greatly affecting that agility. It was no foe to take lightly, even given his powers as a Watcher.

He debated getting Mategaladh involved, but his dear friend might have expended more than anyone else in binding Amphileph, so great was his commitment to stopping that madness. Involving Mategaladh now might serve only to get him killed, for Tophian knew that if Mategaladh had recovered even half his powers, he would never back down from a fight. He did not want to chance it. He would have to stop the Angrodha.

Tophian stopped his horse to pray.

"Creator, how could things have gone so wrong? Forgive us, mighty one, if we have taken one so brilliant and as dedicated to you as Amphileph once was—into an enemy of your creation." He ended his prayer and gave the horse a gentle spur toward the ridge of the mountain in order to see further down its slope toward the valley below.

Such brilliance suffered little with the imperfections of men, Tophian thought. When Amphileph began to profess his belief that men had become a blight upon creation and became intolerant of them, he grew steadily bent on their destruction and cleansing the world of their existence. When the Spellmakers had announced that they would end the time of men and bring about the reign of the Camonra, every facet of the ancient Watcher and Spellmaker relationship seemed to fly apart.

Amphileph had crossed the line with Evliit when he created the Camonra, his *warriors*. Evliit simply would not tolerate the arrogance of Amphileph—this concept that he could create a superior creature, a replacement for the race of men. These things were matters for the Creator alone. *Who did Amphileph think that he was?*

Tophian could see the Candrian warriors approaching from the southwest. He met them at the foot of the mountain. Mordher pulled his horse's bit back with enough force that the horse whinnied in pain.

"What of the Camonra?" Mordher asked.

"Tobor wasn't there," Tophian replied. "I fear the worse." Tophian thought he saw a smirk on Mordher's face, but dismissed it. "We go to the Camonra camp."

"Of course," Mordher responded. "Candrians!" he cried, and the rumble of their horses signaled their presence at his side like a storm.

"Follow me back up the mountain side!" said Tophian. "We'll take the high ground."

As they rounded the mountain, the Camonra camp came into view below him. The Angrodha circled high above it, just below Tophian, so close that Tophian moved behind an outcropping of stone to avoid being seen, but it was no use with the two hundred or so Candrians on horseback. The Angrodha had spotted them.

The Angrodha circled again and landed on a ledge of one of the ridges of the Faceless Mountains, just below Tophian and the Candrians. It screeched loudly, the echo of which Tophian thought he heard twice reverberating from the valley. He leaned out and tried to look more closely at the Camonra camp.

He could see that several of the Camonra had taken cover among the foothills of the mountain, and others were still in the open, one of which appeared to be Tobor.

"Archers! Dismount!" Mordher cried, and a group of about fifty archers dismounted and drew their bows.

* * *

In the failing light, Tobor could just see the riders upon the ridge and yelled encouragement to the Camonra. "The Watcher has found us!" he cried. "Let them draw the Angrodha's attention!"

Tobor's excitement ended quickly, seeing Adheron's eyes widen and turn skyward.

"Father!" Adheron yelled. "Run!"

Tobor ran for cover in the brush, and Adheron moved to his father's aid. The Angrodha swooped down upon the clearing, clipping the treetops with one of its hind legs. The trees burst into pieces, and a large branch struck Adheron across the face and chest, throwing him to the ground. He was instantly buried in the incoming debris.

"No!" Tobor yelled, running toward his son. Tobor's giant biceps strained with the branch in an effort to see Adheron, oblivious to the

Angrodha's imminent attack. "Camonra!" Tobor screamed, hoping their attack might distract the winged predator and give Tobor the precious moments he needed to get to Adheron.

En masse, the Camonra began yelling and shooting their crossbow bolts into the creature's scaled hide, and Tobor took the opportunity to throw the branch to the side.

Adheron's body was bruised and battered. He was motionless, and Tobor could not tell if he was alive or dead, but a gash cut through his brow and split his lips. It was bleeding profusely. Tobor started to grab him up, but the Angrodha apparently had all the crossbow bolts it would tolerate, and it attacked, its encroaching shadow startling Tobor.

The Angrodha's wingspan had grown to fifty feet since their last encounter. It thrust its great wings once, throwing dust in his mouth and eyes, blinding Tobor for a moment. He quickly wiped his eyes and saw the Angrodha lifting a short distance into the air before landing among the attacking Camonra. The Camonra scattered, and the Angrodha lowered upon its forearms and sniffed the ground before him. It snorted and cawed, seemingly happy with finding their scent.

* * *

"Do you have torches?" Tophian asked Mordher.

"Yes," Mordher said. "Torches!" he shouted.

"Light them and draw the Angrodha to me!" shouted Tophian.

Tophian dismounted and moved to a clearing on the mountainside.

Ten or so men removed black, tarry stumps of wood from saddlebags and struck up flints to light them. The light of the torches immediately caught the eye of the Angrodha, who cawed and jumped skyward toward them.

"Come to me!" Tophian shouted, and Mordher waved the torchbearers to do as he wished. He watched Tophian lower his eyes and press his hands together at his chest, and then the Watcher lifted his hands, and the very mountainside shook. A murmur rose throughout the Candrians.

"What is this?" Borian asked Mordher.

"I know not," replied Mordher. He and the other Candrian warriors began to move away from the clearing. They could clearly see the outline of the Angrodha against the moon, collapsing its wings into a dive straight for Tophian.

"Stand clear, but be ready!" Tophian shouted to Mordher. The mountainside shook loose stones that rose up, floating just above the ground beside Mordher, who could not resist the urge to push one of the enormous stones with the tip of his sword. It rotated slightly with his nudge as if it was at once weightless and massive, and then Mordher moved back from it. "The creature comes!" he shouted, pointing up to the Angrodha plunging toward them, turning its body, and opening its claws. Tophian lowered his head, and the Angrodha's wings spread to slow it, blocking out the moon and sky.

"Ready!" Mordher shouted to his warriors, but many had given up their courage, dropping the torches and fleeing, some of them catching the winter grass on fire around him.

The Angrodha screamed, and Mordher saw Tophian's face in the orange blaze, his eyes were set and steady, unflinching. He slammed his hands together before him and the stones took flight, striking the Angrodha with such force that the smaller stones shot completely through its leathery wings, and a large stone struck it directly in the face, appearing to knock it senseless.

The Angrodha folded upon itself and fell upon Tophian with a great crash, one of its wings striking the Watcher and throwing him violently against the mountainside, from whence he slid unconscious, off a sheer ridge, falling to the ground below.

Mordher saw that he lay lifeless there, and called to his warriors.

The Angrodha twitched and kicked, struggling to get its bearings. "Attack!" he screamed. Battle cries sprang up all around it, and the Candrians fired their arrows into it, but its scales were too thick, and the arrows stuck only in the meat of its forearms and legs.

The arrows' pricks seemed only to stir the Angrodha to life, and it struggled to get to its feet. The soldiers stabbed and slashed at it with their swords, but it threw a dozen or more of them off the side of the mountain with a swipe of its forearm. The pike men attempted to stab its less-scaled underbelly with their long pikes, and it roared in defiance. The Angrodha rolled from its side onto its belly to protect itself, and clawed at the mountainside, kicking four other soldiers into the air.

From the encampment below, Tobor could see the commotion upon the mountainside, tearing him between carrying away Adheron and taking the attack to the Angrodha. "Camonra!" he screamed. He ran then for the foot of the mountain, and his warriors followed.

Twice the Angrodha attempted to take flight, but the Candrians hindered it, and then it turned to snatch up its attackers and tear them to pieces. The bodies of the Candrians continued to fly from the mountainside.

"We take too many losses!" Borian yelled to Mordher.

Mordher's face showed disgust, as much for the creature as for the retreat, but Borian was right; his army meant more than his word to the Watcher.

"Retreat!" Mordher yelled, and the order came gladly to his remaining men, who turned and ran for their lives.

Mordher could see that the Angrodha was bleeding from several wounds, but it appeared more infuriated than injured. It turned and snapped up more of his warriors with claw and teeth rather than taking to the air. Just when it looked like the Candrians had met their end, the Camonra reached the mountainside, and Mordher marveled at how much more effective their massive crossbows were against the thick hide of the Angrodha, especially at such close range. They attacked with a ferocity that Mordher had only previously seen directed at men, and the Angrodha turned its attention to them rather than the fleeing Candrians.

"We must flee now while we have the chance!" Borian yelled to Mordher, who had stopped to watch the melee.

"Wait, brother!" Mordher replied. "Wait and see!" He and Borian fell in behind a hunk of igneous rock that protruded head-high from the mountainside.

Borian called for the Candrians to regroup, and the Angrodha traded wound for mangling with the Camonra.

Though the Angrodha snapped at him repeatedly, Tobor bound from rocks to cliffs to boulders, narrowly escaping the clashing of teeth, a spectacle like no warrior of Candra had ever witnessed. The Angrodha killed many of them, until Tobor leapt right upon its back and cut deeply into its back with his great axe.

He struggled to pull the axe from the dragon's thick scales, twisting it to free the blade. The Angrodha screamed in pain and took flight, carrying Tobor skyward. He tried to hold on to the creature's shoulder and swing again, but it soared into the night sky. Tobor fell away, and he and his axe crashed upon the mountainside with a sickening thud.

Several of the Camonra ran to his side and picked him up, and though Mordher could tell he was greatly shaken up, the Camon general was still alive. The Camonra howled their defiance at the fleeing creature and lifted Tobor to his feet, carrying him back toward the encampment. They clanged their weapons in victory and cheered Tobor's praises.

"I must go to Adheron!" Tobor shouted. He just managed to get them to put him down.

Mordher watched the creature fly south into the distance. He watched the Camonra celebrate driving the Angrodha away, and his blood boiled. He grabbed a bow and arrow from one of his archers and stretched it so taut that a few of the horsehairs of the string popped loose. Then he let the arrow fly, and it passed between two of the Camonra, catching Tobor just under his right scapula. Tobor turned and looked back at him, and Mordher could see the arrowhead protruding from his chest. Tobor raised a hand to point at Mordher, and then he collapsed. Two or three of the Camonra attempted to catch his fall, but he slipped between their hands, fell to the ground, and slid down the slope in a heap at their feet. They scrambled to turn him over, but Mordher could tell from their expression that his arrow had done its work. The remainder of the Camonra screamed their battle cries and bound toward Mordher, who still held the bow before him.

"Archers!" Borian cried and arrows rained down upon them, killing a great many of the Camonra, but they continued toward the Candrians without regard for their lives.

"Ride!" cried Mordher, and his men mounted their horses and took flight down the mountainside. The Camonra leapt upon them, shooting across Mordher's field of vision, and ripping soldiers from their horses on either side of him. Mordher spurred his horse without mercy, and the Candrians sped toward Moonledge until the Camonra's battle cries faded in the distance.

* * *

Tophian regained consciousness just minutes after Tobor fell, and woke to hear the war cries of the Camonra chasing the Candrians west. He managed to come to his feet to hear the wailing of the females and children from the camp. They were sifting through the remains of the Camonra camp and had discovered the profusely bleeding, unconscious Adheron, and they had assumed the worse. The younger warriors began to emerge from their hiding places, watching the skies for the return of the Angrodha. They found the body of Tobor, and the camp moved from mourning to utter chaos.

They surrounded Tobor's body, raised it above their heads, and carried him toward the camp. The concubines screamed in sorrow, and Tophian could clearly see the arrow in Tobor's chest. More of the Camonra were returning from the chase of the Candrians, and they began shouting Mordher's treachery to the others, mistakenly calling out that they were the soldiers of Highwood. The chaos of the camp immediately changed to shouts of hatred, and Tophian knew that the mob of Camonra would likely be listening to no reasoning about his good intentions.

Tophian's injuries were life-threatening, and his use of spiritual energy to throw the stones reduced his ability to heal them. Tophian prayed for energy and tried to clear his mind of the pain, but the nerves in his back were on fire, and the bruising in his back and chest muscles made it difficult to breathe. Using all the concentration he could muster, he pushed his aura out from his body, and he could hear the bones in his back popping back into place.

The earth moved away from him, allowing him to pass into the mountain's core. He continued moving through the stone until he entered the void of the caves within the mountain, and he lay in the darkness on the cool, wet stone floor of the cave. The aura dissipated and the mountain closed up behind him.

* * *

Far to the north, Mategaladh woke with a strange feeling that something was terribly wrong. He struggled out of his bed and moved to his prayer room. He breathed in the incense that burned there, and it seemed to soothe his pains.

Hanging on his prayer room wall was a woodcutting of the original group of Watchers. It was sadly happy, Mategaladh thought, made just after the Calling, when nineteen of them had begun their discipleship under Evliit, the first mortals to be called to prophecy. It was a time before the divisions of Watcher and Spellmaker, a time when faces shone with happiness and hope.

His strength was returning, and Mategaladh knew that he had been spared from death at the time of Amphileph's Binding for a reason, and now, his heart felt that part of that reason was coming to fruition. "Creator, thank you for the life I breathe in today," he began. "I thank you for the Binding of evil, for the bountiful harvest when the moons of Sapath are in the house of Ardidhus. I stand ready to use every power you have given me to save mankind from their destruction, and to carry on the good work of Evliit.

"I renew my strength in you, my Creator, and once more, I claim the power you have promised me. Let me be the force that you have made me to be, in this time, according to your plan, and to command all things that grow upon Erathe!

"Show me that I might—" Mategaladh stopped suddenly. Thoughts of Tophian entered his mind. "Tophian?" he said, squinting his eyes, focusing on the images of Tophian and the Camonra forming in his mind.

"Oh!" he said suddenly, as if he had pricked his finger. "Spirit, come to me now! I must come to Tophian's aid."

No sooner had Mategaladh said those words than a rush of energy began to course through his body, and the weakness he had felt previously fell away. A warm sensation in his gut intensified and moved outward through his arms and legs, breaking a sweat upon his brow. Tophian was in trouble. Something had gone very wrong in the land south of the Faceless Mountains. It was if he could feel the distress in the very fiber of the land itself. Amphileph had done something they had not expected, and though he was unsure of the Binding's integrity, he was sure that something . . . some evil . . . had escaped its barrier.

"Keep him safe," he prayed, and he rose to his feet, looking about the room for his things. He had to leave for the Faceless Mountains immediately. Tophian was in dire trouble.

* * *

Adheron woke to the wailing of the concubines, save Lurenda, who was carefully stitching his face, stopping to wipe away silent tears that were impeding its completion.

"The Angrodha!" he said. He jerked forward, stopped by her loving hand.

"My son," Lurenda said. "Everything has changed."

Adheron looked at her, and he thought her face looked sadder than he had ever seen it.

"It has taken Father?" he asked.

She lowered the needle to his face that she had pulled back in his quick movement, and tears welled in her eyes again.

"Let me finish," she said. She leaned in closer to complete the knot of her stitching, biting the horsehair string that she had found in the bows of the dead Candrian archers. "The bowstring has made for a fine stitch, my son," she said, and she placed her hands in her lap.

Adheron put his fingers on her stitch and felt the terribly torn flesh of his face. "Tobor! Father!" he cried, his words marred by the stretch of the stitch.

"Yes, my son, Tobor is gone," she said.

Adheron rolled his head to the side to hide his tears, but the pain grew so that he could not hold it in, and his chest heaved with a long gasp and a cry that sounded for all to hear. "The Father has struck at us even from his prison!"

"No, my son," Lurenda said. "The arrow that killed your father flew from human hands, as sure as the Angrodha was meant to kill us all."

"What do you mean?" Adheron asked, sitting up.

"The humans of Highwood have betrayed us. It is they who killed your father."

Adheron struggled to his feet. "How can this be?"

"It was seen by the Camonra, by our very own eyes! The cowards struck down your father even as he saved us all!" said Lurenda. "They fled west, we know not where."

Adheron screamed at the top of his lungs, his face bleeding afresh with the stress of it. "They have gone back to their Highwood!" Adheron drew his sword. "Camonra!"

Quickly the Camonra gathered at his side, all of them mad with anger. Their grunts and yells slowly drowned out the cries of the females until Adheron raised his sword to silence them.

"We go to Highwood!" he barked. "We will go to Highwood, and we will kill the humans!" A roar of approval sounded around him, but Lurenda called out to him amid the chaos.

"Will you not stay and bury Tobor?" she asked.

"Give my father to the heavens with fire! Let his embers mix with the blackness of night! Let the Camonra remember great Tobor and avenge his death! Bring me fire!"

One of the Camonra brought him a torch, and Adheron ripped a dead branch from a nearby tree. "A pyre for him our worthy leader!"

After they each tore away such kindling, Adheron lay his branch over Tobor's body and threw the torch upon it. The dry kindling caught quickly, until the heat of it was great enough for them to have to turn away.

"We go to Highwood!" Adheron screamed. "Bring me my father's mount, for I command the Camonra now! Have the females and children follow! We leave this land and make our revenge on the humans!" Adheron said. He pointed his sword westward and started in the direction of Highwood, and all the Camonra, warriors, females, and children followed him.

Chapter Twenty-One

Costly Protection

Citanth attempted to communicate with Amphileph within the Binding, but he had no luck. Amphileph had lay in his own vomit for days, and Citanth had come to believe that he might be dying. His breathing seemed to come in short bursts and insects had begun to crawl on his body.

The black rain had almost halved the number of Camonra in the northern camp, and now Citanth was convinced that less than three thousand of the loyal remained.

Though the horrible mutations had slithered and clawed their way west, the Camonra seemed convinced that it all might start again at any moment, and Amphileph's zealots had solidified the loyalty of the remaining Camonra with that fear. They had cried out to Amphileph for forgiveness, confused about what they had done wrong to deserve his wrath. They made sacrifices of the doubters and burned them in his name, but he had not answered them. Citanth wondered at their twisted faith, for they believed that they had done such wrong as to cause his sickness, so much so that they did penance day and night, beating themselves with whips and cutting their chests with knives in hopes that their Father might rise up and be well.

Citanth had watched it all until he could take no more of it, for the tragedy of their misguided love stole away all hope that he had for any absolution with the true Creator. His mind seemed to snap under the pressure of it all, and the days and nights ran together into a blur of flames and sacrifices and howling in the night.

On the fifth day, Amphileph rolled over, causing a great celebration and a frenzy of delight from the Camonra. At the height of it all, the Camonra had lined the Binding's edge, but a flurry of lightning began striking all round inside it, rippling around the inside of the domed Binding. The energy sizzled on the Binding's energy wall, licking it with blinding white forks and flashes that steadily intensified. A dark storm cloud gathered at the top of the dome, and it grew larger and larger, lowering over Amphileph's body until it blotted out everything within the Binding itself. The flashes of light became so intense that they burned skin and blinded the onlookers, and the explosive boom of the lightning strikes ran together into a deafening roar, causing the ceremony to end with the less faithful running in terror to the northern camp.

Just before dawn, the storm stopped, and the dark vapor slowly dissipated. Amphileph's body was gone, and the door was closed on his great Temple. A thin wisp of smoke wafted from the vents in the temple's dome, and the crowd slowly reassembled around the Binding's perimeter, sleeping upon the grounds, fasting until they might see their Father again.

Three more days passed, and suddenly, Amphileph stepped out from his temple. His clothing shimmered and shifted with such splendor that it was hard to focus on him. Citanth exited his small hut and held up his good arm to shield his eyes. The Camonra had fallen to the ground around the Binding, keeping their faces to the ground.

"Citanth!" The master Spellmaker's voice boomed.

"Here, lord Amphileph!" Citanth shouted.

"Our brother, Tophian, remains behind."

"Lord?" answered Citanth.

"Not all of the Watchers perished making this cage!" he yelled. "I have seen Tophian through the eyes of the Angrodha. He hides in the mountains to the north."

"What do you command?" inquired Citanth.

"I must finish what I have started, but the old fool stands in my way. Take the faithful and destroy him!" said Amphileph. "He is weak. Vulnerable. Strike now before he regains his strength."

"Yes, my lord," Citanth said.

"Then go forth into all the lands of Erathe. Destroy this pestilence that is mankind wherever you find it. They have made their flight into the mountains and hillsides, in wood and dale, for neither can they return to Rion. Search them out and kill them all! If you find any that once called us brother, kill them as well, for they have brought this fate upon themselves by standing against me. Do these things and bring me the Sword of the Watch! For I alone am worthy to wield it!" he shouted.

"These, my children, will aid you, for there is purity in the Camon heart. Use the Angrodha, and kill the man Galbard, and then have one of the creatures bring it hither!"

Citanth started to respond, but Amphileph would not have it.

"Do what you must, but do not test me, Citanth! Have I not shown you how I deal with such ineptness?" shouted Amphileph.

The memory of Citanth's dead brethren scattered about the temple grounds, their bodies rotting in the heat of the day—it was a powerful image of the consequences of displeasing Amphileph.

"I will grant you your position over the Camonra once more, but do not fail me again!" said Amphileph.

Citanth turned to the Camonra, who were still prone before the Binding. "Arm yourselves!" he shouted, and the Camonra dispersed, scrambling to their huts. Citanth did likewise, returning to the Binding's edge with his armor and weapons. The Camonra quickly assembled in ordered ranks before him.

Citanth shrugged his chestplate armor into place and put on his helmet. He stepped up upon a short retaining wall that was under construction for the coming colonnade in honor of Amphileph, and then he held up his good hand.

A silence fell upon the Camonra.

"Camonra!" yelled Citanth. "Make ready for war!"

The ranks of the soldiers went mad with delight for the chance to satisfy Amphileph's wishes. They clanged their weapons with such fervor that Citanth almost failed to hear the cackling laughter of Amphileph over it all.

Citanth bowed down to Amphileph, and once again, the Camonra became silent. Amphileph stepped up to the edge of the Binding Spell.

"Yes! Yes! War!" Amphileph cried, and the lines of Camonra formed. "Will you tarry in killing the infidels that have lost faith in their very maker?"

"No!" the Camonra shouted. "The infidels will die!" they cried, pounding their chests and stamping down their spears.

"Fear not!" Amphileph screamed. "I will send the Angrodha to protect you! Go first to the mountains and destroy the Watcher!"

"Yes, Father!" the Camonra bellowed together. Citanth mounted an Azrodh and rode out before them, and then the Camonra rank-and-file fell in behind him, all marching west.

* * *

Mordher and Borian arrived at the entrance to Moonledge Peak, where they startled the craftsmen of Rion with the roar of their horses' hooves upon the rocky ground of the Moonledge foothills.

"How can this be?" Mordher asked one of them. "How is it that you have set such stone?" The arched temple entrance was eighty feet high, with six-dozen steps that rose into three, seventy-foot high openings in a monumental structure whose arched walls set out from Moonledge Peak's mountainside. Each of the openings closed down into the old cave entrance. The immense stones appeared impossible to have been set by any feat of engineering that even Ardhios might have created.

"We have done so with the aid of the Watcher called Tophian," one answered, but the mere mention of the Watcher's name made Mordher's throat tighten.

"The wizard?" Mordher responded.

"You know of him?" asked the other. "His power is beyond compare."

Borian and Mordher exchanged looks.

"This we have heard," Mordher said. "But we had not had the privilege of seeing these, his mighty works."

Borian interrupted. "We must speak to your lord immediately," he said. "Can you arrange such an audience?"

"Our council oversees the Keep of Moonledge," the mason replied. "I will go to them at once. Whom shall I say requests this audience?"

"The Candrians, Mordher and Borian," said Borian. "It is a matter of great urgency."

"At once, my lord," the mason replied. "My men will show you where you can water your horses."

Some of the remaining masons guided them through the sally port on the right side of the thick, curtain wall, and the Candrian soldiers dismounted and watered their horses at a well that was centered among the craftsmen's buildings, which peppered the courtyard within the keep's curtain wall. The masons were silent, and when Borian and Mordher passed them by, they looked away.

Mordher pulled aside Borian to speak privately. "We have set such things in motion that cannot be undone, brother," he said.

Borian's face was drawn with worry. "That we have, brother," he answered. "What now is our play?"

"The Camonra will seek vengeance, that is sure," Mordher responded. "But these people may be persuaded to thin their ranks."

"How so, brother?"

"We will tell their council of their imminent attack, and I will insist that the Watcher's weapon be given to me for their defense! Then we make our way back to Candra while they make war upon the Camonra," answered Mordher. "We test our strength best from within the protections of our own castle, and surely against a lessened foe."

"You would set the Camonra upon the people of Moonledge?" asked Borian. "You go too far, brother."

Mordher grabbed him by the collar and pulled him close. Borian instinctively fumbled for his weapon in surprise.

"You too are in this!" he said in a hush. Several of the Candrian soldiers around them looked on with disbelief. Mordher noticed the attention they were drawing and shouted at them.

"Be about your business or deal with me!"

The soldiers quickly gave him distance and set about busying themselves.

"Let go of me," Borian said with gritted teeth. "Or will your temper foul even this chance?"

Mordher begrudgingly let go of Borian and spat on the ground.

"Don't make as if I'm in this alone, or I'll make it so," he said.

One of the masons appeared through the crowd of Candrian soldiers. "The council is assembling," he said. "This way."

"Of course," replied Borian, straightening his clothing. He let the mason lead the way, and he and Mordher made their way behind him.

They crossed the courtyard and walked up steps to the Keep's opening, a covered area with high ceilings and ornate arches of stone, where several sculptures of the fallen Rion warriors stood in various stages of completion. Apprentices scrambled about the master sculptors, sweeping the floors of dust and small shards of stone.

"Follow me," the mason instructed, and he led them behind another set of stairs that led upward through the arched ceiling, presumably to a deck that jutted out from the structure above them, though the scaffolding blocked a great deal of their view. "Careful," he said. "We're doing quite a bit of construction these days. Everyone is very excited about the new apse." He pointed to the hemispherical dome cut into the mountain, its curved walls having four enormous doors that opened to long naves with arched ceilings. Torches lit the way into the mountain itself. They walked on, the clang of their weapons echoing in the solid stone rooms. Eventually, they came upon an opening to the council chambers.

The chamber itself was alive with movement, and the council awaited their introduction.

They entered the room and the crier announced, "Mordher and Borian of Candra!"

Caratacus sat at the head of the council. "I am Caratacus, and I welcome you to Moonledge."

Mordher and Borian stopped in front of the council table. "We bring you sad tidings, I'm afraid," said Borian. "For it has come to our attention that the Camonra bring war upon you."

There was a general stir that buzzed like locusts in the chamber. Caratacus leaned forward in his chair and raised his hand. "Silence," he said. "How is it that you know of this, Candrians," he said to Borian.

"We have traveled to the east, to the valley that splits the Faceless Mountains on the northeastern edge. There we have seen the Camonra with our own eyes. They make their way toward you and surely mean you harm, just as they did when they marched on Rion."

"It has been said that the Camonra live in peace in the southern part of Etharath, and that the time of Amphileph's reign is past," said Caratacus. "What could bring them north to this place?"

"Conquest, still, my lord, is my guess, but there is more," said Borian. "A creature of the ancients—an Angrodha—accompanies them. My brothers and I have come to warn your people."

Here then, the crowd became unruly, driving Caratacus to his feet. "Silence!" he said. He slammed the council gavel upon the thick stone of the council tabletop. "You have seen the Angrodha?" asked Caratacus.

"Yes, lord," replied Borian. "Though I can tell you that I wish that I had never looked upon a creature such as that, for the ancient stories do no justice in describing the terror it strikes in the heart of even the battle-hardened warrior. Our weapons were useless against it."

Mordher walked the length of the council chamber table, looking each of the council members in the eyes. He could see the fear in their faces. "If only we had a greater weapon still, something truly powerful. Then I would strike down this monster for you."

Caratacus chewed his lip. "What if I could give you Evliit's sword?"

Mordher spun around to him. The chamber erupted until Mordher raised his hand to silence it. "If this is true, than this is the time to produce it. In my hands, it could mean the difference between victory and defeat."

The chatter in the room rose again.

"Quiet!" shouted Caratacus, beating the gavel repeatedly until Mordher thought the old man would break it, but the room did eventually quiet. "How much time do we have?" asked Caratacus.

"A day, maybe two," answered Borian.

"You leave us little time to act, warrior," Caratacus said. "You would take up Evliit's Sword to aid us in our defense?"

"Of course!" interrupted Mordher. "I would wield the mighty sword against all that would make war upon men!"

Caratacus looked around at the council. His face was drawn, and he wrung his jaw with his hand. "Bring the Sword!" he commanded.

Mordher could hardly contain his excitement. He had waited so patiently for this opportunity, and now they were simply going to hand it over to him.

Two of the Moonledge acolytes walked behind the council table, and another man dressed in Rionese Elder clothing stood directly behind Caratacus facing a large tapestry. He raised his hands, and one of the acolytes on either side drew the tapestry open. The second two raised an inner curtain, revealing a marble chest within an alcove, lined around the wall with the figures of the Watchers. A marble statue of Evliit was at the center standing over it, facing outward, his hands opening to the altar upon which the chest rested. The priest began to chant in the ancient tongue, and the four warriors removed poles that were stored on either side of the chest, running them across to each other through rings mounted along its ornate carvings. They raised the chest to shoulder height with some effort and then stepped together out from the alcove and brought the chest around in front of the council's table. An acolyte of the priest moved a golden stand into place under it, and the warriors slowly lowered it with the sanctity of a holy relic.

"Behold, Evliit's sword!" Caratacus said. Everyone in the room fell to their knees at his mention of it, and Mordher and Borian moved just in front of it.

"You have chosen well," said Mordher. "With this weapon, I will crush the Angrodha, the Camonra, and Amphileph himself!" Mordher leaned forward to place his hands on the marble lid of the chest.

"Wait!" the priest cried out. He signaled to another of the acolytes, who produced a basin of water. The priest dipped a small canister mounted on a wooden dowel into the basin, and then he flicked the water on Mordher, much to the defiant, former Guardsman's chagrin. The priest continued to chant and held the basin up to Mordher.

"What does he want?" asked Mordher.

The priest stopped his chanting, looking somewhat annoyed. "Cleanse yourself," he said, and when Mordher didn't move, the priest raised the basin under his hands. Mordher splashed the water over them, and then an acolyte wiped them with a cloth. Then the priest and the acolytes backed away, and Mordher stood before the chest.

He placed his hands upon the marble, and the muscles in his arms jerked taut. He couldn't find the strength to lift the lid from it, and the numbing sensation suddenly changed to an intense heat.

"Barothma!" Mordher cursed. The room collectively gasped.

The priest stepped forward again. "It is said that the Sword chooses who might carry it, and destroys all it chooses not."

"It is said that *I* destroy any who cross me!" Mordher replied. "Don't try me, priest."

Mordher latched onto the lid and gritted his teeth through the pain. The burning sensation in his arms spread throughout his body, the pain so severe that it caused his body to shake; but Mordher pushed the lid open, and he looked inside. For a moment, he saw the Bhre-Nora's adorned case, and then the image of the mountainside flooded his mind. It was as if he was looking from Tobor's view, and he could see himself drawing back the arrow and letting it fly. It crossed the distance to him in slow motion, and he could feel the intense pain of the arrow piercing his skin. It passed through his rib, bursting it into pieces. Then he could feel the arrow pass through his heart and out his chest. He dropped the marble chest back upon the stand and grabbed at the arrow, but there was nothing there, even though the pain remained, dropping him to his knees.

"Mordher!" Borian yelled, but Mordher's chin dropped to his chest, and he drifted forward as if he would fall upon his face. Interceding, Borian caught him.

Mordher struggled to maintain consciousness. Borian's face was coming in and out of focus. "It is cursed," Mordher managed.

"When have we needed magic?" asked Borian. "Our steel is enough to end our enemies! Leave this thing be!"

"No," Mordher mumbled. He reached out for the marble chest again, but his arm fell to his side. He could still feel it, the shaft of the arrow within him, and now his breathing was becoming labored. "Get me away from that thing."

Borian dragged him back from the chest.

The priest stepped in between them and the Sword. "Return the Sword to its resting place!" he said, and the acolytes quickly moved it to the alcove and closed the tapestry.

Caratacus looked even more concerned. "We do not control who the Sword chooses. Surely, you do not hold this against the people of Moonledge. Your friend is correct; you have no need of this magic. Let us speak not of this further, but instead, let our healers look at your friend."

"I don't need your healers!" Mordher shouted, pulling himself up with Borian's help.

"We meant no offense, warrior," said Caratacus. "Please, let us work together against the evil of Amphileph. Will you not gather with us against this evil?"

"We will, but we must first return to Candra to warn the people of the valley. Unlike Moonledge, we have no mountain from which to fend off these threats. We must bring the people into our Warriors Hall, for what would prevent the Angrodha and Amphileph's army from moving on to *our* people, seeing the powerful defenses of Moonledge?"

Caratacus thought carefully about Borian's words. "You are right, warrior. The great caves of the Keep will protect us. The Camonra may pillage and destroy that which lies outside the Keep, but no creature will easily penetrate our defenses. Go, and warn the people of Rion that live in the west. I'm afraid you've no time to return them here, though we would gladly take them in."

"Your offer is generous, my lord Caratacus," Borian replied. "But our best defense is to warn the people of the valley and Highwood. We will ask your leave, and ride west."

Mordher pushed away from Borian and rose to his feet.

"May you ride like the wind," said Caratacus. "We will take the fight to them when they arrive, and buy you what time that we can."

"Your courage inspires us," answered Borian. "May you inflict such damage upon them that they dare not continue!"

"This we will give our finest efforts!" answered Caratacus, and he gestured to them farewell.

"Fare thee well," answered Borian.

Mordher remained silent, and the two of them exited the chamber and returned to the troops awaiting them in the Moonledge outer court.

Mordher pushed on his chest plate.

"Are you all right?" Borian asked him.

Mordher glared at him. "Ready the troops!" he shouted.

"With your leave, my lord," said Borian, and he rode away into the midst of them.

Shortly, Borian returned. Mordher was still holding one hand to his chest. Borian looked down at his hand, but he quickly locked eyes again. "The troops are ready," he said.

"I meant to say 'well done' in there," Mordher said to Borian. "You almost convinced *me* that we would help Highwood."

Borian's face drew taut. "It will take little from us to spare a rider to warn the people of Highwood," he said.

"I'll not spare any of our men for those in Highwood—though your words *were* elegant," Mordher replied.

Borian's face reddened. "We must honor those words or you make their use worthless for all future endeavors."

"I'll not spare a rider for Highwood," Mordher repeated.

Borian pulled his horse around to face Mordher. "I thought as much," he said. The look on Borian's face told volumes of his dissatisfaction.

"What?" Mordher asked.

"I'll not speak for you in the future, my brother. You may make your own commitments," Borian replied. "And you should know that I have already sent a rider to Highwood."

Borian turned his horse and rode west toward the Hall on his own.

"You did what? Borian!" Mordher shouted after him. "I will kill you with my own hands!"

Borian never even looked back.

"To Candra!" Mordher cried, and the Candrians left the Keep at Moonledge Peak for their fortress in the valley.

* * *

Adheron rounded up his fighters to discuss the attack on Highwood in the fields east of the great line of trees.

"Camonra!" he yelled. "The humans have shown their true nature in the killing of Tobor! Amphileph was right to want to destroy them! They are a plague on Erathe!"

The Camonra shouted their agreement with their new leader.

"If the Angrodha hungers, let us line the roads with the bodies of humans so that it may find its feast upon their flesh!"

"Yes!" the Camonra cried in return.

"Fill your quivers with bolts and sharpen your swords and axes! The Camonra have blood on their minds!" Adheron shouted. Then he addressed the females stoking the fire in their hearts by slaughtering one of the Azrodh, placing it on the spit, and dancing madly around a great fire, taunting the Angrodha to come to them right then and there. "Let their scouts see us dancing in the night! Let them make their preparations for war! It will make no difference! Tonight we will add their heads to our belt rings!"

Adheron spurred his Azrodh to ride into Highwood. He could see runners moving in the moonlight, lights flickering in doorways, and Highwood slowly springing to life. He did not care. Surprise was not his concern. "I shall take what I want with only a hundred Camonra!" Adheron shouted. He could see the distant twinkle of torches scrambling about in the trees of Highwood. He gathered his warriors around and pointed to the moving lights. "Look at their fear!" he said. "They should be afraid! They have made war with the Camonra!"

* * *

A runner burst into the commander's quarters in Highwood, where a group of commanders surrounded a map of the lands at Moonledge Peak.

"What is the meaning of this?" his superior inquired.

"My lord, the Camonra are *here*!" he shouted.

"What?" the commander asked.

"Did not the rider from Candra tell us the Inferiors were to strike at Moonledge?" another of the commanders asked.

"That was his message," said the first. "Are they forming ranks?"

"No, my lord, they have built a bon fire, and they are yelling and dancing around it as if to let us know they are here."

The commander looked back down at the map and exhaled loudly. "We make ready to come to Moonledge's aid, and the Camonra come here?"

* * *

Ardhios was waiting outside the Seven Warriors Hall. Runners had told him of Borian's approach, and he had lined the path to the Hall with warriors, thousands of them.

Borian reined in his horse and dismounted. "You've been busy, brother!" he said. "You greet us with an army of your own?"

"There is fear among the people, Borian. They've heard rumor of dark creatures and Camonra on the move. They expect the Hall to protect them for their fealty, and I mean to do that."

"*You* mean to?" Borian replied.

Ardhios did not flinch. "Yes, *I* mean to, as it appears that my brothers are indisposed."

"You have lamps along the road practically all the way to the valley's edge. I hope you've spent your time more wisely than to light the way for our enemies."

"For the Hall!" Ardhios yelled, and the ranks of soldiers to either side instantly echoed his yell, the stamping of their spears in almost perfect unison.

Borian's brows rose. "I see," he said wryly.

Ardhios could see Mordher approaching over Borian's shoulder. He appeared to be riding with abandon until he came into view of the hall, and then he and his warriors slowed to a trot in the light of the lamps on the path.

"Look at him!" Borian said. "He sees that your army outnumbers his own!"

Mordher pulled his horse to a stop and dismounted, walking directly up to Borian and striking him to the ground with his fist. Borian responded by drawing his sword, and Mordher drew his own.

Ardhios saw the confrontation with Borian, and he began down the Hall's stairs. "Oh, Mordher, will you never change?" he asked under his breath. "Cease this at once!" he yelled.

There was a sudden move of soldiers around them, and Mordher and Borian took note of them and held their ground.

"Mordher, what is it now?" asked Ardhios.

"We will continue this later!" Mordher said to Borian.

Borian did not respond, but Ardhios was relieved that they both begrudgingly put away their swords and turned their attention to him.

"What of my proposal to connect our strongholds to Moonledge Peak's southern walls? Did Caratacus accept that such a union would allow us to migrate north beyond the Candra Mountains under the protection of our joint armies?"

"We did not discuss those matters," Borian said. "There was an incident—"

"An incident?" replied Ardhios.

"I killed the leader of the Camonra, and the beasts didn't like it very much," Mordher said.

"What?" Ardhios asked. "You did what?"

"The opportunity presented itself to eliminate the leader of the Camonra, and I took it," said Mordher.

"Our plan was to complete the wall with Moonledge Peak and strengthen our alliance with the people of Highwood," said Ardhios. "Was it not agreed that you would defend the lands north of there until the builders could connect our outpost to their southern wall?"

"The opportunity presented itself," Mordher repeated.

Ardhios paced the floor.

"I'm working to establish rule within the kingdom, Mordher, a sense of safety that might create some source of wealth to fund our growth and prosperity. Have you no idea that the Camonra—"

"The Inferiors!" Mordher interrupted.

"The Inferiors . . . will only be stirred to attack us? What you've done serves only to bring war upon us before all is handily in our favor," said Ardhios.

"I was strong enough to draw the bow and bring him down like a great elk," Mordher said, smiling at Borian. "There is one less Inferior that will attack us."

Ardhios threw up his hands. "Borian, can you not talk some sense into this one?" he asked. "Now rather than draw up treaties with Moonledge and Highwood for a wall that would keep them out of our lands, I'll find myself begging for soldiers. Do you not understand?"

Mordher circled to his left. "We will not beg for soldiers! We'll demand them!"

Ardhios shook his head. "Demand them?" he asked. He had to let out a sarcastic chuckle. "And by what authority will I demand them, Mordher, that I represent the warrior that killed the leader of the Inferiors?"

"This will be a war that none of them can sustain alone," Mordher replied. "They will either join with us or they will surely fall!" he shouted. "You wanted to unify the west? Well, this is the beginning of a great union! A new union that will bring all mankind together against the prophets of old *and* the world they have made for us. This is the beginning of a new kingdom of the west!"

"You gamble everything," Ardhios said. "You've set in motion things that cannot be undone."

"The old ones have controlled us long enough," Borian said.

"There will be a Western Kingdom. It will rise on the ashes of Rion," said Mordher. "Never again will the prophets of old direct the affairs of men, directing wars for this god or that one. We will destroy the Inferiors, and then we will destroy the evil one in the east. Then men alone will determine their destiny."

"*You* may have determined our destiny, Mordher, but it may not be the destiny you envisioned."

"You have said it, Ardhios: it matters not now, none of it! What has been started will only end with a new kingdom or the end of men!" shouted Mordher.

"Everything is black and white, is it?" Ardhios replied. "And even then, I cannot choose, for you have chosen for us." He paced again, biting his lip. "I will send for soldiers, then, send riders to Highwood," Ardhios said. "May the Creator be with us."

"He *is* with us!" Mordher responded. "And you would do well to show that you know that."

"You would do better to keep your temper in check, brother, before you—"

"Before I what?" asked Mordher. "That one is frightened," Mordher said to Borian. "I like my leaders fearless."

Ardhios bristled. "You know less of me than you think, brother," he said, and then turned and ascended the stairs back into the great hall.

"Ardhios is a good man, Mordher," replied Borian. "We've plenty who want our heads without your having to stir up our very camp."

"Very well," Mordher said. "Let them come for my head. I look forward to sticking them like fatted hogs!"

* * *

Mategaladh rode to the northern edge of the Faceless Mountains and dismounted. He could sense Tophian deep within the mountain itself, and struck his staff against the mountainside. The end of the staff moved liked fingers into the stone, crumbling the surface until the staff suddenly straightened, latching onto something. Mategaladh wrenched on the staff and pulled a chunk of black stone out of the rock. He righted the staff, and the end of it curled tightly around the stone, compressing it until it glowed brightly.

Roots sprung up from the place that he struck and rose into the air around him. They paused at the highest point for a moment, and then drove deep into the mountainside, pushing open the side of the mountain. Mategaladh walked toward the inner caves, and the roots drove upward and outward, strapping the stone to the surrounding dirt. The swelling timbers creaked under the weight, allowing him to move into the central cavern.

The roots pushed further and further within the cavern, forming a lattice that pushed away the earth and created a tunnel into the bowels of the mountain. Mategaladh walked into the largest cave within the mountain. He could hear a great popping of stone and crashing of shifting earth. The echoes died down, and Mategaladh thought he heard a groan from within. He pushed his staff over his head and squinted against the light to see as deeply as he could into the darkness ahead.

"Tophian!" exclaimed Mategaladh. Mategaladh ran to him and reached gently around Tophian in an attempt to roll him over. One of Tophian's eyes appeared out of kilter with the other, and his breathing was shallow. Mategaladh brushed the dried, flaking blood from Tophian's face and prayed for him to regain consciousness.

There was a bulge in his lower ribcage that looked as if some ribs might be broken. When Mategaladh touched them, he prayed for healing, and there was a crackling sound of the bones shifting under his fingers. Tophian's eyes suddenly widened, and he looked around the cave walls at the tendons of roots crisscrossing the ceiling of his caves.

"What are you doing, you old fool?" Tophian sputtered. "Are you trying to bring the whole mountain down on our heads? You cannot shift the stone like this—these vines of yours! Stop this at once!"

The root appeared to shrink at his words, and the tunnel to the outside world collapsed with the crashing sound of stone behind them. The dust and debris rushed through the air, until Mategaladh's light was barely visible. Tophian managed to raise one hand, and the dust moved away from them.

"Tophian!" Mategaladh shouted with joy at seeing his old friend alert. "What in the name of the Creator has happened to you?"

"I have much to tell, Mategaladh," Tophian said. "Much indeed."

"Rest, friend, I have you," Mategaladh said.

No sooner had Mategaladh said it than Tophian closed his eyes and took a deep breath of relief. Mategaladh was glad to see it.

"That's right, friend, rest," said Mategaladh.

* * *

Mategaladh tended to Tophian for the better part of two days. Tophian recovered, and he recounted the story of the waking to Tobor's mourners in the valley and the beehive of hate that swirled around the body of Tobor.

"The arrow was Candrian, there is no mistaking it," Tophian said. "The Camonra were completely out of their minds with anger. That much I heard before I crawled away."

"There was no stopping it," Mategaladh said. "Even though we had bound Amphileph, his creation was too far spread to capture them all. It was but a fleeting wish that such a time as this would never come. The Camonra and Man will never co-exist so easily."

"It could have been," Tophian said. "I was so close to moving them to the east, until the fools from Candra ended any chance of it. It's times like this, when I see the treachery—I can imagine Amphileph's loss of hope for men."

Mategaladh was busying himself looking through Tophian's bag.

"Why don't you carry the herbs I gave you? Why must I always find you half dead and without so much as a single good herb? Bah!" Mategaladh said. He put down Tophian's bag and began digging in his own, producing a dark brown, bulbous herb and pushing it toward Tophian's face.

Tophian crumbled his nose. "You know I hate Erdwara!" he said.

"Oh, you old ingrate! Take that and eat it!" Mategaladh insisted.

Tophian grumbled something and sat up against the stone wall of the cave. He took a large bite of the Erdwara herb and acted for an instant as if he would spit it immediately on the ground, except for the short glance at Mategaladh's ever-watchful eye. He let the air slowly exhale from his nose and returned to chewing the root with a grimace.

"There, that will make things better," Mategaladh said.

Tophian held out his left arm, and Mategaladh could see the large indentation in the muscle and bone and a slight bulge elsewhere that indicated a possible break. The properties of the root slowly eased the bluish tone of the bruised skin back to a pink. Tophian straightened his arm out, and the swelling began to subside and return to normal. He tossed another Erdwara root into his mouth.

Mategaladh produced three additional Erdwara herbs from his bag. "I've not enough to heal you as I would like," he added, "but here is the last of it."

"Absolutely not," Tophian said. He shifted his bruised body around to a more comfortable position. "I was unable to destroy the Angrodha, my friend. You'll need a lot more of that herb before the day is done."

"The Angrodha sought to kill even the Camonra, you say?" asked Mategaladh.

"It was clear to me that it meant to kill us all," answered Tophian. "I would never have imagined siding with the Camonra in a fight for my life. I would never have dreamed that I would say such a thing, my brother, but I see the Camonra quite differently now that they have moved away from their worship of Amphileph."

"What?" asked Mategaladh, giving him a strange look.

"I didn't say that their creation wasn't an abomination, but I spoke to the leader of the creatures, Tobor, the one who was killed. He was without malice toward mankind, and when he said that they no longer followed Amphileph's desires to destroy us all, I believed him. As a Watcher, I have sworn to protect the world of men, but I tell you, it was a pivotal moment for me. It was the moment I saw the Camonra as merely the pawns Amphileph used to make his ends possible. They were living, breathing creatures, just as we are, and truly, I tell you, brother, Tobor sought for the Camonra to live in peace with men. They feared the Angrodha as much as the rest of us. Amphileph sent it to destroy them every bit as much as he had sent it for us."

Mategaladh started to respond and then pursed his lips upon the words and looked away.

"If the Candrian has killed their leader, those hopes are dashed," Mategaladh said. "The Camonra will exact swift and terrible justice, without regard for their losses. We need to move to protect the people that will be caught in the middle. Do you think you can travel?"

"Yes, but I question whether I can be much good to you if it comes to a fight," Tophian answered.

The tortured look on Tophian's face told Mategaladh volumes about his injuries. Tophian's spirit was willing, but his body was broken, his powers drained. Mategaladh looked around the cave for an exit, but the darkness swallowed the cave's features. He concentrated for a moment, and the stone on the end of his staff glowed even brighter.

"I will go alone, Tophian. You must regain your strength." He could see more of the cave walls, but he was still unclear on which direction to take. "You know these mountains, brother. Can we follow the caves to the surface, or do I need to push our way out?"

"No, no!" Tophian said. "The caves will not stand much more of your tinkering! You could destroy the weight-bearing members of the catacombs! It is not far."

They made their way slowly, up and around the smooth walls of the cave, where the crystals in the calcium stalactites sparkled in the glow of Mategaladh's staff."

"Quiet, Mategaladh, listen," said Tophian. They rounded a curtain-like formation of stone and could faintly hear the trickling of water. The dim light of the moon parted the cave's walls above them. "There is a way to the surface just ahead. Follow the ridge to Moonledge. The depths of the mountains will care for me. I will rest here for a moment and then descend to the inner catacombs. I know my way in my own home, Mategaladh. You must go. Go to Moonledge." Tophian grabbed his side and winced with the last of his words.

"Then go to your home and rest there. I'll warn the people of Moonledge Peak and Highwood, and you should recover all that you can. I may very well have to call upon your aid in short order, whatever your strength."

"When you call, I will come," Tophian said, but Mategaladh could see in his eyes a desperation that truly frightened him. He could not remember the last time he had seen fear in Tophian's face.

"Fare well, friend," Mategaladh said, and then he turned and made his way toward the surface.

Once above ground, Mategaladh ascended to the highest point he could reach along the southern side of the mountain, and the image before him staggered him. In the distance, to the south, he could see dozens of torches concentrated in the plains before Highwood, and hundreds of torches were west of him, huddled around Moonledge Peaks' Keep. And passing in front of the moon, the Angrodha shrieked its malice, its silhouette appearing for just a moment and then flickering through the stars before Mategaladh lost it in the night sky.

Mategaladh's mouth fell open. "Creator of Erathe, help us!" he muttered.

* * *

Adheron readied to ride into Highwood with a hundred warriors—fifty of his cavalry and fifty foot soldiers. Though Adheron's revenge-driven rage made him oblivious to Citanth and his warriors to the north, it had not blinded his scouts.

One of the scouts approached from the north in haste. "Lord Adheron!" he said. "Lord Adheron, forgive me!"

"Speak!" Adheron demanded.

"Lord Adheron, Amphileph's army moves on Moonledge Peak!"

Adheron pulled the Azrodh's reins, and its lumbering feet shuffled around so that Adheron faced the scout.

"Amphileph?" queried Adheron. He dismounted, and he and his captains moved closer to hear the scout's words over the chaos of the females surrounding the bonfire and the warriors yelling for battle.

"My lord, the Angrodha and four thousand Camonra attack Moonledge Peak!" the scout repeated.

"You have done well!" Adheron said, and the scout signaled his respect and moved away from the circle of his superiors.

This news gave Adheron great pause. He turned in his saddle, looked toward Moonledge Peak, and then back to Highwood. He could see the torchlights of Highwood's warriors dancing between the branches of the massive trees. Adheron waved away his servant and his Azrodh, and gathered with his captains to question their strategy with a patience that would have made Idhoran proud.

"Our scouts tell us that Amphileph's army moves on Moonledge Peak and the Angrodha attacks at their command," Adheron said.

"We stand ready to follow you," the captains replied.

A second scout came to the edge of their circle and dropped to one knee.

"What news have you?" Adheron asked, and the circle opened to him.

"My lord, archers line the trees of Highwood, and the men have set man traps and spikes to stop our Azrodh from riding into the forest," the scout said.

"Very well," said Adheron. The circle of captains closed around him again.

Adheron's new found position of authority suddenly weighed heavily upon him. He wished that he could lean on the judgment of his father and Idhoran. But that was not to be; he knew he must rise to their level on his own.

"Amphileph means to destroy the men of Moonledge Peak," Adheron said, working through things in his own mind. "But they could take heavy losses attacking the stronghold."

The captains looked at each other, and another of them spoke up. "My lord, if Amphileph's army turns on us, as surely it will, we ourselves cannot withstand great losses in a battle with the men of Highwood. No warrior fights as he will upon his own land, and they will fight with the benefit of the height above us in the great forest. If we are to ride into their midst, we will surely lose many warriors. Then our families might stand alone against the victors at Moonledge."

The wind began to pick up northwest, and thunder rolled over the plains east of Highwood. The Rainland seemed to be prodding them on from behind with its unwelcoming weather.

Adheron's head was spinning. He looked back at the orange glow in the distant horizon that pulsated over the rift separating them from Rion. He looked at the anxious faces of the captains of his clan flickering in the torchlights, waiting to hear his orders, and then he looked back at the blackness of the Rainland, and he remembered the creatures of Amphileph. The sound of the Angrodha echoed on the wind.

"We go west around the southern edge of the forest, and then we will attack from their rear," Adheron said. "I will avenge my father's death! Put the torches out! We will travel under the cover of darkness as quickly as we can."

"Yes, my liege!" the captains answered, and the entire tribe gathered their things once again and went on the move.

* * *

The soldiers of Rion scrambled through the trees of Highwood, intensely watching the movements of the Camonra that had appeared on their very doorstep. Then even greater trepidation overcame them. The Camon's torchlights snuffed out, one by one, and the blackness of the night swallowed them up. They had sent the women and children southwest along the Highborne River to the villages in the Dales of Shintower, and now there was an eerie silence in Highwood, broken only by the hushed orders of the soldiers and the distant rumble of the Rainland. Now the occasional lightning provided only brief glimpses of the movement in the grasses, and the soldiers became hypersensitive to the tiniest sound and slightest movement.

"Can you see them?" one of the Rionese soldiers asked.

"No," came the hushed reply. Then suddenly: "To the right, to the right."

* * *

Adheron and the Camonra could see the torches moving in the trees, gathering in their direction. They could faintly hear the men yelling in the woods.

"The grass is higher there," Adheron said. He moved the group further south away from the tree line. He looked back to see the females and children moving in that direction, and the soft *sssip* sound of an arrow passed his ear.

"They've found us!" Adheron yelled. Bedlam broke out, and Adheron could clearly see torches descending the trees and moving toward them. "Epar! Locra! Follow me!" he said, and two of his captains jumped to his side.

They moved toward the tree line, Adheron with his sword drawn and his captains with their crossbows, the sounds of arrows zipping by them.

"Bring light!" Adheron heard them yell, and one of the men suddenly appeared from out of the high grass. Adheron caught him with the tang of his sword, splitting his chin open with the force of the blow. "Ready!" Adheron yelled to Locra, but had no sooner done so than an arrow struck his comrade in the right side of the neck. He staggered and grasped at the shaft, dropping his crossbow.

The winds whipped the grass to the side just enough for Adheron to get a clear view of the men of Highwood, bows drawn, swords at the ready, closing on them. He grabbed wounded Locra and dragged him back into the cover of the grass.

"Be still!" Adheron urged Locra, but the arrow's wound made him writhe in agony.

"They're here!" yelled one of the men carrying a lamp.

"We must go!" Adheron whispered to Locra, whose gurgling sounds stopped suddenly, and Adheron leaned him slowly back upon the ground and took his crossbow.

They were closing upon him and Epar.

"Here! They're here!" they shouted.

"For the Camonra!" Epar yelled, and he jumped up and ran toward them. He parted the grass toward them and arrows struck him, but he closed on them firing his crossbow into the ground before him as he fell.

Adheron squatted down and circled around the men, springing from the grass beside a young squire who, terrified, raised the lamp he carried above his head. Adheron's blade came crashing down, bursting the lamp upon them both in an arc of fire that ignited their clothing and the tall grass. The young squire screamed in agony, running through the high grass, covered in flames. Adheron dropped his sword, beat the flames out on the right side of his head, and dropped to the ground, snuffing those on his chest and legs. He grabbed up his sword, still partially blinded by his burns, and watched the squire collapse some twenty paces away, a trail of flames signaling his path.

The winds instantly whipped the flames into a hellish heat that pushed Adheron to the south and the Highwood soldiers back toward the tree line. He sprang back from the flames into the darkness and ran south toward his tribe. The whistle of arrows zipped by all around him and cries of "fire!" rang out.

The light grew brighter and brighter, and Adheron could see the men of Highwood bringing water buckets from wells in the forest, and archers forming a line to protect them from the Camonra attack.

Adheron burst through the darkness beside his soldiers. "Adheron!" one of them said. The warriors' momentary joy at seeing their leader's return was shortly replaced by the discipline of their race. "Hold still, my liege!" he said, pouring cool water into Adheron's eye and face. Adheron tried to clear his right eye, but it was useless.

The flames were now so high that they had to push back from the intense heat.

Adheron caught his breath. "The soldiers are coming!" he cried. "Take the families further south!"

The warrior pointed back over Adheron's shoulder. "But my lord, look!" the warrior said.

Adheron turned to see the flames crawling into the great forest, illuminating the night sky.

"The northwest winds carry the flames directly to Highwood, my lord," the warrior said.

The heat was so intense that some of the smaller trees exploded into flames, and the fire raged into the branches and wood structures of their Rionese builders. Ash blew like snow in the air, and the superheated air rushed up through the leaves, igniting neighboring trees like a tinderbox. Many of the men that tried to combat the fires choked in the soot and smoke and collapsed, others scrambled west for their lives trying to outrun the intense heat, though many simply could not.

"My father is avenged!" Adheron said, falling to the ground in exhaustion, watching the cinders rise in the curling heat above Highwood.

"My liege, your captains stand at the ready whatever your command!" said the soldier.

"Your allegiance humbles me, but there's nothing more for us here," Adheron said under his breath. He turned back again and looked at the roaring flames devouring the structures of men that crisscrossed the branches of Highwood. "Even if the forest is reduced to ashes, the humans will build again."

Adheron grasped the arm of the soldier, who pulled him to his feet. Several of his captains regrouped before him in the field southeast of Highwood.

Adheron sheathed his sword.

"Gather the women and children, and let us find new lands to the south. My father was right when he said that we must avoid the humans. Their evil is like the poison that runs in the waters of the Rainland."

"We are with you, Adheron, as we were with Tobor before you," one of the captains said.

"Perhaps Amphileph was right; maybe the humans are beyond saving. Let him destroy them if he will, but my father gave his life to protect the clan. I will honor his memory, not with vengeance, but by ensuring the clan's survival. Move the Camonra southwest to the jungles, far away from this evil! We'll drive Amphileph's creatures from our lands and live free from *his* evil as well. We'll live free of it or die fighting for our place in this world, just as Tobor wished."

The Camonra followed him southward into the darkness.

* * *

Mategaladh saw the flames of Highwood roar into the night sky far below the south ridge of the Faceless Mountains. "Oh, no, no!" he said, realizing that he could do nothing about the loss of life or the destruction of one of his beloved forests. "You'll pay for this, Amphileph!" he cried, and he followed the ridge toward Moonledge Peak, ever watchful of the Angrodha overhead.

In the valley to the southeast of Mategaladh, at the rear of the column of Amphileph's army, Citanth could also see the glow in the valley to the west.

"A great fire rages in Highwood!" Citanth shouted. "Hold your positions!"

His orders ran down through the ranks until all his thousands came to a stop on the fields outside of Moonledge Peak's Keep.

"Back away!" Citanth shouted to the Camonra, and he raised his withered hand to the sky. They cleared away from him without question and none too soon. The Angrodha swooped down upon the clearing, now full grown, its wingspan some fifty feet across. It shrieked twice, and the Camonra winced at the sheer volume of it. Citanth moved toward the Angrodha, and it shook its head, the muscles rippling down the length of its neck. The Angrodha leaned its head down near Citanth's face.

"This is most opportune!" Citanth shouted to the Angrodha. "You, my pet, will stay here and kill anything that attempts to come or go from

Moonledge Peak!" he said. "They cannot stay in their Keep forever!" Citanth laughed, making the Angrodha cock its head to one side. It stretched its mouth into a sneer, baring one side of its clenched teeth. "The men of Highwood flee their precious woods! We could walk our full army into the Dales of Shintower! Feast upon these weaklings, and I will signal for you when it is time to attack the men of the Dales!"

The Angrodha snorted, and then it spread its wings and launched itself into the air above Moonledge Peak.

"Turn, great army, turn!" Citanth shouted. "The Creator has smiled upon us! Shortly, we dine in Shintower!" With that, the Camonra sounded the marching drums and turned southward.

* * *

Deep within the Moonledge Peak's caves, Caratacus tried to assure the masses that the Keep was impenetrable. The contingent of soldiers that had remained outside the Keep to delay the Camonra had all but been decimated by an attack of the Angrodha. They had since fled into the courtyard, in and among the buildings, simply trying to avoid being detected. The Angrodha landed among the buildings, ducked its head and folded back its wings to step into the temple entrance on the outer face of the Keep. Its claws dug furrows into the temple steps, it pushed its head against the Keep's lockdown doors, and then it roared a challenge that could be felt through the thick stone. It sniffed all around the door's perimeter for the scent of men, pausing only to snort the dirt from its nostrils.

* * *

Mategaladh watched Amphileph's army head toward Highwood and hurriedly made his way down the mountainside. The sun might rise and set a dozen times before Citanth would reach the Northern Bridge crossing the Highborne River, and it would be another day or so to the Dales of Shintower. *This is my chance*, he thought. Though he feared the Angrodha, taking on both it and the Camonra would be suicide. This could be the only time he might face it alone.

He made his way up the hillside to the temple grounds and happened upon one of the Rionese soldiers hiding between buildings.

Mategaladh moved in beside him. "Ah!" the soldier shouted. "You scared the life out of me!"

"I didn't mean to startle you, my friend. I've come to do battle with the creature," Mategaladh said.

"You?" the soldier laughed. "You, alone, will do battle with that monster? Have you lost your mind? That thing carried off over twenty armed men in mere moments, sir!"

"Stay here," Mategaladh said, and he moved along the building's side, looking for the creature.

"No problem there, sire," the soldier said, pushing his back against the building's adobe stone. He held his halberd tightly to his chest.

Mategaladh rounded the building, and he could then clearly see the Angrodha's back. He stepped into the center of the courtyard and closed his eyes to pray.

The Angrodha interrupted his snorting and stopped instantly. It pulled its head back slowly from the door and turned both eyes on Mategaladh. Its lips slowly stretched back into a snarl that showed all its sharp teeth, still stained with the blood of Rion.

Mategaladh's eyes shot open with a start and the Angrodha sprung toward him from its perch on the Keep's doorway. It bound once and used its wings to hurl through the air toward the old Watcher.

As the Angrodha's jaws spread in anticipation of its kill, Mategaladh raised his hand and a blue aura shot out from his body, engulfing himself and the Angrodha, which slowed to a stop in the thick energy field. The monster thrashed violently, biting and clawing in all directions, but it could only inch itself toward Mategaladh.

"You are an abomination!" Mategaladh cried out, raising both his hands in an effort to stop the beast's approach. The energy field appeared to shift for a moment, pushing the Angrodha away from him, but it roared and snapped, clawing its way back into the aura's field.

Mategaladh cried out, and the Angrodha shot backward from the field, slamming into the stone of the temple. It fell to the side, dazed, but shook its head and curled back around toward him. It roared and shattered a statue of a Rionese soldier with a swipe of its claw.

The Angrodha coiled then and shot toward him with its powerful hind legs, clawing his way dangerously near Mategaladh's face. Bolts of energy crisscrossed the plasma wherever the Angrodha touched it, and the Angrodha shrieked in pain. It jumped back and slammed its wing into the dirt where it had caught fire, attempting to put out the strange blue flames. It pounced upon the aura again and drove its jaws closer and closer to Mategaladh's outstretched hands. The entire valley lit up with the flashing streaks of blue and white.

"I draw my strength from the Creator himself!" Mategaladh cried out. The flashes were so close together now that they became continuous, and the aura exploded outward, throwing the Angrodha against the outer wall of Moonledge, collapsing a section, and falling back through it.

Slowly the aura disappeared, and Mategaladh dropped to one knee. He knew that using his body as a conduit of such energy taxed its ability to remain flesh and blood.

The Angrodha's wings fluttered madly, and it grabbed the wall in an attempt to pull itself up, but more of the stone collapsed under the Angrodha's weight. It rolled forward and screamed, slapping a section of the wall into fragments and falling forward on all fours, and then it lurched forward at the small figure of Mategaladh standing in the center of the courtyard.

Mategaladh drove his staff into the ground before him and a great vine shot up from the ground and back down again between him and the creature. The ground shook violently around Mategaladh, and splinters flew from the Angrodha's attempts to tear through the weaving vine. Other vines shot up from around Mategaladh repeatedly, forming a cocoon that the Angrodha attempted unsuccessfully to rip from its thick base in the ground. It bit upon the cocoon then, and drew back suddenly, shaking its head as if the taste was offensive, and then it roared and struck again, tearing great chunks of it away with its teeth and claws, until all at once it pushed violently away from the mass of vines and gagged.

The Angrodha choked and gagged again. Its left hind leg began to quiver uncontrollably. It squinted its eyes and coughed up a black liquid full of squiggling larvae. It made a mournful cry and vomited dozens more of them, propping up on it forearms, its hind legs folding. The larvae burst open, with small leathery winged creatures that flopped in the filth, trying to find their legs, shaking the filth from their bodies, clicking with their mouths. They squirmed, crawled and jumped through the thick black regurgitation and latched upon the Angrodha like ticks. The Angrodha desperately tried to fly, pushing up into the sky once, but lacking the energy for a second push of its great wings, it crashed back down upon the mountainside and slid into the buildings where a soldier who had been hiding ran screaming.

It rolled to its feet and burst open at its belly, hundreds of the larvae expelled in its dying lunge. The larvae metamorphosed into small winged creatures and one by one, flew into the pre-dawn sky, circling Moonledge for almost an hour and then flying off toward Shintower.

As the morning light revealed the extent of the carnage, the fearful soldier returned to the cocoon, finding that it had died nearly as fast as it had appeared. He cautiously touched it, afraid of the poison it might still contain, but it broke away like a rotted tree limb might, and he searched to see if the old wizard might still be inside.

As he broke away the last of the layers, he could see Mategaladh's face inside, pale and lifeless, but the soldier continued to tear away the cocoon with some hope of rescuing his rescuer.

When he had split open the side, Mategaladh fell out into his arms. The young man carefully lowered him to the ground and pressed his ear against Mategaladh's chest, but heard nothing. The soldier felt for his breath, and Mategaladh made the smallest moan. The soldier quickly threw him over his shoulder and started toward the temple, screaming for help.

Chapter Twenty-Two

Attack on Shintower

Aleris tried the door on Rendaya's cottage, but it was barred, so he got a good running start and flew through her kitchen window with a crash of glass. He ran headlong into and bounced off a pan that was hanging from the ceiling, fell straightway to Rendaya's chopping block that doubled as a general storage area for her herbs and whatnots. He lay flat on his back in the center of the block, scattering several of her glass containers to the floor. The clamor shot Rendaya straight up from her bed. A blue aura appeared to cover her skin and then migrate to her open hand in the shape of a sphere, its blue glow filling the room.

"What in the—Aleris? Aleris, is that you?" Rendaya asked.

Aleris propped himself up on one arm and rubbed his head. "Rendaya! There's a great fire in Highwood! You must come at once!"

"What?" Rendaya repeated. "A fire?"

"Yes, Yes!" Aleris said. He flew to her side and grabbed her sleeve as if he would pull her up from bed. "I fear that Amphileph is moving upon the west!"

"Yes, of course, let me dress at once," Rendaya said, and she threw back the blankets. She opened her armoire and grabbed some of her clothes, throwing them across the chair before unceremoniously beginning to remove her nightgown.

"My lady!" Aleris said. He hovered and turned to face the kitchen window. "I will wait outside!" he said, and he quickly exited back through the missing pane.

When Rendaya stepped outside, she was already sure that there was a real problem. She could see smoke rising to the sky above the Southwood treetops.

"We must go to Shintower; it is time!" Aleris said.

There was a twinge in Rendaya's midsection. Could it be that she would have to cross paths with the Watchers again? It had been a long time, but old wounds ran deep.

"I'm coming," she said. She concentrated on removing her doubts and worries, focusing on the here and now. Her aura shot outward from around her midsection, engulfing her in its vibrant blue glow, and she accelerated upward. She reopened her eyes after clearing the tops of Southwood Forest and concentrated on Shintower, her trajectory arcing in that direction with the mere thought of it.

She landed smoothly in the crop fields south of Shintower and waited for Aleris, who arrived shortly after her.

"They fear you, Rendaya," Aleris said. "Let me talk to them first."

"I'll wait here," she answered.

Aleris nodded and flew toward the gates of Shintower, stopping just outside at the sight of a familiar wagon. Jalin was seated at the wagon's reins, and Ro was helping Tiamphia out of it. Tiamphia's slightly protruding stomach made Aleris sure she was pregnant.

"I feared my friends were in danger."

Aleris turned toward the speaker and saw Galbard walking toward him. His hair had grown long and a little unwieldy, and his beard was full.

"Galbard?" Aleris inquired.

"I could see the flames of Highwood, and I thought my friends might be in trouble. I was going to bring only Ro, but Tiamphia and Jalin wouldn't hear of it. They wanted to be at our sides as we were at yours. I'm afraid I haven't a sword of my own," he smiled. "But if the armory can spare one for an old man and his son, we will raise them for Shintower and the Dales, old friend."

"Galbard!" shouted Aleris. He flew just in front of him and hovered. "We'll find two swords for such good company!"

"I've heard that riders arrived this morning to report of the Camonra's attack on the high wood. There's nothing to stop them from arriving at the Dales in short order."

"Let's us go to the upper deck and talk of war," said Aleris. "Tiamphia and Jalin's rooms remained untouched. Let them take refuge there."

"Very well, my friend, lead the way."

* * *

Seeking order and security, frightened townspeople alerted Cayden in the deep of the night, and he had left Nara to sleep a little longer while he talked with the town council under a street lamp outside the house. The rider said that the Inferiors had set fire to Highwood and the people were fleeing to Candra. Cayden had ridden to Shintower immediately, stopping only to send a messenger to Nara, instructing her to be ready to leave the Dales at a moment's notice.

The sun was rising in the eastern sky. Galbard stood with Aleris and Ro on the upper deck of the great tower, all focused on the huge column of smoke rising from the direction of Highwood and the large flock of strange creatures that crisscrossed back and forth through the black smoke. He heard footsteps and turned to see Cayden exit the deck stairs.

"Cayden! Good!" Galbard said. "I feared I might not have the benefit of your counsel before things got out of hand here."

"Galbard?" asked Cayden. "Do my eyes deceive me?"

"Hello, my friend."

Cayden kneeled. "Sire, we are ready to fight for you," he said.

"Now, now, there'll be none of that. Rise, man, we are brothers." Galbard looked around at them. "This is it, then," he said. "Reminds me of the first time I ever set foot in Shintower, so many years ago. I was convinced then that the Camonra were right behind me. I guess they always were."

"Yes, lord, this *is* our destiny," said Aleris.

"What have we then?" asked Galbard.

"Shintower's defenses are of no use to us without the Sword, but it is still a formidable structure and the Bhre-Nora stand ready to fight for you. The people of the Dales will also be greatly encouraged by your return. They will rally for your cause."

Galbard tried to smile, but the world weighed heavily upon his shoulders. "Have those from the Dales who can fight ready to meet our enemy at the Northern Bridge of the Highborne River. We've no place for everyone within the tower, and we must give the people of the Dales time to get as far away as possible. Have you a map?"

Cayden produced a scroll of parchment, rolling it out upon the altar of the Sword. Galbard watched him do so, and he thought of the power that was lost with its absence. He shook his head as if it might fling such thoughts out of it, for he knew there was no time for such folly.

"We will take the fight to them in waves, falling back among the Dales, and finally to Shintower," he said.

"There is another who is able to come to our aid," said Aleris. "With your permission, I will retrieve her."

"By all means, Aleris," answered Galbard, a bit puzzled by the request.

Aleris took flight and zoomed over the side of the great tower, signaling Rendaya that she should come up. He flew back and landed among Galbard and the others. "She's coming," Aleris said.

Rendaya landed in the center of the tower's upper deck. She stood to greet them, and the glow of her blue aura was still clearly visible in the broad daylight.

"Galbard, this is Rendaya," Aleris said.

"Who is this?" Galbard asked. "A Watcher?"

Cayden saw Rendaya's face, and he cried out. "My lord, this is the one they call the Witch of Southwood! This is the being that landed on the *Merrius!* It's she that told us to build the tower and protect you!"

"Clearly, you know more of me than I do of you, Rendaya," Galbard said.

Rendaya looked them over one by one. "I'm no Watcher," she replied. She walked to the edge of the tower's upper deck and looked in the direction of Highwood.

"I meant no offense," said Galbard. "You have abilities I have only seen in Watchers."

Rendaya turned back to Galbard, and her facial expression softened slightly. "A new creature flies in the skies above Highwood," she said. "They are unnatural, most assuredly Amphileph's work. Do you have archers?"

"Yes," Galbard said. "We've archers."

Rendaya turned to Aleris. "The tower's defenses were designed to repel a ground attack," she said. "It may be difficult to defend from the air."

"We will do what we can, to the last man," said Galbard.

Rendaya paced to the altar and back, looking around the skies. "It is wise that you have sent your people to the north," said Rendaya. "The Dales are abandoned?"

"Only the warriors and our healers remain," replied Galbard.

"The Camonra will not give chase to them as long as they believe that the Sword is here, but there is no sense tempting the likes of Amphileph with easy bloodshed, no matter if their objective lies elsewhere," said Rendaya.

"Cayden, I will entrust the first wave to your command," said Galbard. "Let them know that they have found the Dales!"

"I'll be about that now," said Cayden. "With your leave, my liege."

Galbard touched his shoulder. "Protect your numbers, Cayden. Lead the people to the warriors in Candra if you must."

"Yes, sire!" he answered, and then he bowed and swiftly proceeded down the stairs.

"The Sword lies deep within the Keep of Moonledge?" Rendaya asked.

"Under the protection of Caratacus," said Aleris.

"Now I wish that I had it close," said Galbard. "I feel the fool."

"You did what Evliit asked of you," said Rendaya. "I would've never believed a man would outpace Amphileph's pursuit, but now the next challenge is upon you: *keeping* the Sword from Amphileph."

"We will give Amphileph the sting of defeat," said Galbard. "If only we can greatly thin his ranks, the warriors of Candra and Moonledge will have a fighting chance to drive them back into the east."

"Do not underestimate the Bhre-Nora, for their size is not indicative of their ferocity. You've seen them build, but I've seen them make war. We will give the Camonra a most proper welcome."

"So you believe that they will attack by land *and* air?" Galbard asked. He squinted, trying to bring the distant group of warriors into view.

"Yes," Rendaya said. "You should arm yourself."

Galbard hadn't retrieved a weapon from the armory. In the years since leaving Shintower, he had not even carried a weapon, opting for farming and mason work. "Indeed, that time has come, hasn't it?"

Rendaya nodded. "What of your own family?" she asked. "Have they left for Candra?"

"They would not hear of it. Aleris has seen to them. No one has ever taken over our rooms here in Shintower. My wife and son and his wife are there now."

"Please pardon my frankness, my lord, but you should convince them to leave with the others," said Rendaya. "Your line should not end here."

Galbard considered her words, and he turned from her and descended the stairs.

Far below Rendaya and Galbard atop Shintower's upper deck, Cayden ran without stopping until he burst through the door of his and Nara's home in the Dales.

"Nara!" he cried, huffing and puffing from the run. "Nara!"

Nara pulled back the drape that covered the entrance to their bedroom and answered, "What is happening? The people are all leaving their homes!"

"Galbard is asking for the people to flee to Candra Valley!" he shouted. "Are you ready to leave?"

"Yes, I'm ready, but what of you? Where will you be?"

"The warriors will set out for the Northern Bridge. We'll hold them back from the bridge as long as possible, and then we'll retreat to the Dales and finally to Shintower. Our hope is to thin their ranks as much as possible before they reach the Dales."

"Will the warriors in Candra come to our aid?" asked Nara.

"That is our hope," answered Cayden. "We will beseech them to protect the women and children and send soldiers to strengthen us."

Nara began to cry. "I will not leave you!" she shouted.

"Oh, Nara," Cayden replied. "You must take refuge in the valley, away from these monsters! I'll come for you when they have been defeated and all is safe again in the Dales."

The logic of his words fell upon deaf ears. "I cannot leave you!" she repeated. Tears began to brim her eyes, and her face fell into her hands.

Cayden pushed his scabbard to the side and pulled her to him. "How can I fight while I worry every moment about your safety? You must go—for both of our sakes."

At these words, she gasped and looked into his eyes. She laid her forehead on Cayden's chest then and cried openly. He gave her a moment more, and then he pressed his lips against her hair and kissed her gently. He took her face into both of his hands and lifted her chin so that their eyes met.

"The others will need to see your example," Cayden said. "Be strong, Nara."

"I will go," she said. "I'll go because you have asked me."

They embraced, and then Cayden led her outside and helped her with her things. Several of the women and children were already walking toward the northern end of the Dales, and Cayden urged her to join them. "When you reach the valley, stay with our people. The Highborne will block the Inferiors from crossing into the valley from the north. They'll follow the river to the Northern Bridge."

"Cayden, I'm afraid for us," Nara said. The expression on her face tore at his very soul.

"I've told those leading the people to keep to the western trails. They know the road to Candra well."

"It's not the getting lost that worries me," said Nara.

Cayden wrung his hands. "I must join the other men at the Northern Bridge, Nara. Riders have gone ahead of you to the Candrians. Galbard has asked for their aid in defending Shintower."

"But what if the Candrians refuse?"

"How can they refuse? They know we must act together, for our downfall is theirs. They surely will realize that the Inferiors do not distinguish Candrians from the people of the Dale."

He thought then that she seemed to see the futility in arguing. She bent over to get her things, and a tear trickled down her cheek, but she was quick to wipe it away. "Please be careful," she said, fighting to hold back the tears.

"You must go now!" Cayden said, but then he moved to hold her in his arms, looking deeply into her eyes. "I love you, Nara."

"I've never doubted that for a moment," she said, pulling away from him. "Return to me soon, my love."

Cayden knew that if she asked in that moment to stay, he would have allowed it, but she gathered some belongings and exited their home with him just behind her. Then she moved quickly into the line of people that were leaving the Dales, looking back at him once before disappearing in the crowd.

Cayden looked at their small cottage in the Dales one last time, and he thought to himself that the chances were good that it could be destroyed in an attack. An anxiousness pulled at him to go back inside, to look around one more time for something precious that he might have left there, but he resisted the urge. There was no carrying it with him, no time to hide it anywhere. Everyone was meeting in the fields west of the Northern Bridge over the Highborne River, and he should be among the first to arrive.

Cayden made his way to the eastern end of the Dales, where the men gathered their weapons. They tore down some of the retaining walls on the bridge walks to use the stone for the six catapults they had slaved to get into working order.

"The Inferiors will be forced to narrow their lines to cross the bridge. We'll release the catapults as they funnel inward," Cayden said.

"They'll move on us quickly," replied one of the men.

"Yes, they will," said Cayden. He walked among them listening to them talk nervously amongst themselves. These were mostly masons and craftsmen, not warriors, and Cayden could see in their faces that the likelihood of facing an Inferior in hand-to-hand combat terrified them. He thought a clear directive might ease their minds.

"I have divided the archers into two groups. The first group will release their arrows immediately following the catapults' volley. Reload the catapults and fire them as many times as you can, but the first group of archers will fire only once more before they flee. I suggest that you release one or two more volleys only and then abandon the catapults. When the Inferiors get to the cobblestone portion of the road, the second group of archers will fire their arrows while we all retreat to the Dales," Cayden commanded them. "Don't tarry, my friends. Your only advantage may be that you know the streets of the Dales better than our foes. Our task is to thin their ranks as best we can and allow our people to get as far away from Shintower as possible."

"Yes, sir!" the men responded.

"Well, let's be about it then!" Cayden commanded, and they moved quickly into position with the catapults at the front.

* * *

Citanth watched the strange creatures in the sky to the north of Highwood, expecting instead to see the Angrodha, and the lack of its presence was beginning to worry him.

The Camonra passed alongside Highwood, and rain began to fall. The great forest's blackened, charred and twisted tree trunks reminded Citanth of the withered flesh of his right hand, the constant reminder of his last encounter with the Sword. He couldn't wait to return that cursed object to Amphileph. Amphileph would use it to change the world around them and raise him up to the status he deserved. He would bring the Sword to Amphileph, and everything—even his withered arm—would be made right again.

"Where is the Angrodha?" he shouted to his troops. The flames continued to burn out of control on this side of the Highborne River, but the width of the river had managed to prevent the flames from igniting the western growth.

There was little more than ash where the tree fortress of the Rionese soldiers had been.

"Look! Look at what remains of the fools that oppose Amphileph's power! The men of Rion have only delayed their fate!" Citanth yelled.

In the distance, Shintower rose above the horizon.

"There it is!" Citanth laughed. "We march to Shintower unopposed, my warriors!"

The wind stirred up suddenly, changing directions and raising a wall of smoke from the burning woods that shifted and shaped itself. Even over the roar of the troop movement, Citanth was sure that he heard Amphileph speaking his name. It sounded distant, mixed with the rumble of thunder in the darkening clouds to the east and south of them.

Citanth sat up in his seat and looked around the horizon. He could see the weaponry of Rion among the ashes, scattered beside the remnants of the bodies of Rionese soldiers who had stood their posts to the bitter end. The quiet voice became a little louder, and the winds whipped the smoke into the form of Amphileph floating over the ruins of Highwood, his outstretched arms seemingly reaching to Citanth.

"Bow down!" Citanth screamed, standing up in his carriage.

The Camonra stopped in mid-stride of their battle march and dropped to one knee. The captains reined in their Azrodhs and did the same. Citanth leapt down from his carriage and ran toward Highwood, stopping where the white ash met with the green grass of the Rainland and dropping to one knee.

"My lord, we do your bidding!" Citanth said. He looked down at the ground, but not before he managed another glimpse of Amphileph's wispy form, shifting in the wind.

Amphileph's voice drifted in and out on the winds. "The Angrodha is no more," he said. "Mategaladh has destroyed it."

"My lord?" Citanth responded.

"Silence!" Amphileph said. "It is no matter. His powers were not great enough to end its life force, only alter it. I anticipated as much! What remains now are the Syra, and they will come to your aid in destroying my enemies. Behold!"

The form of Amphileph mixed with the wing wash of hundreds of Syra, swirling above the heads of Citanth and his soldiers. Hundreds of the tiny winged creatures landed among them and spread their mouths open to show their rows of circular teeth, making that clicking sound that drowned out all else. The intensity of their calls rose until the Syra became so agitated that they began to fight among themselves all around the soldiers.

One of the Azrodh's became spooked and rose up on its hind legs. Its rider rose to grab for its reins, and the sudden movement caught the attention of the Syra. A wave of leathery flesh washed over rider and Azrodh and engulfed them. Their tails squirmed in the pile, the awful clicking noises rising and falling with the howls of the Azrodh and the screams of the rider beneath them. The Camon shot up from the pile, throwing half a dozen of the Syra off. The Azrodh shook off the Syra with a twisting quiver that ran the length of its scaly hide.

One of the Syra had driven its spearlike tail into the rider's spine and whipped its body forward, sinking its teeth into the back of his head. The soldier screamed and flailed, and the wings of the Syra flapped madly around his face. The Syra's lower jaw unhinged, and its circular row of hook-shaped teeth stretched the scalp across the top of his head. The Syra's body arched up and its eyes blinked; then the sound of crunching bone could be heard, and the soldier's arms relaxed and fell to his side.

The sound of collective awe caused Citanth to look slowly toward the chaos, when he saw his soldier's torso twitch like a dog shaking water from its coat. His head bobbed, and the Syra seemed to gag. Its eyes rolled back in its head, and its eyelids fluttered closed. The Syra's torso collapsed against the back of the soldier's neck, and it appeared to push its internal organs into the skull cavity of his head.

The Camon soldier fell to one knee and then to the side, his hand barely stopping his toppling over. The sides of the Syra shuddered, it exhaled, and the soldier seemed to gain some bearings and stood back up on two feet. He rose, and the Camonra surrounding him looked in horror at his face. His eyes were lifeless and his mouth was agape, blood drooling its way down the side of his neck.

Citanth could see the makings of panic. The Camonra began moving back from their comrade, exciting the Syra into an even more frenzied state. The winged parasites swirled into the air and back to the ground, shuffling again and making that awful clicking sound.

The Camon with the Syra parasitically attached began to walk toward Shintower. His comrades cleared him a path, and he continued without acknowledging their existence.

The ethereal form of Amphileph folded its arms. "Enough!" he said, and the flock of Syra swirled into the sky.

Citanth let his eyes look up to the mist. "My lord, Amphileph, what is your command?" he asked.

"Make your camp here. I will see through the Syra's eyes as I did through the Angrodha. Let the creatures make their way into the land of men. I'll search them out, and then I will issue your next command." The Syra dove back down, crossing just over their heads in a swarm, and then the creatures shot through the mist that was Amphileph and disappeared into the sky.

The mist dissipated and the figure of Amphileph was gone.

* * *

Ardhios woke to the smell of wood burning. He gently moved Portina's head from his shoulder, got out of bed, and went to the balcony. When he saw the smoke of Highwood burning from the balcony window of his room, he quickly got dressed and went downstairs. There were several of the workers from Highwood in the courtyard outside the Seven Warriors Hall. Their upset was evident.

"My lord, riders come from Highwood! The Camonra have attacked our people, burning them out of their homes, killing many of our kin! Large numbers of them have camped southeast of the ruins of Highwood!"

Ardhios grabbed a runner. "Get Borian at once!" he yelled, and the runner took flight. Within minutes, Borian met him in the courtyard.

"The Camonra move on Highwood and the Dales!" said Ardhios.

"What would you have me do?" inquired Borian.

"Gather your troops and join us. The people of the west must stand together!"

Mordher emerged from the Hall. "A meeting without me?" he asked.

"Look, Mordher! Look what is happening!" cried Ardhios.

There were a great number of the people of the Highwood in the distance, coming from the south toward the Seven Warriors Hall.

"What in the Creator's name have you started, Mordher?" he shouted. One of Ardhios's servants appeared with his horse, and Ardhios practically jumped into the stirrups. "We must defend these people!"

He didn't wait for Mordher or Borian to speak, but spurred his horse to a gallop toward the oncoming horde. There were soldiers and people shouting. Many had burns, and their clothing and faces were black with soot.

"Help us, sire!" they cried. The crowd moved in upon him, and Ardhios reined in his horse and attempted to calm her.

"The Inferiors have burned us alive!" another cried.

"Come to the Great Hall!" said Ardhios. "We have supplies and healers. We welcome you!"

He turned his horse and rode back to the courtyard.

"The Camonra are attacking the people of Highwood. We must ride out to meet them!" yelled Ardhios. "We will combine our forces and drive the Camonra back!"

"My warriors follow no one but me!" said Mordher.

Ardhios was furious, but he fought to think. The people of Highwood looked to him for leadership. "Mordher, have you not seen how I've amassed an army equal to yours? Join me in defending these people, and all will see that I follow you."

Mordher smiled. "Now you need me? Now you need to fight, and I'm once more in your favor?"

Ardhios bit his tongue. "Borian, will you join me?"

Borian looked stunned for a moment, but then he reached out his hand. "Yes, my brother, I will take the fight to the Inferiors!"

"What are you without me?" Mordher smirked.

"Gather your army then, and show me how a true warrior fights!" Borian jabbed.

Mordher leered at both of them. "I will show you how to kill Inferiors!" he shouted, and then he turned to his soldiers. "Get my horse!"

Ardhios turned to the people. "Go to the Warriors Hall!"

"Every soldier stays!" Mordher yelled. "Let the women and children make their way to Candra!"

"They're worn and tattered, Mordher! What good will they be to us?" Ardhios replied.

"They'll make great fodder for the Inferiors, if they do not as I wish! Foot soldiers—that's the place for them!"

Ardhios glared at Mordher. "Depart!" he said to the soldiers. "Join the others in the camp! They've water and food. Gather your strength!"

The Highwood soldiers looked perplexed. "Yes, my liege," they answered and then turned and walked toward Mordher's encampment southeast of the Hall.

When the soldiers were out of earshot, Ardhios shouted at Mordher. "Is this what you wanted?"

"What can you expect from people that build their houses in trees?" Mordher sneered.

"What?" Ardhios replied. He turned to Borian. "Has he lost his mind, Borian?"

"I'll not speak for him," Borian replied. "He happily lies in the bed he has made."

"You've started a war!" Ardhios shouted to Mordher. "The whole of the Spellmaker's army are set against us. We'll band together, the survivors of Rion, or they'll destroy us one by one. With Highwood gone, we've no choice but to go to Moonledge Peak and plead with them to join with us! I don't think you see it. This battle could be our undoing!" Ardhios looked to Borian. "I can't trust him with my army, but I would turn them over to you. Will you lead them in my stead till I return?"

Borian took a moment to enjoy the anger in Mordher's face. "Yes," he replied.

Mordher leaned forward in his saddle, his lower jaw protruding with his distaste for Ardhios. "Let them bring it!" he shouted back. "Take your people to the valley, Ardhios, and leave the fighting to the men."

Ardhios drew his sword, and Mordher did likewise.

"Be still!" Borian said, and they each looked at him as if sizing up his loyalties. "Be gone, Ardhios! There's no shame in the role of savior to the homeless, am I not right? Ignore him and be gone!"

"I didn't survive two years in that Rionese prison to listen to such madness! I will take a company of fifty of my men to escort Highwood's survivors. Then I am off to Moonledge!" Ardhios shouted.

"Take them," Borian agreed.

Ardhios spurred his horse toward the townspeople. "People of Highwood!" he cried, "Listen to me! Women and children are to follow me! Soldiers of Highwood, form up here!"

Ardhios's horse circled to the left, and the people of Highwood did as they were told. Ardhios circled back to his right, closer to Borian and Mordher. "May the Creator protect us!" he said, and he spurred his horse a final time and rode off toward the Seven Warriors Hall.

"Captain!" Borian yelled. "Separate the women and children from the men!"

"Yes, my liege!" the captain replied and the soldiers began herding the weak toward the protection of the Hall, and then Borian addressed the remaining warriors. "Soldiers of Highwood, you are hereby conscripted to fight for Candra! The women and children will follow Ardhios to the protection of our castle, and you will fight the Camonra with us!"

"Soldiers!" said Mordher. "Form up! We make for the Northern Bridge!"

Ardhios watched his army follow Mordher and Borian toward the Northern Bridge wondering if he had done the right thing. He called to his captain. "Take them to the Seven Warriors Hall. I am riding to Moonledge Peak, and I will return as soon as possible!" With that, he spurred his horse and galloped away.

About six hours later, Ardhios stopped at Highborne Falls to rest his horse and refill his water in the clear water of the falls; no sooner had he done this than he began walking him around the end of the Candra Mountains, where he could see the rising Faceless Mountains. He remounted and drove his horse without end for ten hours more, and just as dawn broke the following day, he arrived at the outskirts of Moonledge Peak.

The damage from the Angrodha was everywhere, but the Keep was open, and the soldiers were piling brush and debris upon the Angrodha's carcass to eliminate its stench with fire. The mood was still very tense.

"Who goes there?" one of soldiers asked.

"His colors are Candrian," another said. "Looks like they've sent but one soldier to aid our cause!"

There was a ripple of laughter among the soldiers.

"I am Ardhios of the Seven Warriors!" he shouted, and the laughter immediately ended. "Take me to Caratacus!"

"At once, my lord!" the soldier answered. "Wet down my horse and water it! I've little time before I must ride again!"

Ardhios leapt from the saddle and proceeded up the stairs of the Keep, where he found women bringing gifts of flowers in droves.

"What has happened here?" he asked.

"A Watcher lies near death in our walls," said a women passing by. "He's given his life to destroy the monster!"

"A Watcher?" Ardhios replied.

"Yes, my lord, by the name of Mategaladh," she said.

Ardhios barged ahead and came to the council chambers. Caratacus and the other council members were deep in discussions, listening to healers talking of everything from bleeding to herbs to help Mategaladh.

"Caratacus!" Ardhios called out.

"I am Caratacus," he answered. "You wear the colors of the Candrians. What news have you?"

"My lord, I am Ardhios of Candra. The war is far from over, my lord; we need warriors to drive the Camonra from our lands. Amphileph's army marches on the people of Highwood and the Dales! And surely, when they have finished there, they will march on Candra."

"We've no warriors to spare," answered Caratacus. "We've problems enough here."

"But my lord—" Ardhios began.

"You Candrians. What gall! Was it not enough that we allowed your brethren to try to take the Sword of Evliit? What more do you want from us?"

"The Sword of Evliit," said Ardhios. "Who tried to take it?"

"The one called Mordher tried to take it, but it would have none of his efforts. We will keep the Sword of Evliit until Evliit himself returns for it. It was a mistake to let Mordher even see it, a mistake we made in fear for our lives, a mistake we will not repeat."

"I have little time, my lord. Surely, you could—"

"It is of no use to argue, good Ardhios. We have made our decision, and—"

There was a sudden entrance of the priests from their right, and Ardhios could hear chaos in the wings of the great hall. The priest leaned in to speak to Caratacus in private, but before he had finished, Mategaladh stood propped against the doorway with his staff. The room fell silent, and the people fell upon their faces.

"Praise the Creator!" said Caratacus. "We had thought you dead, Watcher! We never—"

"I am near enough to death, but not ready to let the people of Highwood, the Dales, or Candra die at Amphileph's hands," Mategaladh interrupted. "Give this Ardhios his chance with the Sword! It goes nowhere it wishes not to be!" Mategaladh's knees buckled, and the priests and acolytes caught him up.

"You must rest!" said the high priest.

"I must defend the people of Erathe!" cried Mategaladh. "Give him his chance and do it now!" He coughed and tried to catch his breath. The priest nodded to the guards, who opened the tapestries and brought out the case. Before they could perform their ceremony, Ardhios opened the chest, removed the case, and opened it. Then he lifted out the Sword in its scabbard. There was a collective gasp.

"You are worthy, good Ardhios," said Mategaladh. "Now listen to me: a Calarphian horse is what you need to take this sword to Shintower with all speed. One named Galbard there will know what must be done. Will you do this?"

"I will," answered Ardhios.

"There is no time to lose," said Mategaladh. He swooned with those words, and the priest lifted him off his feet and carried him away.

"Bring this man a horse!" Caratacus commanded, and the room around him sprang to life.

* * *

For two days, Citanth waited for word from Amphileph about the Syra's movements along the Highborne River, but there was no word. He had ordered the Camonra to sift through the ashes of Highwood, but there was little to nothing that they could salvage for war. He walked to the edge of the Highborne River and looked across at the trees on the other side. Items were scattered along a path leading south to the Northern Bridge, but other than the occasional decomposing body, there was no sign of the humans. He knelt over a small eddy and looked at his reflection, almost gathering back some of the humanity he had lost in Amphileph's captivity, but letting it slip away in the next moment.

There was no escaping what he had become, and when he focused on the water's reflection, it began to change, and an image of the Camon appeared, his Syran parasite bored into his head, distorting his facial features. The decaying Camon's mouth hung open, and the Syra pushed its tongue through the opening and lapped at the water. It shifted inside the Camon's head, twitching the wings that protruded out of the back of the Camon's crushed cranium. It too had come upon the river's edge and found no crossing was in sight for its host. The Camon's body was still strong, and the Syra knew it could still feed off it for days, pushing it day and night, up and down the riverbank in search of a crossing. Citanth struck the surface of the water in his frustration, and the vision ended. The wait was driving him mad.

He returned to the main body of warriors, who were also impatient, waiting around a fire they had made from a ten-foot high pile of partially burned remains. The wind rose up suddenly and stoked it into a whirlwind of flame that began to consume the gruesome fuel. It became so hot that those surrounding it had to shield their faces and push back from it. Then, all at once, the Camonra began to shout and chant, for Amphileph's form had appeared in the flames.

"The men protect a bridge that crosses into their lands south of Highwood." Amphileph's voice could be heard coming from the fire. "Destroy them!" the voice wailed. The fire suddenly intensified and then just as suddenly snuffed out, cold. The Camonra leapt to their feet and screamed for battle.

They quickly assembled into a column to march westward. "To the bridge!" Citanth cried. "Destroy them!"

"Destroy them!" the Camonra shouted in response.

* * *

Ardhios rode around the Highborne Falls in little more than half the time it had taken him the day before, and then he had pushed through the Candra Valley at breakneck speeds, at times worried that exhaustion would drop him from his saddle. Then he would find his strength again in the excitement of carrying the Sword of Evliit on his side.

He shot past a line of soldiers coming from Candra, and by midafternoon, Shintower loomed on the horizon. Within the hour, he arrived at Shintower, and he could see warriors of the Dales working diligently to build barbicans of different types around the outer walls of the courtyard. He pulled the proud Calarphian horse to a stop just before them and dismounted, his legs wobbling from the ride.

"I must find a man by the name of Galbard!" he cried, and the soldiers quickly came out to meet him. One look at him, and the soldiers answered together: "This way!"

Ardhios followed the soldiers into Shintower. He kept the sword wrapped in a long rawhide bag until he reached the upper deck where Galbard and the others were discussing their strategy.

"My lord, this is Ardhios of Candra," said the soldier.

"I've no time—" began Galbard, never looking up from the map where they were drawing the lines of battle.

"Unbelievable! Galbard, look!" said Aleris.

Ardhios had taken one knee, holding the Sword of the Watch before him, his head lowered. "I bring this sword to its rightful bearer, in the name of the Watcher, Mategaladh." With his head bowed, footsteps moved toward him, and then the Sword was lifted away from his open hands. He looked up to see Galbard's face stern and determined.

"It seems I cannot escape my destiny," he said. The group behind him looked stunned. "How can we ever repay your efforts, Ardhios? Surely we owe more than we can say!"

"Help me protect my people," said Ardhios. "This is all I ask, good sire."

"You look exhausted, Ardhios. Come, rest a while in Shintower."

"I cannot rest until this evil is driven out of our lands," answered Ardhios. "I leave the Sword in your capable hands, for I must return to the Seven Warriors Hall. My brothers will not understand why I have brought the Sword to you, and the people of Highwood are in need of sanctuary. My place is there."

"May the Warriors of Light protect you," said Galbard, placing the Sword upon Ardhios's shoulders. Spiritual energy poured through Ardhios's body, making his eyes widen and his back arch. "Rise, Ardhios, the first knight of Shintower."

Ardhios felt completely energized, though logic told him he should not even be able to stand. "The power of the Sword in your hands is miraculous!" he said. "I bid you well!"

"Fare thee well, Ardhios!" said Galbard.

* * *

"Someone's coming!" a voice cried from Cayden's front lines.

"Someone's coming!" repeated down the lines, and Cayden made his way forward.

"What do you see?"

"It's a Camon, I think."

Cayden looked into the distance in early-morning darkness. There, slightly to their left was a lone figure running toward them. Cayden slapped the soldier on the shoulder. "Good eye, brother!" he said.

"Four of you, archers!" Cayden commanded. "Ready!"

Four of the archers moved front and center and raised their bows to the sky.

"Steady," said Cayden. The four bowmen drew their arrows taut in their bows. "Fire!" Cayden said, and the bowmen let loose their arrows, arching through the sky. Cayden could see the arrows at first, but then the trajectory was lost against the dim firmament. The lone soldier continued to run toward them.

Suddenly, the impact of three of the four arrows could be seen striking the approaching soldier in the neck, shoulder, and upper chest. He fell to the ground.

"Scouts!" Cayden cried. "Front and center!"

Two slim runners came to the front. Cayden was panged by the fear he could see in their youthful faces.

"See what you can find on him, but don't tarry! There are likely more scouts where that one came from."

"Yes, my liege!" they responded and took off on a dead run toward the fallen soldier. They covered about two-thirds the distance when Cayden saw some movement. The soldier pushed up to one knee, the arrows clearly protruding from his body. The two scouts stopped and looked back at Cayden.

"Hold!" Cayden yelled, waving them back. The two runners gladly obliged him and sprinted back toward the bridge.

"Archers!" Cayden cried again, and the four bowmen once again raised their bows and arrows.

"Fire!"

This time, all four arrows struck the soldier, one just above the knee, twice more in the chest and once in the abdomen. The soldier turned sideways with the impact, and all could see that the arrows had completely pierced his torso and thigh. The soldier dropped to one knee amid a flurry of activity. A winged creature rose up and away from the soldier's body, pushing down upon the ground with its wings and tearing itself from the soldier's head. It flew away, and the soldier remained face down, motionless.

The scouts ran out a second time and cautiously circled the body. Slowly they moved in and investigated thoroughly before they returned to Cayden to report what they had found.

"It's an Inferior, sire, but whatever that creature was, it had ripped open the back of the Inferior's head getting away!" one of the scouts said.

"I rolled him over, sire, and his face—it appeared that he'd been dead for some time. I don't know what to make of it," said the other scout.

"Well done," Cayden said. "Move to the rear—no, you return to Galbard and let him know what you've seen. Inform Lord Galbard that we are prepared to do our part—that the catapults and archers are ready."

"My lord, my brother, Antio, is younger. If it would please, my lord, let him go," the older of the two scouts said.

"Of course," answered Cayden, and the younger of the two scouts raised his hand to his chest and then departed at a dead run.

"Move to the rear, son," said Cayden. "It'll get ugly up here."

"Yes, my lord," the scout said, and he ran for the rear of their column.

"My lord, riders approach from the north!" a voice rang out to Cayden's left. The men recognized the flag of the Candrian army barreling over the nearest hill toward them, and there followed a cheer.

Borian pulled his horse's reins to a quick stop. "Who's in charge here?" he yelled. Mordher stopped behind him, and he raised a fist that halted the army.

"I am," said Cayden.

Borian stepped down off his horse and they clasped forearms. "We've come to kill Inferiors!" he said.

"We're glad to see you!" said Cayden. "We've been charged with delaying their march until our people have fled, and then we're to flee to our tower and make our stand. We've reinforcements and man-traps there."

"Retreat is your plan?" sneered Mordher. He piled down from his horse with a thump. "Why would *we* retreat?"

"We've no idea of their exact numbers, but the Inferiors have mounted an impressive force. We have seen them from the tower's height, and I assure you, they mean to make war upon us."

"Who talks of war, but has no armor?" Mordher asked.

"Mordher—" Borian interjected, looking sternly at Mordher. "Forgive my friend. He means no disrespect."

"We are masons and craftsmen, hunters and farmers," Cayden responded. "But we defend our land, and that should not be underestimated."

"If they cross the Northern Bridge, they'll not stop until they're in Shintower," Mordher said. "We must break up their lines and separate their soldiers to defeat them here."

"We've sent the people of the Dales to Candra. We will draw them toward the tower so that the women and children are furthest away from the battle. The soldiers of Candra will be the last defense if the worst happens. Pull back your soldiers and meet them in the fields north of here if you must. At worst, surely we'll have thinned their ranks."

"We might flank them as they attack the Dales, brother," Borian said to Mordher.

"Flanking sounds good," Mordher grunted.

"But if you meet them here, who will protect our people if they turn north?" Cayden asked.

"We are four thousand strong," Borian answered. "They'll not easily overrun us."

"So what is it then?" Mordher insisted.

"We'll do as we've been commanded by Galbard, but I don't see where that will prevent your plan of attack," said Cayden. "Let us seek the Creator's will."

"You seek the Creator's will, and I will sharpen my sword and axe," Mordher said. He turned around to leave, but another shout rang out from the front of the Shintower's proud few. A runner burst into their midst, panting.

"My lord, Cayden," said the runner. "Thousands of Inferiors approach! Something flies above them in the air! Hundreds, maybe thousands of bat-like creatures, or vultures, I don't know, sire, but they're a creature of the evil one, that's clear by the very sight of them!"

"Spread the word!" said Cayden. "Ready the catapults and archers!" he said to the runner, who sped away. "What say you, Candrians?"

"Ready the cavalry! Archers! Shields, spears, and spikes! We kill Inferiors today!" Mordher hailed, to the delight of his soldiers. His was the battle cry that steeled their will to fight; it seemed for that, Mordher was born.

Borian pointed to the north. "We'll wait just over that hill," he said. "Give them your catapults and arrows, flee, and let them give chase, just as you have been commanded. We'll be watching. When you've taken flight, we'll flank them!" Borian yelled to Cayden, and the two Candrian leaders mounted their horses. Cayden watched them ride back to the main army, leading them back over the hill and out of sight.

Cayden took one knee and called to the heavens. "Creator!" With that one word, the whole of the Shintower fighters did likewise, and Cayden said this prayer:

Holy Creator! We give thanks for your many blessings, for family that we may call our own and neighbor that will stand beside us in our time of need. Thank you for the special blessing of our wives and children, brothers and sisters. Protect us that we may rejoin them in a time of peace! Give us victory over the evil that presses down upon us! May our enemies depart our lands and return to their homes defeated, never to return!"

"And if this be the day that we join our ancestors in the Third Domain, may it be with such a valiant stand that the warriors who have gone before us will certainly smile at our arrival, knowing that we have died well and right!"

Cayden rose up then, as his men did, tightened his sword around his waist, and shouted to his men, "Catapults!"

Cayden removed the glass pieces and thick leather sheet from his pants' pocket. He placed the glass in the leather at either end, wrapping the leather around them to form a magnifier, he watched what appeared to be their leader yelling something, and then a swarm of the winged creatures dove in front of them, speeding toward the Shintower fighters.

"The flying creatures attack!" Cayden shouted. He put away the magnifier and pointed to them approaching. "Archers, fire!"

A hail of arrows rippled through the coming swarm, dropping hundreds of the Syra from the air. Bodies were skipping across the ground toward them, but the vast majority of the Syra spiraled over and around the arrows, moving closer and closer.

Cayden could see that his plan was already falling apart. "Fire!" he screamed, and the air filled with arrows again. His eyes followed their arc downward, and the Syra swirled outward around them, clearing his field of vision. Their evasion revealed the Camonra running toward him, and several of his men turned to look at him. There were thousands of the Camonra, and the men's faces looked as if the urge to break and run in terror was suddenly almost overwhelming. "Hold! Hold!" he shouted. "Fire catapults!" he bellowed.

The catapults let their stones fly through the haze of Syra, splattering them with their force but falling short of the oncoming soldiers by the sheer drag of flesh and wing. The Syra swarmed the archers, their muscled hind legs and slashing claws savaging them. Cayden could see that they were no match for the onslaught. His men were dying in droves. Standing their ground was not dying with honor; it was simply suicide.

"Run!" Cayden exclaimed, and the men tried to flee, but the Syra seemed everywhere. Terror broke their lines, and the Syra landed around them, attacking them in packs.

As the morning sun rose over the eastern skies, Borian witnessed the chaos below him and his troops. "Their lines have broken," he said.

"Archers to the front!" yelled Mordher. "Cavalry will follow with foot soldiers bringing up the rear!"

Mordher and Borian mounted their horses and watched the archers running ahead of them over and down the hill to the Northern Bridge below.

"They've spotted us!" yelled Borian.

"They spread out to secure the bridge," said Mordher.

"Run, you fools!" Borian yelled, as if the fighters from the Dales could hear him. "Look there! The Camon with the winged helmet must be their captain! He signals the others!" A soldier broke and ran from the helmed Camon's side toward the rear of the column of Camonra pouring into the western side of the bridge.

"Form ranks!" cried Mordher, and the Candrian soldiers flooded the hillside overlooking the Northern Bridge. Borian could see that even Mordher gave pause to notice the sheer numbers of Camonra that were spreading out from the bridge into the Dales. "Cavalry to the front!" he cried, and the archers broke ranks and allowed the horses and riders to pass.

Approaching the bridge, Citanth saw that the Candrian army was not taking a defensive stance with the change to their cavalry, and that could only mean one thing: they would attack.

"Syra!" he screamed. "Arm yourselves!" The Syra swooped down upon the dead, many of them finding suitable hosts, and a hundred or so of the carrion became additions to Citanth's foot soldiers, though the Camonra kept their distance from them. The Syra armed their hosts for war from the weapons scattered across the battlefield. Now the living and the dead turned their attentions to the Candrian army.

"What is your bidding, master?" inquired the Camonra captain, eager for war.

Citanth pointed the Syra in the direction of the Candrians. "Let the Syra take care of the Candrians; we will move on the Dales!" he said. The monstrous horde, the dead men of the Dale, shuffled forward toward the Candrian army.

The Candrians met them with a barrage of arrows, only a few of which slew the parasites by striking their host in the head. The greater portion of the arrows maimed their deceased hosts, but did not stop them.

What's more, it appeared to Citanth that the Syra were gaining more control of their hosts with each passing minute. They drew their hosts' swords and continued unfazed by the second and third rain of arrows that struck them prior to colliding with the Candrian cavalry.

"Kill them all!" Citanth shouted. Three and four of them began attacking a single rider at once, clawing, slashing, biting, and stabbing wildly at them, often striking each other as much as the Candrian rider, but taking them and their horses down one by one.

"We're losing the cavalry!" cried Mordher.

"Infantry, attack! Archers to the front!" shouted Borian. The charge followed the roar of his men's screaming battle cries and the rumbling thunder of their feet. A wall of foot soldiers ran down the hill to meet the creatures in the fray; the archers formed a line in front of Borian and Mordher.

The Syra and their hosts did much damage to the cavalry until the foot soldiers attacked them, being no match for their numbers. Several Syra attempted to escape by detaching from their hosts, only to fall to the arrows of the Candrian archers.

The battle in the valley between the two rolling hills raged on, but Borian could see that their leader continued to bring the Camon soldiers into the Dales. When over half of them had crossed the Northern Bridge, Borian could see him ordering the two companies of Camonra that had reached the western side of the bridge to join the Syra's attack.

Borian jumped down from his horse. "Inferiors!" he cried. Mordher did the same.

"Lose the horses! This is going to be up close and personal!" shouted Mordher.

As the two hundred or so Camonra stormed the battlefield, the two thousand or so men gathered together with shield and sword to counter the sheer size and strength of the Camonra. Some of the Camonra simply plowed into the group, battering them to the ground and attempting to pick them off one at a time.

"Come to me, offspring of Amphileph!" Mordher screamed at the Camon closest to him, whose head shot around at the challenge and roared defiantly, spittle spraying. "Come a little closer, and I'll give you your chance to honor the Creator! I'll parade your head around on a pike!"

The Camon charged and swung his great axe laterally across Mordher's face and then swung backhanded up and across Mordher's body, both times narrowly missing him. On the third swing, Mordher used his shield to deflect the blow into the ground, forcing the Inferior to overreach, and Mordher drove his sword into the Inferior's throat to the hilt, pulling it out at an angle that nearly decapitated him.

"Let me get to their leader!" Mordher cried. "I'll rip out his heart with my bare hands!"

Borian swung downward, trying to get a chance to dissuade Mordher from such folly. He wiped his face from the carnage that flew from the head of one of the fighters of the Dales that had a Syra had infested. "Fully twenty companies have made it into the Dales of Shintower. We are no match for those numbers!" No sooner had Borian mentioned it, the bulk of the warriors marched southwest into the villages of Shintower Dales.

"The Camonra go to Shintower!" said Mordher. About two companies of Camonra remained to face them down, and a lull in the fighting emerged, each side allowing some space between the armies. "They mean to just hold their ground, to hold us back!" Mordher and the other Candrians cursed at them, taunting them to do their worst.

"We have taken heavy losses! We must pull back, Mordher, the Dales are on their own now!" said Borian.

"No!" Mordher shouted. "We can take them!" Mordher shouted his defiance, and the jeers had finally boiled over into action. One of the Camonra made good on their threats by charging in among the Candrians and launching three of them into the air with the swing of his great axe. This move emboldened the rest, and the Camonra barreled into the Candrians breaking their lines and killing them left and right.

* * *

The Candrians fought bravely, but even with the advantage of their numbers, they only managed to gain the day with the loss of over half of their army. The last of the Camonra fell to Candrian blades and arrows, and still, Mordher screamed for more.

"Cavalry, mount up!" Mordher yelled. Borian was wounded and bleeding badly, and two soldiers were helping him back to his horse.

"Are you mad?" Borian screamed. The soldiers held his horse at bay and Borian cinched a piece of cloth around a deep cut in his thigh before grabbing his reins. "We lie in ruin at the hands of just a fraction of their army, and you want to follow them? We go to Candra and barricade our doors in hopes that the fighters of Shintower kill them all!"

"I turn away from no one!" yelled Mordher.

"Then you go that way alone, brother!" Borian answered. "We go to Candra!" he yelled to the remainder of the Candrian troops.

"You do not give the orders, Borian!"

Borian eyed him once, but did not respond except to turn his horse toward the Candra Valley and begin a weary trot in its direction. The other Candrian warriors turned their faces from Mordher and followed him.

Mordher grabbed the nearest one and threw him to the ground. "You don't leave unless *I* give the order to leave!" he screamed.

Borian turned his horse around and galloped back, and several warriors surrounded Mordher.

"Leave him be, Mordher!" shouted Borian. "Leave him be or deal with all of us!"

Mordher pulled back his sword as if ready to run the soldier through, but he heard the sound of two dozen Candrians drawing their swords, and he glanced up. The men were slowly closing in on him.

"You would dare challenge me?" Mordher cried. "I will kill you all!"

"Leave him be, Mordher!" Borian repeated. "We are not the enemy, but we'll not let you kill our own!"

Mordher could see the fear in the faces of the men, but there was something else as well: determination. It was clear to him that continuing down this path would not end well. He let loose of the soldier's armor and let him drop to the ground. He whistled for his horse, and it ran to his side. He put away his sword and threw a leg over his horse. "This will not be forgotten!" he yelled, and he galloped away toward Candra.

* * *

Cayden and the remaining Shintower fighters ran into the outskirts of the Dales and fled into the alleyways and side streets, waiting only to hide and allow the Syra to pass over them. Seeking cover, Cayden kicked in the door of one of the little cottages and entered it. His lungs were on fire and his heart was pounding against his sternum, but he managed to push a table in front of the door. Through the window, he saw the young scout, Antio, who passed by Cayden screaming in terror and rushed into the alleyway just behind the little cottage.

You need to hide, boy! Cayden thought. He went to the window that faced the alley, but he could not see the young scout. "Antio? Antio? Are you there?" he called.

"Cayden?" Antio replied. "Is that you?"

"Yes, it's me."

"Did you see them? Are they still coming?"

"They're just behind us. We need to find a way out of the Dales, but right now, you need to get out of the open."

"I saw those flying creatures carry away my brother Marcus," said the young scout. "Several of them latched on to him and carried him away!"

Cayden could hear the desperation in his voice. He thought he heard him choking back tears. He knew panic would rob the boy of any chance of surviving, so he tried to get him refocused. "Have you any arrows left?" Cayden asked.

There was a pause as the clicking of the Syra passed somewhere overhead.

"I have four arrows in my quiver and one with my bow!" Antio replied. The sound of the Syra died out. "What are we going to do?"

"We must get back to the tower," said Cayden. "Have you seen the others?"

"They're scattered throughout the village," answered Antio. They could hear the shouts of Inferiors in the distance as well. "We will never make it to the Gates of Shintower!"

"We've got to keep moving, Antio," called Cayden, but there was no response. He strained to listen, but the clicking noise rose in volume over their heads. Cayden looked around him and saw a back door leading to the alley. He moved in that direction, but then he stopped.

It grew suddenly quiet, and then there was one clicking sound after another around them, each growing louder and then stopping suddenly. Cayden heard the patter of at least two sets of feet on the wooden roof above him. "Antio! On the roof!" he shouted in a hushed voice.

Suddenly the clicking was all around them. Cayden heard Antio scream, and he fumbled with the latch on the back door, and then burst through the door and onto the cobblestone alley between the homes.

Shoulder-high stone walls lined the alley. Antio was against one of the walls with a Syra on top of him, his arrows scattered on the ground, one hand caught in its mouth, and the other trying to grasp the tail that was stuck in his shoulder.

"Antio!" Cayden hollered, but another of the Syra shot past Cayden, slipping on the cobblestone and rolling to its feet. It leapt and narrowly missed Cayden's head with its tail. Cayden dove to the ground, and then the Syra shot back over the house and disappeared.

"Help!" Antio cried. He released the tail and drew a short blade, severing the tail midway. The Syra responded by biting down on his hand, removing the last two and half of his middle finger. Antio stabbed the Syra over and over again, even after it stopped moving.

"Antio!" Cayden yelled, and he rushed to his side. "Get up, boy!"

Antio was in shock. He drew back his blade as if ready to stab Cayden, striping the wall with black blood with the jerk of it.

"Wait!" Cayden said. "It's me, Antio! It's me!"

"Help me!" Antio said. He looked at his mangled hand and back to Cayden in desperation, and tears brimmed his eyes. "Help me!"

Cayden grabbed up the arrows and placed them in Antio's quiver, and then he pushed the bow over Antio's shoulder. They could hear more screaming to the north of them.

"We have got to go now!" Cayden said, and he pulled the young scout to his feet. Out of the corner of his eye, he saw the temple that the Bhre-Nora had built over the escape tunnel that surfaced in the Dales. The temple door was ajar.

"Come, Antio!" said Cayden.

"I can go no further," replied Antio.

Cayden grabbed him around the waist. "Hold onto me!" he yelled.

The Syra could be seen swarming to the east, flying high into the evening sky, and then diving down into the housetops. Cayden and Antio scaled the steps of the temple, and they could hear the shouts of the Camonra entering the town square at the eastern end.

A lone Camonra scout appeared seemingly out of nowhere. "Humans!" he cried. He shot his crossbow bolt, but missed them, and ran toward them reloading. Cayden sat Antio down on the steps and pushed open the massive wooden door entering the temple.

"Humans!" the scout yelled out again, closing the distance between them in bounds.

Antio had managed an arrow from his quiver. He stretched his bow with his chewed-off hand, and tears flowed from his eyes. He and the scout fired almost simultaneously, the scout's bolt striking Antio through the heart, and Antio's arrow shot upward through the Camon's neck.

"No!" Cayden said. He started back outside before realizing that Antio was dead, and then he pushed the temple door closed. Inside, there was a locking mechanism of some kind, but he could not understand how it worked.

Now Cayden was on the edge of panic. He could hear the Camonra battle drums becoming louder and louder. They sounded as if they were just outside.

He turned around and tried to remember exactly what Aleris had told him about the temple. *It was a special place that housed the entrance to their world,* he remembered. *But where was the entrance?*

He ran to the nearest door and opened it to an inner room that housed a large statue of Rendaya. He had no time to ponder its magnificence; he ran along the walls looking for a doorway of any kind, but found none. In desperation, he crouched down to hide behind the statue's base. He could hear the Camonra war drums just outside, and he moved to the edge of the statue's base to look around at the entrance to the temple, expecting them to burst in at any moment. He squatted back behind the statue, where he saw a Rionese inscription on the back of the statue's base.

"For Her Love the War Began," Cayden read aloud, and the stone beneath his feet moved, startling him. It fell away to form stairs descending beneath the statue's huge stone base.

"May the Creator bless your name, Aleris!" Cayden said, and he descended into the caves of the Bhre-Nora.

* * *

Rendaya looked down at the shadows growing across the Dales. "They've taken the Shintower Dales," she said. "They'll make the Gates of Shintower by tomorrow afternoon."

"I cannot see the Candrians anywhere," stated Galbard flatly. "It seems that we are alone in this."

Ronan appeared upon the deck. "I hope that I'm not interrupting, Father."

"Not at all," replied Galbard. "Rendaya, this is my son, Ronan."

"I'm pleased to meet you, Ronan, though I wish it was under different circumstances."

"I have heard that you are here to help my father."

"We work together to keep the sword from Amphileph," said Rendaya.

Ro bowed. "I thank the Creator that you have come. One with your powers is a blessing indeed."

"It will take the sacrifice of many to succeed today," she replied.

Galbard pointed to the flock of Syra, orange in the evening sun, swirling over the town. "A great many of the flying creatures remain."

"You've good archers, you say?" asked Rendaya.

"Deadly accurate archers."

"We must keep the Syra away from the altar, and you must pour the Sword's power into the altar stone. Use the Sword's power, and Shintower will defend you well."

Galbard turned to look at the stone altar. "It has been so long. Release the power into the stone? That was easy once."

"And it will be yet," Rendaya interjected. "You and the Sword remain one. Just concentrate on an even flow. Keep control."

"At the altar, I can't see the courtyard—" said Galbard.

"Worry not about the tower's defenses, for they are things only the Bhre-Nora know. Aleris will captain them. I will defend you with all my powers," said Rendaya.

"May I have a moment with my father?" asked Ro.

Rendaya looked at him for a moment. "Of course," she replied. "I'll speak with the archers. With your permission, I'll have them spread out among Shintower's balconies and bring the best of them to the deck."

"Yes, of course," said Galbard.

"I'll return shortly. With your leave," said Rendaya. Galbard nodded, and she made her way down the stairs.

"What is it?" Galbard asked, searching Ro's face.

"I fear for you, Father," said Ro. "We're placing everything in the hands of Rendaya and the Bhre-Nora, and here upon the deck, there's nowhere to go if things go badly. I know that you have great faith in Aleris, but being cornered upon the deck—it just doesn't seem wise. We should take the Sword to the Candrians, join forces with them; surely then we could push the Camonra back."

Galbard watched the Syra again, swooping in and out of the Dales. He closed his eyes and felt the wind upon his face.

"I've tried to outrun my destiny, Ro, but I know now that this is where I should be."

"Father—"

"Signal the Bhre-Nora," Galbard said, turning to Ro. "And ask your mother and Tiamphia to join me on the upper deck with all haste. I'd like very much to speak with them."

"Yes, Father," Ro replied. He bowed and then descended the upper deck stairs, exiting to the outer balconies two floors down. He told the trumpeters to sound the call for the Bhre-Nora, and then he returned to the staircase that led to Jalin's and Tiamphia's rooms, but before he reached the landing, his mother and his wife emerged.

"We heard the trumpets sound," said Tiamphia.

Jalin spotted Ro. "May the Creator keep us!" she said. "Your father has called upon the Bhre-Nora?"

"Yes, Mother," responded Ro. "Please, both of you, Father would have you come to him at once!"

They ascended the stairs together, and Ro saw a group of the Bhre-Nora flying toward the upper deck through the upper floor's window slits.

Galbard too saw Aleris alighting upon the upper deck just after his family entered from the upper deck stairs.

"It's time, Galbard," Aleris said.

"Yes, Aleris, it is time," Galbard echoed. "Please take Jalin and Tiamphia to the tunnel to Candra. Ro will go with you."

"What?" Ro asked. "Father, I am not leaving you!"

His expression pained Galbard greatly, but he locked eyes with him.

"Take your mother and your wife through the tunnel toward Candra. There is a leader in Candra called Ardhios. He will give you sanctuary. I have the Bhre-Nora and Rendaya here to protect the Sword. Now I need you to protect *the line* of Shintower."

Ro looked at the terrified expressions on Jalin and Tiamphia's faces. He saw Tiamphia's hands instinctively surround her protruding stomach, as if to cradle their unborn son. "It will be done, father!" said Ro. "Come!" he said to them, and they started toward the staircase.

"Jalin?" Galbard said. "Could I speak with you?"

"Yes, of course," she replied, stepping away from the others. Galbard took her hand and led her to the opposite side of the tower's deck.

"I had wished for us so much more," he said, taking her hands in his. "I still remember when you said you'd marry me." He searched her eyes—there were a thousand things that he wanted to say to her. "I'm not sure I ever told you, but that was the most wonderful day of my life."

Her hands were trembling. "Oh, Galbard," she said. "Don't tell me these things."

"I have to tell you . . . ."

"Tell me later, when all of this is past us."

Galbard looked down at her hands, running his thumb over her wedding ring. "The Camonra are . . . ."

"No!" she said firmly, her lower lip beginning to quiver. "Tell me when we're together again."

"Of course," he replied. He leaned over and gently kissed her cheek, just dodging a tear that streaked down. "When I see you again, we'll have much to talk about."

Wiping the tear, she turned and moved away from him. She kept her ring hand in his until the last second, and then she reluctantly let go, rejoining Aleris, Ro, and Tiamphia at the stairwell.

"Fare thee well," Galbard said. He removed the Sword of the Watch and placed it onto the altar, taking a knee before it and praying.

"And may the Creator keep you, Father," Ro whispered back to him, and then he took Tiamphia's hand and led her away behind Aleris and Jalin.

Galbard prayed; Rendaya placed her hands upon him and did the same, and when a blue aura encased him and the Sword, she stepped back from him and looked over the chest-high wall on the edge of the tower to see how far the Camonra had progressed through the village.

The Sword of the Watch began to glow upon the altar, and Galbard remained in prayer. The stone beneath it was becoming hotter and hotter.

Aleris paused to listen as he led Jalin, Ro, and Tiamphia down the stairs. He could already feel the direct heat of the central shaft of stone overcoming the cool draft of air that whistled through the window slits.

Heated air was beginning to rise within the tower. "We must hurry!" he said, and they raced down the tower's stairs.

* * *

Cayden ran through the tunnel that had opened below the statue of Rendaya until he came upon a clanging group of brass piping in every imaginable size, twisting and turning like veins around bone through the adjoining tunnels. Along the walls were smaller pipes that connected tiny glass housings. The little housings eerily lit the tunnel with the greenish light within them, which Cayden could not distinguish between magic and some type of fuel burning. The scene reminded him of the alchemist shop he had visited in the village, with its hissing and banging, shaking and jumping—but on a much larger scale than the little laboratory.

He followed the piping tunnels away from the Camonra though he had no clear sense of direction. All he knew was that he wanted to get back to Shintower, and he had heard the talk of the underground caves of the Bhre-Nora leading miles from the tower in all directions.

The hissing grew louder and louder, and then stone grinding against stone and chains pulling and straining from somewhere within the walls. The pipes themselves rumbled and knocked and whooshed with something moving down them, and then an explosive bang that moved the elbow of the pipe he was standing next to almost halfway across the breadth of the tunnel before springing back into its place. Cayden ran past all these pipes, thinking more than once that they would jump off their mounts or simply come apart in his face.

The heat from the steam in the tunnels was becoming unbearable, and Cayden had stopped to wipe the sweat stinging his eyes when he heard voices ahead. The tunnel opened into a large cavernous space filled with gears and pistons. The noise was deafening.

The Bhre-Nora scurried in every direction, darting in and out of tunnels, adjusting valves and turning levers on the pulsating piping. Water squirted from around the pipes feeding brass tubes that turned round and round the stone shaft. It was a roar of hisses and banging, dripping and spraying and steam.

"Aleris!" Cayden bellowed from a catwalk that extended across the cavern to a center island where many of the pipes and levers came together around the stone column that rose up through the top of the cavern.

One of the Bhre-Nora flew by him. "Lord Cayden?" he inquired, hooking around and hovering in front of him. "You should not be here! It's very dangerous! How did you get here?"

"I came through the temple in the Dales! I'm trying to get to Shintower!"

"Follow me!" the little sprite said, and he shot past Cayden. "Hurry, I must get you out of here!"

Cayden scrambled across the catwalk, and several Bhre-Nora remarked in astonishment of his presence. "The Dales have been breached!" the little elf-like creature yelled to several others who shot by Cayden in what he thought was the temple's general direction. "That way! Hurry!" he shouted again, and he pointed up a long, steep stairwell bored through the bedrock below Shintower.

* * *

Citanth worked his way through the Dales in short order upon finding no resistance, and by evening, the Camonra topped the last of the rolling hills that stood between them and Shintower.

They assembled about a league from the outer set of ring walls that zigzagged through the stone walkways leading to the tower's base. Torches sprinkled along the walkways provided a flickering light with shadows that jumped back and forth, making the stone floors appear to move. Periodically, steam shot from large ports on the side of the tower, and they felt a deep rumble under their feet. The barbicans appeared to be abandoned.

"Master, they run and hide!" one of the Camon captains yelled.

"Quiet!" Citanth said. "They wait for us. Stay together."

The Camonra entered into the courtyard through the gateway and onto the stone pathway leading to the tower, where Citanth waited with his acolytes and a dozen soldiers. The Syra landed around Citanth, waiting for his command.

Citanth looked up at the torchlight dotting the rise of the tower before them. The top of the tower was far above them, merging with the darkness except for a dim, blue glow that seemed to hover somewhere near the apex. He was contemplating the source of the blue glow when a soldier's approach caught Citanth's eye.

"Come!" Citanth ordered. The Syra parted, and a soldier cautiously moved through them and dropped to one knee.

"What is it? Be quick!" Citanth said.

"My lord, we have discovered an entrance to an underground tunnel in the village!" said the Camon.

"Interesting!" remarked Citanth. "Tell your captain to take twenty of the Camonra and investigate!" Citanth said.

"Yes, my lord!" the soldier said, pounding his chest with his fist. He turned and moved back through the Syra to the Camonra.

"Fly, children of Amphileph!" Citanth called to the Syra. "Find where the humans hide!"

* * *

Cayden's calves and thighs were burning, and he was wheezing from the frantic ascension through the bedrock to Shintower's ground floor. Just when he thought he could go no more, the smooth walls of the tunnel widened to a landing illuminated by the same tiny green lights he had seen in the tunnels from the Dales. He felt about the wall on the opposite side of the landing, where he detected the finest of seams in the stone. There was no handle, but when he pushed upon the wall, it opened to the alcove on the tower's first floor, just behind the famous statue of *Galbard's Realization*. The sight of it gave him back his bearings, and he remembered that he still had the remainder of the tower's stairs to climb. "Creator, help me," he said. He stepped into the alcove and turned to push the door closed.

Cayden turned to exit the alcove and almost ran into Aleris, who was leading Ro, Jalin, and Tiamphia to the escape tunnels as Galbard had requested.

"What are you doing?" Aleris asked.

"I came through the tunnels," Cayden answered.

"You did what?" Aleris began, but a ruckus had broken out behind them at the thick wooden gate of the tower base. The group poked their heads out of the alcove in time to see soldiers dropping timbers across three steel mounts, barring the door, and they were wedging posts behind them at an angle with sledgehammers.

One of the archers descended the stairs. "They're coming!" he yelled. There were eighty or ninety of Shintower's fighters gathered on each floor of the tower, ready to stop the progression of the Camonra at any cost.

The Syra circled the base of the tower, dodging in and out of the staggered walls that surrounded the tower's base.

"Cayden, please see to my mother and Tiamphia," Ro said. "I must stay here and defend the tower!"

"Now wait one moment, Master Ro!" Aleris said.

Ro ignored Aleris and kissed his mother's cheek. "I love you, Mother," he said, and then he turned to Tiamphia and kissed her passionately, pausing a moment to look deep into her eyes. "Your husband is no coward!"

"I never thought it even for a moment, my love," Tiamphia answered. She grabbed him and kissed him again. "Please, Ro, be careful!"

Ro pulled away from her. "Go now! Go now and be safe!"

Cayden sighed. "What do we do?"

"Come with me, now!" said Aleris, and he descended the stairs.

Cayden's thighs and calves ached, but he pushed on. "Of course," he replied and followed them through the secret door and back down the tunnel stairs.

Ro stepped outside the alcove and shouted to the soldiers. "We're ready, men of Shintower! Fill your hearts with courage!"

One of the fighters saw that Ro was with them. "Ro!" he shouted. Ro's presence visibly lifted the spirits of the men.

Someone began clanging a loud bell. "Syra! Syra!" Ro ran around the tower floor along the outer walls. The Syra were attempting to force their way into window slits in the lower part of the tower, clawing away at the stone, stopping only long enough to press their heads against the window slit, their black eyes searching for prey. The men backed away from the riotous clicking that echoed from the tiny window openings. There was a sound like someone pounding on the thick wooden doors, a few at first, then faster and faster. The clicking was becoming deafening.

Ro ran to the nearest window slit and stabbed his sword through the opening. His sword jerked in his hand, pulling him into the window slit. Ro placed one foot on the wall to pull it back. It emerged from the slit covered in black blood, and two tails, stingers dripping, wriggled through, stabbing at the air. Ro swung and cut one of them off.

"Be ready!" he yelled. Their claws were chipping away at the opening. "Kill any that pass!" One of them pressed its head through the slit, and he rammed his sword through its face. "Be not afraid! We can do this!"

He ran back toward the main gates. "Hold the gates!" he screamed, pushing upon the supports. He could hear a pecking and clawing sound, and then suddenly, one of the Syra's stingers shot through the wood. "They're destroying the gate!" he yelled. "Archers! We need the archers! Hold the gates!" Several of the men pushed against the wooden supports.

Ro ran up the stairs to the first level to order the archers to fire, but there was chaos there as well. The archers had placed spiked wooden barbicans in the balconies, filling their entire height, and the bodies of the Syra's were impaled upon them so thickly that there was nowhere through which to fire. He began hacking madly at them, cutting an opening through them.

"Archers, fire! Clear these barbicans with your short sword if you must, but fire upon the Syra attacking the main gate!" he screamed.

The order repeated up the stairs, and the archers reacted instantly, hacking their way through the carnage and firing their arrows, crisscrossing the swarm of Syra attacking the gate. The rain of arrows was unending, and hundreds of the Syra fell from the skies, but the Syra's encircling rage slowly ascended the height of the tower until it reached the balconies. The first row of archers fell under attack.

The archers in the balconies above them continued to fire their arrows, but several of the Syra landed on the second floor balcony, and then the third and fourth, while the remainder continued their attack on the main gate.

Citanth could see that the archers were killing off the Syra, but more important, the Syra were keeping the archers occupied. It might be his only opportunity to storm the tower gates.

"Attack!" he screamed at the top of his lungs, and the better part of seventeen companies of Camonra moved into the Shintower courts. No sooner had the last of them entered the outer courts than a loud burst of steam shot out from the sides of the tower. The Syra that could swarmed well away from the intense heat and incredible volume, though some could not escape the superheated steam and caught fire, arcing through the skies in balls of writhing fire.

The Camonra smashed their way through the abandoned barbicans and into the maze of the first three barrier walls, but then the ground shook beneath them and began to move, and they came to a complete stop in an attempt to keep their feet.

"What's happening?" Citanth shouted.

The barrier walls tore turf loose, sliding on their foundations with the distinct sound of stone on stone. The openings to the courtyard were realigning, slamming together to form concentric rings around the tower's base. Suddenly, the Camonra could neither advance nor retreat!

"What trickery is this?" a Camon captain shouted. He moved forward, searching the wall for an opening. He pressed against the stone wall. The stone slab that he stood upon flipped up, sliding him into a nest of spinning gears that grabbed him and pulled him under with little more than a truncated scream and a spray of entrails. The stone flipped back into place, and had it not been for the blood stains, there would not have been a trace that he was ever there.

Alarm ran through the Camonra.

A post rose from the floor of the courtyard, and with a whir of steam, it quickly spun around, slinging out an arm that swiveled out from the top of the post at head height. The power of the swinging arm was enough to burst the skulls of four of the Camonra, and before their bodies hit the ground, it slowed again, pivoting the swinging arm back within the vertical post, and disappearing into the ground, flush with the stone floor.

Groups of spikes shot up from random sections of the grounds, their sharp points cleanly piercing the bodies of the Camonra and returning into the floor of the courtyard so quickly that half a dozen Camonra at a time appeared to fall over dead without cause.

Another explosive burst of steam, and the walls moved again, creating new openings that appeared to be hiding places or possibly exits, but no sooner had the Camonra moved upon them, great stone pistons would close the openings, crushing any who had ventured into them.

The surviving Camonra attempted to flee, clawing the outer walls, leaping for the edge to climb over. Scalding steam sprayed from openings from all along the base of the wall, burning their feet and lower bodies, and slowly forming a haze of steam so thick they could only see a few inches in front of them. The scalding spray and fog collapsed and gathered between the maze of walls, scavenging the oxygen from the air, making it difficult for the winded Camonra to breathe. All manner of Bhre-Nora man-traps consumed the blind and choking Camonra like ravenous dogs.

"No! No-ooo!" Citanth cried. "Stay back!" he yelled to the remaining Camonra, who were helpless to save their comrades. The screams of the

Camonra echoed between the stone walls with cries for help and pure agony.

"Where is it?" Citanth screamed. He looked up the tower's height, and he could see flashes of blue light from its top. "Syra, to the top of the tower!" he shrieked, and the swarm of remaining Syra ended their ongoing battle with the archers and rushed toward the upper deck of Shintower.

"Here they come!" Rendaya yelled.

The Syra attempted to penetrate the blue aura that expanded from Rendaya to engulf the entire upper deck. The Syra dove into the aura repeatedly, piercing its outer plasma shell, and then folding their wings back and clawing through the plasma, struggling to reach Rendaya and Galbard.

"Remember, Galbard! Let nothing stop the Sword's power from flowing into the altar!"

Galbard's eyes remained closed, but Rendaya could see him nod his head with a jerk. He continued to summon the power of the Sword of the Watch, the altar's stone now glowing dimly.

The bodies of the Syra piled up one on the other, their teeth and claws mired in the pulsating energy field. She tried not to notice that the aura's effect was weakening, but they were closing in on her. She could now see clearly that the tooth-lined gullets of Syra hid a second set of teeth for crushing, and they were doing all that they could to latch those teeth onto her.

They tore away at each other in their attempt to penetrate Rendaya's defenses, pushing the bodies of the dead out upon the surrounding deck and over the edge of the tower, where they splattered upon the balconies and stone walkways below. Still, their numbers were overwhelming her.

"Ah!" Rendaya cried, and the outer aura collapsed. Several Syra fell upon her, and she thrust her fist into the tower's deck, blasting them back from her in a black bloody mess. The remaining Syra tried to gain their footing, slipping and flopping on the tissue-covered stone.

The spattered black blood rolled down the sides of the protective aura surrounding Galbard. Rendaya could just see his face. He was grimacing, but still kneeling in prayer.

One of the Syra pounced toward her, but Rendaya drew its life-force in midair, killing it instantly. "Creator!" she yelled. The veins in her arm seemed to flow black for a moment and pain coursed through her body.

* * *

Cayden, Jalin, and Tiamphia had emerged from the descending stairs with Aleris into the main cavern where the Bhre-Nora were still frantically scrambling to control the tower's defenses.

"You must hurry!" Cayden called to Jalin and Tiamphia. Aleris buzzed back and forth utterly beside himself, obviously more than a little bit upset with his being away from the controls for so long.

Aleris pointed to the tunnel on the opposite side of the cavern. "That way leads to the western shores!" he yelled. It was incredibly hot now in the cavern, and they could barely hear him over the rush of steam all around them. "I must return to my duties, Cayden! Follow the tunnel toward the western shores!"

Cayden pulled Jalin and Tiamphia toward the tunnel and motioned them to move quickly. He looked back to signal his thanks to Aleris and saw something out of the corner of his eye behind the pressure controls deck on the central core. It was a Camon soldier in the tunnel coming from the Dales. "Go now!" he shouted to Jalin and Tiamphia.

"Here!" the Camon shouted, and a distant reply echoed from the tunnel behind him. All eyes turned to the creature, and the Bhre-Nora drew their tiny, razor-like swords. The Camon drew his sword and began crossing the catwalk, bounding toward Cayden, Jalin, and Tiamphia, wholly ignoring the Bhre-Nora.

Cayden stepped between the Camon and Jalin, fumbling with his sword.

The Camon reared his sword back to kill Cayden, but two of the Bhre-Nora zipped by his face, slashing each of his eyes. The Camon screamed out in pain, and losing his balance, he tumbled over the side of the catwalk handrail, bouncing off several pipes and falling into the darkness below.

Aleris zipped back to Cayden. "Go now! More of the Camonra will be here any second!" he shouted.

"But—" Cayden began.

"Protect Jalin and Tiamphia! Go now before it's too late."

Aleris rose over Cayden's shoulder, looking over him at Jalin and Tiamphia's terrified faces. "Remember us, miladies," he said, and then his face grew stoic, and he adjusted his goggles. "Bhre-Nora!" Aleris cried, "Attack!" And he flew away toward the center of the cavern.

Tunnels everywhere suddenly emptied of the tiny warriors, and the air became filled with Bhre-Nora. A swarm of them moved to the east tunnel entrance, landing all about the tunnel entrance and lighting upon the walls of the cave, the piping, and catwalks. Many carried their tiny green lamps with them, and the sheer number tinted the entire cavern with a green glow.

For a moment, Cayden could only stare at the amazing sight of them all, a spectacle likely no human had ever seen, and then he turned away from them and ran toward the western tunnel entrance. "Go! Go! Go!" he shouted, and he pushed the ladies into the dimly lit tunnel, disappearing into the darkness within.

* * *

The Syra were recovering from Rendaya's blast of energy and shaking the muck from their bodies. They closed on her position beside Galbard.

One of the creatures flew past her from behind, but Rendaya narrowly dodged it, drawing the life from its body as it passed by. Rendaya could feel her heart skip a beat. The same feeling of despair and fatigue washed over her again.

"Archers!" she yelled, and up from their hiding places just below the upper deck came the archers grasping for arrows and firing at will, dropping three of the Syra closest to her on the first pass, but Rendaya and the archers were still outnumbered.

A Syra struck her arm with its tail, numbing it from just above the elbow all the way to her little finger. It slashed her garment at the shoulder before she resorted to drawing its life force, but the result was the same. She could feel her body slowing, her own life force ebbing.

Another of the Syra struck down one the archers, and Rendaya drew the life from the creature in a desperate attempt at saving him. She fell to one knee. Her lips turned purple.

Galbard's aura also appeared to dim and thin a bit, and the Syra responded immediately, attacking the remaining protective aura that surrounded Galbard with a renewed vigor.

One of the Syra looped high in the air and dove with all his might into the aura. Its tail pierced the inner aura and struck Galbard in the upper back, just behind his heart.

"No!" Rendaya shouted, and she began to draw the life from every Syra in sight, until the last of them fell lifeless upon the upper deck, and then she too collapsed. The aura disappeared around Galbard, and he fell to the ground. The glow around the Sword died away.

The tower's defense stalled. Its pistons ground to a halt, and the Camonra that had managed to survive the courtyard's maze of traps did not know what to make of it. Many scrambled for the outer walls, some working together to pull a few of the survivors over the wall and out of the kill zone. The rest might have done the same if not for the resurgence of stones grinding, the movement of the walls, the reopening of the exits.

Below, in the eastern tunnels, the Bhre-Nora had met over a dozen more Camonra and a handful of the Syra. The Bhre-Nora mercilessly slashed at them, cutting them hundreds of times all over their bodies, but the Camonra flailed the air wildly, and in the close quarters of the tunnel, a single Camon was killing a hundred Bhre-Nora before succumbing in a bloody heap.

The Bhre-Nora were sacrificing themselves to destroy the Syra, who were eating them in whole or in part, snapping madly in all directions to the last.

"Pull back!" Aleris commanded, and his diminutive troops fell back toward the cavern. They fought bravely, but the Camonra were too much for them, pushing the Bhre-Nora from the tunnel and out into the cavern itself. A group of Bhre-Nora managed to push a support column from the cavern wall above the eastern tunnel, snapping the catwalk off the cave wall in a rain of debris and dropping three of the Camonra into the depths below. Two of the Camonra attempted to jump across the missing section to the central deck that surrounded the altar's stone column, but fell to their deaths.

"We must protect the Sword!" Aleris commanded, and the Bhre-Nora swarmed up the stairwell to Shintower. They forced open the secret doorway enough that Aleris burst through, out of the statue room and onto the main floor.

"Ro!" he cried. "Ro, come quickly!"

Ro and the other men were searching the grounds outside the tower through the window slits, trying to see what had happened to their defenses, when Aleris shot past him and back again.

"The Camonra are within the tower walls!" he shouted. "Something has gone very wrong on the upper deck! We must see to your father!"

"Father?" Ro asked. "No!" he said, and he moved to the base of the stairs. "Warriors of Shintower, our time has come!" shouted Ro.

"Go master! May the Creator keep you! Save your father!" said one of the captains.

"Yes, go master!" the men repeated. "We will hold them off! Go to Galbard!" they insisted.

"May the Creator be with you!" Ro shouted, and he raced up the tower stairs.

When Ro arrived on the upper deck, the sight was mind-numbing. Both his father and Rendaya appeared to be dead, her hair drifting gently over her pale face in the light breeze. He ran to his father and rolled him from his side to face him.

"Father!" Ro shouted. Grief consumed him the instant he saw his father's face.

"Ro," Galbard answered. "I cannot move," he said. "The stars fade from the sky."

"Lie still, father," Ro said, curling Galbard up into his lap. "I'm with you." He locked onto his eyes, and the sounds of battle died away. He could see or hear nothing else in that moment.

"We must protect the Sword," Galbard insisted with what remained of his strength, and then suddenly, "Look! Have we driven them back? Go and look now."

"But Father," Ro said.

Galbard's eyes opened wide, and he struggled to lean up toward Ro's face. "I am Galbard, mason of Rion, once slave of Amphileph, and now protector of the Sword of the Watch," Galbard struggled. "There is nothing more for me in this life. Go now and tell me if the Camonra have been driven back!"

Ro fought back tears. "Yes, Father!" he said. He gently laid his father down upon the deck and hurried to the edge. Below, he could see the Camonra climbing over walls, a large group of them rocking the great gate of the tower. They pushed it in then and poured into the tower's lower floor. He ran back to his father's side. "They are coming, Father!" Ro said, but when he sat down beside him, he saw that Galbard was gone.

"No!" Ro cried. He pulled his father's face to his own and gently kissed his forehead. Tears streaked his face, and he groaned in agony of his father's passing. He laid his father gently upon the deck again and walked to the upper deck's edge. The mayhem of the courtyard, with its scattered and broken bodies, the black blood strewn across the courtyard stone, the silent man-traps, now frozen in various positions of actuation—it was all overwhelming.

He squeezed his eyelids closed and when he opened them, the sounds of battle came again to his ears.

Aleris and a dozen or so Bhre-Nora came flying out of the upper deck stairwell.

"Master Ro!" Aleris shouted. "The Camonra have broken through!" Aleris and the other Bhre-Nora saw Galbard's lifeless form. They looked around the deck and saw Rendaya lying among the bodies of the Syra. En masse, they flew to her side and pushed away the Syra carcasses.

"Rendaya!" Aleris cried. He brushed her hair aside and lovingly looked into her face. "She has taken the poisonous souls of the Syra," Aleris said. "Her spirit is weighted down by their darkness."

Below them, the screams of battle continued. Men were fighting in the stairwells, and the Camonra were slowly filling the tower's floors. "She will never enter the Third Domain with such darkness upon her soul! Bhre-Nora, I call upon you, my brothers, to right this injustice!"

The Bhre-Nora gathered around her and placed hands on her, closing their eyes and praying. Aleris saw that Ro was standing alone in shock at the upper deck's edge. He flew to the parapet beside him.

"Ro!" he shouted. "Ro!"

"All is lost, Aleris," Ro said.

"No!" Aleris said as he flew into Ro's chest and pushed him back from the edge. "Do not let them die in vain, Ro! Use the Sword! Call upon the Sword's power!" Aleris stared at him. "We are leaving now, and *you* must defend the Sword of the Watch!"

"Leaving?" asked Ro. "What do you mean, leaving?"

"We give up our spirits to purify Rendaya, Ro. See," he said, pointing to the group surrounding her body. "Good-bye, Ro."

Ro looked at Aleris for a moment, and then the ancient, winged homunculus flew back and took his place among his brethren praying for Rendaya. A black mist lifted from her body, and Ro watched as each of them released their spirits for Rendaya. A soft white vapor appeared to rise from their bodies. Slowly Rendaya's face changed, her blackened veins and dark purple lips subsided, replaced by the pale beauty that she once was. A pure, white vapor befitting her grandeur rose from her as well. There remained only stillness, shaking Ro to his core.

He moved beside the altar and placed his hands on either side of it. His fingers traced the vein patterns in the stone, and then they touched the silky steel face of Evliit's sword. A jolt passed through him, and his mind raced back to the day his father first tested his control of it. A pain passed through his heart, and a sadness swept over him, but then suddenly a warmness followed. It was as if he felt the love of his father pouring over him. He felt the strength of his father's spirit, the very strength that his father must have had to deny the power of the sword and its position, to place his family above all else. Butterflies zoomed around in his stomach. He knew what he had to do.

"Creator, you have blessed me beyond measure, for it is my father's blood that runs through me!" He fell forward and leaned over the stone, motionless. He could feel within it the vibration of the war going on the floors below him, and he could hear the ring of steel and the roars of man and Camon.

He called upon the power of the Sword. "Creator, pour your spirit through me! Use my flesh to impart your power into this, your servant's sword!" He thought of Tiamphia and his unborn child, and he knew in that moment that there could be no peace for them if Amphileph gained the Sword of the Watch. There was clarity in acknowledging it, and Ro felt a heat growing in his core that raced through his limbs and into the altar stone.

A glowing blue mist flowed from his fingers. It danced across the face of the altar stone, pooling around the sword and then overflowing down the sides of the altar. It rose up around him, deadening his hearing as if he were submerged in water. The aura took on a spherical shape, growing about ten feet in diameter. He could see thin lines of electricity jumping erratically between the sword, his body, and the wall of the sphere. His face began to glow and light began to shine from the sword, blinding him to the Camonra that burst out of the stairwell and out upon the upper deck.

The Camonra began to hack upon the aural sphere with all their might, and the impact of their weapons drew bolts of energy from him, rippling through the attackers' bodies and bursting through the stone of the parapets or the tower deck.

Far below Ro, the altar stone grew deep red, and bright red cracks began to show in its surface. The copper tubing began to percolate, and the gears began to turn. The outer walls of Shintower moved again, this time rushing to an explosion of stone as they rammed into each other. The reliefs roared to life, their plumes of white shooting into the night sky.

The upper deck of Shintower flooded with Camonra, and they were unyielding in their attack. They pushed into the aura, ignoring its deadly rejection of their attempts to pierce it.

Whirling deathtraps in the courtyard below began to spin off their shafts, and sections of the courtyard exploded into the air. There was the awful sound of thick steel whining under pressure.

The Bhre-Nora's cave hissed with steam from every direction, interrupted only by the deafening boom of tanks exploding and whole sections of pipe rupturing. Rivets shot from their seams and ricocheted around the cave walls. The entire catwalk broke free and fell, taking the elegant instruments on Aleris' control panels into the depths of the cave.

Ro's eyes adjusted, and he could suddenly see the Camonra, like ghostly glowing forms drifting in the expanding aura. They slowed to a standstill, and he could see their faces clearly. They were all round him, just beyond arm's length, some lifeless, others leering at him as they struggled to destroy him. A steady stream of them continued to appear from the deck stairwell, climbing upon the pile of dead around the aura's edge, clawing and crawling over and around them, pushing toward him through the aura's dense energy field.

He closed his eyes, and he could see the beautiful face of Tiamphia beside the calm waters of Highborne Falls. He could faintly smell the scent of the flowers in her hair.

His head flew back and light burst skyward from the Sword. When he reopened his eyes, he saw the stream of energy parting the clouds in a circle around it, revealing the heavens with a clarity he had never seen before. They were beautiful beyond description. He lifted his hands and reached to them, and arcs of electricity rose from the altar in their wake.

"Tiamphia!" he shouted, and the core of the tower suddenly exploded, rippling down the length of the tower with enough energy to throw chunks of Shintower's stone into the heart of the Dales.

* * *

Citanth had been looking directly at the tower when the bright light of the explosion extinguished his eyesight. The concussion of the explosion followed an instant later, blowing Citanth and his acolytes off their feet.

The concussion was enough to kill the acolytes, but Citanth lived on, swallowed in the darkness of blindness. A wall of dirt and debris swept him almost a half league away to the north. He awoke broken and blind, stumbling as he disappeared into the darkness.

* * *

Steam and fire raced through the tunnels, collapsing long stretches of earth in every direction. The tower's courtyard sank beneath the Dales of Shintower into the fiery depths of the gaping hole left by the explosion. Earth poured like water back into the cavernous gash, pulling the turf from under two-thirds of the Dales like a carpet. Buildings collapsed and fires broke out in what little bit of the village that did not fall, and in moments, the Dales, as anyone had known them, were gone.

* * *

In the tunnel, Cayden could feel the earth beneath them shake before the sound of the explosion reached them. "Get down!" he yelled to Jalin and Tiamphia. The sides of the tunnel collapsed, and the dirt pressed his body to the floor of it. He tried to pull from his mind where each of them had been in relation to each other. He tried to keep moving, to create spaces that he would be able to make bigger until he was freed. But the earth kept falling and the weight of it pinned his limbs. Then it pinned his head. And finally, it filled his eyes, ears, and mouth. Then there was only silence.

* * *

"Over here! There's someone over here!" one of the men of Highwood said. They dug with their hands into the dirt and lifted Cayden's head, wiping his eyes and nose and mouth with their fingers. A group of people converged on his location and frantically pulled the debris away. Cayden was motionless. They dug his body from the collapsed tunnel and laid it onto the ground next to the furrow that had been their escape route. They attempted to wash his face, and Cayden gasped, rising up with a bolt. He screamed loudly, eyes wide and terrified, and it took several minutes before he was calm enough to slow his breathing.

"Another one here, but she has passed," said one of the searchers, and Cayden turned his bloodshot eyes to see Jalin pulled from the earth. They gently laid her on the ground and crossed her arms. "There's another one beneath her!" they cried, and they dug out Tiamphia. Her head had been jammed behind Jalin's knees, which had formed a small void for her face, an air pocket. As they pulled Tiamphia to the surface, Cayden looked at where Shintower had been and saw that nothing was there but a few scattered fires upon the collapsed valley.

"Is she alive?" Cayden asked.

"Yes, barely," they answered. He closed his eyes at hearing it and faded from consciousness.

Epilogue

The old man stood in the doorway with an elderly woman. "We are here to see Tiamphia," he said. "Is she here?"

A young man in his early twenties opened the door to them. "Yes, sir," he said. "I am Strad, son of Tiamphia."

"And Ro," the man interjected. "Your father was Ronan of Shintower."

Strad stood stunned, speechless for a moment. Then he managed, "How do you know the name of Ro?"

The elderly man smiled gently. Clearly he had shocked his old friend's grandson, "I am Cayden, and this is my wife, Nara. We knew your family long ago. May we speak to Tiamphia?"

"My mother has gone to the market . . . but how—"

"We have much to talk about," responded Cayden.

Strad opened the door to them and waved them in. "I am sorry, come in, come in," he said.

Cayden helped Nara to a seat. The kitchen was modest, and there was only the one table and two chairs, so Cayden stood beside her out of respect for Strad, the man of the house.

Strad pulled out the chair for Cayden. "No, sir, sit please," he insisted. "I've a stool I'll be quite comfortable on."

Strad grabbed the stool and sat down. He motioned for Cayden to sit.

"Thank you," said Cayden.

"Would you like something to drink, or perhaps something to eat?"

"No, no, we're fine," said Nara.

"We appreciate your hospitality, Strad, but we've come a long way to see your mother."

"How do you know my mother?" Strad asked.

Nara looked at Cayden, and he caught a glimpse of her out of the corner of his eye, and something unspoken passed between them in the glance.

"I once escorted your mother when she traveled to the southern part of the kingdom, before the Wall had begun, well before you were born," Cayden said.

"My mother will be thrilled to see you, I'm sure," said Strad. "From where are you traveling?" Strad asked.

"I've been searching for old artifacts of Shintower," Cayden answered. "Nara and I have spent most of our years in the southern part of the kingdom, in Southwood."

"In Southwood? Word is that Southwood is haunted," Strad said.

"Don't believe all that you hear," said Nara. "Our home was like a little paradise."

Before Strad could follow up, there was the noise of the latch, and the front door opened. Tiamphia was saying something about the market when she came in, but she was stunned upon sighting Cayden and Nara.

"Mother?" asked Strad. The look on Tiamphia's face appeared to alarm him a little. He rose up from his stool and walked toward her.

"Cayden! Nara!" exclaimed Tiamphia. She put a hand out on the facing of the door to catch herself. Her face went a little pale, but then she regained her composure.

Both Cayden and Nara got up and went to her, and Tiamphia's face melted into a calm smile.

"Have we aged that much?" Nara said jokingly.

"Yes, my dear, I'm afraid we have," said Cayden. A smile slowly crossed his lips as well. "It's good to see you, Tiamphia." He embraced his old friend's daughter-in-law, then Nara did the same, and they all sat down, silent, in awe of each other.

"I've something we must talk about," Cayden began.

"Strad, would you mind getting us some more bread from the market?" Tiamphia asked.

"But you just came . . ." Strad's expression was that of a child being told he was excused from the adult conversation. "Of course, Mother."

"Thank you, dear," Tiamphia replied, and then Strad looked at her to read her intentions, but failing to, he clenched his jaw and then exited their small home's front door. When Tiamphia was sure he was gone, she leaned across the table to Nara and Cayden.

"You've found it then."

Cayden stopped for a moment. He and Nara looked at her.

"Yes," answered Cayden.

"But how?" Tiamphia asked. "It's become a quest to the Candrians, though I had heard they had given up the search."

Cayden looked at Nara and smiled. "Bellows," he said.

Tiamphia reacted, uncomprehending.

"Rendaya's cat," Nara said, smiling in remembrance and then breaking out in a little chuckle.

"Rendaya... I had almost forgotten that name!" replied Tiamphia. Her mind flashed back to the upper deck of Shintower and the brief moment when she had seen the strange sorceress. *"The Witch of Southwood,"* she said.

"'Witch' was a misnomer at best," said Nara. "But that *was* all we knew about her, so we went to Southwood in search of clues to her passion for defending the Sword of the Watch. We'd searched for days in the great forest, when we came upon this black cat, crying incessantly. He stayed right under our feet."

Cayden laughed. "I nearly tripped over him, and when I went to scold him, he ran back from me. I didn't mean to scare him, so I chased after him for a moment. Then I saw it. Deep in the forest. A well-worn path. We decided to explore a little, so we kept going. That was where we met up with a women traveling in the opposite direction.

"When we asked about Rendaya, she laughed and told us she could show us where Rendaya had lived, which delighted us, and so we walked along with her on the path, deeper and deeper within the forest.

"We came to a little cottage, but she said that she could not go in. 'The Bhre-Nora have restored my soul at their own expense, and I must rejoin them in the Third Domain,' she said."

"It still gives me goose-bumps!" Nara exclaimed, pulling up her sleeve to show Tiamphia the skin of her arm. "Suddenly we both recognized who she was. It had been Rendaya walking with us all along!"

"'I knew from the moment we met, you would protect the Sword,' she said. 'Finish that good work, Cayden, return the Sword to the line of Galbard.'"

"I told her that I did not know where the Sword was or even if it yet existed after that terrible night at Shintower," said Cayden. "But she was clear about what she would have me do."

"Return the Sword to the line of Galbard, but warn them to hide it well, for even though many generations may pass, a descendent of Galbard will be called upon to carry the Sword again.' The spirit of Rendaya moved toward Nara then and spoke to her," said Cayden.

Nara tried to hide her tears, but she could not. She recalled the conversation and spoke through the tears. "She said to me that she was sorry she had used me to frighten the people into submission when we had first arrived on the Western Shore, but that she had not known another way. She asked for my forgiveness, and told me to accept her cottage as her gift, and that inside it, we would find many answers to the questions that had haunted us."

Cayden took up the story. "Then she cautioned us again: 'Amphileph will not rest until he has the Sword, and he is even now plotting his return!' Rendaya said, 'You will find the Sword buried deep in the ruins of Shintower. In the cottage, I have left you directions to finding it.'"

Then Nara added another part, remembering, "She called to the cat, which jumped into her arms in two short bounds. 'My spirit would not rest until I told you these things' she said, and then she smiled, and it was the most peaceful smile! 'The Creator is with you,' she said. She cuddled Bellows close to her heart, and then the *two* of them became one vapor that rose into the night sky."

Cayden pressed his hands on Nara's and looked at Tiamphia. "The cottage was filled with scrolls and books, letters describing something Rendaya referred to as *The Watchers' War*, and the absolute importance of keeping the Sword of the Watch from falling into Amphileph's hands. We found the plans Nara had seen in her visions—the plans for Shintower—they were all there, including all the drawings of the Bhre-Nora's caves and tunnels . . ."

"And?" Tiamphia egged him on, on the edge of her seat.

"And there was a map showing where the Sword was buried deep inside the ruins," finished Cayden.

Nara continued. "We had a connection to those things; they had changed the direction of our lives, so we felt that it was meant for us to be there, in that cottage in those woods, at that time. It was no mistake that we were to find the Sword. But even then, we could not go to the site, for the Candrian known as Mordher had soldiers guarding the ruins.

"For twelve years, they pilfered the remains of Shintower. We waited and we watched until the Shintower grounds became too dangerous and unstable, prone to collapses that might drop a hundred feet or more into the caverns below," said Nara.

"And when they assured themselves there was no remaining entrance, the Candrians took everything that might be salvaged from the caves and tunnels. *Everything* disappeared that once marked the great tower's courtyard, the Bhre-Nora's incredible machinery . . . little by little, until nothing remained."

"Each year we watched them, wondering if they might find the Sword, or worse, that the Camonra might return for it," added Cayden, remembering. "When at last the Candrians left, it took us all these years to dig our way to the place Rendaya had marked for us, and there were many times when rock slides and collapses set us back."

"But we never gave up," added Nara.

Cayden pulled the leather pouch out from under his cloak and laid it on the table. He carefully opened it, revealing the Sword of the Watch.

"Hide it well, Tiamphia, just as Rendaya asked. Amphileph will never give up his search for it." Cayden took one knee and held the Sword before her.

"But what will I tell Strad of it, of his father?"

"Tell him that the Sword is an heirloom, tell him nothing, tell him whatever you want, but hide it, Tiamphia, and tell no others," answered Cayden. "As for his father, tell him the truth: he was a brave man who saved a doomed world, tell him that without his father, there would be no Western Kingdom."

"Come with me." Tiamphia led her father-in-law's old friends to her bedroom, where she cleared a keepsake chest that her father, Caratacus, had given her. She removed the contents and took the Sword from Cayden, laying it in the bottom of the chest. She covered it with a dress, some fabric and other whatnots. Then she closed it and locked it.

"I will tell Strad when the time is right," she said.

Cayden helped her set the chest at the foot of her bed, covering it with a quilt, as if it had never been touched.

When Strad returned, they shared wine and fresh bread, and told stories of the Dales and Shintower, Galbard and Ro. They talked for the rest of the night, until Strad fell asleep, overwhelmed by the past. In the morning, they were gone.

* * *

Tiamphia kept her secret until she was very old. Then, when Strad's own son was sixteen years of age, she told Strad that the chest was to be his upon her death, and her single request was that her son would forever keep the Sword in the family of Galbard.

She told him then of that fateful day at Shintower, and his father's bravery. She told Strad that he could bestow no greater honor upon his father than this: when Evliit returned, the line of Galbard would deliver the Sword to him, just as his grandfather had sworn that he would.

After she died that winter, Strad never forgot the oath he had given his mother, and the Sword and its oath passed from father to son, generation after generation, even after the legend of Galbard and the stand at Shintower were long forgotten.